Burt Mueller's Got a String of

Last night, in a highly publiciz̲ someday rival the shower sce̲ episode of *Newhart,* the winner of the hit CBS reality show *Hey, Make Me Over* was revealed. Robin Calvin, a strong second throughout the run of the show, edged out all other competitors, including leader Tori Lyons, to take the crown. In an unexpected happy ending, Lyons didn't win the prize, but she *did* apparently win the heart of the show's bachelor, Professor Drew Bennett. Their romantic "Lady of Them All Ball" kiss wrapped up last night's episode.

But that wasn't the *big* surprise. To the shock of the censors, and the delight of the millions-strong audience who tuned in to see who would be named the Lady of Them All, Robin Calvin revealed herself to be...a *man.* Rob Calvin, a software designer from Tucson, is also a highly dedicated transvestite. During his memorable acceptance speech, he said he decided to compete in the highly touted Burt Mueller reality show in order to share the moment "with all those others out there, like me, who were unfortunate enough to be born in the wrong bodies."

Kudos to CBS for having the nerve to run the show, and not cave in against almost certain controversy in these post-Janet's-breast days of television censorship.

The show, already a smash hit due to the secret agenda of a million-dollar prize for anyone who could win the love of the sexy, brainy professor, is just one in a string of out-of-the-ballpark TV smashes for producer Burt Mueller, an icon of 1970s sitcoms and game shows. Just when we'd all lost faith in reality shows, Mueller has proved there's never too much of a good thing, and he seems to have nailed the perfect reality TV formula.

Which leaves us wondering...what does the legendary Hollywood producer have in store for us next? Here's a sneak peak of what's coming up....

Surviving Sarah

Only Burt Mueller would come up with the idea of mixing two shows—*Survivor* and *The Bachelorette*, to come up with a bright new reality show to tempt jaded viewers. The prize—former teen star Sarah Donovan. But, before they get the girl, these poor guys are going to have to prove themselves—by passing through a gauntlet of grueling trials designed to challenge even the strongest competitor. The question is, will there be enough of them left for Sarah to enjoy...?

The Great Chase

Now this looks interesting...from the wacky reality that exists in the brain of comeback kid and *Surviving Sarah* creator Burt Mueller comes *The Great Chase*, a blatant rip-off of *The Amazing Race* with a healthy dose of *Magnum P.I.* The preview show features a wild and interesting collection of sleuths from amateurs to pros, all trying to out-deduce each other in a transcontinental race for a million-dollar prize.

The episodes feature themes such as Flying High, dealing with airport mysteries, and Sounds of Silence, where all the clues will be of the auditory persuasion. But the cases take a back seat to this reviewer's interest when the contestants start showing their true colors—and their true intelligence. The most promising couple is a team of ex-lovers with some sort of secret past, which may or may not be revealed over the course of the show. Who cares if they locate the owner of the snub-nosed Pekinese? Not me. I want to know what Charlie and Sam are hiding.

The Last Virgin

Good taste isn't the only thing being sacrificed. Just when you thought it couldn't get any more outrageous, the reigning king of reality TV, Burt Mueller, once again proves he knows how to push it over the top with *The Last Virgin*. One unsuspecting ingenue searching for her true love among thirty men. The secret promise of half a million dollars to the man who walks away with her virginity. You'll want to stay tuned for this one.

Really Hot!

Wildly popular as *The Last Virgin*'s almost-winner, Rourke O'Malley, Boston investment banker and the bachelor market's hottest commodity, is back in reality TV's *Money Can't Buy Me Love*. Sequestered in a lavish Hollywood Hills mansion, a bevy of wealthy beauties pull out the stops to win this hunk's heart. As if O'Malley doesn't heat up the screen enough, throw in a catfight or two, director Burt Mueller's signature twist and *Money Can't Buy Me Love* becomes don't-miss TV.

So, viewers, get set for another surprising season of reality TV that is *anything* but real. Don't miss it.

Dear Reader,

The editors at Harlequin and Silhouette are thrilled to be able to bring you a brand-new featured author program beginning in 2005! Signature Select aims to single out outstanding stories, contemporary themes and oft-requested classics by some of your favorite series authors and present them to you in a variety of formats bound by truly striking covers.

You may notice a number of different colored bands on the spine of this book. Each color corresponds to a different type of reading experience in the new Signature Select program. The Spotlight books will offer a single "big read" by a talented series author, the Collections will present three novellas on a selected theme in one volume, the Sagas will contain sprawling, sometimes multi-generational family tales (often related to a favorite family first introduced in series) and the Miniseries will feature requested, previously published books, with two or, occasionally, three complete stories in one volume. The Signature Select program will offer one book in each of these categories per month, and fans of limited continuity series will also find these continuing stories under the Signature Select umbrella.

In addition, these volumes will bring you bonus features...different in every single book! You may learn more about the author in an extended interview, more about the setting or inspiration for the book, more about subjects related to the theme and, often, a bonus short read will be included.

Watch for new stories from Vicki Lewis Thompson, Lori Foster, Donna Kauffman, Marie Ferrarella, Merline Lovelace, Roberta Gellis, Suzanne Forster, Stephanie Bond and scores more of the brightest talents in romance fiction!

We have an exciting year ahead!

Warm wishes for happy reading,

Marsha Zinberg

Marsha Zinberg
Executive Editor
The Signature Select Program

Signature Select™
COLLECTION

Vicki Lewis Thompson

Julie Elizabeth Leto

Jennifer LaBrecque

Getting
Real

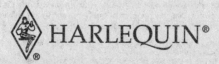

HARLEQUIN®

TORONTO • NEW YORK • LONDON
AMSTERDAM • PARIS • SYDNEY • HAMBURG
STOCKHOLM • ATHENS • TOKYO • MILAN • MADRID
PRAGUE • WARSAW • BUDAPEST • AUCKLAND

ISBN 0-373-83639-2

GETTING REAL

Copyright © 2005 by Harlequin Books S.A.

The publisher acknowledges the copyright holders of the individual works as follows:

SURVIVING SARAH
Copyright © 2005 by Vicki Lewis Thompson.

THE GREAT CHASE
Copyright © 2005 by Julie Leto Klapka.

THE LAST VIRGIN
Copyright © 2005 by Jennifer LaBrecque.

CONTENTS

SURVIVING SARAH
Vicki Lewis Thompson

For Leslie Kelly,
whose fertile imagination knows no bounds.
My kind of woman!

CHAPTER ONE

"I THOUGHT I DIDN'T have to marry anybody." Sarah Donovan paced her suite, picking a trail through twenty-five head shots scattered on the carpet as she talked on her cell phone with her manager, Destiny Germaine.

"Contractually, you don't have to marry anybody," Destiny said in her deep whiskey voice. "You don't even have to get engaged. I mean, the winner gets the million bucks, whether there's a liaison between the two of you or not."

Sarah paused beside an open bag of Kettle Korn and snagged a couple of kernels. "Then why are you telling me to consider the happily ever after bit?" As she ate the Kettle Korn, she reminded herself to glance out the window at the view—miles of uninhabited rolling hills covered with oak and juniper, a scene she didn't get to see every day. Beverly Hills was rolling, too, but inhabited. Really inhabited.

The rugged lodge picked for filming the reality show *Surviving Sarah* sat all alone on the edge of the Cleveland National Forest outside San Diego, and the setting was breathtaking. She wouldn't mind being here on vacation. But she wasn't on vacation, and the contestants she'd be evaluating grinned from the eight-by-tens as if saying *choose me, choose me.*

"Burt's my friend, and he needs to produce a hit show," Destiny said. "Several hit shows, in fact. The guy's drowning in alimony payments. You're my client, and you need a career boost. Both could be accomplished with a wedding."

"Does it occur to you that Burt is living proof that marriage is dangerous?" Still, Sarah couldn't challenge Destiny's evaluation. The woman knew her stuff. She'd arrived in L.A. in the eighties, a brunette named Dolores Hepplewhite. In no time she'd become a redhead named Destiny Germaine, advisor to the stars. She had some big names on her client list.

"I agree that Burt's overdone the marriage thing, but you've never tapped it. There's great publicity value there."

"I wish you'd mentioned this earlier, Des, instead of hours before we're ready to start shooting." Except she suspected that Destiny had intentionally waited until Sarah was already up to her armpits in the project before making this suggestion.

If Des had laid out this marriage idea in the beginning, Sarah would have nixed the deal, no matter how much her manager believed in it. Sarah's parents had married for love, and that's what Sarah intended to do someday. Marriage was not a publicity stunt.

But Destiny couldn't be blamed for wanting to stage one out of desperation. Sarah's career was definitely headed for the toilet. Nine years ago Destiny had taken Sally Debowski from Portales, New Mexico, and turned her into sweet and sassy Sarah Donovan, teen idol. They'd both made a bunch of money, and Sarah had gotten ten quite full of herself.

Believing she knew better, she'd ignored Destiny's advice and accepted the role of a psychopath in *Death Plan,* thinking the character had Oscar written all over it. Instead it had BAD CAREER MOVE written all over it, and she'd been struggling to get back in the game ever since. Destiny thought Burt's reality concept, twenty-five men competing for Sarah's favor, could be her ticket back.

"I've been keeping an eye on this whole reality TV phenomenon," Destiny said. "Except for Ryan and Trista, nobody seems to be staying together and viewers are getting cynical. You could make them believe again. It also would go a long way toward making them forget *Death Plan.*"

Sarah groaned. "Yeah, but will you ever let me forget it?"

"Listen, you'd look terrific in white. Recapture your old image by becoming a blushing bride."

"You think viewers are getting cynical? I can't think of anything more cynical than roping one of these guys into marriage to save a couple of Hollywood careers." She munched on some more Kettle Korn.

Destiny sighed dramatically. "You're looking at it all wrong. Don't think of it as roping in. Think of it as exploration, taking advantage of opportunities. I'm only asking you to keep your mind open. Yes, this setup is artificial, but—"

"Oh, you think? Twenty-five guys I've never laid eyes on, didn't even have a hand in choosing, and my Prince Charming is supposed to be in this batch? Fat chance. And even if a miracle happens and there's a potential candidate, it's not like we could have any real interaction with cameras following our every move. I might be used to it, but he won't be."

"You might be surprised." Destiny paused to take an audible sip of what was probably her tenth cup of coffee. "Personally, I think marriage would be great for you, aside from the jump start it could give your career."

Sarah stopped pacing and stared out at the hills, more brown than green on this January morning. A couple could ride off into the sunset over hills like that. "Marriage is the last thing I need. I talked my parents into moving to L.A. and now I'm afraid they'll have to wait tables to make ends meet. I need a man like Oscar needs an agent."

At the sound of his name, her black Scottie popped up from his bed in the corner and scampered toward her, prancing right over the head shots and making dents in most of them. When the Academy had seen fit to ignore her work in *Death Plan,* she'd decided to buy herself an Oscar. His cute little face with his shaggy eyebrows and adorable whiskers cheered her up more than anything could.

As Destiny started listing all the advantages of having a man around, Sarah reached for her dog, trying to grab him before he ruined any more pictures. Apparently he thought she wanted to play, because he snatched up one of the eight-by-tens and ran off to the bedroom with it dangling from his mouth.

"Just a sec, Des. I have an emergency, here. Oscar's chewing on one of the head shots."

"Maybe it's a sign."

"Oh, I'm so sure." Sarah laughed and started after Oscar. "Hey, you! You could be running off with the father of my children! Des, I hafta go. Burt's bringing the celebrity guest host up here soon so I can meet him."

"Who is it? He didn't have one last week."

"I don't know. He said he'd surprise me. Oscar! Give me that!" As she tried to pull the picture away from her dog, she ripped it in two. "Damn."

"Just keep your mind open on the marriage thing," Destiny said.

"Yeah, yeah. Mind open, legs closed."

"That part's up to you, babe. Just check for cameras before you get naked. You're not Janet Jackson, you know. 'Bye."

"'Bye." Still laughing, she tossed her mangled half of the picture on the bed and pushed the disconnect button on the phone before throwing it on the bed, too. "Okay, Oscar, no more playing. Geez, I hope they don't need those head shots for anything else. Oscar, come here!"

She finally bribed him with a scrap of ham left over from the omelet she'd ordered for breakfast. Holding the bit of meat between her fingers, she coaxed the other half of the picture away from him. It had teeth marks and dog slobber all over it.

Retrieving the other part from the bed and turning it photo-side up, she sat down and connected the two ripped pieces to see if she could tape them. No way. Oscar made a leap for the bed and missed. Knowing how much that embarrassed him, she quickly scooped him up and plopped him down next to her. "There you go, stubs. You really did a number on this poor guy."

Oscar licked her arm as if to apologize.

"We won't tell him. He'll never know he got ripped to shreds before the competition even started." She studied the face in the picture, which looked sort of vulnerable because it was now in two pieces. Or maybe it was because he was the only one of the twenty-five who wore glasses. He was smiling, but just barely, a soft, no-teeth kind of smile. Mostly he just looked into the camera with a steady here-I-am expression on his face. He wore a jacket and tie.

Most of the other contestants had gone casual for the photo, and they'd definitely had their hair styled. She'd noticed streaks and gel and a few punk spikes in the pictures still in the living room. This guy's hair was plain brown, but thick, and cut the way a barber would do it back in Portales. She liked his blue eyes, but she wished he'd smiled a little more. Maybe he had bad teeth.

Yesterday she'd decided to wait until after she'd met the contestants to read their bios on the back of the head shots. That way she wouldn't stereotype anyone in advance. But she'd already glimpsed a couple of things about this guy, so she decided to scope out the rest of his bio. His first name was blurred with dog spit. It could be Dale or Dude, or Duke or Luke.

His last name was Richards, a nice solid sound to go with that steady gaze. Mr. Richards hailed from Indianapolis, and he was the oldest of either three or thirteen. She hoped it was three, for both his sake and his mother's. He had a college degree and was two years older than she was.

His physical description was slightly shredded, too. She hoped he was six-three and not five-three, and that he weighed one-eighty and not one hundred pounds. Maybe she shouldn't be prejudiced against a guy who stood five inches shorter and weighed ten pounds less than she did, but dancing would be awkward.

Not that she'd be dancing with Dale or Dude or whatever his name was. This caper only involved spending time with each guy in casual conversation and awarding points during a series of physical feats. After the first episode the field would be cut to thirteen based on their performances. The second round would reduce the group to seven, and the third would eliminate all but three. When one of those went home, there would be a showdown between the final two, one of whom would win the contest…and her, sort of.

She looked again at the torn bio. Apparently he was a planner, but she couldn't make out what he planned. Weddings? She had a sudden image of Martin Short in *Father of the Bride* and began to giggle. Her Romeo could be a short, skinny wedding planner with bad teeth. It would serve Destiny right if she ended up marrying a guy like that.

LUKE PACED his hotel room in downtown San Diego. Basic room, no view of the ocean. He had twenty minutes before the bus arrived. Being alone fed his anxieties about this gig, but none of the contestants were supposed to meet until the bus ride up to the lodge.

They were all staying in hotels throughout the city and they'd been cautioned not to try and make contact or talk about why they were here. The producer, Burt Mueller, wanted to maintain control of his cast, and Luke could understand that.

Letting a bunch of guys who were all after the same thing get together in a hotel bar could be a disaster. Once everyone was on camera, they'd probably behave themselves, but before that, no telling how greed might affect them. He wondered how many of them were after the money and didn't care one way or the other about Sarah.

Because he'd been here less than twenty-four hours, he hadn't unpacked much, and now everything was back in the suitcase ready to go, except for one thing. He picked up the autographed picture of Sarah at sixteen, right after she'd made *The Slumber Party*, a coming-of-age story about three high school girls dealing with divorcing parents, hormones and demanding boyfriends.

She'd been a brunette in the movie that had launched her career—a tender, vulnerable teenager struggling to balance all the competing forces in her life. Only eighteen himself, he'd fallen helplessly, hopelessly in love with her. Intellectually he'd known she was playing a role, that she might be a total bitch in real life. But he hadn't believed that.

Writing the studio to ask for an autographed picture had made him feel like a groupie, but he'd done it, anyway. After the picture had arrived, he'd written more letters, but they'd gone unanswered. She'd made three more movies after that, changing her hair color each time, but the vulnerable quality had remained, and he'd stayed hooked.

Then she'd starred in *Death Plan,* and he'd forced himself to go see it, even though the trailers hadn't appealed to him at all. He'd hated the movie, even though she'd acted well. She'd convinced him she was indeed a killer, which had made him wonder if the tender, vulnerable characters she'd played in the other movies were also part of an act. Who was she, really?

Death Plan made it clear to him that he didn't know her at all. He'd fallen for someone who might not exist.

So he'd tried to talk himself out of this ridiculous, hopeless crush, one he'd never told anyone about. He had dated over the years, but all the women had looked a little bit like Sarah, with that full mouth and slender figure, those wide-set green eyes and tilted-up nose. Yet they weren't Sarah. He nearly wore out his DVD of *The Slumber Party.*

When he'd seen the ad six months ago for contestants in a new reality show called *Surviving Sarah,* he'd told himself to forget about it. He was the last person in the world who should be in front of a camera. He wasn't into acting, hadn't even taken a public-speaking course. Besides, the challenges would be mainly physical, and he'd never been a jock, either.

But he couldn't resist. Here was his chance to find out once and for all who this person was. Either he would put his demons to rest because she was nothing like he thought, or she'd be everything he dreamed of. In that case, no one would stop him from winning the hand of Sarah Donovan.

WHEN SARAH opened the door of her suite at the lodge, Burt gave her a smug smile. Behind him stood a man who needed no introduction.

"Omigosh!" Sarah threw open the door. "Is Digg Martinez going to be our celebrity host?"

"Yep." Burt's smile widened, making him look like a kid who'd pulled off a prank. Burt did look younger than he was, a prerequisite in Hollywood, especially for a producer trying to make a comeback. He'd handled the aging process by shaving his head and Botoxing his wrinkles. "I thought I'd surprise you."

"Come in, come in." She stepped back and ushered them through the door. "Oscar, stop that barking. This is my producer, and a certified 9/11 hero, Diego Martinez, Digg for short." She and all the rest of TV-land had given their hearts to Digg during the recent reality show *Killing Time in a Small Town,* which had featured Digg in a key role. An NYC fireman and Mr. Tall, Dark and Handsome, he'd been an inspired choice for the show.

Digg walked in and crouched down in front of her dog. "Oscar, you don't seem impressed with me at all."

Oscar gave a last yip and then started wagging his tail, which made his whole body wiggle.

"Okay, now we can be friends." Digg scratched behind Oscar's ears as he glanced up at Sarah. "Some scary guard dog you have."

"Yeah, right. As you can see, he's a pushover. Wow, this is great, that you agreed to be the host for the show. Good call, Burt."

"I thought so." Burt stuck his hands in his pockets and rocked back on his heels. "Still got those instincts."

Sarah hoped so. Snagging Digg really was a stroke of genius, so maybe Burt was on the comeback trail, after all. She peered out the window. "No paparazzi?"

"Not yet," Burt said. "We sorta snuck him in. He's doing this as a personal favor to me."

"Oh, right. You mean because of Jacey." Because Destiny was good friends with Burt, Sarah had heard all the gossip. Burt's daughter Jacey had been the head cameraperson on *Killing Time* and a romance had sprung up between her and Digg. Jacey was also working on *Surviving Sarah,* so it made sense that Digg would want to hang around. "Does Jacey know Digg is the celebrity host?"

Digg concentrated on petting the dog. "Um, not exactly."

"So you're going to surprise her?"

"Something like that." Digg kept petting Oscar and didn't look up.

"Don't worry," Burt said. "It'll all work out. She'll come around."

Sarah decided not to ask any more questions. From the tense set of Digg's shoulders she could guess that all was not roses with Jacey. Sarah had met her yesterday and had picked up on more than a little defensiveness, despite Jacey's obvious skill with a camera. She and Digg were an interesting couple. Jacey carried an L.A.-sized chip on her shoulder, but Sarah thought Digg could handle her if anyone could.

"Have a seat, both of you," Sarah said. "Have some Kettle Korn, too. I'll just pick up these head shots." She gathered the eight-by-tens from the floor.

"Doing your homework?" Burt asked.

"I just looked at the faces. I decided not to read the back until after I'd met them, so nothing would prejudice me in advance."

Burt laughed. "What? You have something against morticians?"

Sarah paused in midmotion. "*Is* there a mortician?" Dale/Dude/Duke/Luke could be a funeral planner. Oh, ick.

"I forget. Sylvie would know."

Sarah hoped that director Sylvie Bradford, known for some unorthodox methods, wouldn't have approved a funeral director as one of the contestants. That would be extremely creepy.

Burt sat on her leather sofa and pulled a pack of cigarettes from his pocket. "Mind if I smoke?"

Well, she did, but she didn't want him getting jittery due to a nicotine fit, either. "Tell you what. I'll throw on a jacket and get Oscar's leash. We can take a walk. It's gorgeous outside."

Digg nodded. "Works for me. I've been on a plane for too long. I could use the exercise."

"Health nuts," Burt muttered as Sarah hurried back to the bedroom for a jacket, Oscar's leash and a pair of shades. Oscar bounced after her.

Both men were standing by the door when she reappeared. "The guys start arriving when?"

Burt glanced at his watch. "The bus should be picking them up about now. They'll be at the staging area in another hour and a half. Then we'll bring them in one at a time by limo, starting at five. Cocktails in the lounge at six."

Sarah made sure the room key was in her pocket before she walked out the door with Oscar. The air smelled like dry leaves, which reminded her of autumn in Portales. Sometimes she missed small-town life, but in general she liked big-city excitement better.

She fell into step beside Burt. "The thing is, I have no idea how to get ready for a date with twenty-five men."

"Heidi from makeup will help you," Burt said as the three of them started down an outside stairway. He lost no time lighting up.

At the bottom of the stairs she zipped her jacket. Up here in the hills it seemed more like winter than down in L.A. The cool air felt good, though. "I didn't mean physically, although I'm grateful for the help. I meant mentally. The concept of entertaining twenty-five guys is intimidating."

"You'll be fine," Burt said.

Digg coughed as a wave of cigarette smoke hit him in the face. "I think you'd better fill Sarah in on the new twist, Burt."

"What new twist?" She stopped walking and gave her producer a wary look. Maybe he'd been talking to Destiny. At least there was a contract, though, and Sarah wasn't obligated for anything additional.

"Sylvie and I have been worried that the concept isn't hot enough, and focuses too much on physical abilities." Burt took a drag on his cigarette. "We want these guys to have to show some brain power, too."

"So you'll stage a wild and crazy chess tournament?" Sarah was kidding. Talk about boring. And Sylvie would never approve anything that dorky.

"No, we'll give them a mathematical equation to solve every night. The winner will be granted immunity from being eliminated. And he'll also get some extra, uh, quality time with you."

"That doesn't sound too bad." Sarah liked the idea of one-on-one better than a crowd, anyway. "You mean I meet him in the lounge for a drink or something?"

"Not exactly," Digg said. "I told Burt you should feel free to veto this."

"Why would I veto it? I'm supposed to get to know these guys."

"Yeah, that's true." Digg's tone was tentative as he glanced over at Burt.

Burt flicked an ash to the sidewalk before he looked at her. "The answer to the equation will be your room number. The winner gets to spend time with you in your room."

"You mean my suite?" She didn't think that would be so bad. The suite was about the size of your average apartment.

"Well, no. The suite would make the answer too obvious. We'll move you to a different guest room each night."

"Oh." Suddenly she got the picture. She was supposed to entertain one of these guys in a bedroom every night. A bedroom equipped with cameras. "I see."

Burt shrugged. "Sex sells."

CHAPTER TWO

SEX SELLS. Sarah had been in Hollywood long enough to know Burt was right. But nothing had to happen if she didn't want it to, and she could keep control of the situation.

"Are you okay with this?" Digg asked, looking anxious.

"I can probably handle it as long as the cameras won't be on twenty-four/seven. Thinking of someone taping me while I sleep would creep me out."

Burt stubbed his cigarette out in the sand of a tall cement ashtray. "We'll rig them to shut off two hours after we get confirmation that someone has arrived at your door. That's assuming we have any guys who can do the math."

Sarah thought of the contestant in the picture she and Oscar had ripped apart. She was probably stereotyping to assume that glasses and a steady gaze equaled math skills. "So they come to my door, and we just talk in my room," she said. "For two hours."

"You can boot them out anytime after they arrive. Up to you." Burt reached in his pocket for his cigarettes.

"If you're hoping to get some nooky on camera, it isn't going to happen. And if any guy gets too aggressive with me, I'll use karate on him."

Burt shook his head. "It won't come to that. I have a

daughter, you know. I can be sensitive. All you have to do is yell for help. Besides, I can't believe a guy would risk alienating you and getting thrown off the show."

"Good point." She reached down and scratched Oscar's back, but he ignored her. He wanted to be off exploring. "And then there's Oscar to protect my honor."

"Yeah, Oscar's your ace in the hole." Digg smiled at the dog. Then his glance strayed to a woman dressed all in black who was walking out to the parking lot. "Oscar's looking antsy. How about if I take him for a little run?"

"I'll bet he'd love it."

Burt followed Digg's gaze. "Sure you want a dog along?"

"Yeah. Good icebreaker." With that Digg took Oscar's leash from Sarah and trotted toward the parking lot.

Burt lit up another cigarette. "Damn, I like that kid, and he's nuts about Jacey. I wish she'd just relax."

"Burt, I have to ask. Was bringing Digg in as the celebrity host a matchmaking move?"

He looked offended. "I did it for the good of the show!" Then, when Sarah continued to gaze at him, he shrugged. "If it helps those two iron out their differences, that's a bonus."

So maybe he was a sentimental guy, after all. Sarah liked knowing that. "By the way, speaking of relationships, Destiny called today and basically told me to think about marrying one of the contestants. How do you feel about that?"

Burt's eyes lit up. "Sarah, if you'd marry the winner of this contest, I would pay for the honeymoon myself. It would be good for you, good for the show, good for everybody."

"We'll be together barely seven days! How could that ever be enough time to make a decision about spending the rest of your life with someone?"

"Don't ask me. I'm no matrimonial expert." But he'd stopped concentrating on the conversation. Instead he was watching Digg approach Jacey, as if trying to read something from their body language. About that time Oscar wandered toward a bush and lifted his leg. Burt chuckled. "There's a romantic moment for you. Two lovers and a peeing dog."

"But it worked. They're both laughing. Oscar was a good prop."

"Yeah, remind me to bring him a doggie treat. Who knows, maybe he'll play Cupid for you, too."

"Not when we're talking about only seven days."

Burt glanced at her. "Digg fell for Jacey in less time than that."

And now they have problems, because love is about more than instant attraction. But Sarah didn't say anything, because Burt so obviously wanted Digg to become his son-in-law.

Later, back in her suite, she noticed a piece of paper lying on her sofa. She guessed it had fallen out of Burt's pocket when he first took out his cigarettes. It was folded in half, but open enough that she could read it.

So she did. The note consisted of two short sentences. *I like the shaved head. Very sexy.* No signature.

Sarah picked up her cell phone and called Burt. She got his voice mail and decided leaving a message would save them both embarrassment. "Burt, you left a note here. I guess you have an admirer, huh? Let me know if you want me to save it."

LUKE CLIMBED DOWN from the bus at the staging area not far from the lodge, but out of sight of any civilization. The white canopy erected in the middle of nowhere looked surreal, especially with the black limo parked beside it and the colorful trays of food on linen-draped tables. He was definitely in Southern California. You couldn't get away with this kind of al fresco deal in Indianapolis in January.

"Hey, Luke, old buddy, I see a bucket of ice with some promising-looking cans sticking out. Think we have beer?" Dino Scarletti, a dark-haired Italian from New York City, had been hanging around the lobby of Luke's hotel, and finally Luke had struck up a conversation with him there, figuring the guy had to be waiting for the same event.

They'd taken seats together on the bus, and Luke had discovered he'd accidentally hooked up with an extrovert. From Dino's seat in the middle of the bus, he'd managed to introduce himself to everyone and had all the guys straight in his mind before they'd gone twenty miles down the road.

Later he'd confided in an undertone that he thought it was good to know your enemy, just like in World War II, when General Patton read his opposing general's book on war strategy. Dino's grandfather had fought under Patton, and Dino insisted this competition was war, minus the blood.

If Luke had felt like arguing, he'd have debated that point. His dad had lost a leg in Vietnam and still suffered from post-traumatic stress disorder. This competition might be vital to Luke, personally, but it wasn't about life and death. But then Luke didn't need the million dollars as desperately as some of these guys. If he kept going at his present rate, he'd retire at fifty.

He found it interesting, though, that Dino had confided in him as if he didn't consider Luke the enemy. Apparently he'd taken one look at Luke's glasses and conservative haircut and had decided he was no competition at all. Luke didn't mind. He liked being underestimated. It gave him an advantage.

Thanks to Dino, Luke had a pretty fair idea about the competition, too. So much depended on whether Sarah was the kind of woman he thought she was. When he'd first fallen for her, he'd been a teenager with a crush on a girl. He'd grown up, and he wanted to believe she had, too. If so, then about half these guys were too immature for her.

They'd spent most of the bus ride telling fart jokes. Of the other half of the contestants, Luke gave five an excellent chance. Dino was in that group. So was Brett, a good-looking blond guy from St. Louis who seemed to have his act together.

"Have a beer, my friend." Dino shoved an icy can in Luke's hand.

Luke eyed the can and glanced around. Everyone else was drinking, and some were on their second. A lot of guys had grabbed handfuls of chips and pretzels, too. Eddie, the instigator of most of the fart jokes, was giving an X-rated puppet show using carrots sticks and black olives.

"Down the hatch." Dino popped the top on his beer.

"Is this a good idea?" Luke said. "Aren't we supposed to meet Sarah in about thirty minutes?" The thought made him a little queasy.

"That's why God invented breath mints." Dino took a hefty swallow of his beer and looked at Luke. "Aren't you nervous?"

"Sure I'm nervous."

"Then drink up. I'll bet that's why they put the beer out here, to relax us."

Conceding the point, Luke popped open his beer. "There's definitely relaxing going on." Eddie had coaxed Cliff, another rowdy type, into joining him in a rendition of "She'll be Comin' 'Round the Mountain." They delivered the lyrics in a way that gave the song a different meaning from the one Luke had learned in elementary school.

So far the only person representing their hosts seemed to be the bus driver, a beefy guy who lounged against the fender of the limo and drank a diet pop.

Luke tried to see through the smoky glass into the limo. "I wonder if anybody's in there."

"Of course someone is. With a camera," Dino said. "In fact, look above you."

Luke glanced up into the canopy's supports and spotted a couple of minicams trained on the crowd. "Not surprising. I figured they were on the bus, too."

"Oh, yeah." Dino finished off his beer. "And choice bits will be made available to Sarah or I miss my guess. Some of these idiots have no idea they're hanging themselves right this minute."

"Unless she likes frat-house humor."

Dino shrugged. "Guess that's always possible. When you get right down to it, what do we really know about Sarah Donovan?"

"Not much, I guess." But Luke wasn't completely

without knowledge of Sarah. For years he'd been comb-ing the Internet for info about her, and recently he'd in-tensified his search. He didn't intend to share his knowledge with anyone here, either.

She'd been born Sally Debowski, the only child of Frank and Lisa Debowski, and had grown up in the lit-tle town of Portales, New Mexico, peanut basin of the nation. On a family vacation to Universal Studios she'd volunteered for an audience-participation skit, and Des-tiny Germaine had seen the tape. Destiny was known to have a good eye.

Sarah had a dog named Oscar, and Luke thought the dog's name had something to do with her getting shut out of the awards. She hated peanuts, probably because she'd been surrounded by them as a kid, but she had a weak-ness for Kettle Korn. He had a small bag in his suitcase.

That was all the personal stuff he'd been able to dig up about her, and he'd concluded she must be a fairly private person. That was fine with him. So was he.

STANDING BY the circular drive in front of the lodge at precisely five o'clock, Sarah wished she'd taken a Val-ium, after all. She hated to depend on stuff like that and had turned up her nose when Burt had suggested it an hour ago. He must have seen her hands shaking. Hell, her whole body was shaking. What had she done, get-ting herself into this?

Burt hadn't mentioned her call about the note, but maybe he hadn't checked his voice mail yet. She'd tucked the note in her cosmetics bag back in the suite, in case he asked for it back.

Digg stood nearby looking cool and incredibly handsome in his tux. He had a list of the contestants and the order in which they'd arrive. Not far away Jacey was positioning her camera crew. She never glanced Digg's way, never acknowledged his presence other than to direct her troops as to which angle to use when shooting him.

He seemed okay with that. After all, the two of them were working, so they couldn't easily exchange melting looks. But Sarah had begun to take up the cause of true love along with Burt, and she hoped they were making progress in their relationship. Thinking about Digg and Jacey also helped keep her mind off the ordeal ahead.

Then Jacey told her to step closer to the driveway, and she was shaking in her Jimmy Choos once again. "I'm so nervous."

Digg smiled at her. "You'll be fine once you get into it."

"I don't know why I'm this way." Her teeth chattered, and not from the cold. She had a slinky black dress on, but for greeting the contestants she'd covered it with a full-length coat of fake fur. "I've performed in front of a camera for years. I should be calmer than this."

"But you were playing a role," Digg said. "Now you're playing yourself. There's a big difference."

"Who knew?" But she thought he'd hit it on the head. These twenty-five men were here to impress her, and yet she was worried that they would meet her and be disappointed. What if she came across as just another blond bimbo?

No one had given her a script for this. Come to think of it, she'd concentrated on her career from the age of sixteen and she'd probably missed some of the normal developmental stages, like how to make small talk.

For some reason she hadn't thought about that when Destiny had come to her with this proposition. Then again, Destiny hadn't wanted her to think about anything but getting back on top, getting her picture on the front of the magazines at the check-out aisle in Ralph's.

She'd been a hot commodity once, but pretty soon she'd be considered too far out of the loop to make a comeback. Producers like Burt could get away with it. Actors were a different story.

"Breathe," Digg said. "And by the way, you look amazing. That upswept hairdo is a real winner."

"Thanks." She drew in a deep breath, but just then the black limo came into view, and she exhaled in a rush. "Oh, God."

"They're probably more scared than you are."

"In that case, they won't be able to get out of the limo without falling down."

Then there was no more time to discuss the matter. The limo stopped, and Digg opened the back door. "Sarah Donovan, I'd like you to meet Dino Scarletti."

Dino smiled at Sarah as he exited the limo. "Hello, Sarah. It's great to meet you." Then he glanced at Digg and did a double-take. "Digg Martinez is the host?"

"Uh, yeah." Digg looked disconcerted. "But I'm not the important person here. Sarah is the one you—"

"Oh, of course, of course!" Dino hurried forward and clasped Sarah's hands. His were as icy as hers. "But Digg! The whole city of New York loves you, man! The whole U.S. of A. loves you!"

Sarah laughed. Maybe this wouldn't be so bad, after all, if she had Digg around. The guys would be too engrossed with him to care much about her.

Dino seemed to realize his focus was on the wrong person, and he swung back to Sarah. "I'm sorry. I've made a total idiot of myself, but I didn't expect to have Digg Martinez open the car door. Let's start over. I'm Dino, and I couldn't be happier to be here."

Sarah smiled at him and felt the knots in her tummy loosen. "I'm happy you're here, too, Dino. I'm looking forward to spending time with you."

"Boy, so am I. Spending time with you, I mean. I've always felt a real connection to you. You, on the other hand, have felt no connection whatsoever to me, because you didn't know I existed. But that's about to change, and I'm babbling, so I'll just take myself on up to the lodge before I make a bigger fool of myself than I already have."

Sarah watched him go. If they were all as cute and flustered as Dino, this might turn out to be more fun than she'd thought.

Unfortunately, not every guy was that charming. Eddie Schnaffle leered at her, and from the way he staggered she'd bet he'd had several drinks before he'd stepped into the limo. Cliff Pettigrew tried to grope her ass. She could only hope they'd be eliminated in the first round.

Several more arrived, and she began losing track of names and faces. But when a guy in a suit, tie and glasses climbed out of the limo, she knew immediately it was Dale/Dude/Duke/Luke. As he unfolded his lanky frame from the limo seat, she confirmed that he was not five-three, as she'd feared, but a full six-three. Nice.

"Sarah Donovan," Digg said, "I'd like you to meet Luke Richards."

Luke. Another point for the tall guy. She liked the name Luke.

"Hi, Sarah." His voice sounded gentle, and his handshake was firm, even warm. "I've waited a long time to meet you."

She looked into his eyes and discovered him looking right back with quiet intensity. "Really? A long time?" The picture hadn't done justice to those eyes. They reminded her of the water in the Sea of Cortez on a hot, sunny day. His wire-rimmed glasses emphasized those gorgeous eyes.

"About eight years," he said. "Ever since I saw *The Slumber Party.*"

"Wow." He was a fan. Maybe he was after the money, but he was definitely interested in her, too. "Listen, you're not a funeral planner, are you?"

He blinked. "Excuse me?"

"I, um—well, my dog Oscar chewed your bio, and all I could read was the word *planner.*"

"No, I'm not a funeral planner."

"Are you a wedding planner?"

"Financial planner."

"Oh." That put a different spin on things, for sure. "I could probably use one of those. My finances are a mess."

"I'd love to help. Usually people aren't in as bad shape as they think. Sometimes all they have to do is shift a few assets around and start evaluating the long-term value of what they have."

"You think so? I've been meaning to have someone look over my situation, but I've been afraid they'd throw up their hands in horror. I—" She paused when she heard Digg clear his throat.

Looking over Luke's shoulder, she noticed that the limo had pulled up with another contestant. She reached out and squeezed Luke's arm. "I'll talk to you later," she murmured.

"Sure thing." Then he smiled, a full smile where she could see his teeth.

And they were beautiful teeth. She sighed. Right now a man who knew how to handle money, and who also happened to be tall, with amazing eyes and good teeth, was very appealing to her.

CHAPTER THREE

LUKE WALKED UP the winding path to the lodge's main lobby, cursing himself all the way. He'd responded like a geek, launching into a stupid financial spiel first thing out of the box. A first meeting was *not* the time to discuss moving assets and calculating the long-term potential of those assets.

He'd started out decently by letting her know he'd waited a long time to meet her and telling her he'd seen her first movie. But when she'd said she needed financial advice, he should have steered the conversation back to something more romantic. Like *finances are best discussed over a good bottle of wine* or *I hope we can have some private time. Then you can ask me anything.*

But no, he'd talked to her the way he would talk to a client. It's a wonder he hadn't hauled out a calculator and started punching in some numbers. *Sheesh.* Given more time he probably would have recommended a few investments she might want to consider. What a fiasco.

He was so upset he almost forgot to take stock of his surroundings. At the last minute, he remembered that this was the stage on which he'd have to perform for the next seven days, if he managed to last that long. He should at least take a quick look around.

The two-story lodge had a rustic log exterior that took on a golden glow in the light from the setting sun. Ahead of him was a central lobby on the ground floor and a large balcony above that. Two wings stretched out on either side, and each room had a small balcony facing the vista of rolling hills and mountains in the distance.

Nice place, but it didn't much matter where he slept. Everything important would take place in the large open area in front of the lodge. For the show it had been turned from a grassy knoll into something resembling a military training camp.

Luke noticed an obstacle course, a rock-climbing wall, a ring for either boxing or wrestling or both and several lengths of thick rope. A pile of sizable boulders stood off to one side. He wondered if they'd be expected to lift them or throw them. The question was whether he'd be able to do either.

After he'd decided to try for a spot on the show, he'd joined a gym so he wouldn't make a complete fool of himself. But six months of twice-a-week workouts wouldn't give him much of an edge over some of these guys. Brett looked like a professional athlete, and a couple of others had obviously made a career of creating muscle definition.

Luke would have to survive mostly on grit. But maybe he'd do better than he thought. He'd even bought himself some sports goggles so he could see what the hell he was doing.

Oh, hell, who was he kidding? He'd been so dazzled by Sarah that he hadn't noticed until he walked away that the guest host for the show was none other than Digg Martinez, certified American hero. Sarah was way more likely to go for someone like that, which meant Brett, or maybe Dino.

She would go for an eye-catcher because like gravitated to like, and Sarah Donovan was breathtaking. He hadn't let that sink in completely until now. Now that he'd acknowledged how amazingly gorgeous she was, he realized how impossible his dream really was.

For this gig she was a blonde, and the color looked terrific on her. He'd take her with any hair color invented, but blond looked fantastic with her green eyes and flawless skin. He'd often wondered if her beauty had been created by a camera lens. Not so. If anything, the camera hadn't done her justice.

"So, Richards, ready to tackle that equipment tomorrow?" Brett Harrison came up the walkway toward him.

"Ready as I'll ever be." Luke wondered if Brett was laughing to himself at the thought of Luke trying to compete with the likes of him. "I'm going to guess you're ready. You look like a pro."

Brett nodded. "Minor league baseball. Sidewinders."

"I figured something like that."

"Yeah, it's a good thing this competition was scheduled during the off-season or I would have been out of luck."

Luke gestured toward the field. "This should be a cakewalk for you."

"Assuming I don't choke." He turned toward the lobby as male laughter filtered out through the closed doors. "I guess we might as well go in and see what tasteless entertainment Eddie and Cliff have come up with this time."

"They sure don't seem like her type."

"I know. But some women like guys like that, guys who make them laugh. I've learned never to count anybody out."

"Good advice." As Luke walked with Brett into the lobby, he admitted that he'd already started to like both Brett and Dino, and that was probably a mistake. In cut-throat competition, you couldn't afford to make any friends.

SARAH HAD NEVER enjoyed cocktail parties, and this one was giving her a major headache. Women might dream of being the center of attention for twenty-five guys, but the reality was exhausting. After an hour she was thoroughly sick of everyone jockeying for position, sick of the subtle and not-so-subtle attempts to touch her and the barrage of suggestive remarks.

There were several men she wouldn't mind spending more time with, but the loudmouths of the group kept inserting themselves into every conversation. She'd tried twice to talk to Luke Richards, but either Eddie or Cliff had interfered immediately. Brett Harrison was another guy who looked interesting, and Dino was pretty cute, too. Not that she intended to get serious about any of them. Not in seven days.

Although the camera crew remained, Digg had left her alone to deal with the contestants. That was what the script called for, but Sarah would have loved having him siphon off some of the attention. She felt as if she'd stumbled into an episode of *Wild Kingdom* featuring the mating habits of bull elk.

When Digg finally entered the room, she heaved a sigh of relief. The first ordeal was nearly over.

"As all of you know from the schedule you were given," Digg said, "Sarah will have room service tonight and remain alone for the evening so she can make notes on her impressions of all of you. She'll also be reviewing tapes of your bus ride and the gathering at the staging area."

A few guys groaned, as if they hadn't realized the cameras had been on then. Sarah could almost predict who had been especially obnoxious and now regretted every crude remark.

"Meanwhile you'll all have dinner in the lodge's restaurant," Digg continued. "After that you're free to do whatever you want. Your suitcases have been placed in your rooms and I have the keys and room assignments for you. Feel free to change into more casual dress for the evening."

Sarah glanced over the motley crew. Most were in casual dress already. Cliff and Eddie had gone beyond casual to sloppy. Brett and Dino had worn suits, but only Luke had added a tie. She was touched by his earnest effort.

"For entertainment tonight," Digg said, "there's a sports bar with a high-definition TV and pool tables. Both the pool and spa will be open until ten. Or you can go to sleep and rest up for tomorrow."

Everyone laughed at that, as if only sissies went to sleep. Everyone, Sarah noticed, except Brett and Luke, her two serious guys. Brett looked like an athlete who believed in the value of a good night's sleep. Luke seemed like a strategist who would take any advantage he could get. She watched Luke specifically as Digg came to the next part of his announcement.

"Aside from all that, we've created an extra competition that's not on your schedule," Digg said.

Luke stood a little straighter and glanced over at Sarah. She looked away, not wanting him to think she'd been staring at him.

Digg cleared his throat. "During the day the competition will be mostly about brawn, so we decided to throw in a challenge that will require some brain power. After dinner you'll all be given an equation to solve. The first person to solve it will be granted immunity from being eliminated in tomorrow's competition."

"Oh, man!" Eddie scowled at the group. "I suck at math!"

What a surprise. Sarah managed to keep herself from smiling. A quick glance at Luke confirmed what she'd suspected. He looked happier than he had since the evening had begun.

"But then that guy won't have to do the competition at all!" Cliff said.

"Yes, he will," Digg said. "The competition points are cumulative, and although the problem solving will still take place between the last two contestants, it won't guarantee immunity. It will be…a perk. Because there's something more you all need to know. The answer to the equation will be Sarah's room number. Whoever makes it there first gets uninterrupted time with her…until she kicks you out."

"Whoa!" Dino said. "There's an inducement."

"Sarah will be switching rooms while you guys eat dinner each evening, and after dinner you'll get the new problem to solve," Digg continued. "That is, the remaining contestants will get the new problem."

The group grew silent as the significance of that sunk in. Tomorrow night a dozen guys would be gone. Sarah already knew of two she'd love to eliminate, but if they scored well at the physical tasks, they'd automatically stay.

"So that's it," Digg said. "Bid Sarah goodbye. Starting tomorrow, one of you will get to spend time with her, assuming we have some math ability here, but everyone else won't see her again until she appears on the balcony in the morning to watch the competition." Then Digg walked over to escort her from the room.

She grabbed his arm like a lifeline. "Whew. Get me outta here."

"Was it rough?"

"I'm ready to thin the herd. Twenty-five is too many to deal with."

He led her to the elevator. "I have a message from Sylvie. After reviewing the tapes, she's all excited about Eddie and Cliff. She wants you to be nice to them."

"Oh, God. I was hoping by tomorrow night they'd be gone."

"I figured as much, but Sylvie says that with some judicious editing, they're good TV. They're so obnoxious that they're funny. Think *Beavis and Butthead.*"

"Believe me, that's not a stretch. Okay, I'll do my best to put up with Eddie and Cliff. At least they won't be solving the math problem."

Digg laughed. "Not likely. Well, here's your new room. All your stuff's been transferred and your meal's been delivered. Oh, and Oscar's been fed and walked. I did that before I came down to get you."

Sarah laughed. "Are you trying to steal my dog's affections?"

"Just doing my job. And he's still a great icebreaker." Digg smiled and handed her a room key. "Have a good night."

"You, too." She opened the door and gave him a wave before going in to greet a very enthusiastic Oscar. "Well, puppy, are you playing Cupid for Digg and Jacey?"

Oscar wiggled happily as she gave him a thorough scratch.

"Well, that's good. As for me, I'm beat, and I have one more obstacle before I can relax for the night." She hoped if anyone solved the problem it would be Luke. She could ask him for some financial advice.

LUKE BARELY TASTED his food as he thought about the problem they'd get after dessert. Maybe he wasn't as screwed as he'd felt a couple of hours ago. The cocktail party had been a zoo, with head monkeys Eddie and Cliff in charge.

Keeping Brett's excellent advice in mind, Luke had tried not to dismiss those two goons. He'd searched for signs that Sarah hadn't liked their over-the-top behavior and found none. She'd kept smiling and laughing, no matter what. But she was, he reminded himself, an actor.

His only consolation was that Brett hadn't had any more luck penetrating the idiot line surrounding Sarah. Dino had done okay, but he was naturally gregarious and had managed to be accepted by both the quiet faction and the obnoxiously loud faction. Luke had spent most of the cocktail hour talking to Brett. Brett had even asked for his card, saying he wasn't sure he trusted the financial advisor he had currently.

Great. So far Luke had netted a couple of clients, which was definitely not his agenda for this trip. He had a truckload of clients. What he lacked was a reason to make all the money that seemed to flow his way without a lot of effort. He needed a serious relationship. He needed the woman he thought Sarah might be.

This problem-solving competition might give him a fighting chance at that. In anticipation of winning, he'd brought a small backpack to dinner. Yeah, he'd been hassled about it, but if the contents of the backpack made headway with Sarah, he didn't care what the other guys thought.

He waited impatiently for everyone to finish the apple cobbler they'd served for dessert. Two members of the camera crew had been assigned to the dinner, and they both looked bored. Luke figured they'd been asked to pan for early alliances and antagonisms among the contestants.

And they were forming. Eddie had tried to bribe him with a check for a thousand dollars if he'd solve the problem and give Eddie the answer. Luke had refused, so no doubt he was on Eddie's shit list.

When Digg walked into the restaurant, the atmosphere immediately became more electric. All conversation stopped as two members of the tech crew set up a screen and projector.

"Here's how the problem solving will work," Digg said. "I'll put the problem up on the screen. You'll work on it right here. Once you think you have the answer, come up and whisper your guess. Then you can leave to find that room number."

"What if we guess wrong?" Dino called out.

"I won't tell you at the moment whether you're right, but a wrong answer will lose you twenty points from the next day's competition. One of the tech crew is coming through passing out pagers. Once the hidden camera records that a contestant has made contact with Sarah, I'll page the rest of you, unless you're still in this room. At that point, even if you solve the problem, you may not approach Sarah's room. If you do, you'll be sent home immediately."

"Can we solve it as a team?" asked Cliff.

"You can, but if you come up with an answer as a group, only one member of that group can look for Sarah's room and be granted immunity from the next day's competition."

No team was going to beat Luke at this game. Teamwork was clumsy and time-consuming. He tapped his fingers on the table as he waited for the numbers to go up on the screen.

"Are you ready?" Digg asked.

"No!" Eddie yelled out. "I don't have a pencil! Aren't you going to give us something to write with?"

Digg shook his head. "You knew this was coming. A pencil and paper would be your responsibility. Here's the problem."

The minute the equation appeared, Luke started working it out. He didn't bother with a pencil, which would take longer. Instead he solved the problem in his head. In twenty seconds he was out of his seat, his backpack over one shoulder, as he headed for Digg.

Digg didn't look surprised to see him. "Got a number?"

Luke leaned close and murmured the answer.

"Go for it," Digg said. "Gentlemen, we have a contender. Anybody else ready?"

Luke heard plenty of swearing, but no chairs scraping or footsteps following him. Once out of the restaurant, he found the stairs and took them two at a time. His heart hammered, but he felt good, strong. This he could do.

SARAH WHEELED her room service cart outside the door and went back inside to change into her favorite pink sweat suit. Then she settled on the bed with Oscar to go over the bios of all the contestants.

She'd already deciphered all she could from Luke's, so she sorted through until she found Brett's. Wow, a professional baseball player. That didn't surprise her, considering his build.

Dino came next, and she learned that he owned a chain of dry cleaners in New York City. She could believe that Dino was a successful small businessman, with his gift for gab. Eddie listed himself merely as a salesman, but he didn't mention what he sold. She suspected not much, or maybe something not quite legal. Cliff said he was in food service, which was equally vague.

As she was about to flip to the next bio, someone rapped on her door. A contestant? Oscar started to bark, and she shushed him immediately. Not many people knew that her dog was here. The lodge hadn't been happy about him, but she needed Oscar, so Burt had worked out a deal and left a deposit.

She looked through the peephole and saw a tall man dressed in a long-sleeved gray Henley, a jacket and casual slacks. He had a small backpack over his shoulder and he was wearing glasses. It seemed that Luke had solved the math problem in record time. She really should consider hiring him as a financial planner.

But that wasn't why he was standing on the other side of her door. He intended to win this contest. The advance information had said the winner was vying for a million dollars and the favor of Sarah Donovan. Destiny wanted that to mean white lace and promises. Sarah wanted it to mean something less, like she'd treat him to dinner at Spago and then add him to her Christmas card list.

She wondered what Luke wanted it to mean. In the next couple of hours, she just might find out.

CHAPTER FOUR

WHEN SARAH OPENED the door, Luke forgot all the things he'd planned to say. The pink sweat suit draped her body in such a soft and inviting way that a number of his brain cells bit the dust. She'd taken her hair out of the elaborate upswept style and put it in a simple ponytail, which looked extremely cute.

"I solved the problem," were the only words that came out of his mouth.

She smiled. "So I see."

Gradually he became aware of the black Scottie standing behind her barking his little head off. "Is that Oscar?"

She looked startled. "You know my dog's name?"

"Um, yeah. I Googled you on the Internet." Buying time until he could remember his own name, he crouched down and held out his hand to Oscar. "Come here, boy. It's okay."

Oscar stopped barking and cocked his head. Then he pranced forward, tail wagging, and shoved his nose into Luke's cupped palm. At least her dog liked him. Maybe her dog liked everybody. The doggie treats in his backpack were probably overkill.

"You Googled me. Every time I hear that I think it sounds like some kinky sex move."

He wondered if that was a good thing or a bad thing. And he had absolutely no idea how to respond. She was so much more sophisticated than he was. He was probably in over his head and she'd kick him out when she got bored in about five minutes.

Nevertheless, he had made it to her door, so he might as well try to capitalize on that. He stopped petting Oscar and stood. "Can I come in?"

"Oh, sure." She opened the door and swept her hand toward one of two chairs on either side of a small table. "Have a seat. You earned it." She eyed his backpack. "Did you bring provisions or what?"

"Just some treats." He unhooked his backpack from his shoulder and sat in the chair.

She closed the door and came toward him, but instead of taking the other chair, she bounced down on the bed across from him and arranged her legs in what he thought might be the lotus position. It was extremely sexy, especially with those hot pink toenails of hers.

"What kind of treats?" She looked like a kid when she said it. Or her face did. Her body was one-hundred-proof woman.

After unzipping the backpack, he pulled out the bag of doggie treats. "These are for Oscar, if he can have them."

Oscar wriggled and whined and tried to get in his lap. Luke had to hold the bag of treats high over his head. "Can he have some?"

She started laughing. "I think you'd better give him one before he attacks."

Still holding the bag over his head, he managed to tear it down the middle and little nuggets went everywhere. "Damn." He dropped to his knees and started grabbing treats and throwing them in his backpack.

"A piñata for Oscar!" She leaped from the bed and helped Luke gather them up.

They were all panting, including Oscar, by the time the treats were zipped safely inside the backpack again.

"I'm really sorry," Luke said. "I think he only got about three."

"It won't be a problem." She scooped up her dog and plopped him on the bed next to her before returning to her lotus position. "He's had much worse. I had one of my rare parties last year and he ate half a platter of hors d'oeuvres before we realized it."

"I wasn't expecting that kind of enthusiasm. Liability doesn't get nearly that excited about doggie treats. But then, Liability doesn't get excited about much of anything."

"Your dog?"

"A basset hound."

"Ah. So let me guess. You have a cat named Asset."

"Nope. But my sister does. She's a stockbroker. Peggy and I were the economics majors. Jeremy's a chef." Like she really wanted to know the job descriptions for his sister and brother. He needed to steer the conversation toward more romantic topics.

"Please tell me you have only two siblings and not twelve."

"Twelve? Why would you think I had twelve?"

"After Oscar chewed your bio, I couldn't tell if you were the oldest of three children or the oldest of thirteen."

"Oldest of three. Thirteen! Think of having to educate all those kids."

"Think of the stress on the mother," she said.

"No kidding." Okay, this wasn't a bad subject. Maybe a little premature, but it never hurt to find out how a woman felt about kids. "I think two's a good number."

She nodded. "Exactly. Two's great. I'm an only, and I would have loved to have a sister or brother."

"Onlies usually do great things, though. I mean, look at you."

"I'm not that big a deal. For a while it looked like I might get really famous, and then…"

"Death Plan." Whoops. He shouldn't have said that. She seemed really unhappy, now. "You did a terrific job with that part," he said quickly. "I don't know why you didn't win an Oscar for it."

Her dog pricked up his ears.

"Thank you," she said. "I can't figure out what went wrong with that movie. Look at how they loved Charlize Theron in *Monster*."

He wanted to offer comfort. He wanted to kiss her and stroke her and tell her that someday she'd be a bigger star than Charlize Theron. But he didn't dare make that kind of move yet. "Do you want to know what I think?"

"Sure. Because I've been thrashing this out in my brain for a long time, and I don't have any answers. I did good work in *Death Plan*. I know I did."

"I think it's because Charlize changed her appearance so drastically that she didn't look much like herself. The weight gain, the bad teeth—she looked pretty unattractive. But you still looked beautiful in *Death Plan*. The audience couldn't forget it was you, and they didn't like the idea of you, the sweetheart from *The Slumber Party,* turning into a psycho. Sort of like if Snow White decided to murder the seven dwarfs."

She grinned. "Oh, God, don't *ever* suggest that premise to Mel Brooks."

He liked that she was joking around with him already. "Okay, I won't."

"But I think you have a point." She sat thoughtfully for a while as if turning the concept over in her mind. "So you think I should have made myself ugly?"

"No! That would have been horrible."

"Not really. Actors do that all the time, for the sake of the part. But it wasn't in the script, and I didn't even consider it."

"I'm really glad you didn't consider it."

She gave him a puzzled look. "Why?"

"Because…" He struggled to think of how to say it without letting her know that he was hopelessly infatuated with her. He couldn't think of a way, so he might as well come clean.

Looking directly at her, so he wouldn't appear to be a coward as well as a dweeb, he told her the truth. "From the first time I saw you in *The Slumber Party,* you've been a fantasy to me. If you changed yourself to look different, it would ruin that fantasy."

"That's incredibly sweet."

"Not really. I—"

"And incredibly stupid, especially considering that you're here, face-to-face with the real me. If you wanted to keep your fantasy, you shouldn't have entered this contest." She held out both arms. "As you can see, I'm just a flesh-and-blood woman. So much for your fantasy."

A flesh-and-blood woman was exactly what he wanted, especially one who looked like Sarah. Besides, he'd discovered she was beautiful *and* modest. Even though she was a star, she obviously respected him as an equal. He shook his head. "You're even better than my fantasy."

SHE MUST BE getting desperate for approval, because the expression in his eyes filled some hollow place inside that she hadn't even realized was there. She had the urge to nestle against him and absorb some of that tenderness.

He was liable to get his gentle self hurt, though, letting his emotions hang out like that. He might have some crazy idea that he could win her hand in the next week. She should warn him that wouldn't be happening—not with him or any of the other twenty-five guys.

But it was such a treat to sit and bask in the warmth of that look he was giving her. For once here was someone who didn't care whether her last movie was a flop and had no stake in rejuvenating her career. Apparently he thought she was great as is.

All the other people she knew seemed to be holding a collective breath, waiting anxiously for her to regain her grasp on fame and fortune. Although her parents had told her a million times that they didn't care if she ever made another movie, she didn't believe them. At her insistence, they'd quit their jobs in Portales and retired to sunny California, thinking their working days were over. She was paying the mortgage on both their house and hers. The money was running out.

Luke shifted in the chair. "Okay, that was lame. I'm sure you have guys saying that kind of thing to you all the time." He stood and slung the backpack over his shoulder. "It must be boring for you. I probably should have given my spot to someone who had a chance, like Dino or Brett. Anyway, I'll take off and let you spend the rest of your evening in peace."

"No, wait." She climbed off the bed, and Oscar hopped off, too, obviously hoping for more doggie treats. "I wasn't bored. I was sitting there thinking how wonderful it was to have someone like you just for myself, even if you don't really know what that self is."

He paused. "I would like to know one thing."

"What's that?"

"The character you played in *The Slumber Party,* Emily. Did you identify with her at all?"

"You mean as opposed to the murdering psycho Amelia in *Death Plan*?"

"That's not what I—"

"Forget it. I was teasing you. Yes, of course I identified with Emily. Luckily my parents love each other, so the divorce thing wasn't an issue in my life, but all that other stuff—boyfriends, peer pressure, wondering where you fit in this confusing world—that felt very real to me. Emily wasn't a stretch. Amelia was." And nobody had ever asked her that question. Luke really was interested in her as a person, not as a star.

"I can't imagine how you played the part of Amelia."

"If you'll sit down, I'll tell you."

He looked doubtful.

"Go on, sit down." She glanced at her watch. Then she leaned toward him and murmured softly, "The cameras go off in two hours. Maybe we can wait it out."

His answering smile made her heart flutter. Her heart

hadn't fluttered in ages. Interesting. This sincere interest on his part seemed to be affecting her libido.

"Okay, I'll stay a little bit longer." He unhooked his backpack and reached for the zipper. Oscar went nuts.

"Just one. I don't want a barfing dog on my hands."

"That isn't what I was going for, although I guess I'll have to give him one, now that he associates the backpack with doggie treats." He pulled a nugget from the bag and tossed it across the room so Oscar had to race to get it.

She'd always loved surprises. "What else did you bring us, Santa?"

"This." And he pulled out a bag of Kettle Korn.

And that was the moment when Sarah began to wonder if Destiny had rigged this competition, and Luke was the chosen one.

"What's my manager's name?" Sarah asked.

Luke blinked, not understanding why she was asking the question. Worse yet, she'd gone from friendly to suspicious in two seconds flat. "Destiny Germaine. But why are you asking?"

"Have you talked with her?" Her green gaze bored into him, as if she was daring him to tell a lie.

"No, I've never talked with her." And a moment ago he'd thought everything was wonderful between them. Maybe she was psycho, after all. "But I remembered her name from Googling you because it was such an unusual one."

"Her name used to be Dolores, but she changed it."

"Oh. Like you changed yours."

She propped her hands on her hips. "Okay, you've talked to somebody."

"All I did was Google you. I swear." He'd intended to let his tidbits of info come out naturally, but the way she was grilling him, he might as well tell whatever he knew. "That's where I got your real name of Sally Debowski, and your parents' names of Frank and Lisa Debowski. And Oscar's name, and the fact you hate peanuts and love Kettle Korn."

"So nobody gave you a bunch of inside scoop? I mean, they added this problem-solving thing which is tailor-made for you. And you arrived here with doggie treats and Kettle Korn. It's almost as if someone wants me to…"

"What?"

"Come here. I want to show you something."

He followed her across the narrow space between the end of the bed and the dresser, with Oscar trotting behind them. At first Luke thought she might be leading him out to the balcony, but instead she turned abruptly, caught him by the hand and pulled him into the bathroom.

She was acting weird, and way too much like the psycho she'd played in *Death Plan*. He found himself crazily hoping she wasn't about to show him the blade of an eight-inch butcher knife.

She waited until Oscar was inside before she closed the door. He glanced around, looking for weapons, but all he saw were jars and tubes of lotion and makeup, plus a toothbrush and toothpaste.

Picking up the toothpaste, he held it out. "Is this what you wanted to show me? That you're a middle-squeezer? Because I don't care."

"No. And keep your voice down."

"I don't get it." God, he hoped she didn't turn out to be nuts.

She spoke in a low murmur. "This is the only place they didn't install a camera. We can't stay here long or we'll arouse suspicion that we're doing the wild thing in the tub."

With that statement, it dawned on him that he was closed in a tiny space with the woman of his dreams. It felt a little bit like the elementary school kissing game, Seven Minutes in Heaven. Girls had always wanted to go in the closet with him. Apparently he was a decent kisser.

"Do you *want* to do the wild thing in the tub?" If he'd been moving too slow for her, now would be the time to change his approach.

"No! I want to explain something and I don't want it to be on tape."

"Oh." Silly him, he'd thought for a minute that she might crave his body.

"Don't look so sad. It's not a terrible idea. But the timing's wrong."

She didn't think it was a terrible idea. With that, his groin tightened. He tried to think about something besides sex, but she was standing very close to him, and from what she'd said, having sex wasn't entirely out of the question.

"My manager wants me to get married," she said.

His heart sank. She was engaged. The reality show was only television hype, not a real chance to win Sarah's hand. "Who's the guy?"

"She wants me to settle on someone from this group."

His brain made a sudden U-turn. All was not lost. "I thought that was the point of the contest."

"Not exactly. The wording's ambiguous and sort of old-fashioned. It offers you a chance to win the *favor* of Sarah Donovan, like they used to do in the days of knights and tights. But the contract doesn't require me to choose a husband at the end, or even a fiancé."

"So what do you plan to do at the end of the contest?" He had a bad feeling about the answer, but he had to know.

"I'll imply that the winner has become very special to me without saying the *M* word. We'll do some press conferences, be seen in public together a few times, and that will be the end of that."

"I see." Disappointment settled in his gut. Obviously he'd read the contest rules and used wishful thinking to interpret them.

"But Destiny thinks that if I found my Prince Charming on this show, I'd reestablish myself as the sweetheart type and people might finally forget about *Death Plan*. So she wants me to pick a husband."

And just like that, his fortunes changed again. Heart thudding, he considered the murky ethics of the situation. Would he agree to marry her as a publicity stunt? Would he be willing to be the trained monkey who walked down the aisle so that she could regain her image in Hollywood?

In a New York minute.

"So that's why I wondered if you'd been coached," she said. "I thought Destiny might have stacked the deck. From your reaction, I can see that she didn't try that, fortunately."

He couldn't make the offer fast enough. "Sarah, if you need somebody to play the role of a husband in your life, I'll do it. I'll relocate. I have a pretty easy time getting clients, so I could build my business up again in no time."

She stared at him. "Um, thanks. But I…uh…wasn't asking that."

Heat crept up from his collar. Life didn't get much more embarrassing than this. "My mistake. I thought, because you told me all this, that you were considering Destiny's plan."

"Absolutely not. I would never marry anyone unless I loved him and wanted us to grow old and gray together. And seven days is not enough time to figure out if that's true or not. Don't you agree?"

He wished he could agree with her. Then he'd sound like a sane person. "No," he said. "I believe in love at first sight."

CHAPTER FIVE

SARAH'S HEART fluttered again. In spite of herself, she was becoming a lot more interested in this guy. Luke might be a financial planner with a mind like a computer, but he also had the soul of a poet. She hadn't realized that she'd be into that kind of romantic approach, but she was.

For her benefit, she wouldn't mind having Luke hang around this week. But he was liable to get hurt. That poet's soul of his could end up trampled in the dirt, not to mention the physical abuse he could take before he was eliminated from the competition.

Putting her hand on his arm, she gazed into his eyes. "I'm telling you this for your own good. Go home. Take yourself out of this crazy contest and go home. Forget me and find yourself a wonderful girl in Indianapolis who wants to have your two adorable children. I'm sure she's out there, some nice person who appreciates all the terrific things about you."

"No."

"You're going to get hurt. I don't want to be the one responsible for—"

"You're not. I'll take all the responsibility. I'll take the responsibility for this, too."

Before she understood what he meant, he pulled her into his arms.

"Wait, Luke. You don't know what you're doing."

"I've been told that when it comes to this, I know exactly what I'm doing." And he kissed her.

Talk about your truth in advertising. Luke did know what he was doing. She couldn't remember a kiss quite this good, and she'd had her share, both on camera and off.

His mouth was not too dry, not too wet, but just right. Oh, so right. The pressure of his lips sent a wave of excitement through every cell in her body, but the main event was taking place between her thighs.

Suddenly the thought of doing the wild thing in the tub had merit. She'd been teasing before, but now Luke was the one doing the teasing, using his tongue like the expert he apparently was. Damn, he was good at this, which suggested he'd be good at the whole program, from start to prolonged finish.

While she was still contemplating whether they'd both fit in that tub or whether the marble counter might be a better bet, he released her.

"I'm heading out," he said.

"Heading out?" That just didn't seem right. "Why?"

"I have to think this through, and I can't think while I'm kissing you."

"That makes two of us. But you don't have to go. We can go back in the bedroom and talk. We can talk about…financial matters."

He looked at her as if she'd lost her mind, which was sort of true. "If we go back in the bedroom, we won't talk about financial matters. I'll see you tomorrow."

And with that, he brushed past her, opened the door and left the bathroom.

She started to call after him, but in the nick of time she remembered that her voice would be picked up on tape. She didn't want all of TV-land to hear her calling out to him like some lovesick fool in a Grade B movie.

Oscar trotted after him, though. Oscar had no shame.

She heard Luke talking to her dog, followed by the sound of the zipper on Luke's backpack. Then a doggie treat landed with a plop on the carpet outside the bathroom. As Oscar ran to gobble it up, the outside door opened and closed with a soft click.

She wandered into the bedroom in a daze. For a guy whose tender feelings she'd worried about recently, he'd made a hell of an exit. She wanted him back. She also wanted more of whatever he was dishing out. But he'd taken that option right out the door.

Glancing at the bed, she saw her consolation prize. Propped against her pillow was a bag of Kettle Korn.

AT FOUR-THIRTY the next day, Luke stood under a hot shower and wondered if he'd have the strength to hold a glass during the cocktail party. At least he knew he wouldn't be eliminated today. Twelve other poor schmucks would be on the loser bus.

That's what everyone had started calling the getaway ride—the loser bus. Luke might not be leaving, but when it came to the physical part of this challenge, so far he sucked. The boulder toss and wrestling matches were scheduled for the next day, and if he didn't win immunity again tonight, he'd be gone tomorrow night, for sure.

At least he'd kissed her when he'd had the chance.

He'd have one shining memory to take home with him. That kiss had sustained him all through the day, when he'd crash-landed on the obstacle course…twice. The third round he'd made it without falling, but his time had been dismal.

He hadn't fallen during the rock climb, which might have resulted in breaking something significant on his body. But no matter how many times he'd tried it, he'd been the slowest guy to the top. What really chafed was how well Eddie and Cliff had done. They had a good chance of lasting to the end, while all that stood between him and a trip back to Indianapolis was a brain teaser.

After all he'd been through today, he might be too tired to tackle that equation. But even if he solved it, even if he won every immunity challenge, eventually he'd run out of chances. That meant he'd have to increase his score in the physical competition, which at this point seemed highly unlikely.

Oh, well. Liability would be thrilled to see him, or as thrilled as Liability allowed himself to get about anything. After last night's most excellent kiss, Luke had allowed himself to imagine a life with Sarah. Along with all the wondrous ways Sarah would change his life, he'd pictured how Oscar would liven up his stodgy basset hound's existence.

So that wouldn't be happening. How he'd ever thought he could compete on a physical level with actual jocks was beyond him. His obsession with Sarah must have blocked out all reason. Now he finally understood why they called it *reality* TV, even though the setup was artificial. A show like this made contestants face the reality of their own limitations. Dammit.

Eventually he climbed out of the shower and dressed himself, although the process was painful. Then he headed for the cocktail party.

"Hey, man!" Eddie walked over and clapped him on the back. "Glad to see you're still alive!"

The slap on the back had jogged some very sore muscles, but Luke gritted his teeth against the pain and smiled at Eddie. "Takes more than that to kill a guy like me." *Not much more, though.*

"You know, I had thought about finding some way to talk you out of your answer to the problem tonight, but after today, I don't think I have to worry about you in the long run. And if somebody else solves that equation tonight, you'll be dead meat."

That was something Luke didn't want to think about. What if some other guy came up with the answer? He hated to think of someone else knocking on her door and going inside for some intimate conversation. If the man was Dino, they might do more than talk. Dino had insinuated that he was skilled at getting a woman into bed.

"Don't count Luke out." Brett came over holding two glasses of champagne. He handed one to Luke. "You showed a lot of courage out there. You'll get a higher score tomorrow."

Luke took the champagne. "Thanks, but I don't have a lot of confidence in that. You did great, though. You should have a shot."

"Of course he did great!" Eddie swigged the last of his champagne. "A guy like Brett shouldn't be allowed on the show. He has a hell of an advantage."

Dino walked over to the group. "You mean because he's a gentleman and you're not?"

Eddie sneered at him. "You'd better be careful, city boy, or I'm gonna have to open up a can of whoop-ass."

Dino took a sip of his champagne before giving Eddie the once-over. "I am so scared."

"I suppose you think I wouldn't try anything, with cameras all around, but think again. I understand they like a little conflict on these shows, and I'm ready to give it to them."

Jacey, who always seemed to know where to point her lens, zeroed in on Dino and Eddie.

Luke caught Brett's eye. Together they moved on either side of Dino, each taking an arm.

"We have urgent business to discuss," Brett said.

"Right. Extremely urgent," Luke added. They maneuvered him to the other side of the lobby.

Dino resisted, but not much. "I can take care of myself, guys. You don't have to save me from that no-neck wonder."

"We're trying to save you from yourself," Luke said. "You'll be a lot less effective tomorrow with a black eye."

Dino bristled. "Maybe he'd be the one with the black eye. Ever think about that?"

"Odds are he fights dirty," Brett said. "Don't lower yourself."

Dino sighed. "Yeah, I guess you're right." Then he glanced at Luke, as if sizing him up. "How're you doing anyway?"

"There's nothing wrong with me that a vat of Icy Hot wouldn't cure."

"Yeah, but you spent time with Sarah last night. And because you've been so damned closemouthed about it,

I've concluded you got somewhere." Dino waggled his eyebrows.

"Nah, she threw me out."

"Yeah, yeah, yeah. That's not the word on the street, pal." Dino smiled. "But if that's true, maybe you should share your answer to the problem and give one of us a chance."

"I like you, Dino, but not that much."

"See, see?" Dino pointed his glass at Luke. "Something's going on! I can see it on your face."

Luke was about to change the subject to something less explosive when Digg and Sarah walked into the room. Everyone fell silent.

As Luke gazed at Sarah standing there in a long silver gown with her blond hair loose around her shoulders, he marveled that he'd been alone with her the night before. And he'd kissed her. Better yet, she'd kissed him back. The concept seemed impossible now, when she looked like a princess surrounded by her subjects, of which he was the lowliest.

Digg waited to speak, as if wanting to build the suspense. Finally he stepped forward. "As you all know, Sarah has reviewed the scores and she will have to eliminate a dozen of you, nearly half of this group, tonight. She'll do that in reverse, by calling up those who will stay and placing a medal around each man's neck. If your name is not called, then say your goodbyes and leave for the bus."

Sarah looked tense, which figured. Luke couldn't imagine that she'd enjoy this part. She took a deep breath and picked up the first medal from a tray sitting near her. "Dino Scarletti."

Luke tried to be happy for Dino. Unfortunately, he kept thinking of Dino solving the problem and ending up in Sarah's room. Tired or not, Luke would have to put forth his best mental effort.

"Eddie Schnaffle."

That name made him clench his jaw, but he'd been prepared.

"Brett Harrison."

Good for Brett. If he solved the problem tonight, he would sit and talk to Sarah. He wasn't a pushy guy at all.

"Cliff Pettigrew."

Unless they cheated, Eddie and Cliff wouldn't solve the problem, so Luke told himself to let any worry about those two go.

"Luke Richards."

Even though he knew he wouldn't be eliminated, he hadn't expected to get a medal. That was for the jocks, right?

Brett gave him a nudge forward. "Get your medal, brainiac."

Luke walked toward Sarah. God, she was gorgeous.

"Congratulations." She smiled gently and held the ribbon open. "Scoot down. I can't reach that high."

He leaned down, which gave him an outstanding view of her cleavage. He shouldn't take advantage of that, but he was a normal guy, so he looked. *Wowza.*

When she placed the medal around his neck, her perfume wafted around him. "Good luck tonight," she murmured.

He straightened and looked into her eyes. Had she really wished him luck with the math problem? Adrenaline rushed through him, and all his aches and pains magically disappeared. "Piece of cake," he said. Then he winked at her.

As he sauntered back to his place, he exchanged a grin with Brett and Dino. He'd winked at her! Maybe he could run with the big dogs, after all.

DESPITE KNOWING she shouldn't want Luke to stay, despite knowing he'd be eliminated once his brain power wasn't an issue, she wanted him to win the immunity challenge tonight. His romantic side coupled with his incredible kissing ability intrigued her. Then she'd watched him struggle through the competition and had been impressed with his courage under fire. She wanted at least one more opportunity to see him alone.

She was just starting to eat her room service dinner when someone knocked at her door. Her pulse rate climbed, although she knew it was way too early for anyone to have solved the new problem. Digg wouldn't give it to them for another hour.

As Oscar barked, she checked the peephole to find Burt standing outside. Quieting Oscar, she let him in. "What a surprise. Come in and sit down. You can help me eat this chicken. They gave me enough to feed a family of four."

"No, thanks." He didn't take her up on sitting, either. Instead he stood and fidgeted, reaching for his cigarettes and putting them back in his pocket, as if remembering she didn't like to be around smoke. "Sylvie's really happy about how the show's going."

"That's good to know." If he wouldn't sit, she'd remain standing, too. "I think the immunity challenge is a good idea." Without it, Luke would have been eliminated today.

Burt nodded. "I'm glad, too. Luke adds something to the mix. I know he stunk it up today out on the field, but he's a whiz at the math, so Sylvie wants to highlight the brains against brawn angle."

"But Luke will eventually lose." She hated to think of it, but after today she couldn't imagine how he'd rack up the scores necessary to stay in to the end.

"Maybe not. Adrenaline is a wonderful thing. He might get his second wind tomorrow. Anyway, Sylvie's *very* curious about what you and Luke were up to when you hid in the bathroom last night."

"I had something in my eye. Luke helped me get it out."

"Yeah, right." He reached for his cigarettes again. Then he shoved them back in his pocket. "Uh, about that note I left in your suite."

"Oh! I'll go get it." She started toward the bathroom.

"That's okay. You can tear it up."

She gazed at him. "Okay. Sure. Consider it done."

He stood there silently for several seconds. "Has anyone ever sent you anonymous notes?"

"You mean there have been others besides that one?"

"Yeah."

A chill passed through her. "Do you think you have a stalker?"

"God, I hope not." He ran a hand over his shaved head. "But these unsigned notes keep arriving. If it's a secret admirer, you'd think the woman would identify herself. Because she hasn't, I'm getting uneasy."

"Shouldn't you notify the police?"

He rolled his eyes. "Nope. When you've had a career like mine, you don't want some gung-ho detective rooting around in your past." He shrugged. "It's probably nothing, just some nutcase with too much time on her hands. Or his hands. I guess I shouldn't assume it's a woman. Maybe I turn some guy on."

"Burt, if you think you might be in danger, you need to get help."

"If I think there's any kind of danger, I'll will. In the meantime, have a good evening with Luke, and don't hide in the bathroom tonight."

She ignored the crack about the bathroom. "You're assuming Luke will solve the problem."

"Sweetheart, Luke will solve the problem. He finished the last one in twenty seconds without so much as picking up a pencil. Nobody else was even close to being done. We checked into his background a little more, and he graduated suma cum something-or-other. The guy's a freaking genius."

"Really?" *And he kisses like the devil in disguise.*

"Really. See you tomorrow. You might want to give our boy wonder a massage, though. The way he staggered off the field, I had my doubts he'd live through the night."

"I'll make sure he doesn't die on you."

"Good. Sylvie will be pleased. See you mañana."

After he left, Sarah did a little dance of joy, which got Oscar to barking again, so she had to calm him down by offering him a bite of chicken. But she could barely contain her excitement. Burt had presented her with an outstanding idea. Her champion Luke probably did need a massage after what he'd been through today. And she was just the girl to give it to him.

CHAPTER SIX

AN HOUR LATER, Sarah was as ready as she'd ever be for Luke to arrive. She'd stripped back the covers on the bed and piled the pillows in a corner of the room so she could use the bed as a massage table. She didn't have any massage oil, but she had some lotion that should work almost as well.

For her role as a massage therapist, she was wearing a light blue tank top and loose white pants. Although she'd never studied massage formally, she'd had enough of them over the years that she could give a decent one when called upon. Her mother swore by her technique and wouldn't even go to a professional anymore.

She'd found a radio station that played New Age music, which she considered perfect for the experience. And she could hardly wait to get her hands on Luke Richards, boy genius. If someone else solved the problem ahead of him, she was screwed, but Burt didn't think that was possible.

Anticipation made her nervous. She wished she hadn't eaten all the Kettle Korn while she'd sat on the balcony watching the competition today, but she'd been nervous then, too. Watching Luke struggle in an arena where he had no business competing and knowing his real talents lay in mental skills—and kissing—she'd suffered right along with him.

She'd also worked up a huge case of admiration for his dogged persistence. Maybe Burt was right, and he'd improve his scores in the physical competition, which would mean he'd have a chance to win, which would mean…well, maybe Destiny's idea wasn't so terrible, after all.

In preparation for his visit, she'd stocked up on beverages. Her bathroom sink was filled with ice and a selection of pop, bottled water, beer and wine. She missed her suite's minikitchen, but the smaller room was more intimate.

When the knock finally came, she jumped and Oscar barked. "Shush, it's only Luke." She hoped she was right in that assumption.

A quick check of the peephole revealed a sunburned Luke wearing khakis, a knit polo and a light jacket. His safety goggles had protected the area around his eyes, giving him a raccoon effect. His nose was bright red. He'd sacrificed himself for her, and he couldn't have looked more adorable.

Her heart did more than flutter this time. Instead she felt the beat drumming through her, making her short of breath. Yet it was *only Luke,* or at least that's what she'd told Oscar. She opened the door, and all she could think about was that kiss in the bathroom.

All that Oscar could think about, apparently, was more doggie treats. He stopped barking and began to wiggle and whine, instead.

Sarah felt like wiggling and whining, herself. Resisting the urge to grab Luke by the shirtfront and haul him up against her eager body, she tried to sound nonchalant. "Hi, there."

"The problem took me a little longer this time." He sounded tired.

"Because you're exhausted! Come in and relax." *Come into my lair and let me have my way with you.*

"Thanks." He stepped into the room and reached in his pocket. "Hey, there, Oscar. I brought you treats, but not the whole bag this time." Crouching down, he fed the dog one nugget. "That's a good boy."

Sarah watched him petting the dog with more interest, now that they'd had a kissing experience. He had nice hands. Chances were they'd be good hands, too. Her skin flushed as she thought about that.

But she was getting way ahead of herself. Luke had walked out on her last night, supposedly to do some thinking. She needed to find out where that thinking had led him.

"Can I get you anything?" she asked. "Pop? Water? Beer? Wine?"

"No, thanks. I'm good."

She thought he might be, at that. "If you change your mind, I have some options chilling in the bathroom sink." The bathroom had taken on erotic overtones, even though it was a different bathroom from the night before. All the ones in the smaller rooms looked identical, anyway, so basically this was the same space where he'd kissed her senseless twenty-four hours ago.

"Ingenious to use the sink." He stopped petting Oscar and stood with a small groan.

"Quite a workout today, huh?"

"I have to admit it was." He glanced at the bed. "I'm curious about this configuration, though."

"As a matter of fact, Burt suggested you might need a massage, so if you're up for that, I thought I'd give you one." Once he was loose and mellow, she'd explore his current state of mind.

He glanced up at the cameras in the far corners of the room. "Uh, maybe not. I appreciate the thought, though."

She kept forgetting how shy nonmovie people could be. "How about just your back and shoulders?" She wanted to get her hands on him somehow.

He glanced from the bed to the cameras and back at her. She could tell from his expression that he kind of liked the idea, but he was the complete opposite of an exhibitionist.

Finally he shrugged. "Okay. That sounds great." After taking off his jacket and laying it over the back of a chair, he pulled his shirt over his head and put it on top of his jacket.

So she'd talked him into seminaked, at least. What a nice, lightly furred chest he had. A girl could relax against a chest like that, one that was solid without being sculpted. Sometimes overdeveloped pecs could get in the way of a good cuddle.

But she was sorry to see that he had several scratches on his arms from his battle with the obstacle course and the rock-climbing wall. A guy like Luke had no business pitting himself against goons like Cliff and Eddie. Luke was a lover, not a fighter. Or so she fantasized.

He nudged off his loafers. Then he took off his

glasses and laid them on the table by the door. "So I should just stretch out on the bed?"

"That was my thought."

"Anywhere?"

"Anywhere. I'll straddle you." She hadn't meant to make it sound sexual, but it must have hit him that way, because his gaze swung immediately in her direction.

His blue eyes darkened. He might have blushed, too, but he was so sunburned she couldn't tell. He cleared his throat. "Okay." He chose to lie across the king-size bed instead of lengthwise.

She wondered if he'd done that on purpose, to make it seem as if they had a job to accomplish and weren't actually climbing into bed together. Silly boy, as if the position on the bed made any difference. But he was safe—she wouldn't attack him, at least not yet.

Oscar made a leap for the bed and missed.

"Stay down, Oscar," she said. Two was company, three was a crowd.

Oscar began to whine.

"Here." Luke rolled to his side, dug another doggie treat out of his pocket and handed it to her.

"Thanks. Oscar, go get it!" She threw the treat to a far corner of the room.

After grabbing the lotion from the bedside table, she climbed onto the mattress. "Oh, dear. You have a bruise on your back, too." Filled with remorse, she gazed at a purple spot the size of a fist under his left shoulder blade. She'd thought having him continue with the show was the right thing, but maybe not. Much more of this and he'd end up in the hospital.

He lay on his stomach, his eyes closed. "I thought I

might have a bruise. It felt sore there, but I couldn't see it very well."

"Luke, I feel terrible that you're putting yourself through this."

"I had an off day. Tomorrow will be better."

"I'm sure it will." She put lotion on her hands and closed the lid on the bottle before laying it down.

Oscar came back, whining to get up on the bed.

She pointed to his doggie bed under the table. "Go lie down. That's a good boy."

He gave her a look obviously designed to make her feel guilty as hell. But he went to his bed and plopped down with a sigh of resignation. She realized she hadn't had a sleep-over boyfriend since getting Oscar, so he wasn't used to this. Luke wasn't a sleep-over boyfriend, but he was in her bed.

She swung one leg over Luke's butt then knelt above him. "I'm going to sit on you, so if that hurts, tell me."

He nodded.

Slowly she lowered herself until they were cheek to cheek, in a matter of speaking. "How's that?"

"Um, fine."

"Am I hurting you?"

"No."

"Is anything wrong?"

"This is bordering on sexy, Sarah."

"Is it bothering you?"

"Never mind. Just do the massage."

She wondered if he was getting an erection, but as long as he was face-down, she'd never know. The idea that he might be getting hard was thrilling, but she wouldn't want to embarrass him by allowing the camera to film his woody.

If he objected to turning over at any point, she'd take that as a signal that he had something to hide. Leaning forward, she started in on the muscles in his neck.

"Mmm."

"Good?"

"Yeah."

It sounded like sex talk, but then massage could be like foreplay under certain circumstances. These circumstances qualified. As she kneaded his muscles, he groaned softly.

"Tell me if I'm being too rough."

"No. This is fantastic."

For once she was grateful for the video portion of the tape, which would document that she was fully clothed and he was still wearing his pants.

"I was afraid I wouldn't solve the problem first tonight," he mumbled.

"It must be hard when you're so tired." She got more lotion and smoothed it over his back. Then she thought about what she'd said and swallowed a giggle. She wondered if he'd figure out the double meaning.

"Yeah, it's hard." He said it with a heartfelt sigh, as if he hadn't thought of that at all.

"Do you work out at home?" Touching him was turning her on. Good thing she was wearing a sports bra under her blue tank top. If she'd gone braless, the camera would be picking up major nipple erection right now.

"Some. Not enough." He winced as she used the heel of her hand to go a little deeper.

"Sorry."

"Don't let up. I need this."

She wondered if he could guess what she needed. She was a little shocked at the thoughts she was having about Luke. Apparently his display of courage when he was so out of his element had flipped a switch inside her, and she wanted to rip the rest of his clothes off, flip him over and go to it.

But the all-seeing camera lens kept her in line. She glanced at the clock to gauge how long before the cameras would shut down. Too long. "So you're sure you'll be up for this again tomorrow?" she asked.

"Assuming I can get out of bed."

"This should help."

"Uh-huh."

She worked on him silently for a while, and gradually his soft moans stopped, so she concluded that the pain in his back muscles had eased. His calves and thighs needed this kind of attention, too, but he wouldn't strip to his underwear while the camera rolled, and she wouldn't insist on it. His modesty was endearing.

"I think that's all the damage I can do from this angle." She remembered her suspicion that he might be disguising an erection on the flip side. "Want to turn over?"

No answer.

"Luke?"

Still no answer.

She leaned forward and listened to his slow, steady breathing. He was asleep.

THE LAST THING Luke remembered was Sarah's hands working magic on his aching back. Yeah, having her so close had given him a minor erection, but even his penis was too tired to rise fully to the occasion. This incredible massage would be another memory to take back to Indianapolis, though. Not every guy could say that Sarah Donovan had straddled his hips and rubbed her hands all over his body.

He woke up in a darkened room and thought maybe he'd dreamed the day of pain and the massage in Sarah's room. But he still hurt all over, so something had happened to him to cause that. He reconstructed the course of events—competition, dinner, problem solving, Sarah's room, massage.

Under the covers he was wearing his boxers and nothing else, which was how he slept when he was in a strange place, in case there was a fire. At home he slept in the nude, but he kept a bathrobe handy for emergencies. On trips he didn't bother taking up suitcase space with a bathrobe.

As his eyes adjusted, he saw that the room looked like his, except that it didn't smell like his. Instead of shaving cream and sweaty socks, this room smelled of flowery perfume. He was lying crossways on the bed, with the headboard beside him. There was also a bottle of lotion on the bedside table.

Slowly he turned his head on the pillow and his breath whooshed out. Sarah was lying there sound asleep, her back to him. If they'd made love and now he'd developed amnesia, he'd kill himself.

He didn't think they had. He wouldn't make love to her and put his boxers back on. Once those came off, they'd stay off until he was required to appear in public again. But she'd undressed him down to the boxers. He had to hope that she'd waited until the taping was over for the night.

He was faced with a dilemma. The cameras were off, and he was in bed with the woman he'd dreamed about for years. He'd fallen in love with her on the screen, but he hadn't dared trust that feeling. He trusted it now. She was everything he'd imagined, and kissing her last night had erased the final doubt.

But she had a lot of catching up to do. She might never catch up, might never return his feelings. And yet, if he didn't take advantage of waking up in her bed, he would miss a golden opportunity to make some progress.

There was definite chemistry between them, unbelievable though that seemed. Was he willing to build on that, knowing that she might want nothing more from him than some mutual gratification? Well, yeah, he was. At least he'd have some outstanding memories.

But there was the issue of condoms. He didn't have any. He'd bet some of the guys had come equipped, but not him, a man who hadn't imagined himself in this situation. So he could wake her up, but they couldn't have sex, at least not full-fledged, anything-goes sex.

As he considered his options, he came up with the only one that made sense. Kissing her and leaving seemed to have made a good impression the night before. Tonight, he'd see if he could go one better.

Rolling to his side, he touched her shoulder. "Sarah?"

She stirred under his hand. "Mmph."

"Sarah." He shook her gently.

Slowly, languidly, she turned toward him, obviously still only half-awake. With a sigh she wrapped her arms around his neck and snuggled against his bare chest. "Mmm."

His arm just naturally had to go around her waist. She was wearing silk. He groaned at the sensuous feel of it. He wanted everything, the whole nine yards, but he couldn't have that. "Sarah, wake up."

She sighed again and wiggled closer. "Uh-uh."

"You're awake."

Her breath was warm against his chest. "Maybe."

He could probably seduce her, and lord, how he wanted to, but he wanted to make sure she knew who was in this bed with her. "Who am I?"

She lifted her face to his. "You don't know?"

"I know. Do you know?"

"Luke." She tunneled her fingers through his hair. "And I want you to kiss me."

His heart thundered. "I don't…I'm not prepared to…"

"It's okay." She drew his head down. "We can make out."

They certainly could. In the darkness he found her warm mouth, and the result was even more spectacular than when he'd kissed her the first time. She was so…accessible. Somehow his hand crept up under the silk, which turned out to be some sort of camisole, and in moments he was cupping her breast. He thought he might pass out from happiness.

She started to moan as he caressed her, and he realized that his original idea was doable. He could give her a gift, something to remember him by.

Deepening the kiss, which seemed A-OK with her, he explored downward, and his breath caught when he discovered exactly what he'd been hoping for—the hem of a pair of boxers. Sleeping in a silk camisole and boxers suited her style perfectly.

It also suited his intention. He slipped his hand under the loose leg of the boxers. Her skin was so soft, softer than the silk she wore. He moved slowly, waiting to see if she would stop him. She didn't.

When he encountered a springy nest of curls, his pulse cranked up several notches. Activity was taking place under his own boxers, but he ignored it as best he could. Probing gently, he found her velvet, dewy vagina and slipped two fingers inside.

She started breathing faster. Instead of stopping him, she shifted her body as if to give him better access.

Yes. He went for it, stroking her rhythmically while also paying special attention to her sweet little clit. She began to pant and her thighs trembled. He picked up the pace, and with a soft, keening cry she tumbled over the edge. He brought her back to earth slowly, caressing her during the aftershocks, until at last she took one long, shuddering sigh.

He kissed her lightly on the mouth.

She breathed his name.

Perfect, he decided. He eased out of bed. Ouch and double ouch. Between his sore muscles and his swollen penis, he was a wreck. He started with his shirt and hoped he'd somehow be able to get his pants on afterward.

"Luke?"

He glanced over at the bed. "Hmm?"

She'd rolled to face him. "Where are you going?"

"Back to my room."

"Like that?"

"Like how?"

"With that big piece sticking out."

Apparently even with the dim light she could figure

out his condition. "Uh-huh." He stepped into his pants and fastened them around his hips. With great effort, he forced the zipper closed.

"I'd be glad to…help you with that."

And he definitely would enjoy the experience. But his instincts told him to leave now, while she was still basking in the glow of her climax. If he lingered, he might outstay his welcome. "That's great to know. But I need to leave."

"You have thinking to do?"

"Yep." He shoved his feet into his loafers and picked up his jacket.

"Don't go. Think here."

He was definitely making progress if she was asking him to hang around. "If I stay, I won't spend the time thinking. See you tomorrow, Sarah." As he went out the door, he did his best not to limp.

CHAPTER SEVEN

ALL THROUGH the next grueling day of competition, Sarah alternated between irritation and longing. When she was in the longing phase, she shuddered every time Luke stumbled or took another body blow. When she was in the irritation phase, she was perversely glad that he was suffering. How could he have left her…again?

Sure, she'd had a climax, but he hadn't. She could have provided that for him, but he'd refused her offer. Of course she'd wanted more than a round of mutual petting. She'd wished for a writhing, sweaty, all-encompassing experience. But he hadn't had a condom. She'd actually found herself impatient that he hadn't thought ahead, but that had been her sexual frustration talking.

When she could think rationally, she admitted his lack of condoms was a point in his favor. She'd classify the guys who brought condoms as players, and she had no interest in becoming one of their conquests. Luke wasn't into that. He seemed genuinely to care about her.

Well, she was genuinely starting to care about him, too, and it wouldn't have killed him to allow her to repay his kindness with a similar gesture. She wondered how tonight would turn out. She became obsessed with the topic of what would happen after dinner.

Judging from what was taking place beneath her balcony, he'd be in worse shape than he had been before. He'd lost three consecutive wrestling matches, and when he'd tried to throw the large boulders across a line chalked into the sand, he'd wrenched a muscle in his shoulder. She could tell by the way he favored it.

This was not turning out well. She was falling for the guy who would never make it to the finals. Destiny and Burt wanted a Hollywood ending, where the best man won the contest and claimed the fair maiden. Sarah just wanted Luke. But this contest wasn't geared for a man like Luke. Poor Burt, there was no way she'd marry the winner, because the winner would not be Luke.

In the meantime, though, she couldn't help but think about what would happen after the immunity challenge tonight. Maybe tonight Luke would bring condoms. But she couldn't count on that, because he might not want to be seen buying them in the lodge gift shop. Consequently, she should probably have some on hand. Unfortunately, she couldn't be seen buying them, either.

The subject of condom-buying occupied whatever spare time she had left during the day. She couldn't figure out the logistics, though. She decided against asking anyone involved with the show to buy them for her. The news would travel through the production crew in thirty minutes.

While she was getting ready for the night's cocktail party and elimination ceremony, she finally picked up the phone and called the front desk. "Could you send a bellman to my room, please? I have some dry cleaning."

"Certainly, Ms. Donovan."

After hanging up the phone, she grabbed an outfit out

of the suitcase she'd already packed for the move to a new room. Then she took money out of her purse.

The bellman who rapped on her door was no more than eighteen. His name tag read *Timothy*.

She handed him her outfit. "Tomorrow will be fine for this," she said. "And, uh, there's another small errand I'd like you to take care of."

"Whatever you need, Ms. Donovan." He looked starstruck.

"You must keep this strictly confidential, Timothy."

He blushed. "Of course."

The request was harder to make than she'd thought. Holding out a fifty, she cleared her throat. "I need a…" She paused, took a breath and finished in a rush. "Aboxofcondoms."

"Excuse me?"

She clenched her jaw. "Condoms."

"Oh." He turned even redder. "S-sure. I can do that. What—what size?"

"Large. And I mean what I said. Don't tell anyone. I need you to deliver them ASAP, before I head down to the cocktail party." Sheesh, it sounded as if she planned to conduct an orgy at the cocktail party.

"Right." Avoiding her gaze, Timothy shoved the fifty in his pocket and started down the hallway.

"And keep the change."

"Okay." He didn't turn around.

Ten minutes later he was back, a small plastic bag in one hand. "Your item." He was still flushed.

"I can't thank you enough."

"No problem. Have a good night." Then his eyes widened as it must have dawned on him what he'd said.

"I mean, enjoy your evening. I mean, *thanks.*" He hurried away, muttering to himself.

She closed the door feeling giddy. She'd scored a box of condoms! Pulling the box out of the bag, she twirled around and lobbed the condoms into her open suitcase. Then she brushed her hands together. There. Let Luke try to weasel out of having sex with her *now.*

TWO HOURS LATER, Sarah had completed the ordeal of narrowing the field to seven. Luke, Dino and Brett remained. Cliff and Eddie had been awesome in the wrestling and boulder toss. That had pleased Sylvie, who still wanted them in the lineup. The other two who'd scored well enough to stay were a redhead named Vance and a burly guy named Jed, both of whom had allied themselves with Cliff and Eddie.

Now she was finally back in her room, awaiting Luke's knock. She'd skipped most of her dinner, not wanting to deal with a full stomach when she had other activities in mind.

Pulling out the heavy artillery, she'd changed from her red cocktail dress to slinky black lounging pajamas. Champagne was chilling in the sink, and she'd found a soft jazz station on the radio. Luke Richards was going down.

Waiting for him to show up seemed to take forever, but eventually the rap came and her pulse rate shot off the charts. Oscar had become used to the routine and didn't bark. Instead he stood there wagging his tail in anticipation of a doggie treat.

Sarah abandoned all pretext of nonchalance and flung open the door. "I thought you'd never get here."

"They're making the problems harder." He gave her

a weary smile as he fished a doggie treat out of his jacket pocket. "Here you go, Oscar."

"But you solved it first, again." She closed the door and looked him over. He had a scratch on his cheek from one of the wrestling matches, and when he crouched down to pet Oscar and had to move his shoulder to do it, he grimaced in obvious discomfort.

"I did solve it," he said, "but Dino and Brett are studying up, and I think they're getting better."

"Enough to beat you?" She liked those guys, but Luke was her evening man and she wanted to keep it that way.

He glanced up at her. "I'm not sure. What if they did?"

"I like having you win." She could say that much with the cameras rolling, but no more.

"Would you like having them win, too?"

She couldn't answer that, not on tape. "I'm going to get you a glass of champagne." Hurrying into the bathroom, she popped the cork on the bottle and poured the champagne into a couple of flutes she'd begged from the dining room. Then she glanced at her watch and groaned. So much time was left before the blasted cameras shut down for the night.

She'd love to get Luke back in the bathroom so she could explain about the condoms and invite him to hang out with her for a couple of hours. Once the cameras went off, they'd have the rest of the evening to themselves. But Burt had warned her about hiding from the cameras, and she didn't want to cause problems for him when he seemed to have enough on his plate with a potential stalker. Besides, she already knew she couldn't give him the finale he wanted.

So she'd have to hope that Luke got her silent message of seduction. Carrying the flutes, she returned to find he'd taken off his jacket and was seated in a chair with Oscar draped happily over his feet. She handed him his champagne. "Here's to your success."

He raised his glass. "I'll drink to that." He took a long swallow and set the flute on the table. "I've been thinking."

"About what?" She sat in the seat opposite him.

"We don't have a lot of time to get to know each other."

"That's why we have to make the most of the time we have." She sipped her champagne and adjusted her position to show off some cleavage.

His gaze settled on her chest and he swallowed hard. "But what about the other guys?"

"You're worried about them?" She toyed with the top button of her outfit and watched those blue eyes of his heat up.

"No." He brought his attention back to her face. "I'm worried that you can't make an informed choice because I'm always winning the mental part of the competition, so you and I spend the most time talking."

"Talking isn't everything." She looked directly into his eyes when she said it, willing him to remember being in bed with her the night before. She wanted his hands on her again. And tonight, she'd get her hands on him, too. She could hardly wait to wrap her fingers around—

"Because you get to watch them perform out on the field?"

"I suppose." If only she could let him know that she barely noticed the other men out there sweating and straining for her benefit. He was the whole show as he valiantly tried to survive in an alien environment. And although he might not perform well in a show of strength, she was convinced that he had incredible talent for performing in bed.

"Hmm." He took another long swig of his champagne.

"When you finish your champagne, I'd be glad to give you another massage."

He drank the last of it and set down his glass. "Thanks."

She stood, eagerly anticipating the joy of touching him again. She'd make sure that this time he didn't fall asleep.

"But no, thanks." He picked up his jacket and put it on. "I'll be fine. I think I'll turn in early. I appreciate the champagne." His glance swept over her. "And that's a fantastic outfit."

She was stunned. He couldn't leave now. Walking over to him, she boldly wrapped her arms around his neck. "I hate to see you go. There's lots more champagne."

She breathed the scent of his aftershave, mixed with the tang of whatever sports cream he was using on his sore muscles. Damn, but she wanted him. When he wrapped his arms around her waist, she thought maybe she had a chance to change his mind.

"I really do have to go." But his eyes had grown hot.

"You're sure?" She edged closer, shamelessly pressing against him to let him know that she had nothing on under the pajamas. In the process she learned that he had a good start on an erection.

"I'm sure."

She wasn't giving up without a fight. "Then let me

kiss you goodbye." Standing on tiptoe, she brushed a kiss against his cheek. "I have condoms," she murmured close to his ear.

He released her so fast she nearly stumbled. "Uh…thanks for the champagne. See you…see you in the morning." Then he was out the door, leaving her staring after him in confusion.

BACK IN HIS OWN ROOM, Luke paced the narrow space between the bed and the dresser, despite that every limping step reminded him of his various injuries. The woman had condoms. Had she brought them along? That question seemed the most important of all. Had Sarah planned to get it on with one of the contestants, and he happened to be handy?

And more specifically, did he care?

So what if she'd figured on getting some action while she was involved in this gig? With twenty-five willing men to choose from, she'd had a good chance of finding a likely candidate. He had the inside track, and if he didn't take what she was offering, maybe another guy would.

He'd been analyzing his role in this contest from the beginning. On a regular basis he'd paused to evaluate what was happening and whether he had a chance to win. After today's miserable performance, he didn't think so.

She liked being around him and there was chemistry there, but in the end, Dino or Brett would win out. If a wedding would boost her career, then maybe she'd actually consider marrying one of them. Luke might be a stop-gap measure, someone she'd make temporary use of. She didn't have much choice because he was the one with the best math skills.

He was still the only contestant who knew her room number and was allowed to visit her there. He was also the only one who knew she had condoms. Hell, the very first night he'd offered to marry her if she needed a husband for publicity purposes. Serving as her stop-gap sexual release wasn't any worse.

Well, yeah, it was worse. If she'd agreed to marry him, he'd have had plenty of time to convince her that he was the right husband, after all. Whether he climbed into her bed tonight or not, he could be gone once the show was over. Having sex with her now would increase the pain later.

But not having sex with her now might be the dumbest mistake he'd ever made.

ONCE SARAH stopped fuming, which took a while because she couldn't yell and scream while the camera was still on, she decided to drink the champagne. With very little food in her stomach, it went right to her head, which was what she wanted. Alcohol made her mellow and less likely to hunt Luke down and kill him.

By the time the cameras clicked off, she'd begun to sober up, which wasn't fun. But she hesitated to order another bottle and risk getting a reputation as a lush. Destiny wouldn't enjoy having to fight off that bit of negative publicity.

Propped up against the headboard of her bed, Sarah gave attention to the only male who cared about her. Oscar deserved a good scratch, or the best she could do when her coordination was a little off. Oscar didn't require perfect coordination. He was loving this.

"At least you appreciate me," Sarah told him. "I'll bet

any one of the twenty-five guys who started this contest would have jumped at the chance I gave Mr. Luke 'I-Have-to-Think-About-It-First' Richards. And I'll bet a bunch of guys all over the country, maybe even hundreds, would jump at the chance."

Oscar's little doggie groan said he agreed with her.

"Damn straight. I went to a lot of trouble to get those condoms, and does he even thank me for taking the initiative? He does not. He *leaves,* as if I'd announced I had cooties. Something's seriously wrong with that boy. He—"

Someone knocked on the door, and Oscar jumped down from the bed and started barking.

"Shush, Oscar. And if it's that rat, Luke, I'm not letting him in." She peered through the peephole. Sure enough, the rat had returned. Ignoring the curl of excitement in the pit of her stomach, she hooked the security chain in place before she opened the door a crack. "Go away."

"I'm sorry."

"That's the truth. You're the sorriest thing I've seen in a long time." Actually he looked yummy, all rumpled and apologetic. But he deserved to pay for his actions.

"You caught me by surprise. I didn't know what to think."

"You think too much."

He nodded. "Yeah, I do. Let me in, Sarah. Let me make it up to you, for being such an idiot."

The thought of how he might make it up to her really got her juices flowing. But she wanted him to suffer. "I would rather masturbate with the showerhead than let you in this room tonight."

He groaned. "Please let me in."

"I don't think so." She closed the door and stood right beside it, her hand on the knob.

He knocked again.

She stripped off her pajama top and threw it on the bed. Then she opened the door a crack, flashing him. "What? I was about to get in the shower."

His eyes widened as he apparently realized she was naked from the waist up. "Oh, God. Sarah, please." He stuck his fingers through the crack in the door.

"Move your fingers before I mash your hand in the door."

"Go ahead. You're killing me, anyway."

"I wouldn't really. Leave your fingers there if you want. I'm taking a shower." And she untied her pajama bottoms and let them fall to the floor, giving him a sliver of a nudie shot.

He drew in a sharp breath. "Sarah, dammit, let me in."

"Nope." She walked toward the bathroom. Once there she turned on the shower, but she didn't get in. She did, however, begin moaning softly. Then she let her cries escalate as she faked an orgasm. Afterwards she turned off the shower and peeked out the bathroom door.

Luke's fingers were no longer visible and the door was shut. She checked the peephole, and he was nowhere to be seen. Shoot! She was too good an actor for her own good. Luke was gone again.

CHAPTER EIGHT

LUKE SPENT a horrible night, waking up every hour or so to relive the agony of knowing that he'd blown what was probably his one and only chance to have sex with Sarah. Instead she'd gone into the bathroom and communed with a showerhead, making sure he'd heard the whole encounter. Maybe it served him right to be tortured like that for always having to think about things first.

Because he got very little sleep, the next day was worse than ever. Instead of wrestling, Sylvie the director, aka the Inquisitor, staged several boxing matches. Luke was groggy, anyway, and couldn't seem to avoid getting punched in the face. Dino gave him a shiner, and then apologized.

Luke told him not to apologize. They were all out to win. But Luke had never had a black eye in his life, and he was amazed at how much it hurt. Unfortunately the pain didn't stop him from thinking. Thinking had become the bane of his existence.

During the afternoon the contest was a tug-of-war tournament. Small wonder that Luke came in dead last. By rights he should have been too tired to think, but whenever he had a moment to catch his breath, he continued to analyze what was happening with Sarah.

By the cocktail hour, he was barely able to stand, so he propped himself up against a wall while he talked with Brett and Dino.

"Luke's in. We've gotta make sure we're the other two who stay," Dino said.

Brett took a drink of his martini. "Yeah, but that means we'll have to compete that much harder against each other. I don't mind pounding on Cliff and Eddie, but I'd rather not wail on you guys."

"Same here." Dino turned to Luke. "How's the eye?"

"It's okay. It was my fault, not getting out of the way."

"Yeah, well." Dino winked. "I'll bet you haven't been getting much sleep lately. Am I right? Or do the two of you spend all your time discussing Plato? Or playing chess?"

Luke didn't know what to say, but fortunately Sarah came into the room on Digg's arm right at that moment, so he was saved from having to comment. She wore royal purple tonight, and she looked like royalty, too, with a crown of flowers in her hair. If he hadn't been such a dope, he could have held her in his arms last night.

But even having sex wouldn't have answered his big question. He wanted to know if she'd wanted him in particular, or a man in general. He desperately needed to know that. The answer would tell him whether he had a real shot, contest or no contest, or whether he was doomed to heartbreak.

Digg gave his usual speech about how the losers were to conduct themselves. Then he left Sarah with a tray containing three medals and walked over beside one of the camerapeople, a young woman dressed all in black.

Luke thought there was something between those

two. They weren't obvious about it, but the air seemed to have sparks in it whenever they drew close together. Luke felt the same thing happening when he got near Sarah, but maybe it was completely one-sided.

Sarah stepped forward, a rigid smile on her face. "It's been a pleasure to get to know all of you." She didn't look at Luke when she said it. "Unfortunately, I can only pass out three medals tonight. Brett Harrison."

"Attaboy, Brett," Dino murmured.

"Dino Scarletti."

Dino gave Luke a thumbs-up before going to collect his medal.

"And the man who continues to win immunity, Luke Richards."

He walked toward her. If only he hadn't blown it the night before.

"Congratulations, Luke. You were very brave out there today."

"Thank you." He leaned down so she could put the ribbon around his neck.

"But you were a jerk last night," she muttered under her breath.

"I know." He met her gaze and lowered his voice. "I wish I had it to do over again."

She smiled for the cameras, but her eyes issued a challenge. "I don't," she murmured. "The shower was great fun. And now if you'll excuse me, I have to bid my departing guests goodbye."

He clenched his jaw and nodded, moving away.

"Hey, we're all in!" Dino held up both hands for a round of high fives.

"Yep, we made it." Brett smiled. "Luke, you should

feel good. You have another chance to solve the problem and spend the evening with Sarah. Show a little excitement, there, buddy."

"I'm excited, okay?" Luke said. But the truth was he was thinking again. He might be in the final three, but he had no chance of beating Brett and Dino in the physical competition. He could win another night with Sarah, though, and despite her comment, he hoped she'd forgive him and let nature take its course.

But if something did happen, he'd never know if she wanted sex specifically with him, or sex in general. The way he saw it, there was only one way to find out. He had to let Dino or Brett solve the equation.

As SHE WAITED in her room later that night, Sarah decided that Luke had suffered enough. Besides, the poor guy had a black eye. He deserved something special. Something special was exactly what she had in mind for him.

She'd tuned in a soft jazz station, and had another bottle of champagne chilling in the sink. When the knock came, she moved toward the door, her pulse racing. At last she and Luke would get naked...after the cameras shut down, of course. She peered through the peephole and nearly cried out in dismay when she saw who was on the other side of the door. How had this happened?

She opened the door and forced herself to smile. "Hello, Dino. Congratulations."

"Believe me, I don't know how I beat Luke." Dino stepped inside the door. "Maybe he took too many blows to the head today."

"Do you think so?" She put a hand to her heart. If competing in these physical games had somehow damaged his top-of-the-line brain, she'd never forgive herself. Even if she wasn't the one in charge, she still might have been able to do something to protect him. But she'd wanted him to stay, for her own selfish reasons.

"I think he's okay." Dino studied her as he took off his jacket. "But from the look on your face, I'd say you really care about the guy."

She quickly wiped off her frown. "I care about each of you. You're all awesome."

"So are you." Dino moved closer. "I've been hoping for a chance to be alone with you, and it's finally here."

Sarah chuckled and edged away. "Yes, it's only you, me and two wide-angle lenses."

"For a while, anyway." His gaze swept over her green cashmere lounging outfit. "You look really gorgeous in green. I don't think you've worn that color since we've been here."

"I'm getting to the bottom of my suitcase."

"Then here's to bottoms." He winked and moved in again. "I like this music. Care to dance?"

"Uh, sure." Reluctantly she moved into his arms, but it felt wrong to be there. For the benefit of the cameras, she had to pretend to like dancing with Dino. She'd been instructed not to show any partiality, because she was supposed to be thrilled with the results of the final episode.

Dino rubbed the small of her back and tried to bring her in closer. "You need to relax."

"Oh, you know what? I have champagne." She whipped out of his embrace. "I almost forgot. I'll get us some."

"Okay." His tone was cautious. "That'll work."

Once in the bathroom she took her time opening and

pouring the champagne. Dammit, she wanted Luke out there instead of Dino. Why had he lost this round?

"Need any help?" Dino appeared in the doorway.

"Nope. Just finishing up." She handed him a glass. "Let's go sit down. You can tell me all about yourself."

He set the glass on the bathroom counter and reached for her. "That cashmere is the softest material I've ever touched."

She dodged around him, nearly spilling her champagne as she left the dangerous confines of the bathroom. "I like it."

"So do I. Very seductive." He came out of the bathroom holding his champagne flute. "I have an idea. Let's put our feet up while we drink this." He sat on the bed and nudged off his shoes.

"Oh, that wouldn't work for me." She began to panic. "I'm so clumsy, I'd probably spill champagne all over the bedspread."

"That's why they have maids." He propped a pillow against the headboard and leaned back against it. Then he patted the spot next to him. "Come on, live dangerously."

"I hate to tell you this, but I think I ate something for dinner that didn't agree with me."

He frowned. "Really? What?"

"I had…shrimp. And you know what happens if you get contaminated shrimp." She clutched her stomach. "It's not pretty."

"Then you should probably lie down. Come on over here and stretch out. You'll feel much better."

"Actually, I feel like I'm going to throw up." And she was a good enough actor that she could talk herself into feeling sick to her stomach.

"Then we should call someone."

"No! Please. Having people around at a time like that is too icky, both for me and them. I just need to be alone and sleep it off. I hate to end your evening like this, but I have to."

"I'd be glad to stay. Barfing doesn't scare me."

"But I would die of embarrassment if you stayed. Please go."

"Okay." With a sigh he put his shoes on. "I'll check on you later."

"Please don't. I'll probably be asleep."

"If you're sure." He walked slowly to the door. Then he turned with a bright smile. "Get better soon. Because I'm planning to solve that problem again tomorrow night!"

"You do that." She smiled back, feeling a wee bit sorry for him. But if she'd let him stay, he would have tried to cuddle and kiss. She couldn't bring herself to do that. Luke had better be in top form the next day. First of all he had to put in one impressive performance on the field. Then he'd have to solve the problem the next night. Otherwise her food poisoning would have to become a bad case of stomach flu.

LUKE WISHED part of the competition included shooting pool. Even with one eye nearly swollen shut, he was clobbering Brett. Brett was good, but Luke was better. Pool could be broken down into mathematical formulas, which made it Luke's kind of game. He concentrated especially hard on each shot because if he didn't, he'd think about Dino in Sarah's room.

But when Dino walked into the sports lounge, Luke completely missed the cue ball. He glanced at the clock. Dino had spent a grand total of twenty minutes with her. A bonfire of happiness glowed inside him, but he had to be careful not to sound too eager to know what had happened. Brett could ask the first question.

"You're back early," Brett said. "She throw you out?"

"Aw, she ate some bad shrimp and now she's sick." Dino walked over to the bar and ordered a beer.

"Sick?" Luke's happiness disappeared immediately. "Shouldn't someone be with her?"

"Yeah," Brett chimed in. "Luke and I aren't supposed to get near her room, but you could. Or we could notify Digg."

"I tried to stay." Dino picked up his beer and walked over to the pool table. "I offered to hold her head, but she insisted she'd rather be alone."

"I still think we should tell Digg, at least," Luke said.

"Me, too." Brett laid down his pool cue. "I'll go find him."

"Tough luck," Luke said after Brett left. "Poor Sarah."

"Yeah." Dino took a swig of his beer. "Food poisoning's no joke. Believe me, I tried to stay and take care of her, but she was having none of it."

"Well, she's a movie star. She probably doesn't want anyone seeing her with her head over the toilet."

"I suppose."

Brett came back into the lounge. "I found Digg. He's going to check on her. If it's anything to be concerned about, he'll let us know. I said we'd be here for a while."

"Might as well shoot some more pool, then," Luke said.

"Yeah, you'd like that, wouldn't you?" Brett laughed. "I'm telling you, Dino, if we had to go up against Luke in this game, we'd be toast."

Dino put down his beer. "I'll bet I can take him."

Luke was in the process of running the table on Dino when Digg walked into the lounge. "I guess it's just mild food poisoning," he said. "She's promised to call me if she feels any worse, but she doesn't have a fever, so I think she'll be okay in a few hours."

"That's good to hear," Luke said.

"Ditto," added Brett.

"I'm glad, too," Dino said. "All I have to say is, I'm in great shape. I won immunity tonight, and if I beat Luke at that math problem once, I can do it again. And I will."

Maybe. Maybe not. Luke played pool for another couple of hours, until the other two called it a night. Once they were headed for their rooms, he took off for the restaurant kitchen. He found a guy dressed all in white with a chef's hat on. He was cleaning the large commercial stove.

The man looked up from the stainless steel surface he was polishing. "Can I help you?"

"Just a quick question. I heard a rumor that we were having shrimp tonight for dinner, and I love shrimp, so I was excited. But we had pork chops, which were good, but my taste buds were set for shrimp."

The chef looked confused. "I don't know who said

we'd have shrimp, because it's not on any of the menus for this week. Sorry about that."

"Maybe somebody thought that if Sarah was having shrimp tonight, we all would."

"She didn't have shrimp tonight. She had pork chops, like you guys. As a matter of fact, we're completely out of shrimp. We're expecting some in next week, but we don't have any right now."

"I see." Luke worked hard to keep from grinning like a kid with a new bike.

"If you can make it back next week, I'll fix you the best shrimp dinner you've ever had."

"Thanks. I'll keep that in mind." As he left the kitchen, Luke couldn't feel a single one of his aches and pains. Even his black eye didn't bother him. Sarah didn't want just anybody—she wanted him. But he'd lost his chance for immunity so he'd have to kick butt in the physical competition. He'd have to beat Brett. And he would. Somehow.

THE NEXT DAY'S competition was even tougher to watch, because Sarah knew how much Dino, Brett and Luke liked each other. And this would be the last day of competition, so they were giving it all they had.

For this day's effort, Sylvie had combined all the previous challenges into one long day of obstacle-course runs, rock climbing, wrestling, boulder tossing, boxing and tug of war. Sarah wondered how Luke kept up the pace, but apparently the days of physical exercise had toughened him, because he seemed to have more energy today than he'd had all week.

Of course, he'd lost his chance at immunity, so he had to do better or be eliminated. Maybe skipping an evening with her had rejuvenated him. That was a depressing thought. She was beginning to wonder if he'd let Dino solve the problem first because Luke didn't want to deal with her anymore. Maybe her last remark to him about the shower had turned him off completely.

Brett, on the other hand, seemed to lose momentum. It was almost as if he'd decided to let Luke have an advantage. At the end of the day, to her amazement, Luke had enough points to edge out Brett. So it would be Luke and Dino. And one more problem to solve, not for immunity this time, but for one last chance to spend the night with her.

Late that afternoon, as she dressed for the final cocktail party, her cell phone rang.

"I've left you alone all week," Destiny said, "but Burt's kept me informed. He thinks you like the financial planner. Is he right?"

"I like them all."

"Come on, Sarah. You know I'm not going to tell anyone."

"But I'm still not sure who will win, so what can I say?" She had no idea who would show up at her door tonight, but she had a strong feeling that Dino would win the competition. Luke had outdone himself today, but he couldn't keep that up.

"Okay, okay. Keep your secrets if you must. But tell me, could you possibly see yourself marrying one of those three?"

"I haven't had enough time to decide something like that."

Destiny blew out a breath. "You're going to drive me to an early grave, girl. Listen, on another subject, I understand you know about those crazy notes Burt's been getting."

"He told you about them?"

"He called to ask if I was sending them as a joke. Unfortunately, it's not me trying to be funny. I don't think that would be a very good joke."

"Me, either. Are they becoming threatening?" Sarah's stomach twisted in fear. Stalkers were a real problem in Hollywood.

"No, but they're persistent. I told him to ask his buddy Patrick Hennessy to investigate. The guy's the head of an excellent P.I. firm, but Burt says he doesn't want to get Patrick involved. He apparently has some skeletons in the closet and he doesn't want his friend to know about them."

"I wish he'd do something. This person could be a total nutcase."

"Just what I told him. Listen, if you get a chance, try to convince him to hire somebody to look into it. If not Patrick Hennessy, then somebody. Whoops, gotta go. As for you, young lady, I hope the winner is somebody you're ready to waltz down the aisle with. It would make your old manager happy."

"'Bye, Destiny."

"'Bye, sweetheart. Kiss, kiss." The line went dead.

Sarah disconnected the phone with a snort of annoyance. Destiny really would marry her off to the nearest guy because it would be a good career move. To hell with love and happily ever after.

She couldn't forget, though, that Luke had been willing to marry her if it would help out. Of course, Luke had probably changed his mind. She'd been a real smart aleck, even when he'd sincerely apologized about leaving her suite. She'd allowed her hurt pride to be in charge. She'd punished him for being exactly who he was—a thorough, thoughtful kind of guy. The kind of guy a girl could fall in love with, given a little more time.

CHAPTER NINE

LUKE STOOD WAITING for Sarah and Digg to come in. He wasn't drinking his margarita, and he noticed that Brett and Dino hadn't made much of a dent in theirs, either. Conversation had lagged, too. Tonight either he or Brett would be sent home. For the first time there were more members of the camera crew in the room than contestants.

"I think I'll be the one to go," Brett said at last. "I ran out of steam today."

"But you're the best athlete," Luke said. "How could I have done so well against you today?"

Brett gazed at him. "Because it's the way it should be. Both you and Dino really want this. I…realized last night that I…don't."

"So you backed off on purpose?" Dino seemed upset. "That's not right."

"Yeah, it is." Brett smiled. "When I got this far, I figured out that winning this contest could play hell with my baseball career. I don't need the distraction. I finally got my priorities straight and accepted that I'm not in love with Sarah. She's a great girl, but I'm not ready to get involved with whatever media circus will come out of this."

"But what about the million dollars?" Dino asked.

"If I concentrate on my pitching, I'll earn a hell of lot more than that. I'd be foolish to screw up my focus right now."

"Thanks, Brett." Luke shook his hand, more relieved than he could say. With Brett out of the picture, he had a fighting chance.

"Good evening, gentlemen," Digg said as he brought Sarah into the room.

Sarah looked stricken. "This is tough for me. I didn't realize how tough it would be." She took the tray holding only two medals as Digg stepped to the side. "It's been a privilege to know all three of you. I wish you each every happiness in the world."

"Same here," Brett said.

"Absolutely," Dino added.

Luke discovered his throat was tight and he couldn't say anything, so he simply nodded. He was suddenly convinced that in spite of his performance today, it hadn't been enough. She'd send him home and keep Dino and Brett.

Sarah took a deep breath. "We'll start with the man who won immunity last night, Dino Scarletti."

Both Luke and Brett clapped him on the back before he went up to get his medal.

Sarah gazed down at the floor for a few seconds. When she glanced up, her eyes were moist. "Luke Richards."

His heart full, Luke turned to Brett. "Thank you. You've been a good friend."

"Now it's up to you and Dino." His gaze was steady. "Go get your medal."

Luke walked toward Sarah and tried to read what was in her eyes.

"Congratulations." Her voice quivered.

"Thank you." He leaned down and kissed her on the cheek. "I feel honored."

"You do?" She sounded surprised.

"Of course." With a smile, he backed away, going to stand beside Dino while Sarah said goodbye to Brett.

"I should warn you," Dino said, "that I stayed up last night working math problems."

Luke adjusted his glasses before meeting his gaze. "And so did I."

"OSCAR, if Dino Scarletti comes through that door tonight, I want you to bite him. Not bad, but enough to cause a ruckus, so I'll have to call Digg, and we can spend a lot of time worrying about the bite instead of me having to deal with Dino. How's that?"

Oscar cocked his head and looked at her as if she'd gone crazy. Which of course she had. She was crazy about Luke Richards, and she didn't know if he still felt the same about her. She'd been a fantasy to him, and that whole silly business with her pretending to have an orgasm in the shower might have ruined his fantasy.

To be fair, they'd both behaved poorly. First he'd run off when she'd told him about the condoms, which wasn't the right move. But then when he'd returned to apologize, she'd been equally stupid in her response.

Tonight she had no champagne, no wine, no beverages at all chilling in the sink. She was wearing an old pair of gray sweats and a ratty Bart Simpson T-shirt. If Dino showed up, she didn't want to look seductive. She'd been caught by surprise the night before, but that wouldn't happen again.

She prowled the perimeter of her room, and Oscar pranced along behind her, as if he thought this was a new kind of game. When the knock sounded at the door, she nearly tripped over him as they both barreled toward it.

Taking a shaky breath, she crossed her fingers on both hands and looked through the peephole. Oh. She had trouble unlocking the door, because her hands were shaking.

"Hi." Luke stood there in a T-shirt, jeans and the jacket that always held doggie treats in its pocket. But instead of reaching for one, he gazed at Sarah. "I made it."

"So I see." Somehow she kept herself from throwing both arms around his neck. Her whole body vibrated at the sight of him. "Come in. Make yourself at home."

"Thanks." He sauntered in. Then he reached in his pocket and pulled out a doggie treat. "Here you go, Oscar." He threw it in the far corner of the room.

Then he stepped forward deliberately, took off his glasses, hauled Sarah into his arms and kissed her.

She was so shocked that he'd do that in front of the cameras that for a moment she didn't respond. Then the warmth of his mouth broke the spell, and she kissed him back. She kissed him back with gusto, sliding her arms under his jacket and holding him tight.

He moaned softly. Then slowly, with obvious reluctance, he lifted his head. "Let's watch TV."

She gazed dreamily into his eyes. "TV?"

"Yeah. One of your old movies is on cable."

"I don't really want to watch—"

"It's a good way to pass some time, don't you think?"

Then she got it. They had two hours to kill before they could do whatever they wanted. Sitting and talking, knowing they couldn't do much else, would be torture. He wanted to be with her for those two hours, but he realized they both needed a distraction.

She gave him a squeeze and moved away. "I'll turn on the set."

While she found the remote and turned on the TV, Luke took off his jacket and propped pillows against the headboard. "Come on, Oscar." He patted the bed.

"You want Oscar up there?" She glanced at him in surprise.

"Sure do." He helped the dog up. "Right in the middle."

So that's how they watched her movie, with Oscar lying happily between them, soaking up the attention. And there was plenty of attention, because they couldn't seem to get enough of petting the dog. Their hands brushed constantly.

"I like your outfit," Luke said about halfway through the movie. He didn't look at her, just kept stroking Oscar.

"It's the real me."

"Uh-huh. That's why I like it."

She hoped he'd like it even better lying on the floor in a heap. God, what time was it? She couldn't see the clock from where she was, and she didn't want to make a big deal out of looking, either.

Then she noticed he was wearing a watch. "I like your watch."

"Me, too." He took it off and handed it to her, making sure they touched quite a bit in the process. "It's got an alarm."

"Really? How handy." She wondered if he'd set it to go off when the two-hour camera session was over. "So you use it to get up?"

"Yeah. Whenever I want to get up. Exactly."

She peeked over at him, and he was gazing at her with so much heat it was a wonder her T-shirt didn't catch fire. Then she remembered the condoms were in the bathroom. When that alarm went off, they wouldn't want to waste any time.

She handed the watch to him. "If you'll excuse me a minute, I'll be right back." Sliding off the bed, she headed for the bathroom. Once in there, she closed the door, as if she might actually have to be in there, as far as the cameras were concerned. Then she had another idea.

Stripping off her T-shirt and sweats, she unhooked her bra and stepped out of her panties, which were already exceedingly damp with anticipation. TV watching as foreplay. Who would have thought it could be? She put her sweats and T-shirt back on and tucked a condom in her pants pocket. Then she flushed the toilet for Sylvie's benefit.

Sylvie would edit that out. In fact, she'd probably ditch most of this tape. The viewers wouldn't care to see two people watching TV and stroking a dog. Sarah climbed back on the bed and started petting Oscar again.

"Nothing chilling in the sink?" Luke asked, still pretending great interest in the movie.

"Not tonight. Do you want something?"

He shook his head. "Not right now. I'll get it later."

She pressed her lips together to keep from laughing. His comment spiked her arousal even higher, and she crossed her arms over her chest to disguise her nipple erection.

"I really like the way you did that scene," he said a few minutes later.

"Thanks."

"I mean, you just threw yourself into that moment. It's electric. It's—" His alarm started to chirp. "It's time."

Her heart raced. "What…what about Oscar?"

"Let's see how long this holds him." Reaching in his pants pocket, he brought out three doggie treats and threw them in different directions.

Oscar leaped off the bed and started foraging.

Then Luke took off his glasses and laid them on the bedside table. "What was that you said about condoms, Sally?"

His use of her real name tugged at her heart. "Only the people who know me really well call me that," she said softly.

He smiled. "And I'm about to become one of them."

LUKE HAD TRIED to play it cool ever since he'd walked into Sarah's room, but when she pulled a condom out of her pocket, he lost all pretense of being cool. He sort of tackled her, pinning her to the mattress and covering her with kisses while he started working her out of her clothes.

Then he discovered there weren't many clothes to work her out of. At some point she'd pared down. Kissing and nuzzling her soft body, he eliminated both the sweats and the T-shirt, until he had one very naked, very gorgeous woman lying under him. "When did you do this?" he murmured, stroking her with both hands, devouring her with his gaze.

"In the bathroom just now."

His heart leaped. For one awful moment he'd been afraid that she'd decided to ditch the underwear for whatever guy showed up. "Thank you." He ran his tongue around her nipple. "Oh, thank you, Sally."

Her breath came in quick little gasps. "You're welcome, Luke. Now take off your clothes."

"I'm having too much fun." He licked his way over both breasts. "You don't know how long I've dreamed about this."

She started fumbling with his belt. "I want you naked."

"Yeah, but you've only wanted that for a couple of days. I've wanted this for years." He dipped his tongue in her belly button. Then he explored lower, and before he knew it, he was settled between her thighs, getting a taste of the best she had to offer.

"Luke…get undressed." Although she was panting and arching toward him, she somehow still managed to issue orders. "Now."

"In a minute. Let me do something first." And then he completed what he had in mind, and from the way she writhed on the bed and cried out his name, he thought she was pretty happy about it.

Unfortunately, Oscar was barking and running around.

Luke placed some more lingering kisses between her thighs. "Your dog's upset."

"He's…he's never…he doesn't understand what's… happening."

Luke liked the sound of that. It meant she hadn't had a serious lover since she'd had the dog. But he didn't want Oscar distracting him from all this wonderfulness. Good thing he'd saved his ultimate weapon for tonight.

He left the bed. "Don't go away."

"As if." She lay sprawled on the mattress in sexy abandon.

He wished that his eyesight was better so that she didn't look so fuzzy. Sarah would be worth getting contacts for. Reaching into his jacket pocket, he pulled out the chew toy he'd brought along. The doggie treats had worked just fine before, so he hadn't felt the need to use it. But now Oscar required something to occupy him for…well…hours. Yeah, hours.

SARAH WAITED IMPATIENTLY for Luke to undress and get himself back into bed. To his credit, he was being very fast about it. And the chew toy for Oscar was an inspiration. Her dog had settled down in his bed and was gnawing away, oblivious to what might be happening.

And plenty was about to happen. Her eyes widened when she got her first good look at Luke's full monty. She hoped the condom wasn't too small. To come this close and then be denied by a skimpy condom would be a crime against nature.

But as she watched, Luke rolled the condom on with no trouble at all. Stretchy little things, those condoms. She might have to write a letter of thanks to the manufacturer.

"You have more than one, right?" Luke climbed back onto the bed and leaned down to brush his lips over hers.

"A whole box." She combed her fingers through his silky hair and held his head still so she could nibble on his lower lip. "Planning to use them all?"

"You never know." Then he moved over her and used that lovely equipment for what it was intended.

From the first deliberate thrust, she could tell she was in for one fine experience. All systems go. Go, go, go.

Bracing his hands on either side of her, he looked into her eyes as he eased back and pushed deep again. "How's that motion treating you?"

She smiled, savoring each delicious shiver running through her. "I can live with it."

His gaze sharpened. "Think so?" He settled into an easy rhythm.

She should have chosen her words more carefully. And now she could barely think at all. "It's a...figure of speech." Oh, glory, glory. He knew exactly how to maneuver in this territory. Ah, yes. She grasped his hips to better feel the pistonlike action.

"Never mind." He picked up the pace slightly, and his voice roughened. "Just let me know what I can do for you."

"You're doing it."

"That means what's good for me must be good for you." His breathing grew more labored.

"Safe assumption." She felt the first twinge of an impending orgasm. "Oh, yeah. Like that. Like *that*."

"No...kidding." He stroked faster. "Ah, so good. So very..."

"I'm...coming...." She grabbed hold and lifted her hips, meeting each thrust as wave upon wave crashed upon her. Her cries of pleasure mingled with his deep groans as he rode her climax, reaching...reaching...and shuddering at last in her arms.

She clung to him, gasping for breath. They were so good together, better than she'd imagined. She thought he might choose this moment to ask what would happen tomorrow. He might not beat Dino in the physical competition. They were alone, as intimate as two people could be, with no cameras to record what either of them said.

But he didn't ask. Through a night of lovemaking like she'd never known, he didn't ask. Early in the morning, he quietly left her room, making sure no one was around to see him go.

She kissed him goodbye, every second thinking he would ask what she would do if Dino won. She would have told him. But apparently he didn't want to know.

THE LAST PHYSICAL CONTEST was, as Luke might have predicted, ambiguous. He and Dino were given staffs and told to fight with them as if they were in a remake of *Robin Hood*. The struggle was awkward, tiring and hurt like hell.

At the final bell, Luke wasn't sure who had landed the most blows, but he felt that Dino had done a better job. Dino was in better shape, after all. But the producer obviously wanted to keep both men in suspense as to the final outcome.

Luke would learn his fate at sunset out on the balcony of the lodge in a few minutes. He waited in a room down the hall, a place which gave him no view of the balcony so that he wouldn't know whether Dino had gone before him and lost, or would follow him...and win.

Win or lose, Luke had promised himself that he wouldn't spoil his and Sarah's night of passion with questions about the contest or their future. He might be the secret pleasure she'd allowed herself before moving on to a more acceptable partner, someone like Dino, or someone totally removed from this contest. He hadn't wanted to press her on that point. It was enough that she'd wanted him, and only him, to hold her.

Even if, by some miracle, she chose him as the winner, that didn't mean they had a future. She'd said that a week wasn't long enough to choose a lifelong partner. And she'd only had a week. He'd had years of loving her from afar, and these few days had been all he'd needed to bring that love to full bloom.

For this final moment of the show, he'd dressed in a tux. At least he wouldn't leave in the loser bus. Making it to the last night meant driving away in a limo. That was the good part. The bad part was that someone with a camera would be in the limo, recording his grief. He vowed they wouldn't get that from him.

He'd lived his fantasy, if only for these few days. Sarah had made love to him all night long, and if that had to last him a lifetime, he'd accept that. He'd given her pleasure—he was absolutely sure he had from her moans and cries of delight. Maybe she'd remember him fondly in the years ahead.

The door to the room opened. "Ready?" Digg asked.

"You bet." Sure, his heart was pounding like a son of a bitch, but he was ready. He could face her and take whatever verdict she delivered, because his real victory had been claimed in the privacy of her bedroom.

As he walked out onto the balcony, the setting sun surrounded her with a golden aura. He couldn't see her face clearly, only that she wore a floor-length dress of gold with a full skirt and a plunging neckline. She looked like a princess. A sexy princess, but a princess nevertheless.

She held out both hands to him. "Hello, Luke."

He took her hands and brought them up to his mouth, placing a kiss on each. "Hello, Sarah."

Holding onto his hands, she drew him closer. "When

this week began, I doubted that I would become close enough to any of the contestants to choose one as my life partner."

"I know." He gazed into her green eyes and saw nothing but good things there. She might be about to lower the boom on him, but she cared about him. He'd take solace in that.

"But I was wrong. I have found someone I would choose as a life partner, if he'll have me. Fortunately he also won the competition today…by a whisker."

He knew he couldn't have won, but he also couldn't believe that Dino was her chosen one. She'd faked food poisoning to get out of spending time alone with him. Yet what if he was? What if he'd won the contest today, and she'd decided to bolster her career with a wedding, exactly as her agent had suggested?

He felt the first stab of grief. He'd thought he could handle it, but now he wasn't so sure. "I'm happy for you," he forced himself to say.

"I want you to be happy, too," she said. Tears glistened in her eyes.

"I will be. I promise I will be." Oh, God, this was going to be bad. He'd be lucky if he didn't blubber like a baby once he got in that limo.

"That's good to know, Luke, because the man I want to spend my life with, the man who squeaked out a victory today…is you."

He blinked. "You're kidding."

"No." She sniffed. "No, I'm not. I love you. I want to marry you, if you'll have me."

"You're serious." He couldn't get his mind around it.

He'd been prepared for failure, but he hadn't given a single thought to how he'd deal with success.

She nodded. "Now you have to say something. Yes or no?"

"Omigod."

"Don't think about it too much, Luke. This isn't a time for thinking. This is a time for reacting with gut instinct. Do you want me or not?"

The reality of it burst upon him. Maybe she was after the publicity, but after what they'd shared last night, he didn't think so. He believed she was after him. "Do I want you? Hell, yes, I want you!" He scooped her up and swung her around.

It occurred to him that, despite his overtaxed muscles, he felt no pain. Then he drew her close and cradled her beloved face in both hands. "I love you, Sally Debowski. Marrying you would make me the happiest man in the universe."

"That's what I want you to be." And she kissed him.

OUTSIDE THE RANGE of the cameras, Burt Mueller watched as the camera crew led by his daughter, Jacey, moved in to capture the final few shots of the happy couple. Then he pulled out his cell phone and punched in a number. "Hey, Destiny, we got us a wedding. Yeah. Luke Richards. Common spelling. Sure, we had to fudge the results a little. She fell for the runner-up. Whatcha gonna do?"

As he listened to Destiny, he observed Digg watching Jacey. He couldn't tell if this ploy of his was working or not, bringing Digg out to be his celebrity host.

But it didn't seem to have hurt. Maybe they'd be inspired by Luke and Sarah.

"No, Destiny, you can't release it until the last episode airs," Burt said. "You know that, so don't push. No, not even hints. But the main thing is, we've got a hit show. The chemistry between these two is great TV, and we'll milk the wedding for all the publicity we can. Okay, talk to you later."

So this one was in the can, and it would be a hit. He'd make money and Sarah Donovan would get offered a good part in a major movie. He was sure of it.

Next week he'd start work on the new project, which, amazingly enough, featured competition among a bunch of P.I. teams. And the best aspect was, as part of the game, he could assign one of the teams to investigate his crazy note writer. God, he was indeed brilliant.

* * * * *

Look for the next book in
Vicki Lewis Thompson's "nerd" series,
NERD GONE WILD,
coming February 1, 2005, from
St. Martin's Press.

THE GREAT CHASE
Julie Elizabeth Leto

To Leslie Kelly, who I can always count on for invaluable friendship and support, an insatiable sense of fun, and brilliant ideas like "Getting Real."

And to the Temptresses, the most talented, hilarious, caring, irrepressible, fabulous writers I've ever had the honor to know and be friends with. Temptation might soon be gone, but it will never be forgotten!

PROLOGUE

"OKAY, BURT, you've got until the espresso comes to deliver your pitch."

Burt Mueller set down his fork and waved for the waiter to remove his half-eaten rabbit food. This was the part of the business he both loved and hated—The Pitch. No more than five stress-filled minutes that could make or break this must-do deal. The man across from him, some richer-than-God investor whose name he'd likely have forgotten if his production assistant hadn't plastered it all over the business plan he had in front of him, wore his aloof expression with practiced antagonism. In reality, investors needed investments as much as producers needed money to create new television shows, and yet the guys with the cash insisted on being wined, dined and, essentially, begged for their coin. Well, Burt had been in Hollywood a hell of a long time. He could beg with the best of them.

"Think *Magnum P.I.* meets *The Amazing Race*."

The man quirked an eyebrow. Good sign number one.

Burt smoothed a hand over his bald head. His skin was smooth and dry, a clear sign that he was keeping it together—and that was pretty amazing considering he'd been holed up with Mr. Moneybags in this Beverly Hills bistro, making ridiculous small talk, for the past half an hour without a cigarette.

Thirty useless minutes. But what happened in the next five was what would count.

"We assemble ten teams of two, some amateur sleuths like mystery writers and *CSI* addicts, and some pros—for example, a few private investigators and maybe a reporter or two. In each episode, the teams are given a case to solve in forty-eight hours. Every episode will have a theme."

He slid a glossy sheet of paper out of his pitch package. Visual aid. Very effective. "This is how I see episode one. The theme is 'Lost in Space.' The teams have to identify the origin of the item and in some cases, return it to its owner. We'll shoot footage of the successful P.I.'s showing up on the doorsteps of everyday Joes who have lost their high school class rings or the $10,000 they left in a forgotten account. Imagine the emotion. The drama!"

The man—God, what was his name again?—turned the paper over, but there was nothing on the back. He frowned and Burt blinked furiously to keep from rolling his eyes. Weren't the slick graphics and key talking points on the paper enough? Of course, they were. If the silent treatment was this jerk's best shot at intimidation, Burt had this deal in the bag.

"And then what happens?" the guy asked. What *was* his name? Skip Something. Shemp? Aw, hell. Could be Curly, Moe or Larry for all Burt knew.

But his question was a good sign.

"The team that doesn't succeed is booted off the show. If there is more than one losing team, we go to an online vote."

"What if everyone succeeds?"

"The online vote goes on. A team has to be eliminated in each episode—more than one on the first few shows—so that we're down to two pairs by the last episode where they play for a million bucks."

"What's the twist?"

Okay, so the bozo with the bling did know his stuff. In reality television, there was always a twist.

"On the final show, the challenge will be very difficult. They'll have to work together to succeed, and yet, when the moment of truth comes, the partners can choose to dump each other and go for twice the cash."

The man's expression was noncommittal. "Why is that exciting?"

"The pairs aren't going to be randomly set. In this case, the betrayals are going to hurt."

Burt fingered through the profiles of the contestant pairs he and his production team had already put together. With the money he'd generated from his first hit, *Surviving Sarah,* which had just ended its successful run, he'd completed all the initial production for the new show, which he planned to call *The Great Chase.* They'd completed all contestant interviews and the screen tests were in the can, ready to show the director. All they needed now was the last infusion of cash to put the show into production.

With only a moment's hesitation, Burt pulled out the profile of the pair he'd personally put together. These two might not win the competition—as producer, he'd have little control over that—but if Burt's instincts proved correct, and they usually did, they were going to fix the personal problem Burt had been grappling with for longer than necessary. If not for the strange, pseudo-threatening notes he'd started receiving just a few months ago, the idea for *The Great Chase* would never have emerged. Now he had a shot to not only find out who was poking around in his private life and threatening to reveal his most carefully hidden secret, but he could also wow television audiences from coast-to-coast at the same time. This incendiary pair was going to burn up the screen.

He handed the profiles to the investor. "Meet Charlotte Cuesta."

The man whistled. Yeah, that had been Burt's first re-action as well. She was a dark-haired, dark-eyed Latina with curves that didn't quit and a fiery temperament that had taken the producers by storm. One grin at the camera from this *chica* and Burt could practically hear salsa music playing in the background.

"Charlie is a private investigator from Florida, running her own business for the past nine years or so. She's done okay for herself, but isn't quite pulling in the bucks of her former lover," Burt teased, then handed the man the second profile, "Sam Ryan."

Looking at the photo the man nodded, then licked his lips. Oh, great. Did everyone in Hollywood swing both ways nowadays?

"Attractive man."

Burt took a second glance, but remained unmoved.

However, even his daughter, Jacey, who was thoroughly whipped on her own on-again, off-again lover, had drooled over the guy. He had all the looks of a Hollywood heartthrob. Combined with the fact that Sam and Charlie had a romantic past that had led them to stop speaking to each other, Burt knew the coupling was going to tear up the ratings—once the show was on the air.

"He's rich, too. Successful. Cocky as hell. Works for one of the top agencies in the South. He and his ex-lover are ocean's apart in the income area, which we're guessing is a bone of contention."

"That's why they broke up? Money?"

Burt grinned. He guessed these two would end up stars on this show, whether they liked it or not. As he'd anticipated, the questions about their private lives would suck people in. And this guy didn't even know the best part yet.

"See? You're interested. You're enticed by the emotional stuff and you haven't even seen how hot they'll be together. And believe me, they'll be like fire. We don't know the details, but something scandalous happened to tear them apart. They were in the police academy together and got kicked out at the same hearing. It was all very hush-hush. But we do know they haven't spoken to each other since. Can you sense the drama? The angst?"

"The sex appeal," the investor said, flipping back to the photograph of Charlie.

"You've got it," Burt said confidently.

The guy smiled. "So do you, my friend. I'm sold."

Burt accepted the man's proffered hand and gave it

a hearty shake. Finally! *The Great Chase* would make it on the air and if Burt's instincts proved correct, not only would Charlie Cuesta and Sam Ryan burn up television screens from coast-to-coast, they'd unknowingly solve his personal problem without anyone finding out what he really had to hide.

CHAPTER ONE

GOD, SHE LOOKED crappy in gray.

Charlotte "Charlie" Cuesta gave herself one last perusal in the bathroom mirror before straightening her thick, black-framed, clear-lens glasses and smoothing her equally dark hair into a slick ponytail. She grimaced at her reflection, making the tiny mole she'd glued just above her lip more noticeable. Wasn't the most flattering disguise she'd ever donned, but though the man she was about to confront was the sexiest combination of male flesh and bravado she'd run across in her entire twenty-nine years, her purpose today wasn't to entice or seduce. She simply had to know how she'd ended up in Sam Ryan's life again when he was the last man on earth she'd ever wanted to call "partner."

Hence, the disguise. Not that she didn't expect him to recognize her. That wasn't her goal. Thanks to the rules of the reality television show she'd been playing for a little over three weeks, she and Sam weren't supposed to meet without a chaperone, preferably one with a camera. But Charlie wasn't one for following rules that could so easily be broken, with a little finesse. Still, to avoid being disqualified early, she had to make sure that anyone she might encounter on the way to Sam's hotel room just down the hall, or anyone watching through the surveillance cameras mounted throughout the hotel, would never suspect that she was contacting Sam outside the perimeters of the game—a game she truly wanted to win.

After three weeks, she should have been able to figure out what was really going on. She wasn't naive. Game shows like this always had a twist, some underlying theme or motive that the contestants were oblivious to while the television audience was privy and entertained. She couldn't help questioning just why she and Sam had been thrown together as partners again, after all this time, with all their baggage. Did the producers know about their past relationship, now a nine-year-old bad memory? And why was Sam letting her call all the shots during the tapings? It wasn't his M.O. Ever since they were revealed as teammates, he'd been acting oddly. As if they'd never been lovers. As if he didn't give a damn that she'd solved all five challenges so far, nearly without his help.

Of course, she didn't gain much satisfaction from the success. Sure, they'd accomplished each and every one of their tasks, but the assignments had been piece-of-cake stuff an amateur could pull off with a good Internet connection and a little shoe leather.

Questions swam in Charlie's brain like sharks on a feeding frenzy. But asking herself the questions with no answers forthcoming wasn't cutting it anymore. She needed a one-on-one with Sam. Privately. With no one watching or listening or recording their every word and gesture to air later for an audience of millions. She glanced at her watch. If she didn't get her butt in gear, she'd lose her window of opportunity.

Her recognizance over the past three weeks revealed that no matter the location of the show, between five o'clock and six o'clock in the evening, the director, a Hollywood cokehead named Rick Ralston, went out for dinner. His meal normally consisted of a tofu salad and a couple of snorts of blow purchased from the doorman or the desk clerk or the guy who sold newspapers outside the hotel. While Rick was out, his assistant's assistant, a plebe named Leon, manned the helm of the control room, which was parked outside the current hotel in a nondescript white motor home capped with satellite dishes. Luckily for Charlie, Leon had his own addiction. *Days of Our Lives.* When Rick went out, Leon caught up on Marlena and the gang in Salem, leaving the monitors on, but unattended.

So for one hour, Charlie had the perfect chance to sneak into Sam's room and find out what the hell her partner knew about the strange turn the reality show had taken.

Loading her arms with towels, she pushed her frustration away at the thought of the word *partner.* Up until now, she'd never had one. Well, that wasn't entirely true. She'd once been partnered with Sam back at the police academy and the utter disaster of that pairing had soured her on such combinations. When she'd signed on with the series' producers, they'd vowed she'd have no one around to cramp her style.

Liars.

She shouldn't have expected any less from television types, but by the time they'd sprung their big "reveal" that Charlie would be figuratively shackled to Sam for the duration of the taping, she couldn't back out. She'd agreed to do the show at the request of Patrick Hennessy, a friend of the show's producer and her potential new boss. The head of one of the largest private investigation firms in the South, Patrick was the only top-level investigator to show interest in Charlie. She'd grown tired of running her own private investigation business, especially since few clients wanted her for more than routine background checks and, sometimes, to track down a cheating husband. If she wanted the tough cases like corporate espionage or celebrity stalking, she needed to be on the Hennessy payroll.

Which she would, Patrick had promised, once she competed on-air. And of course, Hennessy expected her to win. She wondered if he'd known ahead of time about Sam and the child's-play cases. Hell, from what she knew of the guy, he was probably getting a real chuckle out of the whole deal. Sam did, after all, work for Hennessy's biggest rival, Foster and Bragg.

Yet despite their tenuous pairing, they were winning.

In less than two minutes, Charlie had slipped out of her room and down the hall. She kept her eyes down, whistling, as she jangled the keys hanging from her pocket, just one more convincing detail for her disguise. The keys wouldn't open anything of use—for that, she'd swiped a slide-card passkey from the cameraman who'd come into her room an hour ago to replace the hidden camera that had mysteriously stopped working. *What a morooon.* How he'd missed the scent of the nail polish remover she'd squirted into the mechanism was beyond her.

At least not everyone associated with the show was an idiot or an addict. Her personal camerawoman, Jacey Turner, was one sharp cookie. Charlie didn't look forward to explaining her disappearance to Jacey if the goth-dressed camera jockey returned before Charlie had accomplished her covert mission. She'd have to hurry.

She pounded on Sam's door three times. "Housekeeping!"

No answer. She didn't expect one. She'd spoken to Sam ten minutes ago and he'd told her he planned to shower. As loathe as Charlie was to confront Sam Ryan while he was naked and wet, she didn't have much of a choice if she wanted privacy from the game show's cameras. The only place where the contestants weren't watched was in the bathroom.

She clutched the towels close to her chest. *Come on, Charlie. It's not like you haven't seen the man naked before.*

The memories made her quiver.

With a quick glance as soon as she entered, Charlie spotted the camera in Sam's room, angled away from the mirror. Knowing the camera was accompanied by a microphone, she continued her jaunty whistling, but softly, to avoid any unwanted attention.

She walked into the bathroom without hesitation. If anyone witnessed her entry, they'd surely think she had every right to be there.

The minute she caught sight of a naked Sam through

the smoky glass shower doors, she froze. The towels nearly tumbled from her arms, but she caught them. Damn, he was gorgeous. Tanned and buff, he moved with casual grace as he soaped his skin and sang some tune that sounded mildly country-western. She rolled her eyes, allowing his fondness for annoying music to snap her out of her lusty reverie.

From the moment they'd met nine years ago, both rookies at the police academy in Tampa, Florida, they'd marveled at the differences between them. She preferred Latin Fusion to his country twang. He was a vegetarian and she was a devout carnivore. When out of uniform, he wore blazers with his blue jeans. She preferred slinky skirts and tottering heels. His ideal Friday night date had been popcorn and an action flick, followed by a beer at his neighborhood tavern. Though she didn't mind an occasional bust-'em-up movie, popcorn stuck in her teeth and her thirst wasn't usually quenched by hops, malt and barley. No, she preferred dancing herself into a slick sweat, then cooling herself down with an icy *mojito*.

They were apples and oranges. Actually, more like apple pie and mangoes.

"See something you like?"

She jumped, startled as he swiped the glass with his hand, clearing his view. Even beyond the fogged shower door, his blue eyes sparkled above his signature smug smile.

She dropped the towels on top of the sink.

"We need to talk," she answered.

"About your propensity for voyeurism?"

She smirked. "All those big words," she quipped, thickening her accent and ignoring how boldly he stood there in all his naked glory. "Aren't you afraid I won't understand?"

He slid open the shower door, his grin not wavering. Dollops of hot water drizzled off his skin and the steam quotient in the tiny bathroom increased to a dangerous level. Visibility, however, wasn't hampered. Charlie had to concentrate hard to keep her eyes trained on his.

Not that looking into Sam Ryan's eyes was any safer than taking a leisurely perusal of his body. Piercing blue with flecks of gold, his irises could bring a lesser woman to her knees, especially with the frames of thick, chocolately lashes that were two or three shades darker than his hair. When he was dry, that was. When wet, his hair spiked into dark, sharp tips that could only be tamed by a woman's hand.

"Don't play stereotypes with me, Charlotte. You know I don't have anything but the utmost respect for your incredible…intellect."

Even though she was dressed in the dowdiest, frumpiest unbelted housedress in the drabbest gray ever created by uniform manufacturers, his hungry expression made her feel like a hot mama in a halter-top and miniskirt. A leather miniskirt. With fishnet stockings and spiked heels. Moisture tickled between her breasts and her mouth seemed coated with cotton.

"Is that why you're letting me win this game without you?" she asked.

He grabbed a towel, twisted around to turn off the water, then took his sweet time wiping the moisture off his skin. She stood there and watched with as much brazen attitude as she could muster. Just because her mouth salivated at the memories of tasting that hot, tanned, wet male flesh in a shower a lot like this one didn't mean she had to blush or turn away. The pinkening color and flushed heat of her own skin was a simple side effect of talking to him in the overheated bathroom. "You're winning for both of us," he pointed out.

She smashed her lips together to contain a feral growl. His arched eyebrow challenged her to contradict his arrogance, despite her effort not to jump at his bait.

"I'm not doing anything for you," she snapped. "I'm in this because I have a job on the line."

"That's nice," he said, every syllable dripping with condescension.

"I'm so glad you think so," she countered, lacing her words with clear sarcasm. "See, I'm in this for myself, Ryan. I'm not as nice as I used to be."

He stood up straight, briskly brushing the towel over his chest, an amazingly taut expanse of muscle. The steam swirling around her was suddenly infused with a distinct, musky scent. She would have held her breath if she'd thought she could keep from passing out.

"Whoever said you were nice in the first place?" he asked. "Nice doesn't get you kicked out of the police academy for fraternizing with a fellow recruit."

Nice try, but he wasn't going to unnerve her so easily.

"True," she conceded. "I've never been mistaken for a nice girl, just like no one in their right mind would peg you as a nice guy. You were booted to the curb just like I was, Romeo."

He bent down and dried one leg, then the other, his grin flashing. "But we certainly ended up in different places, didn't we?"

Oh, he wasn't pulling any punches. Charlie ground her teeth together, determined not to let him see how his success after their shared scandal irked her to the core. Wasn't like he hadn't had every right to turn his life around. And he'd been damned lucky to land a job with Foster and Bragg, one of the top private investigation firms in the country. She couldn't resent him just because he hadn't struggled as she had, hanging out her own shingle and spending most of her so-called career chasing unfaithful spouses and collecting information on bounced checks and previous addresses.

Well, by all rights of logic and fairness, she couldn't resent him. But hey, she was a woman. Who said she had to be logical or fair?

"We certainly took different paths," she said diplomatically, "but we both ended up in the same place— on a reality television show, trying to win a million dollars. Though I can't imagine why you need the money, judging by your portfolio."

He eyed her warily, slowing his ministrations as he dried between his legs. Even unaroused, which he wasn't entirely, he was impressive. Charlie fought the instinct to lick her lips. He always could push her buttons, sexual and otherwise, like no other man in the world. With a glance, he could challenge her. With a gesture, he could stir any and all of her passions, her competitiveness, her righteousness, her lust. She should be grateful their indiscretions had been discovered early in their affair or she might be nursing a broken…something. Not a heart. They hadn't known each other long enough and emotions had hardly been at play.

For the weeks they'd been involved, the world had stood aside while she and Sam sparred and clashed. They'd taken their insatiable passions from the police academy classroom to the soft-side waterbed in his South Tampa apartment. Well, she didn't have to react now the same way she had in the past, no matter how natural she'd once found flirting with him, enticing him, teasing him until desire overrode her common sense.

"I'm flattered. You poked into my private finances. Shows you still care," he teased.

It took effort, but she grinned. "Your accountant has a hole in his firewall. If you play your cards right, I'll show you how to fix it."

"Oh, so you're a hacker now?" He twirled the towel around his waist and tucked in a corner.

"I've been called worse," she answered.

For an instant, his smile faltered. The pained look on his face instantly transported Charlie to nearly a decade earlier—the last time she'd seen him before they'd both shown up for the first day of taping on *The Great Chase*. Did he remember the scene he'd witnessed the day they'd both been dismissed from the academy after a mortifying disciplinary hearing? God, her father had been enraged. With her. With Sam. With the disciplinary board of the academy that might have forgiven a sexual relationship between two adult recruits—if they hadn't succumbed to their raging hormones in the academy gymnasium after a private workout. Her father's curses had been hard to forget.

Charlie had forgiven *Papi* for calling her ugly names. What father wouldn't resort to such vulgarity when his only daughter's sexual propensities were dragged out for public consumption? Besides, her father had apologized more than any man with his store of pride could be expected to. He'd begged her forgiveness—just as Sam had—and *Papi* had never mentioned the incident again. Slowly her family had healed. But for reasons she didn't quite understand, she had chosen not to absolve her lover. It was so much easier to begrudge him his success…so much easier to harbor anger over the fact that when she'd begged him to leave her alone, he'd honored her request.

At least, it *had* been easy. Since he'd shown up unexpectedly in her life again, the righteous indignation was harder and harder to summon.

"You don't deserve name-calling, Charlie. You never have. You're damned good at what you do."

The warm timbre in his voice shocked her back into the present. She stepped back, her defenses primed. Nothing could knock out her good sense quicker than a jolt of Sam Ryan.

She forced her thoughts back to the matter at hand. "Then why are we getting the easiest cases to solve on every episode? I mean, yesterday, episode four, we had to find the owners of a lost cat that had an identification chip!"

"Well, we had to know how to find the chip," he reasoned.

She frowned. "That's another thing. There was no *we*. Why are you letting me work out the cases without you? I'm making you look like a bigger fool than I look like myself."

Sam stopped his forward movement, dropping his hand to his side with a brow-tilting grin.

"No, love. That's where you're wrong. First, you come across as a brilliant detective who makes everything seem easier than it is. As for me, I'm looking like the sexiest man this side of Hollywood. And I have you to thank."

CHAPTER TWO

SAM WATCHED CHARLIE'S face intently, searching for something more than surprise in her bottomless brown eyes. God, he'd missed those eyes. And those lips— thick and pouty and full. Nearly a decade had elapsed since he'd last tasted her mouth beneath his, but he remembered her hot, spicy flavor with the same famil- iarity as the toothpaste he'd used shortly after getting her phone call.

He was a hopeless, horny fool—he accepted that. Why else would he have gone to all the trouble of ar- ranging so Charlie Cuesta could be his partner on a re- ality television show? He couldn't exactly pinpoint the moment when hooking up with her again had become important. Could have been when he ran across an ad for her private investigation business in the local news- paper. Might have been that time he'd caught sight of her at the courthouse. And of course, the possibility ex- isted that he'd never wanted to leave her in the first place and had done so only because she'd asked.

When his boss at Foster and Bragg had come to him with the reality television show as a means for free pro- motion for the agency, which was losing market shares to smaller firms in a few large cities, Sam hadn't been thrilled—until he'd met with the producers. Once he realized he could get Charlie on the short list of contestants, he'd become much more willing.

He'd known Charlie was struggling to keep her tiny, one-woman business in the black. He'd known her killer body, exotic looks and hellfire attitude would make good ratings. He'd also known that if he played his cards right, he might manage to undo the biggest mistake he'd ever made in his life—letting her go.

Truth was, he didn't give a damn if millions of television viewers all over the country found him sexy or stupid, as long as Charlie Cuesta found him irresistible. Though, so far, she'd been resisting him with a fair amount of ease. Of course, he hadn't been trying that hard. If he turned on too much charm too fast, she'd make a beeline for the door. He'd focused instead on giving her space and showing her he wasn't the same overbearing, cocky bastard he'd been when they'd first tangled.

"Sexiest man in Hollywood?" she asked, adding more shock to her voice than the claim warranted, in his opinion. "What in the hell are you talking about?"

Sam squeezed between her and the vanity, forcing himself to ignore the peppery perfume curling off her skin. He dropped the lid on the toilet, then gestured toward the one and only "seat" in the room. She declined with a sharp glare.

He shrugged and sat. "Ratings, my dear. Ratings."

"The show has only aired once."

"Twice, as of last night. Both times, *The Great Chase*

has landed in the top ten. And did you see the article in *People* magazine? They said, and I quote, 'There's a fire smoldering between Sam and Charlie that could burn the production to the ground if they ever act on it. Let's hope they surrender to the passion very, very soon.' End quote."

She stared at him, wide-eyed. Stunned.

Was their mutual attraction that surprising? Could she be that oblivious?

"Didn't Jacey give you a copy?" he asked. Jacey's assistant, Ed, had beat a path to his door with the article. The ink had practically smeared in his hand.

Charlie's mouth had dropped open in shock, but she managed to shake her head in reply.

"Hmm," Sam voiced, wondering why the producers showed him the article and not Charlie. He may be a fool when it came to women—this woman in particular—but he understood the television business fairly well. Not that he had any experience, but network wrangling wasn't nuclear science. Hell, this was *reality* television—it didn't have the complexity or nuance of, say, underwater basket weaving. The recipe for success was simple. Sex equaled ratings. Ratings equaled money. Money meant power. And nowhere could producers so easily manipulate the action as much as they could with reality TV. All they had to do was maneuver the players, often by giving some information to some players and not to others. Like the article.

For the first time since taping began, Sam experienced a twinge of suspicion. Maybe he hadn't truly gotten his cockiness under control. He'd assumed that his experience at a top agency like Foster and Bragg gave him an edge over the other contestants. He couldn't be so easily duped or manipulated. Now he wasn't so sure.

"Back up," Charlie ordered. "They're talking about us in magazines?"

Sam caught the distress in Charlie's eyes before she blinked it away. For an instant, he witnessed the same expression he'd seen that day at the police academy— the face of a lost little girl disappointing her father with reports of her sexual transgressions. Embarrassment. Shame. Pure mortification. Hadn't her family come to terms with his and Charlie's indiscretion after all these years? Hadn't she?

Suddenly, her actions over the past three weeks made sense. "So that's why you've been avoiding me as much as possible. You didn't want anyone to see."

She straightened, her mouth a tight line. "Didn't want anyone to see what?"

He couldn't resist. God help him, but the woman stirred his senses with the dizzying power of a carnival ride. Before she could fight him, he stood, snagged her by the arms and pressed his mouth to hers.

The heat was just as the magazine predicted—instantaneous and fiery. Her mouth was moist and hungry, opening to his tongue a nanosecond before he decided to go for broke. Their kiss was ravenous and elemental, sparking every lustful part of Sam's body. Blood rushed to his sex so fast, he had to slam one hand against the wall behind her to keep from falling and dragging her down with him.

Though that's what he'd done nine years ago, wasn't

it? Let his dick override his good sense until they'd both been staring at expulsion, humiliation and ruin?

He stepped back at the same moment she did, but he didn't release her arm. He had no desire to feel her palm across his cheek, or worse, her powerful right hook. After a split second, he realized she could knee him to make her point, so he surrendered to the panicked look in her eye and let her go.

"I don't want you anymore, Sam," she claimed, her lips bruised and plump from their quick, but intense kiss.

"Okay," he answered, knowing she was lying, but aware that now wasn't the time or the place for an argument. If he could just hold out for two more assignments, he'd have his chance at reconciliation. What woman wouldn't be more open to the idea of rekindling a lost love affair after she had a check for a million dollars in her pocket and the entire country behind their romance?

"Excuse me?" she asked.

"I said, okay. I shouldn't have kissed you," he said, lying calmly. "I apologize. It's just that, damn, even in that getup, you turn me on."

That part was the honest-to-God truth.

He swallowed a grin as she self-consciously smoothed her tight hair and ugly dress, and keeping her gaze firmly locked with his. No doubt, she'd felt his erection pressed against her belly just as he'd felt the tight points of her aroused nipples against his naked chest.

"Why are you doing this?" she asked.

"Doing what?"

Her hand gravitated to her lips, where she pressed her fingers lightly over her mouth. "Being nice."

"I'm a nice guy."

Her smirk preceded a Spanish phrase he knew meant something along the lines of *give me a break*. "You are a lot of things, Sam Ryan, but I told you, a nice guy isn't one of them."

"Maybe I've changed."

"Maybe you've just refined your singular brand of charm." She tore off her fake glasses and tossed them into the sink, then licked her lips and groaned, her gaze rolling toward the ceiling. "*Pero, madre de Dios,* you're still a good kisser."

Her admission proved that his hands-off policy with Charlie had been a wise strategy up until now. In the past, hands-on had definitely worked much better, but the final outcome had been an unqualified disaster. He'd opted for a different route this time, employing heated glances and innuendo rather than blatant seduction. While Charlie hadn't been swayed—yet—the television audiences were enthralled. Would they? Wouldn't they? How? When? Where? Would it all be caught on camera? The lurid possibilities were endless.

Fortunately, no one but Sam realized how truly resistant Charlie could be. But the *People* article had not only verified that the attraction between them was still palpable—at least to other people—but that the women in the television audience thought the way he was chasing Charlie would ultimately lead to sexual fireworks.

Now, he just had to convince Charlie.

He grinned, heartened by the wistful sound in her

throaty voice. His body still thrummed from the brief but intense contact and he was glad he'd taken the chance.

"But I didn't come here to seduce you," she said, jabbing toward him with her index finger. "I would have dressed differently for that."

He laughed. "That's not exactly your usual choice in fashion. Trying to avoid the producers?"

She crossed her arms and leaned on the wall, bumping her head lightly on the towel rack. "Of course. It's a good thing, too. If I'd worn my regular clothes, you might not have been able to control yourself."

He nodded. "Good point. So why did you come here, Charlie? The rules expressly forbid—"

"Screw the rules, Sam. I have a few questions I'm hoping you can answer."

"Yes, I still want you."

"That wasn't one of my questions."

"Oh," he replied, not the least bit contrite. "Okay. But I thought you should know that anyway. Just in case you missed the subtle implication before."

She smirked, and with a blatant glance at his crotch, verified that she would never miss anything so painfully obvious. "What I really need to know is why we keep getting easy cases."

Sam grabbed his T-shirt and jeans from the hook behind the door. He'd wondered the same thing and he had a working theory on the phenomenon. "My guess is they don't want us eliminated."

"Why not? Without eliminations, they have no game."

He shrugged into his shirt. "Well, we have that whole

sexual tension thing going on. Do you want to read the *People* article? I have it in the other room."

She answered with a stern glare. Those eyes of hers, so round and as brown as fine chocolate, could convey emotion more effectively than any unnecessary chatter. He still remembered the first time they'd met in a dingy, stale-smelling classroom in the back of the police department headquarters. She'd been one of only three women in the class and Sam had no doubt that every male eye had gravitated toward Charlie. She spoke loudly, laughed hard and seemed completely at ease in a roomful of salivating men. She'd sparred with him, flirted with him and enticed him so intensely and yet, when their commander had reviewed the nonfraternization policies for recruits, neither one of them had blinked. They'd simply toned the repartee down, sheltering their banter with secrecy.

Sam remembered looking forward to seeing her every day so he could whisper naughty comments in her ear when no one could hear. He recalled the rush he'd experienced when she'd sauntered past him, oh-so-innocently brushing her hand over his shoulder, down his back or across his backside. Over four weeks, the tension had built to a level that had nearly driven him insane. No wonder he'd ignored his better judgment when she'd suggested they stay in the gym after everyone else had left to review those hand-to-hand combat techniques a few more times.

In minutes, strikes had led to strokes and Tae Kwon Do throws had led to the throes of passion. They'd had the sense that time to leave the police academy prem-

ises for the full hookup, though they hadn't made it farther than the back seat of his car two blocks out of the
parking lot. Their lust had been intense and insatiable.
They had been barely able to exist in each other's presence without hormones overriding their ambitions, their
morals—and their good sense. Getting caught had only
been a matter of time.

But they were older now. Sam liked to think a little
wiser, too. And now, trapped with her in the tiny bathroom,
he knew the attraction arcing between them had only aged
like a fine wine. The flavors had ripened, become bolder
and more intense. He only hoped they had the maturity
now to blithely sip rather than chaotically gulp.

"I don't like operating with so many unknowns,"
Charlie said, pensive. "Why were we paired together in
the first place? Why are we getting easy cases? Why is
Burt Mueller on the set of this show, when he's an executive producer? I did some checking. He hasn't gone
on location with any of his other shows, not the whole
time at least. Yet here he is, watching the two of us, particularly, like a hawk. I signed on to this show because
the Hennessy Group is considering me for a job—or so
they say. If I'm being set up for some big humiliation
on national television, I want to know. Don't you?"

Sam donned his briefs and jeans, considering her
valid questions—and her motives. She'd come to him
instead of trying to find the answers all on her own.
Why? Had she finally realized they could accomplish
more together than apart?

"I did this show for the agency," Sam told her. "Foster and Bragg wants the publicity. But I don't think my

boss would appreciate my becoming a laughingstock among my colleagues because I didn't pick up on some hidden agenda."

Her smile lit her face like a sunrise over a tawny morning sky. "So you'll help me figure all this out without letting anyone from the production crew know we're snooping?"

"If you make me one promise."

She eyed him warily, but he knew she wouldn't refuse. A woman as sure of herself as Charlie Cuesta would never back down from any challenge. He'd already banked on her fierce independence and sneaky propensities to get them this far and he hadn't been disappointed. Now, he just had to start appealing to the part of her she was trying so hard to contain around him— her passionate side.

"Depends on the promise," she said.

He snaked his hands around her waist, reveling in the curves of her hips. He couldn't resist closing his eyes as sensations from the past splashed through him like rapids in a flash flood. He'd given her the split second she needed to maneuver out of his touch, but when his eyes flashed open, she only stared at him with solid conviction.

"Promise me you'll teach me to salsa?" he asked.

Her mouth tilted in a half smile. "You hate dancing."

"Who says?"

"You say. You *said,* anyway."

"When? Nine years ago? Better get ready to put on your spikiest dancing shoes, Charlotte. You're about to find out how much I've changed."

CHAPTER THREE

"YOU WANTED TO SEE ME, Pop?"

Burt Mueller frowned, once again unhappy with Jacey's choice of paternal endearments. She smoothed her tongue over her teeth and suppressed a smile. She may not have known her father for more than a couple of years, but she sure got a kick out of getting under his skin.

"Where's your charge?" he asked, glancing behind her.

Jacey shrugged, with as much innocence as possible. According to the rules of the game, each team of contestants had a cameraperson and an assistant assigned to them. The players could not leave their hotel rooms without taking their cameraperson with them, though the reverse wasn't true. Jacey was free to leave Charlie so long as she was where the hidden cameras and microphones could watch her every move. Of course, they were between rounds right now and as far as Jacey knew, Charlie was resting up for the next challenge, which would be presented at eight o'clock tonight.

But the truth was, Jacey had no idea if Charlie was in her room like she was supposed to be. Knowing the wily private investigator as she did after three weeks, Charlie probably wasn't anywhere near her own room.

"Haven't you learned anything from watching the dailies? Charlie Cuesta could be just about anywhere and we likely wouldn't have a clue. For all I know, she's not in the state anymore. Or she could be under your desk. Do you need her?"

Burt's mouth bowed, but hardly a wrinkle creased his skin thanks to his latest Botox injection. Jacey might personally find the vain practice detestable, but she'd been in Hollywood long enough to understand the sheer necessity of such physical improvements, especially for a man like her dad. Burt wasn't a young man in a business where anyone over thirty-five was considered ancient.

"Of course I need her," Burt spat. He sat, and in a move that made Jacey laugh, glanced under his desk. He responded to her laughter with a growl.

"Look!" he ordered.

Burt whipped a sheet of pink paper across his desk, which Jacey caught and sniffed. The same lemony scent—Jean Naté, according to Charlie's investigation for episode two—and the same faded, woven stationery Charlie had pegged as coming from a specialty store that had been on Hollywood Boulevard back in the late eighties. And though it hadn't been part of her assignment, Charlie had also figured out that the letters the sender had cut out for the message had come from *Variety*.

And exactly like the other six notes Burt had received since taping began on *Surviving Sarah*, this missive provided a similarly unclear message—a few little words and a million possible meanings.

"Roses, roses everywhere and not a petal left for me."

Jacey read the line twice, changing her inflections

each time. Once, she tried to sound happy. The next time, menacing. The dialogue worked fine with both deliveries—leaving them no closer to figuring out who was sending her father these mysterious notes—or why.

"Any idea what this one means?"

"I have no clue."

"Come on, Pop. You have to have some theory. This one is at least a little more specific. What do you know about roses?"

"I know they come in red, pink, orange and yellow. Oh, and white. I know the florists gouge you for them on Valentine's Day. I know there's a whole football game dedicated to them every New Year's Day."

Jacey smirked. Apparently, sarcasm was genetically transmitted.

"Okay, I'll be more specific. What do you know about roses that could potentially ruin your career?"

She hated to be so blunt, but this had gone on long enough. Jacey hadn't known her father her entire life, but she'd been around him long enough to recognize the toll the threats were taking on this vital, but vulnerable man. Long before she'd met her father, Burt Mueller had been a Hollywood legend who, unfortunately, most people now thought was dead. One of the top television producers in the eighties, Burt had been the force behind the hottest game shows during the Reagan-era transition from network dominance to the insurgence of cable television. And though only a few people knew it then or now, Burt had also been involved in a scandal that could have made Charles Van Doren and his *21* dishonor look like a seven-year-old stealing a gumball from the corner grocery.

When she'd stumbled onto the truth, Jacey hadn't known what to think about her father's involvement. On one hand, he'd kept a good friend out of prison. On the other, he'd ruined his own career, which he was only now starting to rebuild. He'd lost every ounce of industry clout he'd built in order to protect a friend who hadn't deserved it. All the money Burt had amassed in his career had gone to paying off huge debts incurred by a show that never got off the ground.

So for the past twenty years, he'd been working his tail off trying to regain some of the luster of his has-been career. He didn't deserve to have his life ruined right now, not when he was so close to success.

Burt's first new show, *Surviving Sarah,* had been airing for six weeks and the ratings were downright impressive. In fact, Burt had been fielding calls from dozens of Hollywood hotshots determined to invest in any of his new creations—*The Great Chase* included. The show had debuted to the same hype and buzz, and initial numbers on the second episode were just as strong. She couldn't let Burt tank now because of some mysterious messages that might mean someone knew his secret and was getting ready to expose it to the world.

Jacey handed the note back to her father. His hand shook as he snatched the paper. She could see how much he wanted to crunch it up, destroy it and pulverize it into nothing. But it wouldn't help.

"I'm wracking my brain trying to figure these out, pumpkin, but they just don't make any sense," Burt said, his frustration hissing through his voice. "I need Charlie and Sam."

Jacey shook her head. "You keep giving them assignments that deal with your mess and they're going to figure out what's really going on."

Burt pressed his lips together. "Maybe that's not a bad thing. She's good, Jacey. So's he, but he's letting her do all the work for whatever reason. Bottom line, she likes you. She might keep our secret."

"That may be, but she's also on national television. If she figures out your secret, so will the rest of the world."

"Not with creative editing," Burt insisted.

Jacey rolled her eyes. Burt knew better. Yes, with creative editing they could manipulate and shape the game into whatever ratings blockbuster they imagined. Unfortunately, editing wasn't done by one person. Burt was the executive producer, not the director—and the director was the force behind the cutting and splicing of the tapes. So unless Burt wanted Rick Ralston to know about his past, he had to keep the investigation more subtle.

"Rick's not going to let you anywhere near his editing room until he's seen all the footage and you know it."

"Then don't shoot her when she's working on my stuff."

Jacey considered that option. She'd already let Charlie get away with more than she should. Rick wasn't wary yet, but she figured even the druggie genius wouldn't take forever to catch on. "He'll get suspicious if I don't keep up."

"Rick's a snake."

"He's also one of the best reality television directors

in the business. You were lucky to snag him and you know it. Keep with the plan. Give the next clue to another team."

"None of them have the fire Charlie has. Together with Sam, they can't be beat, I'm telling you. They're the winning combination *if* Charlie wouldn't be so stubborn about working alone."

Jacey nodded, agreeing with her father's assessment. In the beginning, Jacey had thought Charlie's solo act would be bad for the show, that her independent streak spat in the face of the concept—two private investigators paired together to solve cases and advance to the next round. But then she'd watched the dailies. The sexual tension between Charlie and Sam had been as palpable as tropical humidity. The cat-and-mouse dynamic between them proved more compelling than the cases they needed to solve to move ahead in the game. Because of that, Jacey hadn't objected when Rick had decided to give Sam and Charlie a few easier cases for episodes three, four and five to make sure they weren't eliminated. Jacey hadn't agreed with his manipulation, but things had changed since Burt's heyday. Rick had written the contestant contracts with care. His right to manipulate the show was typed into the fine print. Rick Ralston might be a first-class ass, but he had a nose for two things—snorting cocaine and sniffing out ratings blockbusters.

"Even when Charlie's alone, Sam isn't that far behind," Jacey insisted, confident she'd seen something in Sam's strategy that the others hadn't. According to his dossier, he was a high-powered control freak when on the job. But with Charlie, he was a sly pussycat. Reminded her of Digg. Always up to something. And just like with her long-distance lover, she couldn't wait to find out what. "I have a feeling Sam knows more than he lets on."

Burt's skin paled as he reached for a pack of smokes. In a split second, he was lit up and puffing. "What do you think they'd do if they put all the pieces together?"

Jacey glanced aside, determined not to bug her dad about his smoking habit right now. He had enough stress without her digressing to an old argument. Instead, she tried to formulate an answer to his question.

She liked Charlie and, well, Sam was a major hottie. She also knew their résumés. Charlie and Sam had both been dismissed from the same police academy for some unnamed infraction at the same time, so neither was a stranger to trouble. And while Sam currently worked for one of the top investigative firms in the industry, one with an impeccable reputation, he didn't seem the least bit righteous or stuffy. Charlie, on the other hand, seemed to walk perpetually on the wild side. She ran her own business and a couple of times had talked to Jacey about cases she'd followed that would make tabloid reporters blush. Jacey couldn't imagine the woman being shocked by anything tawdry she might hear or see.

"I have no idea how they'd react, Pop. But maybe it's time we found out."

Burt eyed Jacey with a mixture of wariness and interest. "What are you suggesting?"

Jacey grinned. "A test. A trap of sorts. If they follow the clues we leave, we'll know they're game to help."

"And if they don't?"

Jacey shrugged. At this point, she and her father had nothing to lose. "Then they deserve to be eliminated before the next show. Agreed?"

Burt took a long drag off his lit cigarette, flaring the tip and injecting the air with acrid smoke. "Absolutely. Let's do it."

CHAPTER FOUR

IT WAS ALMOST TOO EASY.

Charlie heard the click and the slight vibration of the tumbler in the lock giving way. Behind her, Sam scanned the parking lot, watching for anyone who might alert security to their presence. Their very illegal presence.

He flicked the blue light on his digital watch. "Fifteen seconds," he reported.

"We're in."

She twisted the knob and with plenty of time to spare before the security guard made his next sweep of the parking lot, they were inside Burt's trailer. In approximately ten minutes, they expected the production crew—producers, director, camera crew, support staff—to return from the tarmac of a private airport an hour outside Los Angeles, the most recent location shoot of *The Great Chase*. While the three other remaining teams of private investigators, the director and a scaled-down crew had boarded a private jet bound for Nevada, Sam and Charlie had hauled butt to the hotel. They had to be done before the remaining crew returned from taping at the airport to prep the trailers and pack up the equipment for the move to Vegas, the location of the most serious part of the taping. It hadn't been easy to avoid getting on the private plane with the rest of the contestants, but Charlie had to admit that Sam had been brilliant. He'd feigned an inner ear infection with total believability, right down to the antibiotics he'd had in his pocket.

The rest progressed in the best tradition of television drama. Would Sam and Charlie be disqualified because he couldn't fly? Could they afford the three and a half to four hours they'd lose due to driving instead of hopping on the jet to Vegas? Would Charlie go without her partner and once again show that she didn't need her ex-lover in order to win the game?

Charlie didn't have time to analyze how easy it had been to make her choice to stick with Sam. He'd agreed to help her figure out what was going on with Burt Mueller. She wasn't about to bail on him, not when she knew that his ear infection had been a ruse on her behalf.

"Any idea where we should start?" she asked, tugging the blinds closed on the tiny window in the door of the double-wide trailer.

"Burt's desk," Sam suggested. "I'll check his file cabinet. Let's just hope that Shandra does her job and keeps Jacey busy for a little while longer."

Shandra Miller had been one lucky break. A waitress with a serious addiction to reality TV, she'd recognized Sam and Charlie the minute they'd walked into her diner to load up on munchies for their supposed road trip to Vegas, with Jacey along to record every mile. Once Sam had turned on the charm, Shandra had easily bent to his will. On cue, she'd spilled an entire platter of chili-cheese fries on Jacey's lap, causing the camerawoman to dash to the bathroom to clean off. One locked door and a hot-wired car later, Sam and Charlie had sped back to the hotel for a quick peek at Burt's trailer before Jacey caught up.

Though Charlie had a feeling her camerawoman was going to be majorly pissed off, she decided she'd deal with smoothing ruffled feathers once they had the information they needed. Jacey didn't seem much like a stickler for rules, especially unexpected ones like "you must not ditch your camera operator at a greasy diner."

Using a penlight clutched between her teeth to see in the dark, Charlie pawed through the files on Burt's desk. She set aside folders marked "Advertising Revenue," "Nielsen," and "Proposed Budget for *The Last Virgin*." Though the last one gave her pause to wonder what manner of craziness Burt was about to unleash next on the television-watching public, she knew these folders wouldn't give them what they needed. They were looking for something more personal—some indication of why Burt was manipulating the game the way they suspected. Ratings were an excellent motive, but both Sam and Charlie guessed that the reasons went deeper.

Charlie continued to search, looking for a handwritten note or a memo from their last production team meeting. Anything to indicate what might be going on in the head of the show's executive producer.

"Here!"

Sam extracted a long, flat lockbox from the bottom of the file cabinet.

"What is it?"

"Don't know until we open it. Can you manage this kind of lock?"

Charlie winced. She'd really only become proficient at doors and windows on houses and cars, mainly as a self-preservation device because she was forever losing her keys.

"I can try, but we may not have time."

Sam engaged the light on his watch again. He turned the face toward her. They had approximately five minutes before they estimated the crew would return.

"Okay, no time to pick it." He shook the box, which rustled in response. "There's paper inside. Could be cash. Could be information. Whatever it is, it's important enough for Burt to lock up. We need the key. If you were the key to a secret box Burt Mueller brought with him to a temporary, mobile office, where would you be?"

"On Burt's keychain," Charlie guessed, imagining the collection sitting snugly in Burt's pocket.

"Keys make noise. I've never heard any of the crew walking around with keys."

"You think he'd keep them here?"

The search began anew. They had two minutes left before the crew would return to the hotel when Charlie found the key ring stuffed inside an extra pair of shoes Burt kept in his closet. Sam fumbled through the collection, inserting the smallest one into the lock.

The box clicked open with a sharp snap.

He lifted the lid.

Charlie grabbed the first piece of paper. "This is the

note I identified in the "Beginnings" episode where we had to find the origins of something. Remember? The stationery came from the shop in L.A."

Sam nodded and took out the second sheet—the brown paper wrapper of the package Charlie had identified in episode one as coming from a post office outside of Phoenix. Beneath that, they found a gold chain with a square-shaped charm dangling from it.

"What is this?" Sam asked.

Charlie focused her light on the gold chain.

"That's the necklace from episode one."

"We didn't work with a necklace," he reminded her.

"No, the team from Biloxi did. Remember, the woman had a brother in the jewelry business. He was able to identify that it had been a mass-produced fourteen-carat chain and charm likely sold in department stores in the early eighties. They got that one, but were eliminated on show three when they couldn't find the luggage lost on that flight from London to New York."

Sam nodded. "That's two trinkets from the eighties, you know. Three if you count this CD," he said, gesturing into the depths of the safety box. "It's the radio broadcast the husband and wife team from Dallas figured out for episode five."

"Right, the radio station in Los Angeles. KLAS or something." She dug deeper and found the compact disc. "But these aren't all the winning clues, are they? Where's the mug with the fingerprints the brothers from Chicago identified in episode two? And the pictures of the missing dog from episode four?"

Sam blew out a frustrated breath. "Don't know. But all of these do have something in common."

"Two somethings," Charlie concluded. "The city of Los Angeles and the Reagan years. That connection can't be random, not when all the clues that don't connect are mysteriously not in this locked box. What do you think is going on?"

The sound of a truck pulling up outside sent Charlie and Sam into covert mode. Penlights flicked off and they worked in quick silence. While Sam put the clues back into the box and returned them to the cabinet, Charlie eased to a window and peeked through the blinds. The door of a white pickup swung open and Jacey stepped out, her camera hanging wearily from her tired arm. She turned and walked directly toward Burt's trailer.

"Damn," Charlie cursed, ducking beneath the window. "Jacey's headed over here. We're busted."

"Not on my watch," he whispered.

From the darkness, Sam grabbed Charlie's hand. In a split second, they were tucked into Burt's closet, hidden by the collection of tobacco-smelling slacks and jackets and coats. Sam shut the door at nearly the same moment that Jacey walked into the trailer. Adrenaline kept Charlie from immediately noticing how Sam had crammed himself against the wall, then pulled her completely flush against his body.

"Pop?"

Jacey's voice was muffled, but clear.

"Pop?" Sam's question floated on a warm breath tinged with the nutty flavor of the coffee he'd drunk at the diner before the great chili spill. The scent of his cologne, spicy with sandalwood and musk, had already begun its assault on Charlie's senses. Coupled with the feel of his hard body pressed against hers, she had to work double time to figure out why he sounded so surprised.

Jacey was Burt's daughter?

Charlie opened her mouth to speak, but then figured they should stay as quiet as possible. The trailer was not large and the walls were thin. Surprisingly, though, Jacey didn't seem very angry over them dumping her. If Charlie wasn't mistaken, Jacey was humming.

The chair behind Burt's desk creaked, followed by the rattle of Jacey lifting the receiver off the phone. While she dialed, Charlie tried desperately to calm her heart and tame the wild flock of buzzards zooming through her stomach. This was what she wanted from her career, right? The rush of excitement? The inherent danger of covert operations? Playing for stakes that were normally out of her range?

"Jacey is Burt's daughter?" Sam asked, his voice barely audible, even with his lips pressed intimately to her ear. Common sense told her to move out of his range, but the situation forced her to stay where she was. "Think that's a big secret?"

Charlie turned her head and her cheek swiped his jaw, igniting her flesh with the rough feel of his late-night beard. When her breath caught, his lips parted so that even in the darkness, Charlie could sense the nearness of his mouth.

"No. Jacey probably just wants to be her own woman," Charlie replied.

"You should understand that, shouldn't you?"

On the other side of the door, the volume of Jacey's voice rose, but she was laughing. Charlie knew she shouldn't risk moving in the small closet, but she used the moment of Jacey's distraction to turn slightly, scraping one of the hangers on the pole.

She stiffened, but Jacey's string of conversation didn't break.

"Don't move," Sam warned.

"I can't stand this," she whispered back.

"Can't stand being so close to me?"

"No."

"Do you hate me that much?"

"I don't hate you. I've never hated you."

"You've never exactly loved me, either."

"There was hardly time for that," she murmured.

"There's time now."

"Not if Jacey finds us in this closet."

"She won't."

But Charlie doubted his claim the minute she felt his hand easing up her side. "She will if you don't stop touching me."

"I can't help myself."

He slid his palm up the side of her jeans, then around her waist. Her top, a cropped black sweater, had ridden up, leaving him two exposed inches of flesh to arouse. He took complete advantage, smoothing her bare skin with a light touch, skimming the waistband of her low-slung jeans, igniting sensations that flashed through her body like fire. He didn't play fair, she concluded, but why would she expect him to? He never had before.

His fingers inched beneath the hem of her sweater. At the same time, her breasts filled with want for him, and her nipples peaked, scraping the top of the lace demi-cup of her bra. She closed her eyes, knowing that if he touched her where she wanted him to most, she'd likely jump right out of her skin and reveal their hiding place.

"Sam," she hissed.

"God, your skin is so smooth."

"Sam, please."

"Just one touch."

"Sam!"

That plea caught both their attentions, since the half-amused, half-shocked shout came not from Charlie, but from Jacey, who'd thrown open the door. Charlie propelled herself out of Sam's reach, pushing past the camerawoman. She was halfway to freedom from complete humiliation when Jacey's question cut through the silence.

"Why were you groping Charlie in my father's closet?"

She spun around. "He wasn't groping me!"

Sam looked completely irrepressible. "Yes, I was."

She jabbed her finger in his direction. "No, you weren't. You didn't touch anything important."

"Not yet."

"You're a pig."

"I once read that pigs can have thirty-minute orgasms."

Charlie opened her mouth, but what possible response could she offer to such inane trivia?

"Okay, let me rephrase the question," Jacey asked, chuckling. "Why were you hiding in the closet to begin with?"

Why was the closet so damned important? Didn't Jacey realize she should be bitching about being dumped in a diner? About being lied to about Sam's ear infection?

"You got here quicker than we anticipated," Sam answered.

"Shandra let me borrow her truck."

"She was supposed to be on our side."

Jacey grinned. "Shandra just wanted to be on television. I taped her handing over the keys to me."

"You can't air any of this," Charlie insisted.

"Why not? After all these weeks of you ditching Sam, making the production crew and the audience question your loyalty to the game and Sam's ability to keep up with you, you two pull a classic bait-and-switch to get off the plane then dump me at some roadside grease factory to sneak into the executive producer's trailer. You're suddenly loyal partners in crime. This is good stuff. Before we disqualify you, the ratings are going to go through the roof."

"You aren't going to disqualify us," Sam said, shutting the closet door behind him.

Charlie's eyes widened. They'd been caught red-handed. Burt would have no choice but throw them out of the game.

But the smug smile on Sam's perennially cocky face caught her attention. He knew something she didn't— and he was going to milk this moment unless she pushed.

"Sam, what do you know?" Charlie asked, stalking toward him.

"I know what Burt has been up to."

Charlie lowered her voice, forcing intense eye contact in hopes of discovering if he was bluffing again or if he'd lost his mind. "We found nothing."

"Didn't we?" He glanced around to Jacey who, still chuckling, was wiping the skin beneath her eyes carefully so as to not smudge her smoky eyeliner. "Care to clue her in, Jacey?"

The door from the outside opened and Burt strode inside, his hands deep in the pockets. Like Jacey and Sam, he wore an inscrutable grin. What had Charlie missed?

"And here I thought only Charlie was the good investigator on this team of two," Burt remarked, shutting the door carefully behind them. He gestured toward two other chairs shoved up against the wall, then moved around to his seat behind the desk. "I underestimated you, my boy."

"Yes, sir. You did."

Sam moved the chairs Burt had pointed to, then grabbed Charlie by the hand and in her confused and cautious state, led her to sit. Just what did the notes, the chain and the CD mean to him that they didn't mean to her? So what if all the locked-up clues pointed to the city of Los Angeles and the decade of the eighties. Los Angeles was the center of the entertainment industry and the eighties…

Well, the eighties were Burt's hey day.

"It's you," she said, the connection finally dawning on her. "You're the key that connects those clues from the show. But what's the connection to us?"

CHAPTER FIVE

SAM LEANED FORWARD and winked. "She's a little slow on the uptake sometimes, but she's quicker than most."

"I'll say," Burt said with a smirk. "Why do you think I didn't give you both all the clues at once? I wasn't sure I wanted you to figure it all out, and I was fairly certain you would if you had all the information."

"Figure out what?" Charlie slammed her palms on the arms of the chair. "This is about you, Burt, clearly. But what's the big secret? What are you trying to hide from everyone besides us?"

Burt stalked to the file cabinet and retrieved the lockbox. When he moved to the closet to retrieve his keys, Sam took a second to wink at Charlie again. If things didn't go as Sam anticipated, Burt would have no proof they'd broken in to his private papers. Sam had returned the key to the shoe while he and Charlie had been holed up in the closet.

The interlude in the closet had been too brief. Unbidden, his hand drifted to his face where he pretended to scratch an itch on his nose when he was really inhaling the lingering scent of Charlie's skin on his. If only that closet had been a little larger and they'd had more time.

Since taping had begun, Charlie had been careful to avoid any personal or intimate contact with him. Even when he'd kissed her in his hotel room earlier, it hadn't been enough. Now that he'd touched her, he knew he was even worse off than he'd suspected. The brief contact had his body craving hers with overwhelming intensity. One kiss and a short press of bodies would not be nearly sufficient to satisfy his needs. Or hers.

Sam forced his thoughts away from amorous possibilities as Burt unlocked the box and withdrew the contents. He split the clues and handed one batch to Sam and the other to Charlie.

"I've been receiving these messages for over two months. I haven't used all of them on the show, so look carefully. Notes, letters, trinkets—some mailed, some delivered to whatever location I'm on. They mean something, but I don't know what. And the time has come for me to find out."

Sam pawed through the clues, noting that his were the ones from the bottom of the stack, which he hadn't gotten to during their brief peek. The one that caught his eye was an old business card of Burt's, back when he was a producer on a show called *The Bermuda Triangle*.

He showed the card to Charlie, who looked at it with equal confusion.

"*The Bermuda Triangle?* I've never heard of it."

Burt's lips straightened into a thin line. He sat briskly and grabbed a pack of cigarettes from a drawer. "No one has. No one but trivia buffs over the age of forty, that is."

Sam handed Charlie the card. "You produced the show?"

"I was the creator and producer, but the show never aired."

"Why not?" Charlie asked, examining the card carefully. Sam had already noted that nothing was written on it, yet the paper was curled on the edges and well worn, as if someone had handled it frequently.

Burt glanced quickly at his daughter, but his expression revealed nothing. "There were complications."

With a sigh, Jacey looked at her watch and then stood. "Don't screw with them, Pop. Tell them the whole story. They'll put it together sooner or later, and frankly, I'd like this whole matter settled." She turned and stepped in front of her father's desk, as if to waylay any objections he might voice. "*The Bermuda Triangle* never saw air-time because my father's partner, a man named Linc Firestone, took bribes from an advertising agency to make sure certain contestants won— some of them plants from families of advertisers, which was illegal. Pop had had a bunch of hits running at the time. He was on top. *The Bermuda Triangle* was going to put the *$25,000 Pyramid* out of business."

Burt grumbled, but his curses were unintelligible. Still, the sound made Jacey press her lips tightly together. She crossed behind her father's desk and placed her hands on his shoulders. "The show never aired, but they had taped over a dozen episodes and had spent a whole lot of money for sets, salaries, etc. Someone found out about the scam and told Burt. He shut down production, but that same snitch then blackmailed my father, threatening to implicate him in the scandal and call in the Feds."

"Who was the snitch?" Sam asked.

This time, Burt's words of disgust were completely understandable. "Never found out."

"How do you know the snitch was the blackmailer?"

"I don't know that for sure. All I know is that after I paid cash, the blackmail stopped. I never heard another word. Until a few months ago. And it's so similar, right down to the notes with letters cut out of magazines. I should have called the cops back then, but I was trying to keep myself out of jail, not to mention retaining at least a part of my reputation."

Sam couldn't believe what he was hearing. How could the man sacrifice his life's work when he'd done nothing wrong? "You hadn't broken any laws, Burt. This Linc Firestone guy had."

"Doesn't matter," Burt insisted. "If this scandal had come out, Linc would have gone down hard and taken me with him. No one would believe I didn't know. I should have known. My reputation would have been shot to hell no matter what."

Charlie blew out a frustrated breath. "Your reputation was shot to hell anyway, wasn't it? Took you over twenty years to get back on top again."

Burt shook his head. "The shutdown of production on *The Bermuda Triangle* hit me hard, but that wasn't the whole story of my downfall. Television changed. My brand of entertainment just wasn't hot anymore. Game shows were for old people eating dinner at three o'clock in the afternoon before they went to bed at six. Sitcoms were replaced by glitzy dramas. But tastes shifted again when *Who Wants to Be a Millionaire* hit the scene—and got even better with *Survivor.* My time is back and I'll be damned if I let some asshole with a long memory ruin things for me again."

Jacey pushed harder on Burt's shoulders and Sam watched the producer force himself to calm down, his gaze connected to his daughter's. For all her goth makeup and shadowy clothes, Jacey Turner had a strong effect on her father. A soothing, rational effect.

She was also a very clever woman. He now realized why Jacey had made a phone call to her father as he was on his way to the airport. She'd deliberately made remarks that he and Charlie would overhear about ensuring that everything was locked up tight in Burt's office. Then she'd left the production schedule in plain view. Sam had noted the time lapse highlighted in neon yellow and that's when he'd decided to pull the ear infection scam to buy them time to snoop in the office. Damn, but he'd been duped! And by an amateur! Well, that wasn't entirely accurate. He figured Jacey Turner had been pulling scams for a very long time.

And what had been her goal today? Enlisting their help in figuring out who was sending the stuff to Burt? Why else?

Sam glanced at Charlie, who'd reached for the papers Burt had handed him from the lockbox, the ones she hadn't seen. "Where is Linc Firestone now?"

"Dead," Burt answered, his voice betraying a hint of frustration. "I did a quick search of the Internet when my old business card arrived. I found an article about him biting the dust in a car crash outside Vegas."

"Vegas?" Sam asked. "Is it a coincidence that Sin City is our next location?"

Burt tapped a cigarette on his desk. "I thought you might want to verify my story, so I arranged for the next set of challenges to be in a casino that's bucking for some publicity. I convinced them that taping a reality television show there would bring in the easy marks."

Charlie leaned forward, her keen eyes narrowed on Burt and his daughter. "Why would we need to verify your story? We're not cops."

"We're well aware of that," Burt replied. "You're even better. You're private investigators who won't try and arrest me for complicity in a twenty-year-old crime. Discretion is part of your job description."

Sam sat back in his chair, smiling as the foggy picture he'd had in his mind from the beginning about this whole affair cleared. "So that's why you've been feeding us the letters and trinkets you received during the challenges. You were secretly trying to get us to figure out who was sending you this stuff. In fact, I'll bet big money that's why you came up with this show in the first place."

Burt steepled his fingers on his desk. "You are a smart one. Jacey and I hoped we could figure out what was going on by feeding clues to the teams on the show. We finally realized that we couldn't solve anything if you and your partner here, or any of the other teams, couldn't make all the right connections."

"What was tonight then?" Charlie asked. "How did you know we'd break in here?"

Jacey cleared a spot on the corner of Burt's desk and

sat. She kept one hand on her father's shoulder and Sam would have bet his collection of Clint Black CDs that the gesture of affection wasn't for show. He could see the concern in her kohl-rimmed eyes.

"We had a hunch," Jacey admitted. "Charlie, I saw you talking to Leon at lunch yesterday."

"So?" Charlie responded innocently.

"Leon mans the cameras during the dinner breaks. I heard you asking him about *Days,* when you distinctly told me during a taping two weeks ago that you were a *One Life to Live* junkie. In most markets, those shows run opposite each other—and frankly, you don't seem the type to follow them all."

"Why, Jacey Turner," Charlie said, feigning surprise, "what a fine investigator you would make."

"Watching people is my business. Anyway, I went to check on Leon earlier and saw a maid with a very familiar walk coming out of Sam's room. I figured you two were scheming something."

Sam wondered if Jacey didn't have the stuff for a second career. "So that's why you were so understanding about my—" he faked two coughs "—ailment."

Jacey just smiled. "We decided that we wanted to see if you were more interested in winning the game or solving the case. We thought your ear infection story might throw a wrench in our plan—we'd decided to set things up in Vegas so you could get the information— but this works just as well. You bought us time to explain, though dumping me at the diner could have been done a bit more neatly," she groused, swiping at the damp spot on her T-shirt. "However, your method gave you the time you needed to get here. And now you know the whole truth. So the question now is, will you help us?"

Sam shifted in his chair. "Is that why you fed us the easy stuff? To keep us on the show so we could eventually work for you?"

Burt rubbed his palm over his stylishly bald head. "Keeping you on at all costs was Rick Ralston's decision and simply worked to our advantage. You guys add a sexual edge to the show. He didn't want to lose that."

"You mean ratings," Charlie corrected, her voice gravely with annoyance.

"Sex, ratings…same difference," Burt said with a shrug. "Now you know the score. You in?"

Sam glanced at Charlie, who wore a smirk on her face that was part pride and part anticipation. Oh, yeah. She was in. Which meant he was in, too. He'd come here for one reason and one reason only—to win Charlie back. He had nothing to lose and everything to gain by continuing to play sidekick to the woman of his dreams.

"What do you want us to do?" Sam asked.

"We're going to give you everything and see if you can make a connection we're not seeing," Jacey said, her smile widening beneath her inky lipstick. "We'll give you all the equipment you have for the show—the wireless computers, unlimited phone calls, transportation. But this can't be done on tape. If Burt is being primed for another round of blackmail, we need this hush-hush."

"One thing I don't get," Charlie mused, her fingers toying with a strand of hair. Did she always do that when she was thinking? Was this a quirk of hers he'd missed before or simply forgotten? He figured they'd have less than forty-eight hours to do this job for Burt and Jacey, since the show was drawing to a close. There was so much he still wanted to learn about Charlie. Would two days be enough?

"Just one thing?" Jacey asked, her brow cocked.

Charlie chuckled. "Why didn't you just hire someone to investigate this case? Why create a reality television show around it, when exposure might result? Aren't you friends with Patrick Hennessy? Isn't that why I'm on the show?"

Burt glanced down at his lap, where he'd folded his hands. "First of all, it was a damned great concept. The ratings are incredible. And I'm actually more acquainted with Patrick's uncle, who started the firm, than I am with the nephew. Besides, I didn't want him to know what a fool I'd been all those years ago. And I couldn't risk hiring some unknown P.I. who might turn on me and use the information to bleed me dry yet again. I'm just now getting back on top."

"So, since you have us over a barrel on the whole disqualification thing now," Charlie surmised, "you figured you could get us to do your dirty work on the QT?"

Jacey and Burt's matched frowns brought their familial resemblance to the forefront. Charlie was a damned good investigator, but she was close to crossing a line. Sam moved to interrupt, but Burt had already taken up the gauntlet. Apparently, he was just as competitive as Charlie.

"That wasn't our intention, but it does give us some

bargaining power, doesn't it?" His obvious disappointment at her attitude washed from Burt's expression with one easy Hollywood smile. "You figure out who is sending me these little reminders of my dubious past and I'll forget that both of you should be disqualified for ditching Jacey and breaking into my trailer. I know the execs at Foster and Bragg wouldn't be too happy if one of their top detectives couldn't go the distance and I'm certain the Hennessy Group wouldn't appreciate a new employee who can't follow rules."

Charlie snorted. "Obviously, you don't know the Group very well."

Burt's grin widened. "Actually, I do. They've been known to bend a few laws in his pursuit of a case. The difference between you and them is that they don't get caught."

Charlie sat, silenced, with only Sam knowing how deeply that swipe had cut. The producer knew that he and Charlie had been dismissed from the police academy together, but neither of them had divulged why, no matter how many times the producers and director had tried to coax the information from them.

Charlie crossed her legs casually. Only Sam likely noticed the stiffness in her shoulders. The job with Hennessy obviously meant a great deal to her. She wouldn't let this chance go so easily, would she?

"I could just quit," Charlie said. "Patrick Hennessy's operation isn't the only game in town. I don't like to be manipulated."

"Then you should have stayed clear of Hollywood all together," Jacey quipped. She moved around the desk and took Charlie by the hand. "Come on, Charlie. I promise that if you crack this case for my father, Hennessy will know that you did a big favor for a good friend. I've taken care of you so far, haven't I?"

Sam watched the women expectantly. Charlie might have a great deal of pride, but she wasn't stupid—and she wasn't cold. Compassion would drive her, whether she would admit it or not.

Still, he thought he should clarify a few points.

"So you just want us to find out who is sending the notes?"

"Yes, that's it. Just a name." Jacey dug into the pocket of her black leather jacket and extracted a small envelope and handed it to Charlie. "This was left for my father on his chair at the taping tonight. Looks like everyone wanted to speed up the time frame, even our blackmailer."

CHAPTER SIX

CHARLIE ACCEPTED the invitation-size envelope, turned it in her hand and sniffed it. She wasn't surprised to inhale the same sweet, lemony scent as the notes from before.

"Whoever this is keeps using the same stationery. It doesn't mean anything to you?"

Burt shook his head. "I don't notice that shit. I'm not a sentimental person, so if it's supposed to have significance, it's lost on me."

Charlie stood and held the envelope out. "Smell it again. This time, concentrate. Olfactory memories are incredibly powerful."

Burt opened his mouth to protest, but Jacey took the envelope from Charlie's hand and shoved it toward her father. Burt sighed and did as instructed. After a couple of seconds, he peeked one eye open. "Sorry."

"This is a woman's scent. Was Linc married? Did he have a girlfriend you flirted with, maybe had a thing for?"

Burt rocked forward and returned the note. He didn't answer her question, though. Interesting.

Sam stood and rounded behind Charlie's chair as she slipped her hand inside the envelope. Her fingers connected with a slim matchbook—and nothing else.

Charlie turned the glossy flesh-toned promotional item around in her hand, then handed it to Sam over her shoulder. "This isn't from the eighties and it's definitely not from Los Angeles."

The lettering, in gold, read *Lucky Chances*. On the flip side was a Las Vegas address and the phrase, "Where the Strip Strips."

Sam couldn't resist repeating the words aloud with his eyebrow cocked and his voice full of sinful possibilities. Charlie barely managed to ignore the tingle that rippled over her skin, especially when the hard impression of Sam's body flush against hers, still lingered fresh in her mind.

"I called from the set. It's a clothing-optional resort," Jacey replied.

Sam glanced down at Charlie. His wicked grin nearly sent her into sensory overload. She willed herself to match his stare, but when he licked his lips, she couldn't help but turn away.

"I've never been there before," Burt insisted without prompting. "Never even heard of the place before tonight."

"You sure? Those eighties could be really crazy times." Charlie was glad her sarcasm wasn't lost on Jacey, at least, who snorted appreciatively.

"Positive. I'm not the nudist type."

Charlie sifted through the pile of notes and clues, hoping to jog his memory a little. For a man who'd made and lost millions, he didn't notice many details. "But you have been to Vegas, right? Did you make any of the payoffs while there? Maybe meet up with your former partner at some point?"

Burt shook another cigarette out of the pack after he'd crushed the first one with his incessant tapping. "Once I fired Linc's ass, I never saw him again, never even heard from him. Vegas was his playground and I've avoided the place since."

"So that's why you think someone is trying to black-mail you again," Sam said. "The Vegas connection is too coincidental."

"Exactly. Prior to the success of *Surviving Sarah*, I was a bloodless stone. Now, I've actually got some cash coming my way. The details of *The Bermuda Triangle* scandal have been buried pretty deep. Most of the major players are dead or out of the biz. Only someone with prior knowledge would be hinting that they know something."

"And that's what you think these all are?" Charlie asked, not entirely convinced. "Hints?"

"It's a possibility," Sam conceded.

Charlie figured he had a point. It wasn't the most clear or concise way to put a man on notice that all his newfound wealth might again be in jeopardy, but it was obviously effective. "So we find out who is behind the notes and trinkets and you keep us on the show."

"With no guarantees you'll win, of course," Burt re-plied. "I made Rick promise the last two episodes would be totally on the up and up—all challenges equally hard. If you win, you'll do it on your own. But if you get me a person before that—just a name—I'll have what I need to stop this harassment. We wouldn't put you in any danger."

As she pawed through the clues one last time, Char-lie scrunched her nose. Something wasn't jibing.

"None of these notes are very threatening," Charlie said.

Burt sneered. "They don't have to be. There's only one thing they could mean."

Charlie shook her head. "No, that's not true. They could mean anything. Even something romantic."

Burt chuckled heartily, as if the idea was absurd. "The kind of women I hook up with aren't this subtle."

Jacey glanced at Burt and hopped to her feet with a clap that injected the air with a sense of sudden urgency. "We need you to focus on the Lucky Chances clue first. The show will leave Vegas in two days for the final challenge. This will be your only shot."

Charlie's heart skipped a beat. She hadn't worked this hard to end up booted now.

"How are we going to work on your assignment without getting disqualified?"

Burt pulled out his lighter and ignited the tip of his cigarette. "You give me a name and you'll get time to work out the next case for the show. No one will have to know you haven't been working on *The Great Chase* assignment the entire time."

"How are you going to pull that off?" Sam asked. "Doesn't the director get dailies from the camera operators?"

Burt came around the desk and patted Sam amicably on the shoulder. "Let me worry about Rick Ralston. The next location after Vegas is relatively remote. You only have forty-eight hours." He glanced at his watch. "The other contestants have probably already arrived in Nevada. They'll be escorted to the Athens Bay resort where the first taping will take place. The portfolios with your next assignments will be delivered to a private room in the casino in two hours, one o'clock Vegas time. You'll receive your instructions along with the others, then go off on your own."

"In two hours?" Sam asked. "I like a fast ride as much as the next guy, but even I can't condense four hours driving time by half."

"You won't have to." Jacey picked her cell phone out of her pocket and pressed a speed dial number. After a few moments, she asked, "We good to go?"

She grinned at the response on the other end, then disconnected the call. "Charlie and Sam, you're about to embark on a very wild ride."

JACEY HADN'T been kidding. Their wild ride arrived in the form of an Agusta 109C luxury helicopter sent by the casino. Charlie did her best to hide her surprise after Jacey had ushered her and Sam to a landing pad atop a nearby bank, but she couldn't help but wonder when the bombshells were going to stop falling from the sky. Just a few weeks ago, she'd flown to California with little more on her mind than winning a televised contest of skill against other private investigators, thereby landing her dream job with the best firm in the South. Yet from the moment she'd stepped out of LAX, unexpected twists had been the order of the day—starting with a production company limousine occupied by her former lover.

If that ride had been awkward, this one was downright unbearable. The limo had been about grappling with nine-year-old memories of a lover who'd changed her life forever. She'd experienced all the predictable emotions—disbelief, anger, suspicion, fear. She'd known from the start that her pairing with Sam Ryan had been no accident, but she'd possessed equal certainty that his presence would not distract her from her goal. Not this time. She was older, wiser, more aware of how her uncontrollable desires could land her in the kind of hot water that scalded you for life.

Now, she was in a much more dangerous place. The emotions that had initially ensured her safety from Sam's charm had slowly dissipated. Disbelief had been replaced with a sense of irony. *Of all the P.I.'s in all the world…*

Her own confidence in herself had helped her forget about her anger. Though they'd been stuck together, she'd managed to outshine him in nearly every task. Her mind had shifted from questioning Sam's sudden reappearance in her life to figuring out, first, what Burt's agenda was, and, now, who was bringing back bitter memories for the producer.

Her last unwanted emotion, fear, was the only one hanging on with a vengeance. And it was the one feeling Charlie hated most. In her book, fear equaled weakness. To be fearless was to be a risk-taker, an adventurer. To be fearless was to be strong. So despite the lurching sensation deep in the pit of her stomach, which she knew wasn't entirely from the pitch and shimmy of the helicopter ride, she adjusted her headset so she and Sam could talk.

"I'm not convinced that the person sending these notes has any intention of hurting Burt Mueller."

Sam looked up from his notes and laptop, then adjusted the thin, wire-rimmed glasses he'd perched on his nose shortly after take-off. The gold frames encircled his eyes in such a way that even the dim lights of the helicopter's cabin managed to sparkle in their deep blue depths.

"Burt said he didn't have any former lovers who would do all this."

In the headset, his voice became an intimate whisper. Since they'd already decided to discuss the case on the way to Las Vegas, they'd engaged the privacy mode on the headsets. The pilot, separated from them by the floor-to-ceiling backs of the luxury seats, couldn't hear a word they said. And despite Charlie's objections, Jacey had insisted on sitting in the co-pilot's seat rather than joining them in the lavish cabin—which consisted of two long seats facing each other, a small bar and a television. For the next ninety minutes, she and Sam were completely alone.

They'd even swept for hidden cameras before take-off. So unless the casino employed tactics for watching and listening to their luxury passengers that neither Sam nor Charlie was familiar with, this trip was an opportunity for privacy that neither she nor Sam had experienced in three weeks.

Dammit.

"What men don't remember about their former lovers could fill the technical manual of this helicopter."

"I beg to differ," he said, scooting across the slick leather seat facing hers. In the cramped space, his knees couldn't help but brush against hers. And yet, she had no room to pull out of his range, not that she really wanted to, despite the logic that told her she should. "I remember everything about you."

"That's not what I was talking about," Charlie clarified, looking back down at the collection of notes and trinkets.

"Maybe, maybe not." He paused, then leaned forward so she could see the sincerity in his gaze. "Charlie, I'm sorry. Really, deeply sorry."

She swallowed. How could he do this to her? Now? When they were alone? She knew what he wanted…and damn her, she knew that if he said all the right things, he might get it.

"Sorry for what?" she asked, playing as dumb as her pride would allow.

"For playing a part in the most painful moment of your life."

"What? Our dismissal? Sam, I've experienced worse."

"Name one thing."

Charlie bit her lip, trying to conjure a life experience that had scarred her more deeply than having the career she'd dreamed about since childhood yanked away at the same time that her family learned she wasn't the good, virginal, modest girl they'd raised her to be. She'd always known that her tastes leaned toward the hot and forbidden, but she'd never broadcasted her preferences to the world. Until that day.

She swallowed, flushing the lump in her throat into her stomach, which suddenly felt the pitch and wavers of the helicopter flight with dizzying sensitivity. *Dios mio,* what did she think she was doing? Alone with

Sam, finally facing her most painful memory and trying to act as if none of it mattered.

"I don't want to talk about this, Sam, We need to talk about Burt and what we might find when we get to Vegas."

She grabbed the stack of file folders and envelopes and pulled them onto her lap, but wasn't surprised when Sam scooped up the entire collection and placed it out of her reach.

"Sorry, Charlie," he said, a smile teasing the corners of his mouth. "I've always wanted to say that."

"Funny. Original, too. You should write for, oh, I don't know, tuna commercials."

"Sarcasm will not get you out of this."

"Out of what?"

He slid directly in front of her. He opened his knees to encompass hers and grabbed her hands. She might have resisted if not for the sweet tenderness of his light and tentative touch. "Out of putting our past to rest. I know you think you have, but you haven't. And I'm going to show you how I know."

CHAPTER SEVEN

"I'M OVER IT, Sam. I'm over you."

"That's a shame, because I can't say the same."

He wasn't surprised when Charlie looked at him like he'd sprouted a new head. In reality, he had. Not a new noggin, per se, but definitely a new brain. His old one hadn't provided him with the sense to hold onto a woman who challenged him, excited him, pushed him beyond the limits of his admittedly conservative lifestyle and upbringing. Try as he had over the past nine years to find a lover who would fulfill his needs the way Charlie had in just a few weeks, he'd come up empty. Until fate and reality television had lent a hand.

She braced her hands on the headphones. "You're insane," she claimed.

"Am I?"

He switched seats, ducking to avoid banging his head on the low ceiling. He thought she might attempt to move out of his way, but in the tight confines of the helicopter, she had nowhere to run, nowhere to hide. He'd already wasted a good twenty minutes of this ninety-minute trip, although, that was short in comparison to the time he'd wasted over the past nine years.

He was done waiting, done biding his time. He had her trapped in ultimate privacy, high above the ground and away from anyone who could hear them or see them. Jacey and pilot occupied the cockpit, but the coach of this particular Agusta 109C had been designed for both luxury and discretion. The seats—soft, tawny, padded leather—extended from floor to ceiling. The small window separating the pilot from the passengers was covered with a thick curtain, accessible only on their side. The headphones could be tapped into by the captain, but on their current setting, what he said to Charlie and vice-versa remained between them.

The time to make his move had come.

"Charlie, can you honestly tell me that you don't wonder what might have happened between us had we not gotten caught by the brass and kicked out of the academy?"

Like it or not, they had to deal with the past completely—put it to rest—before they could move on to any sort of future.

"I don't have to wonder," she answered. "If we hadn't been caught, you and I would both probably be detectives right now, pulling in crappy pay and working long hours on cases that test our faith in humanity."

"And that differs from our current lives, how?"

"Well, you don't exactly get paid in bubblegum wrappers, Sam."

He nodded, conceding that point at least. He made

great money at Foster and Bragg. "I wasn't talking about our careers, anyway. I was talking about us."

After a moment of careful maneuvering, Charlie crossed one leg over the other. "You never struck me as a romantic."

He grinned ruefully. "I've developed a taste for the sentimental over the past few years."

"I'd have to check out your little black book and see if that's true."

He dug into his jacket pocket and retrieved his PDA. With a glib smile, he tossed her his handheld computer. "You can check anything you want, but you won't find anyone to vouch for my new romanticism in there."

"Is that so?"

"Oh, I'm sure none of the women I've dated have any serious complaints," he answered, confident he'd been a relatively great guy to date, even if he hadn't fallen in love with any of the women he'd wined, dined and in some cases, seduced. But while commitment had eluded him, he'd become completely open to the possibility of settling down. Especially if he could entice Charlie to join him.

"Then why aren't you married yet?" she asked, one step ahead of him, but not by much.

"I ask myself that question with growing frequency, and I finally know the answer. I'm looking for a different kind of woman, one who isn't so easy to find. One who is more adventurous than I am. One who is strong enough to put me in my place when I get too cocky. One like you. You inspire me, Charlie."

"Inspire you?" She scooted back the inch or so that

was left between her and the door, which was thankfully secured and locked. "To what? Ruin your life? Throw all your good judgment out the window?"

"That was nine years ago, Charlie. You said you were over that."

She pressed her lips together. "I am, dammit."

"Then why are you still angry with me?"

"I'm not angry."

Even in the dim light of the cabin, he knew she could see his dubious expression. Such a ridiculous claim didn't deserve a verbal response.

She took a deep breath and after a long glance at her hands in her lap, she turned toward him. With only a few inches separating them on the seat, he couldn't miss the sincerity in her round brown eyes. "Seriously, Sam. I'm not angry with you. We were equally responsible for what happened. My anger has been at me."

"For what?"

She laughed, but the sound echoed hollowly in his headphones. "For not exercising better judgment."

"Everyone makes mistakes."

"Yeah, when I make them, I make them big."

"But you don't make them often. And I like to think that we can learn from our mistakes. That some good can even come from them. In fact, when you happened in to my life again, I saw that as a chance to *make* some of that good happen."

"As if you didn't have something to do with my appearance on the show. Come on, Sam. Admit it. You got me on."

His grin widened. Smartest move he'd made in a long time. "I may have made a little suggestion to the producers."

"Why?"

"Because I wanted to spend time with you and I knew you'd never agree if I just called you on the phone one day."

"You don't know that," she claimed.

He rolled his eyes. "You ordered me not to call you. You begged me. You forbade me. Give me some credit, Charlie. I tried to honor what you wanted."

"So instead of seeing if maybe I'd softened on that request after nine years, you used the reality television gig to circumvent my wishes?"

"You've got to admit I was creative."

She pushed on his chest and snickered. "Creative he calls it. Okay, I'll concede that. But I can't help going back to 'why?' We didn't have any earth-shattering, heartbreaking affair. We had sex a couple of times in really stupid places."

"We had an attraction neither one of us knew how to ignore," he clarified, taking a chance by placing his hand on her knee.

She glanced down at his touch, but didn't balk, not that she had any room to go anywhere. However Sam knew that Charlie had the physical dexterity and strength to twist out of even his smoothest moves. "I'm ignoring it now."

"Are you? Really?" He traced his hand up her leg, loving how the denim softened the taut muscle of her thigh. "Or are you just fighting extra hard to stop that spark? That fire? You're a passionate woman, Charlie, and the past is just that—the past. We've both grown beyond it, learned from it. But when we left the hurt behind, we also left what might have been good, what might have been right."

Charlie pressed her lips together, unwilling to release the moan of pleasure brewing in the back of her throat. He was doing nothing more than tracing his hand up and down her leg, but the delicious sensation reminded her vividly of what she'd given up when she'd walked away from Sam. When she'd been with him, she'd channeled some brazen seductress she'd never known before. Sure, she'd had lovers before Sam and after, but none that so effortlessly invoked the sensual woman she kept hidden deep inside.

"Tell me you aren't attracted to me," he said, leaning so close his breath teased the tendrils of her hair.

"I won't lie."

"Okay," he said, slipping his other hand up her back and exerting just enough pressure so that her breasts arched against his chest. "Then tell me you don't want to make love to me again, find out if we've still got that special rhythm."

She licked her lips, undeniably aroused. In a split second, she weighed what she had to lose—a little self-righteousness—against what she had to gain. No one seemed to know how to make love to her the way Sam had. Just his scent and his taste pushed her beyond limits that every woman should explore once in her lifetime.

Or in her case, twice.

"I said I wouldn't lie, Sam." She swallowed, and

forced the words out of her mouth. "I want to make love with you."

He shot a quick glance around them. "Here?" His grin kicked up on one side of his mouth.

The lights were dim, the space tight, but intimate. And truth be told, she'd always wondered what it would be like to make love in the sky.

The blatant thrill in her eyes made him laugh. With a quick tug, he removed his headphones, but made one last speech into the microphone that had hung beneath his chin. "I wouldn't want the pilot or Jacey breaking in to speak to us at the wrong time."

She turned and secured the curtain separating the cockpit from the cabin, then removed the headset herself. The captain and Jacey might suspect what was going on behind them, but they wouldn't be able to prove a thing.

CHAPTER EIGHT

THE STEADY BEAT of the blades slicing through the air provided a soul-strumming bass for the droning melody of the engines. The thrumming of the airborne machinery and the whistle of the wind outside created a soothing atmosphere unlike any Charlie had ever known.

And the minute she looked into Sam's eyes, electric expectation shot through her. She knew this man. She knew his body, and in the past few weeks, she'd caught glimpses of his soul. Yet even if he'd still been a cocky show-off instead of what he'd become—a confident man comfortable in his own skin—she knew she'd want him again. She wondered if her need for him had been somehow written into her genetic code. She couldn't deny him. She couldn't deny herself.

Sam's gaze flashed—hungry, territorial and eager. His transparent need, so like her own, transported her into a world of pure sensuality. With her ears muffled by the noise of the chopper, her other senses intensified. Her flesh tingled, the goose bumps reaching for Sam's touch. Her mouth watered, anxious for a taste of his hot, musky skin. Her eyes, even in the darkness, feasted on the sight of his muscled arms and sexy smile. Suddenly,

the scent of fuel and motor oil became a wild, intoxicating blend.

She whipped her black sweater over her head.

His eyes widened, and his hands were on her in a split
second. He cupped her greedily, his callused palms
pressing through the filmy lace of her bra. She gasped
and briefly wondered if the helicopter had lost altitude
or if he simply still remembered precisely how to send
shock waves rippling through her. Her nerve endings
throbbed from the tips of her breasts, which he plucked
through the fabric, to the seam of her jeans, which
bunched tight against her intimate flesh. She reached between their writhing bodies and released her button and
zipper, feeling his hardness against the back of her hand.
Her breath caught at the full length of him, but knew he
couldn't hear.

She forgot her own jeans and concentrated on his.
She loosened them, then slid her hands into the waistband and luxuriated in the tight muscles of his buttocks.
She pulled him close against her, losing her breath when
his sex pressed against hers. Even with clothes as a barrier, she knew she wasn't far from hurdling over the
brink of sexual release.

With obvious reluctance, Sam backed onto the seat
opposite her and stripped down to nothing but his smile.
The blue and red cabin lights cast a violet glow over his
smooth, hard chest and long, muscled legs. Her fingers
ached to tangle in the smattering of hair surrounding his
thick, male nipples and to ease down his belly to stroke
him to an even more impressive length and thickness.

But she resisted temptation and instead took off her

own jeans, determined to match him skin to skin. When she twisted to unhook the bra, he stopped her with a ravenous look that said, "Let me."

She complied.

With the space so tight, he crawled across the seats to reach her. He took advantage of her stretched-out position, swiping kisses up her ankle, calf, knee, thigh and belly on the way back to her breasts. She curved toward him, giving him access to slip his hands behind her and unhook her bra, while pressing her flesh nearer to his mouth.

He released the hooks, but didn't move the material out of the way. Instead, he let the fabric fall aside as their bodies writhed and melded. Charlie flamed from the inside out. Sam's hands stoked her, pleasured her, reignited the heat they'd discovered so long ago.

Without words, they explored and aroused. The hum and beat of the helicopter blades became more than just sound—the vibrations absorbed into her, burning through the boundaries of their bodies. He slipped her panties off with as much grace as the small space allowed, then slid his hand between her curls to find her wet and ready. He retrieved a condom from his jeans, which she rolled on with slow, tortuous attention. When he finally slid into her, Charlie doubted she'd ever experienced such intense eroticism—such an undeniable connection.

His lovemaking taunted her, lured her to the brink of orgasm, where the sensation of falling was amplified by their liaison in the sky. He grabbed her hands, braced her, then pushed them both beyond the limits of air and space and time. When they crossed the line between sanity and nirvana, she cried out. He matched the sound with a deep groan of her name against his ear.

They remained together, entwined and sated, until the helicopter started its descent into the desert.

SAM WINKED at Charlie conspiratorially when the pilot swung open the doors just as they finished frantically buckling and zipping and covering all their previously exposed and aroused body parts. From the bored look on the guy's face, Sam figured he either didn't give a damn what had happened in the back of his bird or, more likely, he and Charlie weren't the first lovers overcome with amorous intentions in the back seat of the luxury chopper. Either way, Sam didn't much care. He'd tasted Charlie again and knew the flavors would remain indelible on his tongue.

She was not getting away.

As they went silently down the elevator from the helipad into the Athens Bay hotel, Charlie stared stoically at the doors, avoiding his gaze. He fully expected her to begin the process of pulling away now. Not that he figured her the type to turn shy after they'd pushed the limits of propriety yet again, but he had a sinking suspicion that something more than lust and desire had come into play on that ride from L.A. to Vegas—and that would send her running.

So unless she'd drastically changed since their last encounter, Charlie would only run scared when her emotions were involved. She didn't mind the kind of conflict she could confront with fists or intellect, but the type that tore at her heart sent her scrambling.

He knew that was why she'd asked him to leave her alone all those years ago. It was so much easier to deny her struggle with her attraction to him versus her family's disappointment than to confront the trouble head-on. At the time, he'd agreed that they'd both be better off taking the easy way out. Now, he knew they'd been wrong. What they'd started in the back seat of his car had lasted longer than either of them had imagined possible. He couldn't let her go until they'd at least seen their attraction all the way to the end—if there was an end.

"The teams are meeting in a room just off the casino, where the poker games are usually played," Jacey announced, glancing at her watch and shrugging beneath the weight of the equipment she'd lugged from the helicopter. "We have just enough time to get you both into makeup and wardrobe before we start taping."

A production assistant met them in the lobby and handed them both room keys, which Jacey confiscated the moment the young man turned to rejoin the crew.

"You won't be needing these," Jacey said.

She tilted her head toward the casino and they followed. At the third bank of dollar slots, a hotel concierge appeared.

"You Jacey Turner?"

She dropped the camera to her side with a grunt. "I'm the only brunette lugging a television camera, aren't I?"

The hotel employee smirked and handed her a manila envelope, which she immediately flung over her shoulder at Sam.

"What's this?" he asked, looking over the unmarked package.

"Reservation for Lucky Chances. You have late check-in. Nudist resorts can be very accommodating."

Jacey lifted the camera and resumed her march, but Charlie grabbed Jacey's sleeve and pulled her to a screeching halt. "*Nudist?* You said clothing-optional!"

"What's the diff?"

Charlie threw down the overnight bag she carried on her shoulder. "Don't play airhead with me, Jacey Turner. You grew up in California. You sure as hell know the difference. Which one is it?"

Sam watched with great interest. Clothing optional meant just that—optional. Nudist, on the other hand, denoted no clothing at any time. For a brief moment, he wondered how the staff distinguished themselves from the guests. He winced, imagining how they might affix their nametags.

Jacey put the camera down and rolled her shoulders, then her neck, which cracked loud enough for them to hear over the rings, dings and whirls of the casino apparatus.

"There won't be any cameras," Jacey reminded them.

Sam pressed his lips together to cover his smile. Just when had this assignment become so incredibly delicious? Oh, yeah—the minute the producers had taken him up on his brilliant suggestion to include Charlie Cuesta in the game.

"That's not the point," Charlie insisted.

Jacey leveled a disbelieving stare at Charlie. "You're telling me you've never seen Sam here in the buff? Ha!"

Charlie stepped closer to Jacey. If Sam hadn't known that the two women had developed a genuine affection for each other, evident by their barely contained smiles, he might have thought a catfight was about to ensue. "That's none of your business."

"The whole world is speculating," Jacey said, sing-songing her words.

Charlie matched her melody. "The whole world can go to hell."

Jacey bit her lip. Sam could see the questions dancing in her curious eyes. But Charlie was right. What happened between him and Charlie, ultimately, had to remain between the two of them. He wasn't beyond using the television audience's interest to fuel flirtations with Charlie, but in the end, what happened between them in private mattered most.

And he wasn't going to get Charlie in private any time soon if this showdown didn't end.

He broke in between them, sliding his hand gently behind Charlie's back. "Jacey, I don't think Charlie gives a damn if I see her naked, but it will certainly be hard for me to concentrate on solving your father's problem if I'm so…distracted."

Charlie bristled under his carnal look. He chuckled, knowing he'd pay for his salaciousness later.

"It's clothing optional, Charlie," Jacey finally admitted, the joke over in light of their assignment. "Just play it like this is your first time and no one will look twice at you."

Charlie nodded, snagged her bag and stalked in the direction that the production assistant had taken. Jacey glanced furtively at Sam, then without a word, followed.

Only once he was alone did Sam say the words dancing on his tongue. "I don't know about everyone else, but I plan to look twice, three times, four times…"

He'd counted all the way to fifty-three by the time he reached the staging area for wardrobe.

CHAPTER NINE

SURREAL DIDN'T BEGIN to describe the scene in the Lucky Chances disco. Until Sam had ushered her into the lounge, complete with spinning mirrored balls, strobing colored lights and pounding music from a live, nude band sporting more tattoos than native tribesmen, Charlie thought she'd seen it all when it came to clubs and nightspots.

How wrong she'd been.

With the notable exceptions of her and Sam, nearly everyone in the club was buck naked. Ages ranged from college co-eds to the silver-haired set. As the music surged, assorted body parts jiggled, jostled and swayed. She wondered if she'd ever listen to Gloria Estefan again without conjuring this bizarre image in her mind.

Luckily, Sam rejoined her quickly and took her attention away from the dance floor. He tossed a coaster onto the table in front of her, then delivered a tall, icy glass stuffed with mint leaves. He pulled his chair directly beside hers and slid into it with the same ease as he sipped his beer.

"Your *mojito,* señorita."

"Extra sweet?"

"Of course. You didn't think I'd forget, did you?"

Well, yeah. Why would he remember? Then again it's not as though he likely dated many *mujeres* with hankerings for rum, sugar, water and mint.

She took a sip and the crispy sweet concoction trickled down her throat and soothed the parchedness within. She held the glass away from her and took a close look at the size. Yup. If she polished this baby off quick enough, it would be soothing more than just thirst.

"Why are we here again?" she asked Sam, gulping down generous sips through her straw.

"Scoping the place out. Everyone seems to be in here or in the casino. We'll swing by there in a few."

She pictured someone winning big at the craps table and jumping for joy. The mental image made her reach for her drink again.

She sucked down half of it, then focused on Sam. "What are we looking for?"

Sam chuckled and shook his head. So what if she was trying to make conversation? They both knew exactly what type of person they were searching for—someone as equally uncomfortable in this clothing-optional resort as she was. They'd learned a few important facts since arriving in Vegas. First, Burt insisted he didn't know any nudists. Second, Lucky Chances had only been in business for two years. The building, however, had been around since the seventies. Originally called Casino City, then Sirens, then Cupid's Corner, the business had changed hands more times over the past thirty-five years than a ten-dollar poker chip. Burt could have been here before and he simply hadn't made the connection. He'd followed them from Los Angeles with the full production crew, so they expected him to arrive soon. But chances were, whoever had tried to arrange for Burt to meet him or her might not have anticipated the change in…atmosphere.

In his tropical attire—a breezy white *guayabera,* tan slacks and sandals purchased at the Athens Bay hotel—Sam exuded the same touristy vibe as the rest of the partiers in the room. Even with clothes, the man looked confident and relaxed, as if he owned the whole world and everything in it—and loved every inch with equal relish. What woman wouldn't want to spend time with him?

"You look beautiful," he said, scooting nearer. His nose skimmed the skin on her bare shoulder as he took a whiff of her perfume. "You smell delicious. I wonder how you taste."

She grabbed her drink and took another hearty sip, resisting the urge to dump the entire frosty contents over her head. She needed to cool down. They had work to do.

"I still think Burt is on the wrong track with the whole blackmail angle," she said, avoiding a personal discussion. They'd gotten personal enough tonight, thank you.

Sam sat back, sipped his beer and complied with her change in topic. "He has precedent for believing this is a prelude to extortion. The Vegas connection is too co-incidental to ignore."

Charlie fiddled with the coaster, flicking the cardboard with her nail. "I don't know. The matchbook was delivered to the set at the airport, right? That means that whoever was sending the notes has direct contact with someone on the production team—or other contestants. Since the notes began arriving long before the players of *The Great Chase* were chosen, I think we can eliminate our competition."

"I had Jacey run us a list of everyone working on *The Great Chase* and *Survivng Sarah*. She said she'd have it faxed to the front desk by morning, but Burt says he's not working with anyone he knew before. He's been very purposeful about that."

Charlie eyed him warily, surprised they'd think along the same lines, even in business. Sure, they made great lovers—they'd established that nine years ago and confirmed that truth earlier in the helicopter. Didn't mean they had anything else in common. Right?

And yet, he didn't seem any more satisfied with the situation than she did. Something in his narrowed eyes said his hackles were up.

"What are you thinking?" she asked.

"Well, this last clue might be just that—the last clue. Delivering it to a closed set was either a major miscalculation or an indication that the person is about to reveal him or herself, probably to make his or her demands clear." Sam scanned the room, his glance never lingering long in one place. "If we're lucky, we'll figure out what's going on before Burt arrives. But if we don't spot someone that we recognize as connected to the show, or someone who is out of place and suspicious, we're going to need him to take the meeting. We can help him out from there."

"He just wanted a name," she reminded him with a grimace, unable to kick her disappointment at such an unsatisfying task. She'd rather deal with the matter more thoroughly.

Sam tilted his head toward hers, his eyes gleaming with what she could best identify as expectation. "Just a name. That's an awfully simple and boring request, don't you think?"

A thrill surged through Charlie, one nearly unrelated to the sexual excitement of having Sam so close. This buzz stemmed from something less personal—and yet intimate in its own way.

"Yes, I think just giving him a name would be incredibly dull. I'd much rather provide our client with the person and whatever ammunition they might have to hurt him."

Sam nodded, downed the rest of his beer and then stood. "Much more bang for his buck. And I have a very good idea of where we should move on our search next."

She jumped up and immediately smoothed down the miniskirt sarong she'd purchased at the other hotel as well. Like Sam, she'd chosen an outfit that exuded casual comfort. She'd also gone to great pains to make sure the miniskirt and off the shoulder top, paired with spiked red sandals, would drive Sam absolutely insane with desire.

"Where to?"

"The dance floor."

"What?"

He grabbed her waist and tugged her close, then took one hand in his. She nearly melted against him thanks to the heat radiating from both their bodies.

"You promised to teach me to salsa, remember?"

THE DANCE LESSON hadn't lasted more than the three minutes of the latin-rhythm song, but Sam learned a great deal. Which was easy, since Charlie was such a great teacher.

"You need to start drinking *mojitos,* too, Ryan. Maybe the rum will loosen those hips of yours."

"My hips are plenty loose when they need to be," Sam shot back, pausing as Charlie slung her purse over her shoulder and finished her drink with two gulps. She didn't so much as waver on those tottering heels as they wound their way through the crowd. She could drink, dance and drive him insane with lust all without missing a beat.

"Can't argue there. Where to next?"

"Front desk. I've got a hunch."

They exited the disco and then cut through the blackjack tables to reach the relatively quiet front desk. It was nearly three o'clock in the morning and the older woman manning the hotel desk looked sleepy and bored. Fortunately, she hadn't been on duty when Sam and Charlie had checked in over an hour ago, so he could use a check-in ruse to get the information he needed.

"Hi," Sam said, turning up the wattage of his smile.

The woman blinked, but that was the scope of her response to his charm. "Can I help you?"

"Yes, you can. We need to check in."

He glanced at Charlie, but she kept her eyes on the clerk, a smile plastered on her face.

"Name?"

He should have thought of this earlier, but apparently, the prospect of spending a few hours with Charlie in a clothing-optional resort had waylaid his thought processes. "Burt Mueller. I have a reservation."

The clerk fiddled with her keyboard, typing and scrolling through screens Sam couldn't see from the other side of the desk. "Here you are. You have one room, a single, adjoined to a second room. But that can't be for you," the woman said to Charlie. "The other party has already checked in."

Sam cleared his throat, determined to hide any sense of surprise. "Yes. She's a good friend of both of ours."

The woman nodded, but released no further information. "She put your room on her credit card, Mr. Mueller. All you have to do is wait while I program a key for you."

After yawning, the woman grabbed a plastic card from a drawer then scooted down the long desk to punch in the numbers. Luckily, Sam was tall enough to turn the screen of the woman's computer monitor and catch the name of the mystery guest, the person obviously expecting Burt to check into the room connected to hers.

"Kelly Laurens."

Charlie's eyebrows popped up. "So it *is* a woman."

"Means nothing."

"To you, maybe," Charlie said, "but we'll see when we give the name to Burt."

CHAPTER TEN

"OKAY, BURT," Sam said, glancing over his shoulder. They'd commandeered a dark paneled room just off the lobby, dimly lit and unused at somewhere around 4:00 a.m. Sam stifled a yawn. It had been a long night for all of them and his patience was wearing thin. "Time to come clean."

"I told you!" Burt insisted for the fourth time since arriving with Jacey twenty minutes ago. "I don't know anyone named Kelly Laurens. And I don't appreciate your interrogation tactics."

Charlie threw Sam a smirk, but continued to circle Burt just as she'd been taught way back at the police academy. At this point, they hadn't made the good cop-bad cop distinction, but they'd established an easy rhythm in their questioning that surprised even Sam.

"Burt, you want us to figure this out, right?" Charlie asked, her voice firm, yet distinctly feminine. She was leaving herself room to take whatever tack Burt required—soft and friendly or stern and insistent. Sam folded his arms over his chest, impressed.

"We have a name that you say doesn't mean anything to you. How could that be? The name was on her credit card. And we know it's legit."

"Could be an alias," Burt argued. "A stolen identity."

"True, but I don't think it is. Why would a black-mailer send scented notes, Burt? That has bothered me from the beginning. I think you knew Kelly Laurens. I think you knew her intimately."

"I have a lousy memory," Burt insisted.

"Apparently," Sam quipped, aware they were running out of time. They had to solve Burt's case and reserve enough time to complete the challenge for the show, which wouldn't be so easy this time. Apparently, some-one at the Athens Bay casino was cheating at blackjack. Not only did they have to find the cheater, they had to catch him or her red-handed. On top of that, Sam was exhausted. "But this has to be someone significant. Did you ever know any women with the first name of Kelly?"

Burt scoffed. "Of course. It's not exactly an uncom-mon name."

Charlie charged on this piece of information, stop-ping her pacing. "Did you know anyone named Kelly during the taping of *The Bermuda Triangle*?"

"No! I mean…" Burt slowed down, rubbing his un-shaven jaw. "Wait. Yeah, I think I did."

Finally! Sam glanced at Charlie, who didn't bother to hide a grin. She grabbed a chair and scooted it for-ward, so that she was nearly knee-to-knee with Burt.

"That's progress," Charlie said softly. "What do you remember about her? Can you tell us her last name?"

Burt squinted, his lips scrunched as he thought. Sam estimated that Burt wasn't fooling around and feigning a bad memory. He had too much at stake to play games. He really didn't remember this woman, whoever she was.

"I'm such a dog," Burt said, shaking his head. "But we really didn't know each other for very long. We hooked up for a couple of weeks just after *Triangle* bit the dust."

"But she wasn't just some lover, was she?" Sam guessed. "She *was* tied to the toughest time of your life." Sam kept his tone stern, but after crossing behind Charlie, he couldn't help but lay his hands as casually on her shoulders. He couldn't fathom Burt's situation. He'd been Charlie's lover for only a few weeks a long time ago, but he hadn't forgotten one single detail about her.

Charlie snuck a look up at Sam, one that included a tiny smile. Now they were getting somewhere.

She spun back to Burt. "Come on, think. She worked for you. You signed her paychecks. What was her full name?"

"Kelly, but not Laurens," Burt said, confident. "She was on the production crew. A seamstress. Her husband had just left her."

"You had an affair?"

Burt shook his head. "You couldn't really call it that. I was in a rough place. Just lost my business partner and a show I'd known would be a huge hit. My career was in the toilet. She was a distraction. I haven't thought about her in years."

"Did she know about the scandal?"

"No. I never told anyone. Especially not once the blackmail started."

"Why did you break up?"

Burt paused. Sam could practically see the cogs in his brain spinning backwards, back to a time the producer would obviously rather not remember.

"We just lost track. I was all caught up in trying to salvage something of my career and I think she moved, or got a new job. Kelly Maitland. That was her name!"

"Then you do remember me!"

Behind them, an attractive woman, not much younger than Burt, floated into the room. She was tall, graceful, with thin fingers that Sam could easily see manipulating threads or intricate beading. Her skin and hair were pale and her smile reached her soft green eyes, the same color as her breezy sundress.

"Rachel?"

Burt stood and so did Charlie. Sam moved the chair out of the way, then softly touched Charlie's elbow. They, along with Jacey, faded into the background. Any answers they needed from this point on would likely reveal themselves without any prodding from them.

"What are you doing here?" Burt asked.

Her smile quickly morphed into a deep frown. "You don't remember."

"What are you talking about? Did you know Kelly?"

"I am Kelly."

Burt stumbled back a step, but recovered at once. He strode forward, his eyes trained on the face of a woman he obviously knew, but didn't know.

"You're Rachel Shaw. You worked wardrobe on *Surviving Sarah*. You've worked for me on several shows in the past three years." But then, a connection formed the minute the words tumbled from his mouth. "Good Lord. You sent all the notes, the trinkets. Rachel, what is this all about?"

The woman's smile tilted downward with shy embarrassment. "It's about the past, Burt. And the present. We were supposed to meet here, at this hotel, for one last fling, remember? It was the Dolphin Cove back then. You never showed up."

Burt rubbed his hands over his head, clearly not sharing the same recollection. "Damn, but I don't remember leaving things so open between us. You got a job. You moved on."

"I took up acting."

"Is that why you changed your name? Your hair?"

Rachel took a deep breath, still obviously deflated by Burt's lousy memory. She clasped her hands in front of her and pushed the words out with clear emotional effort. "There was already a Kelly Laurens in the Guild and there was no way I was going to use Maitland after what my ex-husband put me through. So I took my mother's name, Rachel. Shaw was my second husband's name. I got married. And divorced. Again. But I have a daughter."

Burt's face lit with realization. "Jasmine! Jasmine Shaw. I never made the connection."

Burt turned to Jacey, Charlie and Sam, who had formed a quiet line in the back of the room. They nodded, understanding. Jasmine Shaw was the current wardrobe mistress on *The Great Chase*. Obviously, she'd been the contact to the set that they'd searched for.

"Why did you send all the notes? The necklace and

other mementos? Why didn't you just tell me who you were?"

Rachel glanced at her sandals. "I expected you to remember me when I interviewed for that pilot three years ago, but you didn't."

"You could have just told me your name," Burt said.

"Would that have meant anything to you?"

Burt cleared his throat. "Maybe not. I've tried very hard to forget that time in my life."

Hurt darkened the woman's expression, but Burt recovered and grabbed her hands. "Not because of you! Because of the scandal regarding *Triangle*."

"Scandal? What scandal?"

Sam jumped when Charlie, sporting a smug grin, elbowed him in the ribs. From the get-go, she'd guessed the clues might not point to blackmail. Okay, so Burt had been paranoid. A guilty conscience tended to cause that reaction.

Sam rolled his eyes anyway, but secretly decided that the woman's instincts were every bit as honed as her interview skills.

Jacey, Sam and Charlie slipped out of the room. When a drunk assortment of naked conventioneers, complete with tasseled purple fez hats, tumbled out of the casino into the lobby, the trio scrambled for the front door. Once out on the terrace, Jacey drew both Charlie and Sam into a group hug.

"Wow, you guys are good. She was never trying to hurt my dad, just trying to jog his hopeless long-term memory."

Charlie patted Jacey on the back and released her. "Burt

must have meant a lot to Rachel, er, Kelly, for her to go to so much trouble to rekindle an affair from the past."

Sam took the opening she'd unwittingly given him, slipping in behind her with his hands around her waist. "I think I like how that woman thinks."

Jacey chuckled. "I'll bet you do. Charlie, the time has come for you to know that when Mr. Wonderful over here saw your name on the list of possible contestants Patrick Hennessy had provided, he told the director he absolutely wouldn't do the show unless he was paired with you."

Charlie glanced up over her shoulder. "Is that so?"

Sam nuzzled closer. "Again, guilty as charged."

She twisted around in his arms, a sly smile on her face. "You are guilty of quite a few transgressions, Mr. Ryan. One would think you have trouble following rules."

"Just one of the things we have in common."

She licked her lips. "One of the more innocent things."

"Well, innocent or guilty, you two still have a challenge to complete," Jacey said. "I think Burt will be occupied for some time playing blast from the past with Rachel. I have my camera in the car. Think you can drag yourselves away from this hedonistic hotspot long enough to work?"

Sam groaned in protest, but Charlie laughed and slapped him on the shoulder.

"Of course we're ready to work."

"Can't we sleep first?" Sam wasn't so much tired as he was anxious to spend quality time alone with Charlie.

Charlie lifted onto her tiptoes and kissed him on the

chin. "Let's give Jacey a few hours of interesting footage, then we'll sneak back here and utilize that room we still have available. You won't tell, will you, Jacey?"

"Me? Tell what? You saved my dad from a whole lot of worry tonight. You think I'm going to begrudge you one wild night at Lucky Chances?"

Behind them, the fez-topped naked men were playing an interesting game of Red Rover in the lobby, and despite the security guards that had just descended on the scene, Sam wasn't deterred. "I'll grab the laptop. Be right back."

"Be sure that's all you grab!" Charlie teased.

He didn't bother to respond. For a night alone with Charlie, he'd brave a whole lot worse than what Lucky Chances had to offer.

CHAPTER ELEVEN

FOR THE LIFE OF HER, Charlie couldn't think of a more straightforward yet brilliant final challenge. The goal was simple—find the liar. In a posh three-bedroom suite on a scenic, cliffside beach on the east side of the island of Puerto Rico, the final two teams—Charlie and Sam and the Rosco brothers from Chicago—had to mingle with a cache of runway-worthy beauties and determine which one was not telling the truth about who she really was.

Charlie had to give the creative team on *The Great Chase* some serious credit. All three guys were so distracted by the tall, well-endowed, elegantly dressed women, she wondered if they had enough brain power between them to remember one-tenth of the chitchat they exchanged with the hired goddesses. She, on the other hand, had to grapple with that green-eyed secret all women denied but still experienced in the presence of such unnatural beauty—jealousy. With so much sex thrown into the mix, someone was bound to screw up. She only hoped it wouldn't be her. Or Sam.

At times, Charlie couldn't believe that she and Sam had made it to the final challenge at all. Not that the easy cases hadn't been a snap, but they'd had so much work-ing against them—including but not limited to her im-mense distrust of her former lover and partner. But at other times, like right now when Sam caught her eye from across the room and his hungry expression made her feel like the only beautiful woman who existed in the world, she wondered why the hell she'd wasted so much time resenting his success, and therefore, him.

But that negative association was gone now. The hurt, disappointment and embarrassment from the past had washed away like water down a drain. She'd even spoken to her father, who'd been watching *The Great Chase* as if he was the one with a million dollars on the line. If Papi remembered who Sam was, which she was sure he did, he hadn't said a word. Instead, he'd simply pointed out that she and Sam made a very good team.

"Got any clues yet?" Sam asked, sidling up beside her from such an angle that the cameras placed through-out the suite wouldn't pick up the way he smoothed his palm over her backside.

She bit her bottom lip and shook her head, trying to ignore the thrill his touch sent through her. "They're *all* phonies as far as I can tell. Does plastic surgery count as a lie?"

Sam chuckled. "Not unless they won't admit it."

Exasperated, Charlie huffed. "Well, then it's no clue at all. I just got a twenty-minute rundown from at least three of them on all the work they'd had done."

"Which ones are real?" Sam asked, his eyes nar-rowed in curiosity.

She socked him in the arm.

"What about our competition?" she asked. "Do they seem to be getting anywhere?"

Sam leaned around to get a better view. "Looks like they're both more interested in collecting phone numbers."

"Maybe you should try that. Maybe one of them will transpose a number and we'll have our woman."

Just then, the host of the show burst into the room. Jacey followed close behind with her camera and the crew pushed several lights into position. Charlie looked at Sam, then at her watch. According to the rules of the game, they had slightly less than an hour more to conduct interviews.

"Time's up!"

The Rosco brothers pushed to the front. "What? We have another fifty-five minutes!" Allen Rosco insisted.

A grip handed the host a hot mike and in seconds, they were live. Charlie couldn't believe they'd changed the rules, but kept her protests to herself. Since she'd been breaking rules left and right since the show's first taping, she didn't have much of a leg to stand on in the self-righteous department.

"This is Cal Carter of *P.I. Files,* taking up the hosting role tonight on *The Great Chase.*"

Charlie shook her head, then smoothed her hair and checked for lipstick on her teeth. She might as well look good since they weren't going to win. She had no idea which of the women in the room hadn't been truthful in the interviews and Sam, who always looked confident, wore a somewhat shell-shocked expression.

Damn, damn, damn. She'd had at least two more

women to interview when Cal burst in. Since she and Sam had split the twelve women into two groups, she didn't know which portion he'd finished or not.

Great. She'd always wanted to be humiliated on national television.

Cal instructed the players to gather in the center of the room. He handed each of them a small leather portfolio, which had nothing more than a pad of paper and a pen inside. At his urging, the models formed a line across the wall near the balcony. Each was presented with a card that bore a number, one through twelve.

"For the past four weeks, the detectives of *The Great Chase* have dealt with the typical cases real P.I.'s face every day. In episode one, 'Lost in Space,' the players searched for the owners of long-missing keepsakes. In episode two…"

Cal continued the recap, which Charlie figured would be paired with a prerecorded montage of the previous six episodes. She'd worked so hard, utilized every trick in her book to get this far.

Now, they were going to lose.

"Okay, detectives," Cal said, grinning with practiced expectation. "Tonight, we've shortened the time allotment so the detectives can work using gut instinct just as much as skill. Each of you has a sheet of paper, but you now have a hard choice—work on your own or with your partner."

Cal paused, allowing what he'd said to sink in. After weeks of being forced to work with a partner, Charlie now had the choice to work alone. Choice and, she'd bet, financial incentive.

"If you opt to work together, your total possible win-
nings will be cut in half. In other words, the million dollar prize reduces to five-hundred thousand, split two
ways—so two hundred and fifty thousand each…unless
you both have already found the liar. If you have, then
you'll get the full amount. If you work separately and
only one of you gets the challenge correct, you'll get the
million bucks all to yourself. So, do you remain loyal
to your team or do you go it alone?"

If not for the cameras, the audience might have
missed any hesitation the Rosco brothers experienced.
They separated faster than bullets shot from the clip of
an automatic.

Charlie and Sam didn't move so quickly. Neither of
them could deny that they made an awesome team. They
were stronger, smarter and more confident when they
worked together. He listened to her instincts and she respected his experience. Should they go for the million,
or stick together and possibly walk away with less
money, but the pride of having won?

"Let's go for it, Charlie," Sam said, winking.

Funny how she knew what he meant.

They stepped apart.

"Everyone is going for the big bucks, ladies and gentleman. So much for team efforts. Okay, players, you
have thirty seconds to write down the number of the
woman you think is the liar. Ready, go."

Charlie scanned the women she'd interviewed,
knowing Sam would cover his half. She replayed the
main points from their conversations. She skipped numbers four and seven, since she hadn't exchanged as

much as a word with either of them, though she did take a quick perusal of their body language, which yielded nothing. For the most part, the women stood like twelve mannequins in haute couture.

"Ten seconds," Cal announced.

Charlie's throat tightened. Her heart pounded as if she'd run two miles at top speed. A chill chased along her spine and she shifted from foot to foot, trying to concentrate on her task. She threw a quick glance at Sam, who was standing with his hands crossed in front of him, his portfolio dangling lazily from his fingertips. His grin exuded relaxed confidence.

He knew. Or if he didn't, he'd be damned if he'd let anyone else know.

Charlie took a deep breath, then slipped the pen back into the little leather loop inside the portfolio. With utter surprise, she realized that even if she and Sam walked away without one red cent, they'd already won. Not only because they'd both performed with skill and expertise, but mostly because they'd found each other again. Charlie couldn't imagine that they'd both go home and not continue to see each other. They'd become lovers again, and more importantly, they'd become friends. She'd found the only answer she truly needed— one she hadn't even been hunting for.

"Time's up!" Cal announced.

He started with Allen Rosco, who surrendered his portfolio to Cal's waiting palm. He flipped open the notepad and announced Allen's choice.

"Number seven."

Damn. One of the ones Charlie hadn't interviewed.

"Why do you think it's number seven, Allen?"

Allen ran down his reasoning, which sounded like a crock to Charlie. He was bluffing. And he wasn't doing a very good job.

His brother, Pete, apparently had all the real deductive reasoning skills. Unfortunately, his knowledge about women was sorely lacking. He'd chosen number two, based on the fact that she'd claimed to be a professional surfer even though her hair was dark brown and didn't have a single sun streak. Had the guy never heard of hair color? Granted, the dye job was clearly professional, but if that woman was a natural brunette, Charlie was blond in very hidden places.

Cal Carter milked the moment for all it was worth. He scanned the line of beauties, watched the Rosco brothers with keen interest, then cast a glance at Charlie and Sam.

"Sorry, guys, but neither of you made the right choice. It's up to our former lovers now, Charlie Cuesta and Sam Ryan, to take home the cash. Charlie, let's start with you."

Despite the fact that her paper was blank, Charlie handed the portfolio over forcefully. He flipped it open, then stared at her with exaggerated shock.

"You don't know who the liar is?"

"Other than the producers of this show who guaranteed us two hours of investigation time? No, I haven't a clue."

Cal cleared his throat and ignored her pointed quip. "Then it's all up to your partner. Sam Ryan, do you know who the liar is?"

Sam stepped forward, his perennially cocky grin tilting high on the left side of his face. He handed the pad to Cal but before he could flip it open, Sam snatched it back.

"You can't change your choice now," Cal warned.

Sam shoved the portfolio into his back pocket. "I'm not changing anything. I'm just going to tell you and your audience who I think the liar is myself."

He turned toward Charlie and snagged her hands in his. "It's her."

CHAPTER TWELVE

"WHAT ARE YOU DOING?" she asked, grinding out her question through a frozen grin.

Had he lost his mind? Did he not know who the liar was, so he was trying to finesse? It would be just like him. Should she play along?

"You're a liar, Charlie Cuesta." He lifted her hands to his mouth and brushed soft kisses over the knuckles. "You claim you don't love me—and that's a lie."

Charlie's legs vibrated, her bones from skull to toe quaking as disbelief crashed through her. Was he crazy? Was he serious? Did he really think she could love him after only a few weeks together?

Did she really think she could resist?

She swallowed deeply, trying to forget the lights, microphones and cameras zooming in for a tighter shot. She concentrated on the keen, expectant look in his blue eyes, in the ever-so-slightly uncertain tilt of his smile. She heard a whimper from the side and caught sight of Jacey behind her lens, trying to contain her tears.

"I've never said one way or another how I feel about you, Sam."

"Lies of omission," he said simply.

She narrowed her gaze. "Then you're guilty, too."

He reached up and crooked his finger beneath her chin. A flash flood of emotional waves rippled through her, causing a swell of moisture to pool in her eyes.

"Not anymore. I'm going to tell you and the whole world. I love you, Charlie Cuesta. I probably loved you nine years ago, but was too much of a self-absorbed fool to figure it out. But now, I know the truth. I love how you want everyone else to follow rules, but you buck the system whenever you can. I love how smart you are, how sexy you are. I love how you aren't afraid to say what's on your mind or go for what you want. You're the perfect partner for me, and cash or not, I'll have won this game if I can get even five more minutes in your life."

In the corner of her eye, Charlie caught sight of Rick Ralston and Burt Mueller slipping into the suite, each of them whispering in deceptively hushed tones. She laughed, realizing that Sam had probably just increased the show's ratings and advertising value by huge percentage points. Not that she cared, but Burt and Rick were beaming so brightly, Charlie figured they could douse the stage lights and the production would still proceed.

"You're a real charmer, Sam Ryan."

"So I've been told."

"Has any woman ever told you she loved you?"

He shook his head. "No one that I wanted to hear it from. Let me hear it from you, Charlie. If you mean it."

The words caught in her throat, so she followed her heart and slipped her hands around his neck, then planted a hungry kiss on his lips. The minute their mouths met, the tears she'd held back splashed down her face. She'd lost the money and more than likely, she'd lost the potential job with the Hennessy Group because she'd failed to win the game, but she'd gained a man who was willing to put his heart on the line in front of the whole television-watching world—all for her.

"I do love you, Sam," she whispered.

If everyone didn't hear, Sam's response let them know what she'd said. He whooped like a cowboy and swung her around so that Pete and Allen Rosco, the nearest camera operators and Cal Carter all had to jump back to keep from being slashed by the heels of her shoes.

The entire crew and cast, including the models, burst into applause. Jacey handed her camera to Ed, her assistant, then leaped in to hug both of them, her heavily lined eyes leaking dark liner down her face.

Charlie's face was hot with both happiness and awkwardness. Apparently, she was never going to get a hang of the whole discretion thing.

"We didn't win," Sam said, his arms still locked around her waist.

"Nobody did," Charlie answered. "I wonder if there was even a liar in the room at all."

Sam shrugged, but something in his eyes told her he knew something she didn't. This happened more times than she cared to admit and, unfortunately for her, increased her attraction to him. But she had skills he couldn't anticipate, either. With deft hands, she removed the portfolio from his pocket, then spun out of his embrace. She ducked behind Ed as she flipped the top to reveal the answer he'd taken out of Cal's hands.

"Number twelve!" she shouted.

The woman squealed. Ed spun the camera on Charlie while another operator focused on the woman Sam had identified as the liar. Rick dashed out of the room, undoubtedly to the production truck where he could direct the action.

Cal jumped back in to the craziness, adjusting his ear piece. "Sam Ryan chose number twelve? Are we going to allow…yes! Okay, Sam, tell us why you think number twelve is the liar?"

He shoved the microphone in Sam's face.

"Simple. She has a tattoo."

Charlie blinked. The bob-haired blonde shook her head in obvious amazement while the others crowded around her.

"Why is a tattoo significant?" Charlie asked.

He leaned down and kissed her cheek. "Look at her earrings."

Charlie crossed the room, with Jacey on her heels taping every moment, every expression. The woman glanced aside, then curled her hair behind her ear, giving Charlie a clear view of her jewelry. Two dangling Stars of David.

With a gasp spawned by his brilliance, Charlie turned to Sam and applauded. "Amazing. Did you ask her where she got the earrings?"

Sam nodded, his smile classically smug. "At her *bat mitzvah*. Any girl who goes through that type of religious training would know that a tattoo would be seriously frowned upon, if not forbidden, in her religion. And since I know that the wardrobe department on this

show is very interested in each and every piece of clothing and jewelry worn on the set, I knew the earrings
weren't an accident. So I asked her where she got them.
She said she was Jewish…but she lied. True?"

The woman, who'd been shaking her head at Sam's
clever deduction, suddenly realized he was speaking
directly to her and began nodding furiously. Again, applause thundered through the room. Even the Rosco
brothers clapped, albeit reluctantly.

Sam opened his arms and Charlie snuggled in, pretending for a second that they were alone instead of surrounded by well-wishers. Even as the models
surrounded them and Cal presented his final lines to the
camera, Charlie closed her eyes, leaned her cheek on
Sam's chest, breathed in his warm scent and absorbed
his racing heartbeat.

"You won," she murmured.

"We won," he corrected, gently kissing her on the top
of the head.

"I'm not taking any credit for this one, Ryan. You
pulled it off all on your own."

"Just like you pulled off all the cases before this. I
was trying to give you space then, let you shine on your
own, you know that, right?"

She laughed. She wondered when his ego would
sneak back into the situation. "You did all this to prove
something, didn't you? That you can be generous but
you're still a great investigator."

He clucked his tongue. "I did all this to prove to you
that I love you more than winning, more than my career
or my reputation."

Their kiss was long and gentle, but as much of an exhibitionist as Charlie had been tonight, she desperately wanted to retreat from the crowd. But Cal was already ordering a setup for private interviews and the makeup and wardrobe crew had descended, insisting that she and Sam hit the chairs for touch-ups. She kept her hand in his as a production assistant ushered them out of the crowd.

"So, what are you going to do with all that money?" she asked, loving how his hand surrounded hers so naturally. "Start your own firm?"

"Me? Nah. I like working for someone else. I was thinking about making a serious jewelry purchase. Diamond solitaire. Maybe a carat or two or…ten. What do you think? Do you like square-cut or pear-shaped?"

The question stunned her so thoroughly that she hardly felt him pull her into a private courtyard on the other side of the suite. He locked the gate. The ivy around the fenced-in area ensured no one could see where they'd run off to. Amid a collection of hyacinth and birds of paradise, with the moon sparkling high over the Puerto Rican mountains behind them and a fountain burbling just a few feet away, Sam dropped to his knee.

"Marry me, Charlie."

She slapped her hand on her chest, certain she'd lose her ability to breathe if he didn't stop throwing shock after shock in her direction. "You can't mean that. You're caught up in the moment, Sam."

"No, I'm not. Well, yes, I am, but I'm still thinking clearly. I love you and you love me. I know we have a special connection and we'd never abandon each other again, no matter how tough things get. I would like to stop chasing you, Charlie. I just want to love you."

Charlie tugged until Sam stood. She flattened her palms on his cheeks and knew in her heart that his plea was sincere. This had all happened so fast, and Charlie had to admit that her natural impulsiveness usually landed her in big trouble. However, that same brash nature made her who she was, bolstered her strength and kept the world fresh and exciting.

Just like Sam would.

"Yes, Sam," she answered. "I'll marry you."

This time, Sam didn't whoop or holler. He simply pulled her into his embrace and whispered, "Then now, we truly have won it all."

EPILOGUE

"Busy?"

Rachel sauntered into Burt's trailer, those elegant hands of hers lingering on the doorjamb, then following behind her with the same fluttery grace as the chiffon scarf she wore around her neck. Even with the bangs and shouts from the crew outside breaking down the set of the post-show special for *The Great Chase,* Burt couldn't help but appreciate the visual. Damn, she was one breathtaking woman. How he'd forgotten her would remain a mystery even the best private investigators in the world wouldn't be able to explain.

"Never too busy for a beautiful woman."

She slipped onto the corner of his desk, allowing the slit in her skirt to part just enough to give him a generous glimpse of thigh. She might be twenty years older, but Rachel hadn't forgotten how to work him over but good.

"Any beautiful woman, or just me?"

"You're fishing for a compliment," he said, closing the file he'd been reading and scooting it out of his way.

"So what if I am?" she countered, her smile adding sparkle to her already glowing eyes.

"Then I'm the man for the job."

Burt scooted his chair over, feeling a whole lot younger in the past few days than he had in years. And it had nothing to do with the fact that he was quitting smoking, at Rachel's request. No, it's just that somehow everything suddenly seemed right with the world. He'd known that bringing Charlie Cuesta and Sam Ryan together had been a good idea. Not just because they'd solved his little problem, but because their whirlwind romantic reunion had swept up everyone on the set, spinning amorous ideas in their heads. Since the post-show wrap just last night—which informed television audiences everywhere that Charlie and Sam had enjoyed a large and boisterous wedding in their home-town, followed by a fairy-tale honeymoon at the same resort in Puerto Rico where they'd taped the final episode—everyone from the key grips to the executive producer seemed to have romance on the brain. Burt had even caught Jacey chitchatting on the phone with that Latin lover of hers more than usual. And since Rachel had sauntered into his trailer, he couldn't help but wonder how much time he really had to spend on the set of the next show. He was, after all, just the executive producer.

"What are you working on?"

"Last minute details for *The Last Virgin.*"

Rachel winced. "I'm not sure I like the concept of that show. It sounds so…crass."

"It sounds crass because it is crass. And the American television audiences are going to eat it up with a spoon."

She nodded, but her gesture was noncommittal. "You know, you're three for three."

"You mean in the ratings? Yeah, I'm pretty hot. Does that turn you on?"

Laughing, she hooked her slim arms around his neck and then slid into his lap. Funniest part was, his sciatica didn't protest one bit.

"No, I mean, yes, it turns me on," Rachel said huskily. "Just being around you does that to me. But I wasn't talking about ratings. You realize that on your last three shows, the end result has been romance."

Burt stopped to think. She was right. *Hey, Make Me Over, Surviving Sarah* and *The Great Chase* all had, without any planning on his part, spawned three interesting relationships, each with a damned good chance at making it for the long haul. Somehow, though, he couldn't see that happening on his next venture.

"Well, don't start calling me Cupid yet. I'm about sure the next show won't end that way."

"The virgin show?" she asked, surprised. "Why not? Virgins can't fall in love?"

Burt chuckled, dipping his nose against Rachel's neck and inhaling the tart lemony scent of her perfume. "What do I know about virgins? I guess anything can happen on television."

And they were living proof.

THE LAST VIRGIN

Jennifer LaBrecque

To the Baja Babes and the best life therapy
and wetsuit inspiration I've ever had.

CHAPTER ONE

"YOU PROBABLY QUALIFY as the oldest virgin in Brooklyn." Janine, the self-appointed Dr. Ruth of their Tuesday lunch group, was back on her favorite 'subject, Andrea's sex life, or more accurately, the lack thereof.

"Nah. All five boroughs, I'm sure." Andrea glanced around the noisy restaurant where they met each week. Two tables close by were oblivious to any conversation but their own. The table closest to Janine…well, all Andrea could see was a newspaper. Hopefully the reader was engrossed in something more interesting than her virginal status. No one seemed to be paying any attention to their conversation, but still… "Hey, why not just run a piece in *The Times?* In case anyone in here missed it."

Her friends patently ignored her sarcasm.

"Andrea's problem is she's waiting for Mr. Right to drop into her life," Tina said, gesturing with a garlic breadstick.

"She could be more proactive," Donna chimed in with a nod, her close-cropped strawberry-blonde curls bobbing, looking every inch the suburban mom she'd become since she'd married, started a family and moved to Westchester.

Okay. Enough was enough. "Hel-lo. Could you maybe not talk about me as if I weren't present? I'm a virgin, not comatose." That was part of the problem with girlfriends you'd known since diapers and *Sesame Street*. They felt free and easy to mind your business—and do it as if you weren't there.

"You're too picky." Donna licked the salt off the rim of her margarita glass.

"Picky? I'm too *picky*? Please tell me I didn't just hear that. It's asking too much that a man's capable of more than fogging a mirror?" She had an ideal man in her head and he was out there somewhere. It'd be primo if she could find him sooner than later though.

"I'm all for mirror fogging," Tina said. But then again, Tina's sex life was a thriving enterprise.

"Are men capable of more?" Janine asked, her impending divorce echoing in her question. "Don't look to me for confirmation. Gary lived in a fog."

Everyone laughed. Gary was a loser with a capital *L*. They'd all celebrated when Janine had kicked him out.

"All I want is—"

"Someone with a really big…" Tina waved her breadstick suggestively.

"Oh, baby." Donna smirked.

"Size does matter." Janine's divorce was not amicable. "Gary's breadstick was more along the lines of a crouton. The next time around I'm going for a stromboli."

"Mr. Big?" When they were all sixteen they'd found Janine's cousin's porno stash. Mr. Big, one of the "stars," had dropped his pants and it had been immediately, impressively apparent he was aptly named. Mr. Big had set a standard.

"You got it. Mr. Big."

"Good luck," said Tina. "There're some nice breadsticks out there, but you just don't find that many strombolis."

Tina *would* know.

"Oh, yeah," Donna said. "But we got off topic. We were talking about Andi's dream man."

"That is so not off topic. Stromboli, breadstick or crouton—that's an important criteria," Tina said in one-track mind fashion.

"Okay. So Andi wants *a man with the soul of a poet*," Donna intoned because they'd all heard it so many times before. "And a nice breadstick," she tacked on with a smirk.

Andrea knew her friends thought she lived in a dream world. Perhaps she was something of an idealist, because honest to God, she didn't see why business had to be so cutthroat, why cynicism was as de rigueur for city life as a little black cocktail dress and why she shouldn't hold out for *the* man. She knew he was out there. But geez, how many toads did she have to kiss before she found her prince?

"Andrea's holding out for Nicholas Cage."

Oh, baby. Now there was a prince, but her head wasn't so in the clouds she was waiting on Nic to show up. One day she'd meet her prince and she'd know it. There'd be a sign. "Nic is unavailable in this lifetime. So how about just a guy with an ounce of romance and a hearty dose of testosterone?" And just to shake the girls up, Andrea added, "And maybe I'll start out with a stromboli."

"Don't go there." Tina shook her head. "You'd be ruined for other men for life. You've got to work your way up to the stromboli."

Andrea laughed. "You're insane. But I love ya."

"What about that photographer where you work? That British guy I met yesterday?" Janine asked.

Aha. Janine had dropped by Hendley and Wells Advertising yesterday just as Andrea's team meeting had broken up. She thought Janine had seemed interested. Andrea was her team's graphic artist and Darren was the team photographer. She knew Darren a little too well to be interested.

"Darren's fun to go clubbing with, but he's got too many tattoos and his mouth makes the New York sewers seem clean." And there was something about a guy who showcased his breadstick in tight leather at work…*ewww*.

"So he's available?" Janine asked.

Janine was welcome to him. Andrea grabbed a breadstick and dipped it in marinara sauce. She was starving. "Go for it," she told Janine. A big blob of marinara landed on her boob. "Damn. This shirt's new." And white.

"I thought so. Silk?" Tina asked.

"Yep." She'd known better than to blow a wad on DKNY white silk, but she'd wanted it and she'd meant to skip the marinara.

Donna shook her head. "Andi, at the rate you spill food on yourself, you should only buy synthetics."

"Or at least dark colors," Janine tacked on. "I don't know if that big red stain is gonna come out of that white blouse."

"Maybe you should look for a guy in the dry cleaning business. It'd save you a bundle," Donna said.

"There you go. Sex for laundry," Andrea said. Maybe it wasn't such a bad idea considering she paid a small fortune on a weekly basis for Mr. Chu to remove her food stains.

"How about Vinnie?" Tina asked.

"He's gone into the dry cleaning business?" Janine asked, a confused furrow bisecting her forehead.

"Geez, Janine." Tina rolled her eyes. "No. He's available. My cousin Vinnie."

"That sounds like a bad movie," Donna said.

"That *was* a bad movie." Janine winced and shot Andrea a sidelong glance.

Andrea, the avowed movie buff of the group, took the bait. "It was okay. Joe Pesci's brilliant," she replied in defense of the film. Janine, with her pop psychology take, had accused Andrea more than once of living vicariously through movies.

"Forget the movie." Tina waved her hand. "How about Vinnie? He's been asking about you."

Uh-uh. She'd much rather talk about the movie.

Andrea had met Vinnie at Tina's parents fortieth wedding anniversary party. Vinnie had cornered her and suggested they "hook up and check out the Poconos one weekend." And then he'd tried to stick his tongue down her throat as an incentive.

"You didn't mention…my, uh, *status*…did you?" Andrea asked.

"God. No. Why?"

Vinnie worked with numbers—and he wasn't an accountant or actuary. "Did you know Vinnie was running numbers on whether I'd go out with him or not?" Sweet Jesus, she could only imagine the numbers he'd run on scoring her virginity. What a nightmare.

"He's a businessman. What's wrong with a little ambition?" Tina took familial loyalty to a new degree.

"Nothing. It just didn't strike me as particularly romantic."

Tina shrugged with a little bit of attitude. "Okay, *ixnay* Vinnie and we'll move on to another candidate. There's a whole sea of men out there. Dive in, Andi, the water's fine."

"You almost slept with Ricky. It was close." Donna said, in the same tone she used with her two-year-old when Devin had fallen short of the mark and she wanted to try to find something positive to say.

"Give me a break, I found out he was gay," Andrea said. Again. As if she hadn't already told them numerous times.

"Are you sure?" Donna wouldn't let Ricky and his sexual preferences go.

"Hel-lo. He was trying to decide if he could go straight. I didn't want to be his test run. No thanks. But he always kept me in touch with the Filene's Basement sales." And he'd found her a kickin' pair of Bruno Maglis for next to nothing. She didn't want to sleep with him, but they did great shopping together.

"What about…"

This was not making her feel any better. She was here to enjoy lunch. "Face it. I'm not picky. I'm just a loser magnet. There's a giant *L* imbedded in my butt that attracts them," Tina's eyebrows hiked north and Andrea scrambled to correct the insult, "…all except Vinnie of course and he's just not my type."

"You know, you're lucky we're not an ancient culture. You'd be prime sacrificial material," Janine said.

Janine was lucky Andrea didn't reach across the table and smack her. "I for one would like to move on to a topic other than my sex life. You guys are far more interested in it than I am."

"That sounds perverse."

"It is perverse, if you ask me." She was just waiting for the right guy. And a sign somewhere along the way would be nice, too. "How's Devin doing in preschool?" Andrea asked Donna.

Donna immediately launched into her toddler's exploits. Tina kicked her under the table. What? Tina could've changed the subject at any time, and Andrea personally liked little kids. She hoped to have a couple of her own one day if she found a guy before she hit the expiration date on her eggs.

They ran through Devin's update and Tina's latest sexcapade carried them through lunch. Andrea had her fork poised over a mouthwatering cannoli, when a stranger approached the table.

"Excuse me, ladies." A brown-haired man wearing a T-shirt and jeans interrupted their conversation. "My name is Todd Phillips and you ladies caught my eye when I was walking by." He gestured toward the sidewalk on the other side of the floor-to-ceiling window behind Donna. "I'm a reality TV scout." *No kidding?* The man looked Andrea dead in the eye. "You wouldn't happen to be single and interested in auditioning for our upcoming episode of a bachelorette-type show, would you?"

Andrea glanced over her shoulder. Nope. Nobody there. "Me?"

"You."

Her fork clattered to her plate as her stomach did an elaborately slow three-sixty. Her? A bachelorette?

Donna squealed. "Shut up."

"You're for real?" Janine asked, her eyes narrowed in suspicion.

The man handed over a card. "I'm for real. We put out a casting call but we also use scouts. Sometimes the perfect participant is someone who wouldn't come forward on their own steam." His eyes held Andrea's in a very nonthreatening, nonsexual way. "I saw you and I thought you'd be…well, perfect."

"You have no idea," Tina smirked.

"She doesn't have to take off her clothes or anything does she?" Janine quizzed him.

No way she'd appear before millions of people. Dating was hard enough without having an audience. But…

The *but* niggled in. She pushed others into adventure but hung back herself. What'd she have to lose? She'd be the one culling through the men who would be trying to impress her. Her. Andrea Scarpini. And her job? Like Hendley and Wells would turn down the exposure. Life was short and opportunities to star in a TV show didn't exactly fall in a gal's lap every day. If she walked away from this, she'd spend a lifetime wondering "what if." Not to mention the major ca-ca she'd take from these three.

All of that aside, she'd asked for a sign. What was this if it wasn't a sign? How smart would it be to ask for a sign and then turn your back on it when it smacked you upside the head? Ignoring a sign might curse her to a virginal state for the rest of her life. And face it, she wasn't doing so hot on her own.

You could've heard the proverbial pin drop at their table. Tina, Donna and Janine's faces said it all—they expected her to turn it down. "Where do I go and what time should I be there?"

The table erupted. Andrea and Todd Phillips exchanged information and Todd left, looking extremely pleased that Andrea had promised to show up at a screening Friday after work.

"Since you're about to have a boatload of men

dropped in your lap, can I sort through your discards?" Tina asked.

"You're going to be a celebrity," Donna said.

"I still have to pass the screen test," Andrea reminded them, and herself. She was a candidate, not the chosen one. But somewhere, deep inside, she had a feeling her life would never be the same.

THE KID—he didn't remember the name his secretary, Sharon, had called him—shoved his hands in his pockets. "Yes, sir, Mr. Mueller, thank you for seeing me. I feel sure I've got the next reality TV hit. Just the spin we were looking for on this bachelorette deal."

Burt Mueller leaned back in his chair, popping a peppermint in his mouth. Giving up smoking sucked. But then so did getting nagged to death by the women in his life. Women in his life? Still hard to believe. His daughter, Jacey, a tough young woman who favored Goth attire, incongruently tried to nurture him, though in her own smart-ass abrasive way. Rachel, a former lover who was now a current lover, said she only wanted him to stop smoking so he could go longer in the sack. They were whacky women, but hell, he was a whacky kind of guy, so somehow in a weird way it all sort of fit.

And he damn well hoped the kid in front of him had a hit. So far *Make Me Over, Surviving Sarah* and *The Great Chase* had scored big ratings. Burt wouldn't admit he fell into the trap of Hollywood superstition, but if he could turn out more than three hits in a row, he'd finally feel like he could breathe. And if there was one thing he'd learned in the hard-knock world of television production, you never knew when a blockbuster idea was gonna fall in your lap. And if this kid had the next winning spin on a bachelorette show, well, he was all up for it. "Knock my socks off, kid."

"I was having lunch in New York yesterday. Four women were at the table next to me, talking about how this one woman was probably the oldest virgin in New York."

Burt sat up straighter and fought the urge to light up a smokey joe. He could smoke the lines into this face faster than his plastic surgeon could Botox them out. Not to mention Jacey and Rachel would raise hell. "You've got my attention. How old is she and what's she look like?" She needed to be older than a teenager and that was a stretch in the virgin department.

"Prime time. I'd guess somewhere between twenty-five and thirty."

"Blond?"

"Brunette."

Ha. He knew there couldn't be any blond virgins left. "Dog?"

"No! She's not howling at a full moon." Burt shot him a look and the kid straightened up, once again suitably respectful about being in the executive producer's presence. "Makeup could give her a decent hair-cut and that'd help. Thin. Pretty. Big brown eyes. Very expressive face. Outgoing. Perfect in front of the camera."

If this was for real, it definitely showed promise. Burt could feel it in his gut, and it wasn't that damn ulcer acting up again—they were on to a winner. "A virgin over the age of consent in New York who's not a dog? How do you know it wasn't all a joke?"

"I stuck my head in the newspaper and listened. And then I slipped out. Came down the sidewalk as if I'd just spotted her and whammo."

"It's a helluva twist." It was tacky. It was tawdry. It was perfect. "So, she thinks she's picking the man of her dreams but the real winner is the guy who makes her. We'll bill her and the show as *The Last Virgin*. Beautiful." Some viewers would be outraged. Some would be intrigued. But everyone would tune in to watch. This was fresh and outside the box. A little risky, but then the best things usually were. "You sure none of them saw you at the table next to them?"

"I had my head stuck in the newspaper. She never even noticed me."

The kid would make a great private detective or criminal. He was the sort of average Joe that blended into a crowd.

"What'd you say your name was?"

"Todd. Todd Phillips, sir."

"So, Todd, you think you can find this virgin and persuade her to be America's next reality TV star?"

Todd allowed a small triumphant smile. "Better than that, sir. Her name is Andrea Scarpini and she's screening Friday afternoon."

"Good job, Todd. Now you bring me Andrea Scarpini and I believe we'll have a hit on our hands." Burt dismissed Todd, already mentally pulling the program together. They'd film in the South—cheaper production costs would give a better margin. He'd turn the show over to Eric Lauchmann. He definitely wanted Jacey on the filming. Not only was she his daughter, but she was one of the best damn camera operators in the business. And if he could get Jacey's boyfriend, Digg, to come in for a cameo appearance or two, well, that might help his daughter get past her commitment hang-up.

Yeah. It was sort of late in the day for Burt to win Father of the Year, but what the hell, stranger things had happened. At least they had in his life.

Burt rolled the peppermint around in his mouth and looked up. "Todd."

The kid stopped with his hand on the doorknob. "Sir?"

"This is going to work best if we keep the element of surprise for the end. I don't want anyone else to know about this other than the two of us. Not until I decide it's time."

"Yessir."

"I need you to fly back to New York and sit in on that screening. Tell them you're acting on my authority and have the final decision." Burt smiled. "Just make sure Andrea Scarpini's the final decision."

"I can do that." The kid smiled in return. "There is one thing. What if she sues us afterwards?"

So, maybe the kid could sniff out an angle, but he

still had a whole lot to learn about the business. "We should be so lucky. It'd put us at the top of the charts. It'd be publicity. And there's no such thing as bad publicity."

ZACH ROBERTS whistled beneath his breath as he took his apartment steps two at a time. Today was his lucky day. He could feel it. He'd found a penny on the sidewalk—heads up.

He stopped at the first-floor landing of the aging brownstone. "Can I get your door for you, Mrs. Kravitz? Do you need a hand with your shopping?" he asked the stooped woman with her white hair in curlers, fumbling for her door key. Mrs. Kravitz invariably went to the market in curlers. Zach always wondered where she was going afterwards that was so important she'd let the whole world—or at least the part of it that thrived between 37th Street and Zebrowski's Grocers—see her in curlers.

She turned and smiled at Zach, revealing a full set of perfect dentures, as she opened her door. "I've got it, but you're a nice boy for asking." Beyond her, the apartment was a smaller replica of his grandmother's house, complete with plastic covers on the sofa arms and a crucifix next to a rendering of a saint he should know but didn't, "Come back later. I'm making strudel. My granddaughter, Bergita, is coming by." She shot Zach a coy look. "The pretty one." *Only if she'd recently waxed her upper lip,* he thought. "You stop by later."

"I can't make it today." He headed toward the next flight of stairs leading to his floor. "But how about saving me a piece of strudel?"

Mrs. Kravitz waved him up the stairs. "A piece just for you, Zachie."

Today he was on top of his game. A piece of Mrs. Kravitz's strudel and finally, the break he'd been waiting for. He wanted a scoop on reality TV but he wasn't *Survivor* material—let's get real, his idea of camping was the Holiday Inn and he was making no apologies for it. He just wasn't a wilderness kind of guy. And he didn't want a job with The Donald. He also wasn't into solving any mysteries. No. He'd been waiting for something he had a chance in hell of winning, or just staying in the game long enough to get a story.

Like *The Single Girl.* And tomorrow they were screening male applicants for the show. He wasn't the best-looking guy, but women seemed to find him passably attractive, he could talk to a wall and he was determined.

Definitely determined. First, he'd worked his ass off to put himself through school. Then he'd worked his ass off to move up at work only to find his career jeopardized by a corporate buyout and reshuffle. This story would either save his job and earn him a slot on the editorial staff, or he'd be sending out résumés or, worse yet, writing on spec as he'd done when he'd first started out. Proving reality TV was rigged was either going to make or break him. And he had no intention of winding up broken. He'd felt out Ned Hopkins, the senior editor, and he'd been open to a story if Zach could get an inside scoop. He grinned to himself. There were much, much worse ways to research a topic than wooing a pretty woman.

He let himself into his apartment and stepped around the duffel bag of clean laundry that hadn't made it to his bedroom. Keeping his job and moving up the food chain at the magazine would mean a fatter paycheck and that would translate into a bigger place. A place where he could actually have a dog. Coming home to an empty place sucked. Either a lab or a golden retriever. A big dog who'd sprawl on the couch with him, run with him through the early-morning city streets, lie on his feet when he was writing at the computer. Yep. A bigger place and definitely a dog. Hearth, home and a hound.

First things first, he needed a decent cover. He could hardly waltz into the auditions announcing he was a journalist. The only place that'd get him was out the door. Fast.

Zach tossed a frozen dinner into the microwave and snagged the portable phone. His sister answered on the second ring.

"Zoe, hey, how's it going?" He flipped through the stack of mail—all junk except the electric bill and he'd rather not have seen that.

"Zach. I was just going to call you. You must be psychic. Eddie called in sick today. Strep. I'm short for tomorrow. Any way you can help out?"

Zach pitched his lucky penny in the air. "I could

help out my sister the business owner if she could help out her brother the journalist. I need a cover. How about theoretically I work for you full-time as a salesman?"

"This isn't a cover for something dangerous, is it?"

Zach laughed. Zoe needed to have a couple of kids so she could mother someone other than him. At thirty-three, she was only four years older than he was, but she acted like it was a lifetime. "Nothing dangerous. With a little bit of luck," he tossed the penny into the air again, "you're looking at one of the new bachelors vying for the hand and heart of TV's next Single Girl. And then yours truly will write a brilliant piece on reality TV and get the promotion he's been working his butt off for." He didn't mention saving his job. Zoe'd just worry about it. And Zach wasn't going to let it happen.

The microwave bell dinged and he pulled out his steaming meatloaf dinner.

"Are you eating frozen again? That stuff is loaded with sodium," Zoe admonished.

Zach pulled back the cardboard corner. "It's hot and easy and I'm starving." He forked in a mouthful of instant mashed potatoes and burned his tongue. No kidding it was hot. "Oomph."

"Burned your tongue, didn't you?" Zoe didn't wait for him to answer. "Well, what are the odds of you making it onto the show? I wouldn't think great."

He loved his sister but she wasn't the most optimistic soul. "I think I've got a good chance." He laughed. "Better than if I don't show up."

"Well, if you make it that far, remember that a woman just wants a man who'll listen and pay attention to her." Uh-oh. Zoe and Greg must be fighting again. "You know, if you men could just manage to move past your own self-absorption, you'd do a lot better with women."

Oh, yeah. Greg had definitely stayed out too late last night or committed some other male sin. And Zach had learned some time ago not to get sucked into Zoe and Greg's quarrels. And they happened often enough. His sister and brother-in-law weren't exactly the poster couple for marital bliss. Of course, neither had his parents been. Right up until his old man had packed his bags and left while the family was at church one morning. Life seemed easier just avoiding that whole commitment schtick.

"I do okay with women. Getting rid of them is usually more of a problem than finding them," he said.

"It's a good thing you don't suffer from low self-esteem."

Zach speared a chunk of meatloaf. He'd let this bite cool down before he shoveled it in. "I guess I did sort of sound like a schmuck. You know what I mean." It was more accurate to say that the women he'd dated had always wanted to go farther faster than he was ready, willing or able. "Remember Tracey?"

Thinking about Tracey still gave him cold chills. They'd only dated two months when he found a *Brides* magazine in her bathroom with pages turned down. And she didn't have any close friends planning a wedding. A big sign that it was past the time to vamoose.

"Lots of women look at bridal magazines."

"That's cool—as long as I'm not dating them. What about Tara? Two dates and she wanted to live together?" No could do. "And Gigi who wanted to spend Christmas together after I met her at a holiday party?" And Felicia who'd tattooed his name on her…well, at least the whole world wasn't getting a look at his name on Felicia, but he was sure it made for some interesting bedroom conversation with her next boyfriend. And there were some things his big sister didn't need to know.

"Okay, okay, Romeo. You're good with women." At least he'd managed to get a laugh out of her.

"I like women." He did. He just didn't want to live with any of them or get married or otherwise tie himself down. No thanks.

"And they like you. You're right, you'll do okay."

"Trust me. Give me a chance to get in front of TV's bachelorette flavor of the month and I'll be better than okay."

"LADIES, YOU ARE now looking at television's next Single Girl. Can you even believe it?" She'd given herself the pinch test so many times, her arm was sore. The call had come yesterday and she'd barely managed not to spill the beans 'til they were all together for lunch.

"Get out."

"Shut up."

"For real?"

"For real. Me, Andrea Scarpini, TV-land's newest bachelorette. Go freaking figure."

"Oh. My. God. This is too cool," Donna said.

"I still can't quite believe it. When I saw all the other candidates, I almost turned around and went home. But the casting director said there was something about me. I had a special something the others didn't." There'd been some gorgeous women there, but apparently the studio had seen something in *her*. She still wasn't sure what, but she was rolling with it.

"Just think, I'll see your face on the tabloids at the newsstand," Janine marveled, motioning the waiter over and ordering a bottle of champagne. "It's not every day one of us becomes a celebrity overnight."

"Details. We need details," Tina demanded. "How many men do you get to choose from?"

Leave it to Tina to want to know that. "I really can't remember. I was in a state of shock," Andrea said.

"What'd they say at work? I'm guessing Eve said go for it," Janine said.

Still giddy—her feet hadn't hit the ground yet—Andrea laughed. It didn't hurt that her boss, Eve Carmichael-LaRoux was also one of her best friends. However, Eve seldom made their Tuesday lunches because she traveled a lot, even more now that she'd been promoted at work. Andrea had pushed Eve into an adventurous romance that had turned out very well. She'd worn a Cheshire cat smile as she'd told Andrea it was her turn and ordered her to go find herself a man. "I have a leave of absence from work, and they're cool with that. And I'm hoping Janine won't object to taking care of my little darling?"

Her friend nodded. "I promise you'll come home to a bright-eyed and bushy-tailed ferret."

The waiter arrived and served champagne around the table. The next question came on the heels of a toast and a quick sip.

Janine eyed her over the rim of her glass. "What about money? I mean you'll miss work. And you're going to lose your privacy. At least temporarily."

"That's another cool part. They're paying me more than I'd make at work. Of course, there is that loss of privacy thing. But that'll only last for a couple of days, maybe a week or two, and then everyone will move on to the next pop culture phenomena and I'll have a tidy sum of cash and hopefully a man in my life."

"We all hope you know what to do with the man." Tina said with a leer. "What're you gonna do with the cash?"

"Well, if this were a beauty contest, the correct response would be that I'd give it to my favorite charity. But I plan to take me and my best friends shopping." She paused while they all cheered. "Then I'm going to send my parents on that cruise they've always wanted to go on, finish paying off my student loan, and what's left over will go in the bank."

Donna held her empty glass out for a refill. "What'd your parents think?"

Her parents hadn't been nearly as enthusiastic as Eve, but in the end they'd supported her decision. "My parents were," she waffled her hand back and forth, "and grandma said that it was a sign." She'd trained Andrea from an early age in the power of signs. "She's going to light a candle for me at mass and pray to the Virgin Mary that I'll finally meet a nice man." She polished off her bubbly. It went down smoothly.

"Grandma's a hoot," Donna said. "She would say that."

Grandma Franchetti had lived with Andrea's family since Ompa had died when Andrea was five. She'd been as much a part of Janine's, Tina's, and Donna's lives as she had Andrea's.

"Yeah, yeah. We all love her. Now tell us the rest of the deal," Tina demanded, impatient as ever.

"I'm leaving on Friday. We'll start filming on Saturday somewhere near Atlanta at an antebellum plantation. They say it's a lot warmer down there than up here." Everything was happening faster than she'd anticipated, especially since she hadn't anticipated winning the spot. And she'd never been to Georgia. Romance, travel, excitement. "Maybe you'll come back with a hunky Georgia farmer." Donna rubbed her hands together.

Janine rolled her eyes. "Don't be a spaz, Donna. They bring guys in from all over the country. Don't they?" she looked to Andrea for confirmation.

"Yep. All across America."

"There's no way around it. We need to go with you.

I could screen them for you," Tina offered, waggling her brows.

"I wish, but for the next two weeks, I'm incommunicado."

Tina sighed. "With a bunch of hot guys. It's a tough job, but somebody's got to do it."

CHAPTER TWO

"IF YOU GENTLEMEN will line up along the driveway, we'll bring her out momentarily," the producer instructed them.

Zach fell in line with the other guys on the semicircular drive. The drive fronted a white-columned mansion that could've been lifted directly from a *Gone with the Wind* stage set, complete with enormous oaks dripping Spanish moss. Thank God, they weren't doing period costumes.

He'd spent the afternoon with his eyes and his ears open, observing the production crew and watching them interface with the cast, looking for any signs of collusion, and generally getting a feel for who did what. One of the camera crew, a Goth princess named Jacey, positioned herself in front of him and the mass of hopefuls. She panned the male meat market and then zoomed in on the door.

"Here she is gentleman, Andrea Scarpini, the Single Girl you'll be vying for," announced Dirk Sherwood, the aging B-movie star who was emceeing the whole schmeel. Dirk actually brought a touch of class to the set with his genteel Southern drawl and droll sense of humor.

Zach, along with the other guys and the entire crew, watched the door in anticipation. A woman walked through. The woman. Okay. A slight wind rustled through the trees, ruffling her hair against her cheek.

This was going to be sweet. Average height, slender, shiny dark hair that begged for him to run his fingers through it, huge dark eyes framed by dark lashes, a delicate line to her jaw, and a scrumptious pair of lips. She was a little on the flat-chested side for Zach's taste—so shoot him, he preferred women with a little more curve—but this was business and wooing Andrea Scarpini so he could stay on the set didn't look as if it would be a hardship. He'd wondered if the "twist" on this particular show was to set the guys up with a "plain Jane" but that obviously wasn't the case. Not that it would've mattered because he simply wanted his story.

Since they'd lined the men up alphabetically by first name, Zach had plenty of time to observe her reactions as the bachelors approached her one by one. She smiled at each of them graciously. Zach had pretty much memorized the bio he and the other guys had been given. Andrea was twenty-six, she worked as a graphic artist for an ad agency, and lived in New York. She liked movies and she had a pet ferret. Zach had drawn a mental image, but there was a hint of reserve and delicacy about her that surprised him. She wasn't as in-your-face as he'd anticipated in a New York single.

And then it was his turn. Zach approached the

woman who was about to unwittingly aid and abet his career. Confident, his lucky penny buried in his pocket, he began to introduce himself.

"I'm pleased to meet you Andrea. My name is…" He took her hand to shake it. It was delicate and felt incredibly small in his. A jolt of something shook him, his world tilted on its axis, and he couldn't recall his own name.

Her eyes, dark and fathomless, widened slightly, a smile hovering in their depths. "You're not going to make me guess, are you?"

He was lost in the luminosity of her eyes. "What?"

"Your name." Her lips twitched. She seemed dangerously close to laughing at him.

Damn. He unscrambled his brains and mentally righted himself. "Zach. Zach Roberts."

For a second longer than necessary her fingers wrapped around his. "It's nice to meet you too, Zach."

"Uh, yeah." Brilliant. He'd have been better off not saying anything else. He turned to take his place in line again, passing a beefy ex-jock named Brian along the way. Brian smirked at him. So much for suave and composed.

He took his place back in line and the guy next to him shot him a sympathetic look mixed with triumph. "Tough break, dude."

Zach shrugged. Inside he didn't feel nearly so calm. He'd never reacted so strongly to a woman. Never felt such an intense, instant slam of attraction. Never had his wits scatter. He hoped Andrea Scarpini liked guys who occasionally geeked out because he'd just had his first geek experience. And unfortunately, it'd be aired in front of millions of viewers. He wasn't exactly off to a stellar start.

"HERE'S THE LIST and we've included head shots next to all the names." Portia Tomlinson, the show's associate producer, handed her a sheaf of papers. "Now you just need to narrow it down from thirty to twenty and we'll be on to the next phase."

Andrea sank back onto the not-so-comfortable, but very elegant sofa in the very elegant parlor. It seemed a fitting location for the first-round cuts. The house, and this room in particular, exuded an aura of romance and nostalgia that spoke to her. She'd guess this room had seen its fair share of love and sorrow over the years. She shuffled through the papers.

"Thank God, you included head shots because I would've never remembered which one was which. I think I was more nervous than they were…well, except for Zach." She felt flushed simply saying his name.

"So, you don't need any help remembering his name?" Portia asked with a teasing laugh. She and Andrea had clicked the first time they'd met. Close to Andrea's age, the other woman wasn't beautiful but she possessed strikingly exotic looks to go along with her unusual name. Almond-shaped eyes and the rarity of natural blond hair, a genuine kindness offset her intimidating sophistication. And any woman who'd wear

Jimmy Choo's on a Georgia plantation was her kind of people.

Andrea shook her head. No. She remembered Zach. She'd had the weirdest reaction to him—tumultuous. When she met her ideal guy, it wouldn't feel this way. Rather, it would be a strong, steady certainty. "He wasn't really my type, but how can you forget a guy who forgets his own name? It was sort of sweet." And that sweetness helped to diffuse her volatile response to him.

"Sweet, huh? I guess that means Zach…" she consulted her copy of the name and faces list "…Roberts survives the first round of cuts, even though he's not your type."

"I think he has to." She hated to vote him off her private island and have him think it was because he'd freaked on the introduction. And she hated even worse to be a chicken just because she'd reacted so strongly to him.

"Okay, who else?"

Andrea must've looked a little shell-shocked. She felt a lot shell-shocked.

"I've found the best way to do this is not to think about it too much. Glance over the list once and then go back to the top and start marking out. That way you're running off gut instinct. If you spend too much time on it, you just confuse yourself. Trust me, I've seen this enough times to know." Portia smiled, her eyes crinkling at the corners. "And a couple of deep breaths don't hurt either."

Andrea took the prescribed breaths and was almost relaxed until she caught sight of the camera stationed on the fireplace mantel, angled to catch any action in the room except perhaps the far corner. And doubtless the place was wired for sound. Damnation. She'd forgotten about the ever-present video/audio feed. She gnawed at her lower lip. Had she said anything too dweebie?

"Forgot the camera was there?" Portia asked.

"How'd you know?"

Portia smiled. "Maybe it was the sudden deer-caught-in-headlights look."

Great. Hopefully that footage would wind up on the cutting-room floor. And at least there wasn't a camera-person in her face. "Uh, yeah. The cameras take some getting used to."

"That's okay. Pretty soon you won't even notice them. Just think of it as shopping at the mall. You're caught on tape in every store and mall security now has its own cameras in the thoroughfares. But when you're shopping, you don't even think about it."

"Okay. Mall shopping. But instead of shoes I'm shopping for men. I can do that."

"That's it. Shopping for gorgeous men. And if it helps, talk it through with me."

That could work. She knew it was part of the other woman's job, but Portia was easy to talk to and she possessed a sense of humor, a nice surprise for a Hollywood studio exec on the rise. Andrea tapped the red marker against her pursed lips, concentrating on the men on the page.

"*Ixnay* that guy. When he met me he told me he thought I'd be a blonde."

"What an idiot." Portia indulged in a little eye-rolling.

"Yep. And that was supposed to make a good impression?" Andrea also crossed out the last guy on the first sheet. "Clammy hands. The poor guy was probably just nervous but those clammy hands grossed me out. They pushed my ick-factor limits."

Portia wrinkled her nose. "Can't really imagine those hands touching any of your other body parts, can you?"

It was such a Tina-esque comment, Andrea liked the other woman even more. "Exactly." She flipped the page and zeroed in on the middle of the page. "He's history. Stripping a woman naked with your eyes is so not sexy."

"Sorry about that. We try to screen them carefully, but…"

Andrea shrugged. "They're guys and you're not miracle workers. How many did you screen to come up with thirty?"

Portia shook her head. "Honey, you don't even want to know. The stories I could tell you if we had more time."

Andrea got the subtle prod and went back to culling through her prospects. She hated to do it, but she crossed out the dark-haired man right below Mr. Let-Me-Undress-You. "He's probably a very nice guy, but he's a dead ringer for my cousin Tony and I can't go there."

"It usually works best to avoid incestuous associations," Portia deadpanned.

Andrea laughed and continued going through the sheets systematically until she got to the last one.

She handed the list over to Portia. "There you go. Done. Not as difficult as I thought it would be."

Portia shuffled through the papers twice and then handed them back. "Sorry. You've only eliminated nine. I need one more."

"Okay. Now it's getting harder." None of the others had stood out as needing to go. She flipped through the papers. Rourke O'Malley. No. Definitely not him. He was a hottie. Nice eyes. Nice smile. Great body. Sexy voice. And she hadn't felt as if she'd just grabbed a lightning rod when she shook his hand. Pretty much the ideal man. Rourke was a keeper.

Her hand hovered over Zach Roberts's photo and she reconsidered him. With sandy brown hair and green eyes, he was a bit leaner than she usually went for and something about him both attracted and disconcerted her, but he had a nice smile and a great butt—oh, yeah, she'd noticed when he was walking away—and if she cut him now the poor guy would forever think he'd botched it on the name thing. And quite frankly, she'd never had a guy react that way to her. And it had been her. The camera hadn't bothered him. No, he'd lost it when he'd touched her. She could handle Zach Roberts. She'd keep him for now and if she decided to, she could take him out in the next round.

Oh, such power. It was sort of a turn-on.

"HOW THE HELL did you not get cut?" Brian, the I-am-a-hot-jock, wasn't smirking at Zach now.

A couple of the guys nearest them stopped what they were doing to listen.

Jesus, talk about a sore loser. Zach shrugged, "I don't have a clue how I slid through that one." He was just damn glad he had. The majority of the women he knew would've tossed a guy who screwed up like that so fast it'd leave their head spinning. Must've been the lucky penny.

"What a loser. You royally screwed up the introduction," Brian nagged on. "Maybe this is rigged."

Unfortunately for his article, Zach hadn't found any sign of it being rigged. And he'd had enough of Brian's mouth and bad attitude.

"Obviously she prefers losers to jerks." Zach delivered the insult with a smile. No one said a word. An expectant hush hung in the room. Christ. Brian probably had close to a hundred pounds on him. When would he learn to keep his mouth shut? He sure wouldn't have had the shit beat out of him nearly as often as a kid or as a teenager.

Brian started toward him, curling his hands into what looked like near-lethal fists, wearing a mean grin. "This is going to be fun."

Double shit. How far was he going to get with a black eye? But Zach had never backed down and he wasn't about to start now. Brian was big, but Zach knew he'd be faster than the beefy guy. He hoped anyway. "Bring it on, big guy."

Rourke, another first-round survivor grabbed Brian by the arm. "Hey, man. The cameras are on. And if you're bringing it on, I hope you've got enough for both of us because I think you're a jerk, too."

Brian shook off the restraining arm but backed off, picked up his suitcase and contented himself with giving both of them the finger on the way out the door.

They'd all come with a suitcase, prepared to stay, but they'd been instructed not to unpack until after first-round eliminations.

"Thanks, man," Zach said to Rourke. Being flipped off was definitely preferable to having his ass kicked.

"No problem," Rourke shook his head at Brian's retreating bulk. "Definitely a jerk."

Zach shrugged. "There's one in every crowd."

The other guys started milling around, chiming in that Brian was indeed a jerk.

Dirk Sherwood strolled into the room and everyone quieted, shifting their attention to the man. "Gentlemen, congratulations on making it through the first round. As you might anticipate, round two is going to be a bit more challenging than introducing yourselves—"

"Sorry, Zach." A tall guy named Pete ribbed him, but it was good-natured as opposed to Brian's earlier belligerence.

Zach grinned and shrugged. "It's okay. I'll give it a shot."

Dirk cleared his throat, regaining control of the

conversation. "Those of you who move on to round three will enjoy a nice surprise."

"That's more like it," someone said from the back.

Dirk frowned at the interruption. "I'm glad you approve, but you've got to make it through round two. Your challenge now is to write a poem which you will then have the opportunity to read to Andrea privately."

A mixed chorus of groans and one or two words of profanity arose from the group. Zach bit back a smile.

Maybe he'd forgotten his name, but writing was his business. Not that he spent his time composing love poems, but writing was writing. And he planned to succeed, because he had every intention of sticking around a little longer to prove that there was nothing real about reality TV. Surely this program wasn't as straightforward as it seemed so far.

Move over, guys, he was on his game now.

"JACEY'S ON line two for you," Sharon announced over the speaker phone. "Can you talk to her now?"

"Give me a minute." Burt pushed aside the budget reports and the treatment proposal for an upcoming program. He'd been expecting this call from his obstinate, prickly daughter who'd suddenly materialized in his life. He, who'd never aspired toward pursuing lasting relationships and certainly never fatherhood, was still amazed at how quickly he'd adapted to the role. And genetics astounded him. Jacey was a chip off the old block. She called 'em like she saw 'em and she didn't take crap from anyone—him included. When he'd sent Digg down to the Atlanta location, Burt had known she'd be on him like white on rice. And hell, since he was on some weird reforming kick, why not include matchmaking. Digg and Jacey were perfect for one another and he didn't want to sit around and watch Jacey screw it up because she was scared and insecure beneath that tough-girl role she played so well.

Burt hit the speakerphone button and punched line two.

"Hi, Pumpkin." Might as well try to soften her up with the nickname. She didn't remotely resemble a pumpkin, but when she was decked out in that Goth crap she favored, she reminded him of Halloween. And she'd appreciated his warped sense of humor when he'd slapped the name on her.

"You're interfering in my life. You might be my father, but you're not my keeper. I needed some time away from Digg."

Yep. She was pissed.

"I've got ratings to think about. Digg pulls in viewers. So shoot me."

"There's an idea," she said darkly.

"How's it going? I haven't heard from Lauchmann yet today."

"Then I guess you ought to call him."

Sheesh. She was really pissed. "Don't be a smartass. How'd the filming go on the first segment?"

"Fine. The only real stroke of excitement was when a fight almost broke out between one of the losers—who was a total loser in every sense—and a guy who made it to round two. Chuck found it on the video feed."

Excellent. "Any heavy contenders right out front?" Jacey had a good eye for people and situations, one of the reasons she was so damn good behind a camera. She only seemed to have a blind eye when she turned it on herself and Digg.

"Right off jump street, I'd say it'll come down to two guys."

"Yeah?"

"One's eye candy but seems decent enough beneath the caramel coating. Female viewers will freak over this guy and he comes across hot on the camera."

"And did our Single Girl think he was hot?"

"She was breathing, so I'm guessing she did." Okay, if she was cracking smart-alec jokes, she wasn't as pissed as she had been.

"And the other one?"

"Not a hottie but there's sizzle between them. You know that chemistry between Charlie and Sam, and Sarah and Luke? It was there during the introduction. And he was the one that almost brawled with the loser."

Good deal. He'd make sure Lachmann threw the hottie and the firecracker at The Virgin—that's how he tended to think of Andrea.

"Make sure you keep the camera on those three."

"Thanks. I think I know how to do my job. Speaking of chemistry, how's it going with Rachel?"

Rachel. Shit. He was too old and jaded to get this

warm fuzzy feeling when he heard her name. And he was about as damn close to loving that woman as a man like him was capable of loving any woman. "She's okay. She's been in Arizona for a few days." And he'd missed her more than he liked to admit, even to himself. It was damn foolish to let anyone mean that much to you. First Jacey, now Rachel. He was losing it.

"Arizona?"

"Visiting her ex-mother-in-law."

"Oh." Jacey didn't even question it. That was the kind of warm, giving woman Rachel was. God knows what she saw in him.

"So what's the deal with this show?" Jacey asked.

"The deal?"

"Yeah? What's the catch? The twist? Reality TV's gone way beyond a chick picking a guy after he's jumped through a few hoops. What's the ratings buster?"

Burt had decided from the show's inception to keep Andrea Scarpini's virginal status from cast and crew until there were only five men standing. It'd keep it fresher and there was less likelihood of someone slipping up and giving the game away.

"That's my girl. We've got a helluva twist coming, but you'll have to wait along with everyone else to find out just what's so special about this Single Girl."

CHAPTER THREE

THE HEAVY mahogany door muted the mix of male voices waiting in the dining room on the other side.

"Deep breath," Portia instructed.

Andrea braced her hand on the cool plaster wall and inhaled. She'd been doing a lot of this today, but it helped calm her nerves. Still, she hesitated, bathed in the soft glow of the hall sconce.

"*This* I'm not looking forward to—dinner with twenty men. And I'm pretty sure I won't make it through the night without spilling anything or dropping food down the front of me." How had she managed to forget that she couldn't make it through a meal without spilling something? That alone should have kept her from that screening.

Portia brushed aside her angst. "You're gorgeous. And if you do spill anything, I'm sure any of those men would jump at the chance to clean it off of you." She eyed Andrea with motherly approval, despite being close to her age. "That cut and color are great on you."

Andrea glanced at her plunging neckline. She'd considered it invasive when wardrobe had taken over even her underwear. Now she was simply grateful. "I'm buying stock in the push-up bras wardrobe supplied." She looked again at her new-found boobs, amazed. She'd never worked up the nerve for implants and now for the first time in her life, she didn't feel so lacking in the chest department. "Who knew I could fill out a dress like this?" She wasn't a conservative dresser, but the short yellow dress with its plunging neckline was one step sexier than what she would've chosen on her own.

"That's why we pay wardrobe the big bucks."

"It's amazing what it does for my self-confidence having a wardrobe and makeup staff behind me."

Portia nodded. "Like I said, if you drop something all over the front of yourself, those guys'll just be wishing they were that spill."

Portia's surety further bolstered Andrea's confidence and soothed her nerves. "Hmm. No wonder you have this job. You know just what to say to calm me down."

"That's why they pay me the big bucks," Portia said with a teasing glint in her eye. "Just remember we knocked ourselves out to find you thirty gorgeous guys and now twenty of them are waiting to knock themselves out to impress you." She winked. "Except the one who made the dumb comment he was hoping for a blonde. And you sent him home."

"I could get used to this."

"Thatta girl. That's the attitude. You're gorgeous and any of those guys would be lucky to have you pick them. Just keep telling yourself that." Portia took her by the arm and drew her toward the closed door. "Deep breath."

Andrea did as she was instructed.

"Now turn on that one hundred-watt smile and we're in business, Ms. Single Girl."

Andrea embraced her newfound spirit of adventure and didn't have to force a smile. This was pretty fun so far and it was cool being in control of a relationship—well, an impending relationship. She opened the door and walked into the room.

Wow. This was serious dining. Forget the haphazard mayhem of Scarpini family dinners. A gleaming wood table, replete with candelabra, sparkling crystal and old world china, seemed to stretch forever.

As if a switch had been flipped, the cacophony of male voices ceased. All eyes trained on her. Thanks to Portia's pep talk, she was more amused than wigged out. Dirk Sherwood escorted her to the empty chair at the head of the table and seated her with a gallant flair. The white linen tablecloth brushed against her bare legs. She glanced down the table. She had brothers and male cousins out the wazoo. She knew what all these men wanted. "Hi guys. You must all be starving. I know I am. Whadaya say we eat?"

Mercifully, the men resumed conversations. Yep, she'd been right. Men were interested in sex and food. Since the sex was out right now, she knew they were all dying to eat.

She glanced at the opposite end of the table. Zach Roberts. His eyes smiled a hello and she silently returned the greeting. Even separated by the table's long expanse, heat rushed through her in response. She was suddenly aware of the comparatively cooler air against her flushed skin.

What was it about him that shook her up so? He wasn't the best-looking guy in the room. After that introduction earlier today, she knew he definitely wasn't the most polished. But there was something about him…something sexy and appealing in the lean lines of his face and startling green eyes. He stirred something in her that felt dark and mysterious and on the other side of safe. And she didn't particularly like feeling this way. Deliberately, she looked away from him.

And found herself face-to-face with Rourke O'Malley, hands down the hunkiest guy in the group.

"How are you tonight?" he asked. Bedroom blue eyes fringed with dark lashes. Short black hair. Tall, broad-shouldered. Nice, deep voice. A total hot package.

"I'm great. How about you?"

"Lucky." He smiled. "I got the seat next to you." His light flirtation and slightly crooked smile put her at ease. "I'm Rourke O'Malley."

Even the name conjured up a romance novel hero. She barely caught herself before she said she knew exactly who he was. "It's nice to meet you. Again."

Someone touched her arm, startling her.

The guy seated on her left shook out her napkin and leaned over. "I'm Guy. Here. Let me help you with your napkin."

Too surprised to object, she merely watched while he spread the white linen over her yellow dress. She'd been insane to agree to wear yellow. Yellow would showcase every morsel of food that found its way down the front of her and wound up in her lap, or worse yet, on her chest.

"Thanks. Actually, I need a bib," she said, joking.

Her humor, however, seemed to bypass Guy altogether. He reached for her lap, eyeing her dress's neckline as if working out where he could tuck in or tie on the napkin.

"It's okay. It was just a joke."

Guy, about two beats too late, laughed. "Oh, yeah."

Andrea barely managed not to roll her eyes. Her skin prickled and she looked up. Zach watched from the other end, his eyes alight with amusement. It was a moment that caught them up in the same joke, a bit of shared intimacy at a crowded table. She felt connected and disconcerted, all at the same time. Andrea looked back to Guy.

"I like a woman with a sense of humor," he said. Maybe he'd simply missed her attempted humor because he was nervous.

The man seated beside Guy leaned past him and flashed a really nice set of pearly white teeth. God, his parents must've spent a fortune on orthodontia. And wasn't that a romantic thought for her to have? But, she had a hard time moving past his teeth. They were so white. And shiny. And so…there.

"I'm Timothy."

"How are you, Tim?"

"Timothy. It's Timothy," he corrected.

Got it. Timothy. "Sorry. How are you Timothy?"

"I'm a male model." O-kay. "I do a lot of mouth work." He preened and managed to look suggestive at the same time.

God, she could never really get into kissing a guy who made his living flashing a smile. What if she got carried away or in a moment of supreme uncoordination chipped his tooth or busted his lip? And she'd have to call him Timothy. And she bet Timothy spent more time in front of the bathroom mirror than she'd ever thought about.

"Do you enjoy modeling?" she asked.

"I love it. It's fascinating." Not. Being in advertising had debunked that myth pretty early on. It was a lot of standing around and retakes. Try boring. But it told her all she needed to know about Timothy. *Ixnay* Timothy White Teeth. "Maybe you've seen some of my stuff…."

Andrea had a sudden mental image of Ashton Kutcher's *Cheaper by the Dozen* character, a model/actor totally self-absorbed by his scene in a commercial. And Ashton was better looking.

She shook her head, "Sorry. I don't think I've caught those."

The waiter brought out a bottle of wine—she'd already been quizzed on her preference before the show—and poured a glass of merlot.

"You know you could've had white," Guy informed her.

Uh, yeah. "I prefer red."

"Really?" Guy apparently was only convinced of her bad taste.

"I tried white. It was my rebellious phase. I wanted to leave my Italian roots in Brooklyn so I only drank white for a while, but you know what they say, you can take the girl out of Brooklyn but you can't take Brooklyn out of the girl."

Guy pretty much looked at her as if she'd sprouted a couple of heads. "I'm from the Upper East Side."

Andrea swallowed her instinct to tell him she lived in Manhattan now. Guy was a tight-ass snob and who cared what he thought of her? He could be Alfred Lord Tennyson when he wrote his poem and it wouldn't make any difference. He was so out of the running.

"I prefer red as well," Rourke said and saluted her with his glass. In addition to being gorgeous, he seemed like a nice guy. She needed her head examined. She was seated next to this dream guy and she was still excruciatingly aware of Zach at the other end of the table. She tried very hard to look elsewhere but every now and then, she couldn't help but look at his end of the table. And each time, her pulse fluttered.

"I'm from Phoenix. But I live in L.A. now. Better opportunities for my smile." Timothy flashed his teeth again. She hoped they made him a lot of money because he sure was proud of them.

Silently, servers moved around the table, delivering dinner salads complete with croutons, along with, oh, God, no, bread sticks. She couldn't even go there now.

While everyone dug into their salads, some with more enthusiasm than others, her end of the table talked about where they were from and what they did.

In the midst of Timothy telling them all about his start in tooth modeling, a monstrous glob of dressing dropped onto her, dribbling down her front. Surreptitiously, she swiped at it with her napkin, hoping no one noticed. She looked up. Zach had noticed. She'd felt him watching her. She forced herself to look away from him and concentrate on the men at her end.

Timothy and Guy and the dark-haired man next to Rourke—she thought he was Tyler from Texas, but he could've been from Tyler, Texas, she really didn't know—all chimed in with their careers and how well they were doing, each one obviously set on impressing her with his accomplishments. Rourke listened quietly.

Not once did they ask her about herself. Such typical guys. Surely finding a manly man with the sensitive heart of a poet wasn't just a pipe dream. She glanced down the line, past Rourke and Tim…uh, Timothy…well, maybe it was a pipe dream.

Once again, she wound up looking at Zach at the other end. No. Her Mr. Right wouldn't leave her feeling as if she was one step away from the edge of a cliff.

ZACH LEANED against the post, deep in the night shadows, on the covered walkway that connected the house with the garage, welcoming the anonymity of the dark.

Early spring evenings in Georgia beat the heck out

of Chicago. He'd still be freezing his cojones off back home. It wasn't exactly balmy, but it was warm enough with only a hint of chill lingering in the air.

He'd spent his time at dinner talking to the guys at his end of the table. So far, they all seemed legit. None of them seemed like a setup or a plant. More than once, he'd found himself distracted by the woman at the opposite end of the table. Not a good idea since he wasn't here to sit around in a state of lust, but to dig beneath the surface of reality TV.

A couple wandered out of the kitchen and into the dark night, obviously not seeing Zach.

"So, you're through for the day?" Zach recognized the guy's voice. Digg something or other had won on a reality show last year. A fireman who'd lived through the hell of 9/11. Seemed like a decent guy who hadn't let fame and fortune go to his head.

The woman turned to face Digg, and Zach recognized the dark-haired camerawoman from earlier in the day. Jacey. "I'm done for the day. Unless something exciting comes up. You know these sets are a 24/7 thing."

"I do know. And I love to watch you work, Jacey. I love your intensity…the way you give it a hundred percent." Digg wrapped a possessive arm around her shoulders, pulling her close. "What's the twist on this show?"

Zach stayed where he was. This was, after all, what he was here for.

"None of us knows. Yet. Or if some of them do, they're not telling. But Burt says it's a good one."

"I knew there had to be something going on."

"Hey, that sounds bad."

"You know what I mean. Burt's not going to just put out another pick-and-choose show."

"I know, that's the same thing I said to him. I told him Rourke's going to be a big draw so they put him next to Andrea at dinner tonight."

"You think he'll win?"

"I didn't say that. I think he'll have a little competition. I like Andrea. She actually treats the crew like human beings instead of one step above galley slaves. I hope she winds up with a decent guy."

"Someone who'll appreciate her for the woman beneath the exterior? Who'll laugh with her when she's happy and hold her when she's sad? Someone who'll believe in her when she doesn't believe in herself? Someone who'll convince her they're right for one another, even if she can't see it? Someone who believes there isn't any obstacle that can't be overcome if two people genuinely love one another? Is that what you hope she finds?"

She turned away from him. "Yes."

Whoa. They'd taken a sharp turn from discussing the show to something that seemed very personal. And Zach had no idea how to announce himself without them knowing he'd been eavesdropping.

"So you do believe in those things?"

"Yes."

He cupped her shoulders in his hands. "Just not for yourself?"

"Digg—"

Gently, as if she was made of fragile porcelain, he turned her around to face him again. "Listen. Just listen for a minute, Jacey. There's not a day that I'm not thankful to be alive. I've wondered how many of the guys we lost from the station, how many of all the people that died on 9/11, never had a chance to say 'I love you' again to the people that mattered most in their lives. Too many of them didn't. And I've realized that every day is a gift. Hell, every moment is a gift. I know your concerns with my family are real to you, but it's no reason for us not to be together. What we have together is special and I can't bear to waste it."

"You've never talked about that day this way before."

"I'd seen people die before. You don't work as a firefighter and paramedic without it. But that day…I'd been to Phil Chang's kid's birthday the week before. I worked with Phil, and he went into the south tower and he never came back out. He'll never watch any of his kids blow out their birthday candles again, he'll never kiss his wife Patty goodbye or listen to her tell him about the kids' day before falling into bed after twenty-four hours on duty."

"Stop." She scrubbed at the tears coursing down her cheeks.

"Phil gave up his chance that day. But you and I, we still have a chance. I love you, Jacey. And I'm damn certain you love me."

"What if you leave one day? What if you check out in a fire or just get tired of me?"

"What if I did? Would it hurt any less because you'd turned me away today? Honey, we can go through life using the 'what if' barometer but that's not living life. I'm going to try damn hard not to check out in a fire. I can't imagine growing tired of you. But tomorrow's not even a promise. All we've got is the here and now. We can plan for tomorrow, but we have to live in the moment."

"So, does this mean you're gonna keep turning up on my sets 'til I tell you what you want to hear?"

"Pretty much," he said.

"Ya know, you can be a pain in the ass."

"Your sweet way with words is just one of the things I love about you."

Zach barely managed to choke back a snort of laughter.

"I'm not going to get rid of you, am I?" Jacey asked with a faux grimace.

"Nope. You might as well marry me."

"Digg…"

"Just think, you could hook up with a hoser for life."

She laughed. "Easy, ladder-boy. I need to walk before I run. How about I list your address in New York on my next job application?"

"It beats the heck out of you heading back to L.A."

"And we'll work on that living in the moment thing."

"Works for me. Let's find someplace a little more private so we can live a little more fully. Are there any cameras wired out here?"

"It's a little late to be asking, don't you think?" Jacey laughed. "No, there aren't any cameras here. And there aren't any cameras out in the stables."

Digg stroked his hand down her side. "How'd you like to hit the stables for a little horsing around?"

Jayce slid her arm around his waist. "Don't ever think about giving up firefighting for stand-up."

The couple melded into the night, and Zach moved forward out of the dark recesses. He didn't want to witness any more liaisons. He was glad they'd decided to take the hot and heavy somewhere else and he could avoid the awkwardness of speaking up. It was also good to know there were two spots he could enjoy without his every expression being captured for posterity.

And he'd gleaned some interesting info—like there was a twist coming down the pike and the seating arrangements at dinner tonight hadn't been the luck of the draw.

And, hell, he'd been touched listening to Digg and Jacey. Of course, he didn't know many people who wouldn't have been. Zach agreed with Jacey—the guy should skip stand-up, but Digg had a future in evangelical preaching if he wanted to go there. Zach was convinced he needed to do a better job of making every minute count.

Somewhere in the dark night an owl hooted and Zach jumped. This place was so different from the city. He'd thought he'd never miss the noise of a metropolis. But he couldn't recall ever being so alone. Noise in the city was like a constant presence, the pulse, the push of humanity.

Now, there were no taxis, no trains, no cars honking, no neighbors shouting two doors down. Only the distant murmur of a television and male voices interrupted the night. Unless he was mistaken, the boys were watching a rousing game of Monday night football in the common room.

The kitchen door opened and closed. Welcome to Grand Central.

"Oh, I didn't know anyone was out here." Andrea. He recognized the tenor of her voice with its faint Brooklyn undertone. Even more telling, he felt her. He turned. She stood a few feet away, a slender cameo in the dark. The night carried her scent, light but sophisticated. No cloying, flowery scents for this woman.

"It's a nice night. Stay and enjoy it," he invited. His heart thudded against his ribs at her nearness. This woman had the most curious effect on him. "Enjoy a break from the cameras and lights. This place isn't wired."

"How do you know that?"

She definitely sounded suspicious. Did she think he was trying to hit on her?

"I overheard two of the production crew talking to one another. And that comment about the lack of cameras wasn't a come-on."

Andrea laughed. "I didn't think it was."

It was the most damnable thing. It was as if Andrea Scarpini carried her own force field with her that sucked him in. Something about her tugged at him, threw him off balance. Notwithstanding that she was opposite him at the far end of the table, he'd found his attention drawn to her again and again over dinner tonight. She had a beautifully expressive face that could get her into all kinds of trouble.

"Did you enjoy dinner?" he asked.

"The food or the company?" Her voice, as expressive as her face, conveyed amusement.

"How about both?"

"I thought the food was excellent. But it was weird being the only woman and the focus of everyone."

"Wasn't that what you expected?" Otherwise, why had she signed on for this gig? He was a little surprised that she didn't exude more ego.

"I should've expected it. I guess I did. But the reality of it, no pun intended, is a bit of an adjustment," she said, wrapping her arms around her middle.

"Why'd you sign on for this?" he asked. It was purely research and not because he wanted to know on a personal level.

"I'd never thought about it. I wasn't hanging around thinking, wouldn't it be cool to be on a reality TV show? A scout approached me. I push my friends to be adventuresome, but I tend to hang back. That day I decided what the heck, went for the screen test and here I am. What about you? Why'd you sign on?"

Zach laughed at how different their approaches had been. He'd come as close to the truth as he could without giving away his assignment. "I *was* thinking wouldn't it be cool to be on a reality TV show. I'm not a jock and I'm not a *Survivor* kind of guy, so this seemed like a good format to pursue. And hey, I made it through round one."

Her mood shift was almost palpable. "Well, I don't want to…I guess what I'm trying to say…wow, I'm botching this," she stumbled around.

Hmm. This didn't sound good. "Just say it."

"You seem like a nice guy, so don't take it personally if you don't make it through round two."

Talk about a sucker punch. "I'm not sure how I should take it if it's not personal," he said, keeping a light tone.

"The thing is I didn't want you to think you got cut because of the introduction thing."

He was a freaking sympathy save? Yeah, he'd call that barely sliding by. "Ouch. I was a sympathy save."

"It sounds bad put that way…." Apology softened her voice.

"But true." This was going to be one short stint, not nearly long enough to get any dirt for his piece. And that didn't even take into account all the bruises on his ego.

"You seem like a nice guy," she'd said that before and it wasn't making him feel any better, "but you're not really my type."

He laughed softly in the dark, scrambling for an angle, and remembered something she'd said earlier. "Well, if you're looking for adventure, maybe you should be looking at the guy who's not your type." He stepped closer, drawn to her despite her declaration that he didn't do it for her. After all, he'd caught her glancing his way more than once at dinner. He didn't think this attraction was a one-way thing. "If you'd found what you wanted in your usual type you wouldn't be here, would you? Maybe it's time you expanded your boundaries when it comes to men, Andrea Scarpini."

What the hell, if he was about to be kicked off of the show, what did he have to lose? And after listening to Digg, he decided to roll with the "live in the moment" philosophy. So he did something he'd wanted to do since dinner. He cupped Andrea's jaw, her skin warm and soft beneath his fingertips. He couldn't contain his hiss of indrawn breath.

Zach felt almost dizzy from her scent. She tilted her head back and the silky strands of her hair teased and clung to the backs of his fingers. He'd never been so aware of the sensual details of a woman.

She could have stepped away from his touch. Instead, she moved closer. "Maybe I *should* expand my boundaries, Zach Roberts." Her voice, low, soft, sexy, wrapped around him. She didn't look any happier than he was at this attraction, this force that drew them to one another.

Zach always had a plan. He lived by plans. But this time he woefully lacked a plan.

This time he was operating on instinct and want. Based on that, he shouldn't kiss her. The only way he should be lip-locking with this woman was because it would give him a competitive advantage. Instead, he wanted to kiss Andrea for the sheer pleasure of the experience. Did she taste as good as she smelled? Was her kiss as honest as she was?

He bracketed her shoulders in his hands. She felt delicate and fragile beneath his fingers, but he also sensed a core of steel. "I want to kiss you. If that's a problem, just say so now and it won't happen."

She leaned toward him, only a slight movement, but his body surged at the faint brush of her hip against his. "Is this a trying-to-sway-me kiss?" she asked, her lips mere inches from his.

"No. Definitely not. This is simply a kiss borne of a beautiful woman and a moment of privacy." That was no angle, just the truth.

"Oh." She wound her hands around his neck.

He shouldn't care. He should just take what she was obviously offering. But as much as he wanted to kiss her, *her* motives mattered to him. "Is this a sympathy kiss? A consolation before I'm given the boot?"

She tilted her head. "No. This is an I-want-to-kiss-you kiss." She was so close, her warm breath fanned against his mouth and he inhaled her scent.

"Good answer," he murmured as he bent his head. He brushed his mouth against hers. A trial run. A sample.

She sighed against his mouth. And then her lips melded against his in a long, slow, lip-clinging kiss that fired through him. He slid his hands along her back, drawing her closer and she pressed against him, winnowing her fingers through his hair, pulling his mouth into firmer, more intimate contact.

Where Zach had been inundated with the details before, now everything fused into a collage of sensation. Her scent, her heat, the press of her body, her taste, the smoldering heat filling him, surrounding them.

Something happened to Zach that had never happened before. He lost himself in a kiss. Time. Space. Circumstances.

Andrea pulled away, her breathing not quite in control. But then again, neither was his. "Expanding my boundaries was an excellent idea," she said with a note of self-consciousness.

"I'm glad we both wound up out here," he said.

She slid her hands from his neck and he missed her touch. She took a step back and he released her. If it was up to him, they could stay out here all night kissing. But that was a really bad idea. They might've only just met today and he might've botched the introduction, but there was an obvious chemistry between them. Chemistry might keep him in the game, but he couldn't afford for chemistry to muck with his assignment.

"So am I. You won't…it'd probably be best if you didn't mention this to the other guys."

He tried not to feel too insulted. She really didn't know him. "I don't kiss and tell."

"Neither do I." She leaned up and brushed a featherlight kiss against his mouth. "Good night, Zach." She slipped away and Zach stood alone once again.

He realized he'd lied to Andrea. Writing his article would be the ultimate kiss-and-tell. And he, as well as anyone else in the entertainment business, knew that sex sold.

CHAPTER FOUR

THE NEXT DAY, Andrea soaked up the warm Georgia sun on the veranda overlooking the formal gardens behind the house. She'd already changed her dress once this morning, having dropped egg down the front of her at breakfast. Thank goodness the guys weren't bringing her chocolate or food or anything. They were simply reading her their poems.

"Three more and then we'll take a break," Portia called from the sidelines.

The camera operator gave Portia a thumbs-up without taking her eye from the lens. Andrea gave a mental thumbs-up. Her butt was numb from sitting on the wrought iron settee. It looked good but it wasn't the most comfortable seat in the house.

A tall guy named Pete folded himself onto the settee next to her. "It's a good thing you're sitting down already because you're about to be wowed."

She liked his manner. Unfortunately, his nearness didn't send her pulse into overdrive. "I'm ready if you are."

Pete plunged into his poem. "Like the deep depths

of a bass lake, like the brightest sky on a cloudless day, your bright blue eyes, a mess of me make."

That was one muddy lake and one overcast sky, she thought. Her eyes were dark brown. Pete was either seriously color-blind or seriously unobservant.

"I lie in bed and think of you, and in that darkest hour, only a cold shower will do," Pete finished with a dramatic flourish, obviously very sincere.

Ack. She could handle tongue-in-cheek, but Pete the Perv was serious. This guy considered a cold shower romantic prose?

"I'm not sure what to say."

"I told you," he said. "It came to me while I was in bed. Actually several came to me, but I thought this was the most eloquent while offering brevity as well. You're very inspiring you know."

"Thank you." At least his poem hadn't contained a wet dream.

Pete left with a promise to see her later.

This was her fifth poem this morning and she found herself only half-concentrating on them because she'd been so busy checking out each guy's mouth. One was too big. One was too thin. So far, none had matched Zach's. She was still reeling from that kiss. All morning she'd run on an incredible edge of sexual energy.

It was insane to think she was besotted with a man's mouth, but...wow. She needed to check with Portia and see when she'd get around to kissing the other guys, not that she planned to mention last night. But as of now, she'd muddied the waters by kissing Zach Roberts.

She'd read once that men look at women and try to picture themselves in bed with them. Women look at men and try to picture themselves kissing the guy. And Zach was immensely kissable. Those sexy lips, nice teeth… His mouth had been warm, his breath faintly flavored with after-dinner port. Mmmmm….

"Hi." As if her silent musings had conjured him up, Zach appeared before her.

She started, momentarily losing herself in his sea-green eyes. They reminded her of the waters in the Sea of Cortez, off the Baja coast where her family had vacationed one year. Not aquamarine. No hint of blue. Beautiful, translucent green.

"Hi," she said. Zach sat down and her heart raced as awareness shivered through her. Andrea controlled the impulse to lean forward and give him a reality-check kiss. Maybe kissing him wasn't as awesome as she remembered. Maybe she'd simply romanticized it in her head, built it up to be better in memory than actuality.

"You looked as if you were somewhere else. Was Pete's poem that good? I'm in trouble," Zach said, his voice dropping a notch on the last word, sending her hormones into a feeding frenzy of lust. He glanced at her lips as if he too was reliving kissing her.

Yeah, she was somewhere else…mentally making out with him. And sexual arousal with a numb butt felt weird. "Pete's poem was…different. And I'm sure

you're trouble." Damn. Talk about a Freudian slip. "I
meant I'm sure you're not in trouble."

"Maybe you're not ready for what I've got?" A
teasing, challenging gleam lurked in his eyes.

"Bring it on and we'll see how it stacks up against
the competition."

"I had plenty of time to work on it because I
couldn't sleep last night. Sometimes a walk relieves
tension and sometimes it just makes it harder to sleep."

Her entire body tightened at the memory of his lean
body against hers—some parts harder than others—his
scent, the taste of him and the feel of his hands in her
hair. Sweet heaven, this guy struck sparks off of her.
And, she reminded herself, the camera crew was right
there, film rolling, everyone wired for audio and video.
She chose her words carefully. "I hate to hear that
your night was disturbed."

"Not disturbed, or disturbing. Invigorating. I'm
looking forward to walking again tonight."

It had been both terrible and wonderful. Wonderful
because kissing him left her feeling more alive than
she'd ever felt before. She felt goofy admitting it even
to herself, but it was as if she were some fairy-tale princess and Zach's kiss had awakened a part of her that
had always been asleep. Today colors were brighter.
Smells sharper. And that was just from a kiss. Imagine if they actually… And then there was the terrible
part. The restlessness and longing that plagued her.
You'd think she'd never been kissed before. She had.
But never like that.

And he'd be back there tonight. And she'd be there, too. "Perhaps I'll run into you."

"That'd be…" the heat in his eyes spread through her, warming her inside and out "…nice."

For the span of a heartbeat and a breath, everything stood still. No cameras, no microphones, just her and a man with intense green eyes connecting. Getting real.

Zach looked away first. "Dirk is giving me the high sign. I think I need to read my poem."

"I'm ready."

"Roses are red, violets are blue, I hope you pick me, cause I'm the guy for you."

"Oh." Laughter burbled up. "That was beautiful. And original."

"You liked it?" He looked boyish, sexy and slightly insecure all at the same time.

Actually she did. She liked a guy who could laugh at himself. And after all that sexual tension inside her, it was a relief. "Yes. It was wonderful."

"Mr. Roberts, there are other contestants waiting," Dirk admonished from the doorway.

"They're kicking you out," she said with a smile.

"It looks that way," he agreed, making no move to leave.

Dirk crossed the room, a mixture of annoyance and amusement warring on his face. "We need to wrap this up *today*, Mr. Roberts. Now bid lovely Ms. Scarpini adieu."

A devilish light glimmered in his green eyes. Zach

stood and clasped her hand. In a Puckish manner, he bowed and kissed the back of her hand.

A tremor ran through her as his lips branded her hand, his fingers curled around hers.

"Adieu, fair lady. Until lunch brings us together again."

Andrea watched him cross the patio, admiring the play of khaki slacks across his rear. Zach Roberts left her confused, bemused, amused…and wanting more.

"SO, ARE YOU READY to send another ten packing?" Portia asked after they'd wrapped up the morning filming and returned from a picnic lunch by a meandering river.

"It sounds awful when you put it that way," Andrea said. "Especially after we all had such a blast at the picnic." Even Pete the Perv was fun when he wasn't quoting gross poetry at her.

"It was fun, wasn't it?"

"Some of the guys seemed surprised to find out I drink beer and throw a mean disc." She'd realized today that part of her problem was that while she liked guys, she'd always been their buddy, more interested in hanging out than making out or getting naked with them. Except Zach. She'd like to do more than hang out with him, which was rather confounding. Rourke was much closer to her long-standing ideal.

"I guess they were expecting you to be a sideline cheerleader or a pretty princess."

"I think you're right. But they were great once they

figured out I don't do the sideline thing real well. They really are a pretty nice group of guys. I hate to give any of them the cut."

Portia laughed. "Sorry, honey, but you can't wind up with all twenty of them. It's part of it. And all the guys know the deal when they sign on. What'd you think of the poems?"

Andrea waffled her hand back and forth. "There were some really funny ones and some were really lame."

"Did any sweep you off your feet?"

Portia didn't have to know everything. And really, Andrea felt rather foolish. One kiss and she was smitten by a pair of green eyes and a sexy butt. Finally, she had a horde of men vying for her attention and she'd plunged into the throes of some weird preadolescent crush. And it *was* a preadolescent crush. Normal human beings didn't fall in love in one day based on one kiss. Didn't happen in real life. Too silly to contemplate. "No. I haven't been swept off my feet."

"Aw. That's too bad." Portia studied her French-manicured nails. "Not even the awe-inspiring Rourke? And I thought I detected some sizzle between you and Zach."

Hmm. Was there just a hint of sarcasm when Portia mentioned Rourke? Andrea shrugged off the thought. She'd probably just imagined it. Everyone loved Rourke. Andrea had to admit she was a bit infatuated with him, even if he didn't send any tingles down her spine. "They're both okay."

"Mm-hmm."

Maybe Rourke would send tingles down her spine if she kissed him the way she'd kissed Zach. And Tyler from Texas might well incite a tingle or two if she gave him a chance. And, to their credit, none of those guys set her on edge the way Zach did. She'd been aware of him every second of the picnic, the sound of his voice, the occasional brush against him.

"When can I kiss these guys?" Andrea didn't see any point in beating around the bush.

Portia's head whipped around at that. "What?"

"You know, when do we get physical?"

Portia stared at her for a moment like a lab specimen and then threw back her head and laughed. "Andrea Scarpini, I love you. You can get physical whenever you want to. There aren't any rules regarding physical contact."

"Do the guys know this?"

"They should. But you learn to never take anything for granted. I can follow up with Dirk and make sure he covers it with them." Portia smiled. "So, is it getting to you, all these gorgeous men under one roof and you the only woman?"

"Seems like I've noticed you and quite a few other women here."

"Granted, but you're the only woman that counts," Portia said.

"That's wickedly warped, but I like it."

Mischief gleamed in Portia's eyes. "I'm assuming you have a let's-get-physical list."

"I do." A very short list thus far, but she was willing to expand it. Maybe that'd be her new motto for this whole experience—expand her horizons.

Portia waited expectantly for a few seconds. "Does this mean you don't plan to share your list?"

"A girl has to have secrets."

"That's fair enough. How about giving me ten guys who aren't making the to-be-kissed list?"

No problem. She'd looked them all over today with a kissability meter going in her head and narrowed it down to three, with Zach being at the top of that list. But she had to leave ten men standing. "Do you have that cheat sheet?"

"We thought it'd be best if you consulted your stack of poems and culled that way."

Nuts. "Don't make it easy."

"Since they had to come up with the poems, we thought it was equitable if they were judged on them."

"Fair enough." She beat Portia to the next line. "I know. And do it quickly."

"See, you're getting to be a pro at this." She handed over the list with a sly smile. "And I suspect it'll get easier once you've kissed a few."

LAST NIGHT she'd simply wandered out to the breezeway. Tonight she was much more careful to leave the house undetected.

She'd gone back and forth over whether she'd show up, but really, she'd known all along she'd meet Zach.

She felt his presence before she saw him. It was as

if they shared some weird cosmic connection. She'd dated her share of guys and kissed more than her fair share of toads, but she'd never felt this incredible rush, this surge of attraction. "Hi," she said softly into the dark.

"You came," Zach stepped forward.

A sweet shiver of anticipation stole through her. "Yes." A soft breeze shifted her hair against her neck. Zach's scent whispered over her, masculine, fresh, tantalizing. A sliver of pale moon hung suspended among the pinpricks of starlight. Looked like she couldn't blame her insane obsession with last night's kiss on a full moon. "It's another beautiful night."

"It is now that you're here," he said. "There's a small walled garden tucked behind the terrace and formal garden. Want to check it out?" He held out his hand.

She slipped her hand into his, his touch warm and sure, his palm faintly calloused.

For a few minutes there was only the sound of their footsteps crunching in unison on the graveled garden path. The dark cloaked them, wrapped them together in intimacy, even though only their hands touched. On one hand, it was comfortable, lovely really, walking quietly together, his lean warmth next to her. On the other hand, a taut expectation hummed between them. Escaping into the dark night lent a hint of illicitness that excited her.

Somewhere in the distance a dog howled. The faint smell of cigarette smoke drifted on the evening air along with the indistinct murmur of voices. The crew had a designated smoking area at one corner of the house.

"This is a little different from New York, isn't it?" Zach asked, a cricket chorus singing backup.

"You mean the total absence of night noise? It's like another planet. It must be for you as well. You're from Chicago, aren't you?" She'd read his bio.

"Yeah. And where I'm from, we prefer red wine to white," he said.

"How could you have possibly heard that at dinner?"

"I didn't. I lip-read. You could say I was eavesdropping from my end last night." His low sexy laugh wrapped around her.

A man who paid attention. She fell a little bit harder.

"Where'd you learn to lip-read? And pay such close attention?"

"My grandmother's hard of hearing. When I was a kid, I thought she was a witch. She could be across the room and I'd still get in trouble for something I said. It wasn't until I was a little older and wiser that I figured out she was lip-reading. So, I taught myself because if Tante could get all that good dirt on me, I could do the same." He laughed and Andrea laughed with him. She envisioned a young boy with light brown hair and startling green eyes teaching himself to lip-read.

"You lived near your grandmother?"

"Oh no. We lived with her. My father booked when

I was a baby. No one had a clue where he was, or is. My mom, my sister Zoe and I moved in with her after my father left. Tante's the daughter of Lithuanian immigrants who stuck closely to the customs of the old country. I come from a long line of strong women. We're close."

Andrea heard the level of respect and admiration in his voice when he spoke of the women in his family and knew "we're close" was an understatement.

He was also from an ethnic family and had grown up with his grandmother. Andrea felt an instant bond. She so knew where he was coming from. But where Andrea's Italian roots were evident at a glance, Zach could've been an F. Scott Fitzgerald descendent with his sandy brown hair and green eyes. "I would've never guessed you had a Lithuanian background."

"I'm a dead ringer for my WASP father according to my mother and the photos. My mother's a smart, strong woman but he was her one mistake."

"I'm sure that she didn't see it that way if she wound up with you and your sister."

"That's exactly what she says." Zach laughed, sounding a bit awkward and self-conscious. "And I'm sure that's more than you wanted or needed to hear about me. What about you, Andrea Scarpini? Let me take a wild guess that you're Italian?"

Andrea laughed, sensing Zach had let her get as close to him and his background as he was willing to. "Was it the name or the nose that gave it away?"

They entered a small walled garden. A fountain

gurgled in the middle and espaliered trees lined the walls.

"Just a lucky guess. Do you have a big family?"

"Is the Pope Catholic?" Grandma'd give her the evil eye for that comment.

Another one of those laughs that sent a shiver down her spine. In a good way. "Big, huh?"

"There are six of us. I'm the second youngest. I have a younger brother. I'm going broke buying presents for all of my nieces and nephews at holidays. I have twenty-three first cousins. My parents' house is insane in a totally good way. I grew up with my grandmother also. She moved in with us when I was five."

Of one unspoken accord, they stopped at the fountain.

"So, what's a nice girl from Brooklyn doing on a reality TV show? Was it the fame or the fortune?"

Maybe in another time and place she would've given the rehearsed answer, but he seemed genuinely interested and this was a guy who'd grown up with a Lithuanian grandmother. So, she offered him the truth. "The fame's not a plus in my book. The money, that's nice enough and I've already got ways to use it. But the real reason I decided to do the show…" She paused and then stepped off into the deep end. "I got a sign. My grandmother's always believed in signs and I guess I do, too."

Andrea held her breath. Please don't let him laugh at her. A true Manhattan sophisticate wouldn't confess to the guy who left her weak-kneed that she based monumental life decisions on signs.

"Yeah, I can see that." He pulled something out of his pocket and held it up for her to see. "My lucky penny. I found it outside my apartment the day I read the notice for try-outs for the show." He grinned in the sliver of moonlight and something inside her shifted. "So, what do your parents think about you doing this?" Zach asked.

"You mean looking outside the hood for a man who's not a good Italian boy?"

He chuckled. "I wouldn't have put it so bluntly, but yeah."

Had she ever met a man who could make her shiver with just a laugh, but was so easy to talk to? "A hundred years ago, they would've already stuck me in a convent. Now, they just want me to find someone and they're okay with it if he's not Italian. I'm different from my brothers and sisters. I'm lucky. In so many large families there's no room for nonconformity, but my parents have always been great about letting me be me."

"That's very cool. And what is it that you're looking for in a man, Andrea?" Their hands were still clasped and he stroked his thumb against her wrist in lazy pulse-accelerating motion.

In the span of the past half hour, all her preconceived ideas of the right man had begun to change. What was she looking for in a man? *This. Him.* She reminded herself to breathe and play it cool. "If I told you that, you'd have a distinct advantage, wouldn't you?"

"You're tough."

"Look at it this way, I'm out here with you now, instead of with someone else."

"But how do I know this isn't a sympathy walk before you dump me tomorrow?"

"Is that how it feels to you?"

"No. It feels like I'm a lucky guy to be walking with a beautiful woman on a beautiful evening." His voice shifted, husky without the previous teasing note. Andrea's heart slammed against her ribs.

A soft, misting rain began to fall, adding to the surreal, sensual night.

"Dance with me in the rain, Andrea." Zach turned to face her, opening his arms.

Who but a man with the soul of a poet would dance in the night rain? Heedless of the lack of music, she stepped into his arms. At this moment she'd probably follow him to hell and back if he asked in that way, half-command, half-request.

"What are we dancing to?" she asked. As if anything mattered other than the touch of his hand on her waist, the nearness of his lean body, the intoxicating scent of him, the whisper of his breath against her hair, the mist clinging to her heated skin.

"Do you know the theme from *Dr. Zhivago*?" he asked.

"Yes." Her heart seemed to be stuck in her throat.

"It's playing in my head. Let's dance to that."

She placed her hand on his shoulder, reveling in the flex of lean muscle beneath her hand. In a pleasant tenor, he hummed a few notes and then they silently moved about the garden, dancing to the music in their heads that linked them.

It was wildly romantic to dance in the rain in a moon-slivered garden with this man who made her feel safe and terribly dangerous all at the same time.

The longer they danced, the closer they drew to one another. Finally, they stopped and simply stood wrapped in one another's arms.

Slowly, with a tenderness that left her aching inside, Zach framed her face in his hands, his fingers stroking the contours of her face as if committing her details to memory. He opened his mouth, as if to say something, then he changed his mind and leaned down instead, slanting his mouth over hers.

He kissed her the same way he'd touched her face, as if he was memorizing the feel of her mouth, the shape of her lips against his.

He pulled away from her. His boyish charm had vanished in the moon shadows. Zach Roberts was all man—intense, arousing, his hair gilded silver, his lean face all angles and slopes, his green eyes glittering.

Andrea felt the powerful tug of attraction surge through her. She echoed his movements, tracing the lines of his face, feeling the inherent strength of bone and sinew beneath her fingertips. She slid her thumb along the fullness of his lips, his breath warm against her hand. She smoothed her hands along the strong column of his neck, feeling the pulsing of his blood, the rhythm of his breathing. She linked her hands behind his neck and pulled his head down, pressing an open-mouthed kiss against his lips.

He splayed his hands across her back, pulling her tight against him. She swept the wet warmth of his mouth with her tongue.

That was all the encouragement he needed. His tongue explored her mouth with a sensuality that left her hotter than she'd ever been. *How could you feel so damn good, enjoy something so much, when it made you ache?*

His mouth consumed her as if a ravenous hunger drove him. He nibbled along her jawline and trailed kisses down her neck. She moaned when he licked the rain from the sensitive spot where her neck met her shoulder, spreading a wanton heat through her.

She tugged his shirt loose and slid her hands beneath the material to discover lean, sinewy muscles covered by warm satin skin. Andrea pressed closer to Zach, confounded by the clothing barrier. No matter how close she was to him, it wasn't enough.

Oh my God. She wanted this man with a desperation bordering on pain. *This* defined true desire. She'd kissed men before and been kissed. It'd been fun, mildly arousing. But nothing like this absolute need to make love to Zach. To feel his mouth, his hands all over her. To take him deep inside her. To give and take in equal measure.

Zach buried his face in her neck, inhaling against her. "Andrea."

"Zach."

"I didn't mean...I didn't know..."

"I know," she murmured.

"You do?"

"Uh-huh."

It began to rain in earnest. Fat drops slid down her face and plastered her hair to her scalp.

"You're wet," he said.

"Yes, I am." Some spots were wetter than others, she almost said, but she felt sure he had a pretty good idea already. Water ran down his face and darkened his hair. She smoothed his wet hair back. "So are you."

Andrea wasn't sure whether it was her or Zach that initiated it, maybe it was a joint effort, but then they were laughing and kissing again. It was primal and arousing—the taste of fresh spring rain combined with the moisture of Zach's mouth, the feel of cool water and wet clothes against her hardened nipples contrasting with the heat of his body against her, the smell of damp earth and the musky aroma of arousal, the chill of the rain against her skin and the inferno raging inside her.

Her blood thundered...

Zach pulled back. "Come on." He took her by the hand. "That was thunder."

"Oh." She thought she and Zach had created their own private storm.

They ran back through the gate, along the manicured garden paths, past the silent marble statues and Andrea laughed from the sheer pleasure of being alive and running through the rain with Zach. He looked over at her and they shared a smile. When they came to the back of the house, Andrea slowed and pulled her hand from Zach's.

"I'll go into my room through the French doors off the terrace," she said.

Zach pulled her to him, his fingers molding against the back of her head, and kissed her one last time, long, slow and hot. "Thanks for the dance. Sweet dreams." He grinned, once again looking boyish. It was doubly sexy because she knew what lurked beneath that boyish exterior.

He released her, turned and loped toward the breezeway, swallowed by the dark night. Andrea touched a tentative hand to her kiss-swollen lips, destined to dream of dancing in the dark and of Zach's rain-soaked kisses.

CHAPTER FIVE

"Zach, MAN you just missed the most exciting play of the season. You've got a dismal sense of timing," Tyler called out as Zach walked down the hall, almost making it past the group gathered in front of the boob tube. Instead of the solitude of his room, he stepped into the TV room. "And you're wet."

"It's raining out." He gestured toward the big screen. "Just my luck." Although he'd say he had great luck and an excellent sense of timing. Nothing on TV could touch the time he'd just spent with Andrea. Hell, forget TV. He couldn't think of anything that compared. Not that he had any business feeling this way. He'd always been laid-back with women, but Andrea made him crazy. Sent him over the edge of sanity. Not that he was sharing that information with anyone.

"Dirk came in with our next game plan but you were M.I.A." Pete paused, giving Zach an opportunity to tell where he'd been.

They might've discussed the next step, but they still didn't know the mysterious "twist." That was reserved

for the final five. Zach shrugged. He didn't owe anyone an explanation. "And our next assignment is?"

"Massage. And I hope you like to give as much as
you like to receive because we're on the giving end,"
Rourke spoke up.

He was an okay guy, even if he did send all the
women into drool mode. And Zach wasn't sure he
liked this massage business. "Okay. So how does this
work? All ten of us give her a massage at one time?"

"Not quite. We drew for body parts," Tyler said.

What the hell? They drew for body parts? He was
none too happy to think of any of these guys putting
their hands on her parts. "So, what part do I get since
I wasn't here when you drew?"

"Don't worry, good old Dirk oversaw the drawing
and some guy wrote down all the assignments. Sorry,
man, I can't remember what part you got, but hey,
there aren't any bad parts on a woman's body, so…"

Damn, what was wrong with him? The thought of
these guys touching Andrea made him physically sick.
Whoa. He needed to put a red light on his brain. Just
because he'd kissed her twice, ostensibly in the name
of research, didn't give him any rights. He reminded
himself he just needed a scoop. Nothing more. He was
here to save his job, not find a love life.

Zach pasted on a smile. "I'll track down Dirk in a
minute or two and find out what part I drew." And
though it galled him, he even managed a smirk. "And
no, I don't believe she has any bad parts." Okay, so
maybe his first impression was that she wasn't chesty

enough, but a guy could revise an opinion and he had. She now struck him as nicely proportioned. His body was still humming from how nicely proportioned. Damn near perfect, actually.

Tyler chuckled. "I'm just messing with you. She's going to give us our body part assignments when we walk into the room. We didn't draw any parts. And then for the lucky final five, they have to wine and dine her with a meal they plan. I'm planning—"

Zach cut him off. "You may not make it to the final countdown."

"I'm thinking positively. And I plan to be prepared with a French dinner, complete with some chilled bubbly. Rourke's treating her to a Boston seafood bake. How are you going to wine and dine the delicious Andrea?"

Maybe he should give up journalism and go into acting because he actually managed to paste on a smile and laugh. "Like I'm gonna tell you schmoes what I'm doing."

"Come on, man. What? You scared of a little competition?" Tyler said.

"Hardly. I just don't want anyone taking my ideas," Zach said.

"How do we know you won't sponge some of ours?"

Zach shrugged, palms up. "I guess you don't. But I don't need to. I'm fine coming up with my own original stuff."

"Piss on you then, man. Yours can't top mine anyway. After a champagne-soaked dinner, I plan to make my move. I'm more than ready to sample our bachelorette first-hand. And she's got that sexy voice. I can't wait to hear her moaning my name."

Shit. He could barely stand the thought of any of these guys spending time alone with Andrea. Kissing her the way he'd just kissed her. Or worse yet, her kissing any of them, running her hands over their naked back, the way she'd just done with him.

Zach's gut instinct was to rearrange Tyler's face for him. Tyler came across as suave and sophisticated in front of Andrea or any of the crew members. He'd revealed his true colors now. What a fricking moron. Well, the guy might just be digging his own grave. In the first place, the whole conversation was being caught on tape, so Andrea just might see it. Second, if Tyler had paid any attention, he'd know Andrea preferred red. Zach figured the odds of her moaning for this moron were nil. At least he hoped.

"I think your chances of getting a moan are slim to none," he said. It wasn't as satisfactory as rearranging Tyler's face, but it still felt good.

Tyler bristled. "You think you stand a better chance?"

Yeah, he did, cause he'd just been there and done that. "I didn't say that."

"We think you and Roy are goners after tomorrow."

His gut tightened at the prospect of not seeing Andrea again or spending any more time with her. Plus, it would mean she was left with jerk-offs like Tyler.

Although, if she knew about Zach's article, she might consider him a jerk-off as well. And there was the little matter of him being unemployed if he didn't get this damn article. "Any particular reason why?"

"You guys aren't connecting with her like some of us."

No wonder women thought guys were clueless. They basically were. He'd never been so tempted to kiss and tell in his life. He'd like to wipe that smirk off idiot-brain's face by telling him just how connected he'd been with Andrea less than half an hour ago. But Zach's own self-respect wasn't worth putting Tyler from Texas in his place.

"You may be right. I guess we'll all find out after tomorrow night. I'll just have to work harder on connecting with her."

"I'd like to connect with her," Tyler said with a leer and a hip thrust.

"You're a pig," Rourke said, shaking his head.

Someone laughed. Zach wasn't laughing.

"We boys from Texas learn to ride at an early age. Dirk told us all the only rule about getting physical was everything had to be consensual. Apparently she asked that lady producer, Patricia."

It was Portia, but Zach let it slide. Man, this show had short-changed Andrea in the choice department and that included him as well. He wasn't feeling like any prize himself. He was just here for the story.

Tyler smirked when Zach didn't respond. "Obviously, a couple of us do something for the little lady. Personally, I'd like to do a lot for her—all night long."

She'd asked this afternoon, after he'd kissed her last night. Had she asked to make sure of the rules or because she wanted to check some of the other guys out as well?

The thought of Andrea getting physical with any of the guys in the room had him grinding his teeth. He told himself it was merely a reaction based on self-preservation. The bigger his advantage with her, the farther he'd go, and the better his material for his article. It really wasn't anything personal.

Yeah, right.

THE SMART THING to do would be to go to bed. However, Andrea felt neither smart nor prudent. She considered last night's restlessness child's play compared to the longing gripping her now. She was drowning in heavy-duty lust.

Pathetic that mere kissing reduced her to this. It wasn't as if they'd progressed to heavy petting. Maybe that was the problem. Was that why she could only toss about on the soft, cool sheets in her lonely bed and imagine Zach's mouth on her breasts, his hands soothing the tormenting ache for his touch? Imagine him between her thighs, filling her, touching her the way she longed to be touched?

If this was what physical lust was all about, small wonder her friends thought she was a freak. She now understood their obsession with her sex life, or lack thereof.

Confused, restless, she flung back her covers and

climbed out of bed. She opened the French doors and swallowed her apprehension at the possible animals lurking in the dark depths of the Georgia wilds. There was something so civilized about the steel and concrete hustle and bustle of the city. City dangers were a known quantity. It was a measure of her restlessness that she'd brave the Georgia wilds of her patio to escape her room. The air held a cool freshness, compliments of the earlier rain.

If she hadn't spotted Rourke before he saw her, it might've scared her witless when he walked by on the lawn.

She considered hanging back in the shadows. Heck no. Making herself known was the wise, bold move. Maybe it didn't matter where you got your appetite, as long as you got what you wanted to satisfy it. She'd told Zach he wasn't her type. Rourke was much more the kind of guy that usually attracted her. Tall, broad shoulders, arms that looked as if he pumped iron at a gym, dark hair, blue eyes, professional. Rourke was packaged nicely. What had she overheard the wardrobe mistress saying that first day to Portia? Oh yeah. If you looked up tall, dark and handsome in the dictionary, you'd find Rourke O'Malley.

He looked as out of sorts as she felt, with his hands shoved into his pockets. She called his name and for a moment he looked startled. Then he collected himself and sauntered across the wet grass to her patio.

"What are you doing out?" she asked, terribly

aware that she was naked and hot and bothered beneath her nightgown.

"Just a walk. I'm used to getting more exercise than this. I worked out in the gym earlier but I miss the handball court," Rourke said. Aha. She'd called the gym addiction correctly. Muscles bulged beneath the clinging knit of his shirt. Not too long ago, she would've admired his build, now it seemed almost obscene compared to Zach's lean, sleek physique.

"Yes. I can tell you work out."

He nodded as if her observation embarrassed him. "What are you doing out tonight?" he asked.

Most guys she'd met built like Rourke would've treated her to a little flex show. At the very least they would've gone into more information than she wanted on their workout. Instead, Rourke had quickly changed the subject. How often did you find gorgeous men who weren't totally self-absorbed? Like never, that she'd noticed. She shrugged and answered his question. "Maybe the same thing. A lack of exercise. A need for some fresh air."

"It's a nice night now that the cloud cover's cleared. You don't see stars like this in the city," he said, tilting his head back to study the night sky.

"Umm. For sure. It's lovely," she said. Something was seriously wrong with her. She stood there practically naked, sharing a star-studded sky with the hunk de jour and she might've been standing around with her cousin Nick talking Yankees stats.

He stepped closer. "I'm enjoying the view."

Part of her felt kind of creepy out here with Rourke after being with Zach earlier. But, on the other hand, she was here to choose a guy and she was shooting herself in the foot if she didn't give them all a chance.

Hel-lo, dweeb girl. Wake up. Think romance. He looked good. He smelled good. He sounded good. Round out the sensory experience—check out taste and touch.

She stepped into his shadow and lightly placed her hand on his chest. Yep, he felt pretty good, darn near a rock beneath her hand. But so far, she wasn't experiencing any heart palpitations. Maybe that came with the tasting.

Rourke trailed a finger down her bare arm. "You look like a late-night goddess kissed by the moon. One of those alabaster statues waiting for the right man to come along and kiss you. Bring you to life."

That was certainly the right thing to say. Romantic. Poetic. A pretty speech. She should be going all warm and gooey inside. But then again, that earlier rain-kissed dance in the garden was a tough act to follow.

But Rourke was saying all the right things, even if it wasn't doing a thing for her. He was a good test run for whether her infatuation with Zach was situational or man-specific.

"Maybe I *am* waiting on the right man," she said softly in the night. They both recognized it as an invitation.

His arms circled her, drawing her to his muscular

body. And then he kissed her. Nice mouth. Fresh breath. Great bod.

And nothing happened. He was good at it. Technically all his moves were right, but he wasn't engaging her gears.

When his tongue pressed against the seam of her closed mouth, she pulled back. If the lip action wasn't doing it for her, they weren't progressing past that. She didn't want to insult him, but this wasn't working. It had been pleasant but the chemistry just wasn't there.

She took a step back. "I'm more tired than I thought."

"I understand," Rourke said, smoothing her hair back from her face in a gesture more paternal than sexual.

In her ideal world, he'd be her man. But she'd been handed yet another sign. This was the real world, and he wasn't the man for her.

"You're a sweetheart," she said. "I'm sor—"

He cut her off with a gentle finger to her lips. "Don't. It's okay."

She could easily be friends with this man, but never lovers.

He leaned forward and kissed her forehead. "Sweet dreams, Andrea Scarpini."

Andrea retreated to her room, closing the French doors on Rourke's receding silhouette.

She shook her head over her lack of response. Not even a tingle. Nothing like kissing Zach. An increasingly familiar ache filled her. She was in a bad way.

Just *thinking* about Zach left her hot and bothered, achy and needy.

Why had she ever agreed to this? All the cameras? Microphones at every juncture? Incommunicado with friends and family? Although she didn't really need to talk to Janine, Donna and Tina to know what they'd say if she confessed to being in the throes of dark, desperate lust.

"Do something about it."

"Go for it."

And why not? How much more of a sign was she waiting for? Maybe a meteorite to land on her head? She'd been hanging around, waiting for the ideal man to show up. Why sit around dithering when he did? Because he wasn't the man she'd had in her head? Because it was scary to feel so intensely about someone she'd known so briefly? Because she was more than a little in love with him?

Yes. To all of the above. But Zach felt right. The timing felt right.

Andrea climbed back into the four-poster antique bed hung with a tatted canopy, a sense of resolve and calm stealing over her.

She'd seduce Zach Roberts and this time tomorrow night, she'd be a different woman. And she'd finally be free of her "oldest virgin in the five boroughs" title.

"YOU'RE UP NEXT, Mr. Roberts. And what are you hoping to massage for Ms. Scarpini?" Dirk asked, winking and hamming it up for the camera.

"I'd consider whatever body part I get to be a lucky choice." Zach offered his best happy-go-lucky smile. Inside he seethed. This qualified as the longest morning of his life, watching the other guys file into the room where they rubbed their hands over her silken, bare skin. *Lighten up, Zach, old boy,* he reminded himself. And while there weren't any camera operators in the massage room—they wanted to preserve the mood according to Portia—they'd stationed several cameras and audio equipment in the room.

"That's a good answer. And let's hope you're good with your hands since only five of you will go forward."

"I guess we'll know after this," Zach said. Story or not, he possessed some male pride. And for better or for worse, somewhere along the way this had shifted from a mere assignment to something far more personal.

"And you've picked out your music?" Dirk asked.

Oh, yeah. It was a deliberate choice. He held up the jewel case. "Right here."

"Well, I've just been given the signal. Mr. O'Malley finished a few minutes ago, Ms. Scarpini's had a break, and she's ready for you now."

Don't think about Rourke, the bastard, touching her. Especially don't think about Rourke, the bastard, kissing her. Unable to sleep, Zach had stumbled on Rourke and Andrea last night. His gut knotted anew at the thought. The only thing that had kept him from making an ass of himself and tearing the two of them apart was that Rourke, the bastard, was actually a decent guy. If it had been Tyler….

Zach pushed aside the thought and focused on the opportunity at hand instead of the jealousy that gnawed at him.

He walked into the massage room. Since the shades were drawn, the flicker of several votives scattered about provided the only light. The aroma of exotic scented oils hung in the dark, warm room. Andrea lay on a sheet-draped table, covered by a blanket and a robe. A white turban contained her dark hair. Her brown eyes were enormous in her face. She looked like a sexy model advertising a spa.

Everything about the room, the woman, the setup screamed sex and every fiber of him answered the call.

Portia stood to one side of the room, a knowing, amused look in her eyes. "I just wanted to remind you the room is wired for video and audio. If Andrea feels uncomfortable with you or the situation, at any time, and asks you to stop, please respect that. Otherwise, you have half an hour to make her feel as good as you can. I encourage both of you to enjoy the experience." She opened the door behind her and slipped through it, still wearing that knowing smile.

Without a word to Andrea, but feeling the weight of her dark-eyed gaze on him, Zach loaded his CD into the player. The unmistakable sound of falling rain filled the room. Andrea smiled, an intimate quirk of her lips that slid over him. Instantly he recalled the taste of her mouth and skin washed by the fresh rain.

"That's a nice choice. I'm partial to rain these days," she said.

"I like it, too. Why don't you close your eyes and imagine the rain falling over you? And then tell me where you want me to touch you."

"My legs and feet."

That definitely worked for him. When he'd dated Felicia, before his name showed up tatooed on her derriere, she'd taken massage and reflexology classes. He'd been only too willing to let her practice on him and in the process had picked up a technique or two.

"I'm going to start with your right leg first." He slid the blanket and robe aside and tucked it between her legs. She had gorgeous legs, long, slender with delicate ankles and narrow tapering feet. "Relax and enjoy."

He picked up a bottle from the small table next to the CD player.

He poured a measure of oil into his palm and then rubbed his hands together to warm it. The exotic scent filled the air. He started at the top of her leg, the sensitive area just below her buttock. She tensed when he first touched her. But as he began to knead her with slow, rhythmic strokes, she relaxed. Touching her proved a subtle torture as he worked his way down her shapely leg, his fingers plying the back of her thigh, the sensitive area behind her knee, the curve of her calf, the delicate indent of her ankle. With precise care, he rotated his thumbs along the lines of her foot, paying special attention to the heel since it linked to the pelvic area. Her soft sigh mingled with the sound of rain and the occasional soft rumble of thunder.

Zach covered her right leg and repeated the process again on her left side. From the moment he'd touched her, when he'd first met her, he'd been besotted. Now he found himself caught up in the texture of her skin, her scent, the feel of her muscles, the art of pleasing her. With each touch, the tension inside him mounted. He'd love to repeat this without the presence of cameras or microphones and follow his hands with his mouth, tasting every inch he touched.

Long before he was ready and long past the point of sanity, he was through. Touching her without responding the way his body was inclined to had taken an enormous toll on him. But there was no way in hell he was going to be caught on-camera with a woody for everyone's viewing pleasure. Nuh-uh. That thought alone effectively kept a hard-on at bay.

He skirted the table and hunkered down at the top, putting his face level with where Andrea lay on her stomach. "Andrea, I'm done."

She lifted her head, her face inches from his. "That was wonderful, thank you," she said. "Come closer." She obviously had something to say she didn't want captured on audio/video feed.

He leaned in and her lips touched his ear, the contact ricocheting through him. Her warm breath whispering against his ear almost rendered him incapable of coherent thought. Luckily, he managed to process what she said. "That was the closest I've ever come to an orgasm just by being touched. Meet me in the stables, the tack room, at ten tonight."

"I'm glad you enjoyed it," he said while his whole body screamed a response to her invitation. He stood and realized his mistake. Standing put her face at crotch level. *That* put his body on red alert and sent his pulse into warp mode.

He turned and left the room, only maintaining his control by constantly repeating to himself, *don't wear a woody for the world.*

CHAPTER SIX

ANDREA SLIPPED the three-pack of condoms into her pocket, silently thanking her wise-guy friends for their send-off gift.

Her heart pounding with a crazy mix of fear, excitement and anticipation, she slid out of the French doors onto the patio. She wasn't nervous about what was to come with Zach—that part excited her. She just didn't want to run into Rourke or Portia or one of the other multitude of people populating the house. All she wanted to do was meld into the darkness and wind up in the stable with Zach and rock his world. And her world. And the wonderful world in general.

She grinned into the night, hugging the shadow of the house as she moved through the damp grass. A stable, well, tack room, held an earthy, sensual appeal. Most people might've preferred a bed the first time round, but she'd always been rather unorthodox. No kidding. A twenty-six-year-old virgin was the height of unorthodox. But she clearly saw why she was still a virgin at twenty-six. She'd never met Zach. Any man who'd dance in the rain without music on a moonlit night possessed the soul of a poet and any man who touched her the way he did had an ample supply of testosterone.

Of course, the downside to being a twenty-six-year-old virgin was that having watched movies, read books and run through quite a bit of fantasy in her head, disappointment was a distinct possibility. But she didn't think so.

Andrea slipped into the barn. A few horses nickered softly, sensing her presence. Otherwise it was quiet. Her hand shook as she turned the tack room doorknob and stepped inside.

The scent of oiled leather and horses permeated the room. Rows of saddles lined one wall. An assortment of bridles hung from pegs on the other wall. A stack of horse blankets sat atop a table. In keeping with the house and the rest of the grounds, the room was immaculate. Even more important, a single mattress sat atop a platform with a small lamp beside it.

Actually, that made sense. She recalled during their briefing on the house and grounds that occasionally a stable hand or vet bedded down in the barn if there was a touch-and-go situation with any of the horses.

Behind her the door creaked open. Zach came in and latched the door behind him. He turned to face her.

"Andrea…"

"You were expecting someone else?"

That was *not* what she meant to say. She'd planned to say something sexy, seductive. Even a simple hello would've been better than her smart-ass comment, but damn it, she was nervous. Twenty-six-year-old virgins had had lots of time to hype up the momentous event and right now she registered a tad high on the anxiety chart.

What if she bombed in bed? What if the whole thing was…well, a big disappointment? What if Zach packed a crouton? It hadn't felt like a crouton the other night pressed against her, but you never knew. Janine's cousin Donnie, the same perv with the porno stash, used to strap a zucchini to his thigh before he went clubbing.

Maybe that sounded shallow. In a perfect world, if you'd fallen for someone, whether they were endowed with a crouton, breadstick or stromboli should be immaterial. But hey, in the real world it mattered.

She was one breath away from hyperventilating. And she'd just been a bitch to this awesome guy who made her melt from the inside out. Spiraling into virginal histrionics was too lame. *Pull yourself together, girl.*

"Oh, no. You are just who I expected—just who I hoped to find waiting," he said. Ye gads, he didn't have a clue how long she'd been waiting. But the look in his eyes and his husky tone soothed her nerves. Anticipation replaced anxiety, desire curling low in her belly.

She laughed softly when they reached for one another at the same time and she went eagerly into his arms.

His mouth branded her, declared her his own with

a possessiveness in his kiss that hadn't been there before. Likewise, she staked her claim. For tonight at least, he was her man.

She ran her hands beneath his shirt, delighting in the feel of his bare flesh. Impatient, she tugged his shirt up, eager to have it off. Zach dragged his mouth from hers, his green eyes fathomless, serious, questioning.

"Am I undressing alone?" he asked.

"That hardly seems fair." He felt great beneath her fingertips. Her entire body craved contact with his.

He cradled her head in his hands. "No. It doesn't. But then sometimes life and situations work out that way."

She took one step back. "Not tonight. Let's make this fair." She tugged her shirt over her head and stood before him in a skirt and black lace bra.

His green eyes were on fire. For her. "That seems more than fair. Are you sure you want to do this? This isn't against any rules?"

She wound her arms around his neck, delighting in the feel of his naked chest against her breasts. "I've never been more sure of anything. I've had all of last night and all day to think about this. And there are no rules." She tilted her head. "What about you? I don't want you to feel pressured to do this or risk jeopardizing your spot on the show."

Zach gave a short bark of laughter. He splayed his hands along her back, sending her internal heat skyrocketing. "You're beautiful and standing in front of me sexier than any woman I've ever known. I've ached for you since this morning, make that since I met you, and you want to know if I feel coerced? No. I feel like the luckiest guy in the world. Especially since I saw you and Rourke last night." When she tensed, he added, "I wasn't spying, just out for a late-night walk."

Zach's comment that she was the sexiest woman he'd seen bolstered her past what she saw as her physical shortcomings—she was thin and could eat all the junk food she desired, but she wasn't toned and fit, just sort of skinny, and she didn't have any boobs to speak of. Of course, as her friend Eve said, better flat and skinny than flat and fat.

Zach witnessing Rourke's kiss was a stroke of bad timing. Tina would've said leave him wondering, but that wasn't Andrea's style.

"Rourke's a nice guy. I really like him, but it was his kiss that convinced me I wanted to be here with *you*."

He laughed low and sexy in the back of his throat. "Then I'm glad I didn't knock the hell out of him, which is what I felt like doing. I guess I should thank him. I just wasn't sure where that left us."

"This should clear up any lingering doubts." She unzipped her skirt and stepped out of it.

"Oh, honey, that clears up a lot of things." He reached for her and she placed her hand against his chest.

"There's one more thing, Zach."

"Okay."

"What if I don't pick you in the end?" She had to

ask. She needed a little reassurance he wasn't just sleeping with her to press an advantage.

He took her wrist in his hand and brought the soft underside to his mouth. He nuzzled the sensitive skin where her pulse beat a frantic tattoo. "I'd still be grateful you picked me to be where I am right now. Let me say it again, I'm a lucky guy."

Good answer. And it seemed unlikely he could feign the level of...uh, enthusiasm apparent by the strain against his zipper. Of course, a gigolo could... "You're not a gigolo, are you?"

"What?" He looked astonished and then he laughed. "You are one nutty woman."

Thank goodness he seemed to think she was funny instead of frightening. If she could manage to keep her mouth shut, they just might have sex. And that's exactly what she wanted. In a bad way. "Yeah, I'm a nutty woman who's feeling pretty lucky myself. So why don't you kiss me? Ya know, keep my mouth occupied so I can't make any more stupid comments?"

He grinned, boyish and sexy, and want coursed through her. "I love your sense of humor. But I love kissing you as well, so that, Ms. Scarpini, is no hardship at all."

And then he proved just that by kissing her thoroughly, his fingers against her scalp, the nearness of his bare chest turning her inside out.

"Zach," she murmured against the warm column of his throat. The combination of his skin's slight saltiness and heat was a potent aphrodisiac. She nuzzled lower, caught up in the play of lean muscle beneath the satin of his shoulder.

"Oh, Andrea," he said with a groan. His heart pounded beneath the sleek plane of his chest. She flicked her tongue against his flat brown nipple and was rewarded with a soft gasp. She gave herself over to the delight of exploring him—the taste of his skin, the various textures of his body, his scent. She lost herself in a sensory wonderland.

His hands smoothed across her back. She sighed. Zach had the most incredible way of touching her, as if he were learning her, memorizing her, committing her to memory. His touch permeated her skin, reaching soul-deep.

They made their way to the mattress, covered by a worn patchwork quilt. Andrea perched on the edge and watched as Zach unzipped and stepped out of his pants. Dark green boxers. She'd never, ever before considered boxers sexy. Zach instantly converted her. And that was no crouton tenting the front.

"Mama mia," she said.

Zach looked at her. His slow, sexy, wicked smile made her glad she was already sitting. "You have the most expressive face. And I hope I'm reading you correctly—you're not disappointed."

"Not by a *long* shot." All lean, hard male arrogance, he flashed a smile at her bad pun. "At least not so far," she said, teasing him.

He was beautiful. She was more than ready for this. For him. For them. She'd thought she'd be shy about getting naked in front of him, but he seemed so in tune with her—sharing in a light banter underscored by intense sexual awareness—she slipped off her bra and panties without awkwardness.

For a second Zach closed his eyes and then slowly reopened them. "Nope. I'm not dreaming. You're even more perfect than I'd imagined."

She smiled and leaned back, bracing herself on her hands. For the first time in her life, she felt as if her small breasts were more than adequate, and even downright sexy. "Hmmm, flattery will get you a lot places."

"Honey, forget flattery. It's the truth, and there's only one place I want to be." His gaze raked her from head to toe.

Impatient, not willing to sit on the bed and wait like a good virgin, she stood.

"Let me help you get there," she murmured, emboldened by her desire and the hot promise in his eyes.

She slid her hands over his shoulders, down his chest and the flat plane of his belly, savoring the texture of his skin, his scent, his ragged breath stirring against her hair. She pushed his boxers down past his very impressive erection. No hidden zuchinni here. Slick, wet heat pooled between her thighs. She stepped closer, trapping Mr. Happy against her damp curls, which was pretty rewarding in and of itself, but then she reached around and did what she'd wanted to do since the first time she'd watched him walk away. She skimmed the taut, smooth skin of his buttocks.

"Oh. Just as awesome as it looks," she said. His green eyes dancing with mischief, he flexed his stunning gluteus maximus. Sexy and funny. "Show off."

"Temptress. And now it's my turn." He bent his head and teased his tongue against her nipple. She sucked in a harsh breath, her entire body going tight as a bowstring. "Oh honey, just as tasty as it looked."

One step and they were at the platform bed. Andrea hadn't exactly been shy about this whole endeavor so there was the possibility that Zach might move faster than she'd like. But, once again, they seemed to be tuned into one another.

Andrea lost track of time as they explored each other with hands and mouths, pleasing and being pleased, inflamed by the erotic slide of bare skin against bare skin. Need mounted with each touch of hands and mouth, until she shook with an intensifying ache, the need to take and be taken.

As she welcomed Zach into her, she looked into his green eyes and realized this was more than just a toss in the hay. *This* was making love.

Then she wasn't thinking anything. She only felt— the sensation, the connection that grew with each thrust, pleasure so intense she cried out. She almost couldn't bear anything that felt this good, but she certainly couldn't bear it if it stopped. Zach shifted, and mother of God, he must've hit that elusive G-spot she'd read about in every woman's magazine since she was seventeen, because what she didn't think could feel any better became phantasmagorical. She was spinning, flying, dancing, caught up in something that took her far beyond where she'd ever been before. Still quivering from the aftershocks of registering off the chart on the orgasm scale, she drifted back to the real world.

Oh. My. God. Small wonder Tina was a nymphomaniac. Phe-freaking-nomenal. Incredible how much better an orgasm shared with Zach was than a vibrator. Andrea laughed aloud, giddy from the sheer pleasure of the moment. She'd never, ever felt better in her life.

Zach propped on one arm and looked at her. Oops. Lesson number one. Don't laugh after sex without offering an explanation. "That was better than great."

He looked immensely relieved and grinned back. "Yeah. Definitely somewhere the other side of great."

A sound intruded on the cozy cocoon of intimacy. If she'd had the strength, she would've raised her head to hear better. "What's that?" she asked.

"I believe it's rain." The sound intensified and his beautiful face blossomed into a sexy grin. "Maybe more along the lines of a deluge."

The rain pounded against the red tin roof. Perfect timing. Lyrics played in her head of her favorite Norah Jones song—a woman lying in her lover's arms to the sound of rain on a tin roof.

The lights flickered and then went out, plunging

them into utter darkness. A tremendous clap of thunder shook the building.

Andrea sighed with utter contentment. "I love thunderstorms."

"Me too. You're my kind of woman."

She bit him playfully on the shoulder. "You're just deciding that now?"

"It just drove it home," Zach said.

"Hmmm." The rain performed a staccato dance overhead, punctuated by outbursts of thunder. "I don't think we'll be going anywhere for a while." She plied her instep along his calf.

He slid his hand along her buttock and around to the juncture of her thighs. She quivered with renewed interest.

"I consider that good news," he said.

Andrea moaned against his shoulder as his fingers found her. She knew a whole lot more than she had an hour ago, but the one thing she knew for certain, she was a lot of things, but she was no longer the oldest virgin in Brooklyn. She smiled her immense satisfaction against Zach's naked shoulder.

She'd just disqualified herself for the title.

ZACH LAY in the dark, surrounded by Andrea. That had been like nothing he'd ever experienced before. And maybe it was the dark, or maybe it was the emotion, or perhaps a combination of both, but he found himself saying things he'd never said before. Or maybe it was simply that he'd never felt this way before.

"Making love to you with the light on was incredible because I could watch your beautiful face and your body's reaction to mine. I got off seeing myself between your thighs, your body opening for me, taking me. It was hot. But this is almost better in a different way."

Her hand wrapped around his sex and he shuddered. Without warning her wet tongue flicked against his nipple. "In what way is it better?" Her fingers tightened around his burgeoning member. He wanted her just as intensely as he had half an hour ago. Perhaps more, now that he knew the prize in the Cracker Jack box.

The poetry that had eluded him before now poured out. "It's the brush of your hair against my arm, the sweet scent that tells me you want me, the sound of your breathing mingling with mine in the darkness, the feel of your skin against mine." He couldn't lay himself bare enough to verbalize the rest. But it was also the easy way the two of them could lie together, as if they'd done this before, as if they'd do this again, as if they belonged here.

"Yes." Her breath whispered across his cheek. He was at full attention now and she shifted across him, straddling him.

Zach's breath caught in his throat and his heart pounded. His article focused on how there was nothing real about reality TV and the situation into which they were all thrown. But this, Andrea climbing on top of him, sheathing him now with her nimble, capable fingers, *this* was intensely, achingly, emotionally real.

Where did this fit into his article? What would she think when she found out about his assignment? If she sent him packing, how could he bear to let her go? He, who had only ever worried about how to get rid of a woman, suddenly realized he had no clue as to how to hold on to one. And he wanted to hold on to Andrea. Desperately.

He cupped her breasts in his hands, fondling the turgid points that were so responsive. She mewled deep in her throat and impaled herself on his rigid member.

With noisy abandon, the rain continued to fall on the tin roof and Zach Roberts both lost and found himself in Andrea Scarpini.

CHAPTER SEVEN

ZACH CLOSED his bedroom door behind him and acknowledged he was dangerously close to being in over his head. He'd made it through to the final elimination—despite what Andrea had said last night, Zach knew she couldn't eliminate him when they'd been that good together.

He shuddered at the thought of four other guys wining and dining her, trying their damndest to get physical.

And now Dirk had called another meeting, this time with the show's executive producer, Burt Mueller, the big kahuna.

Zach made his way to the assigned meeting place, the billiard room. He entered the dark-paneled, depressing room that held the stench of a hundred years worth of cigar smoke. Burgundy velvet drapes blocked any hint of sunlight. A magnificent, ornate billiard table commanded one half of the room. The other half contained five wing-backed chairs arranged in a semi-circle before logs in the massive gas-burning fireplace. It wasn't cool enough for a fire, but Zach supposed it made for a dramatic backdrop. Jacey, her handy-dandy camera ready, had positioned herself to the left of the mantel. A sound guy stood behind her, his mike boomed out far enough to pick up the conversation.

Zach dropped into one of the two remaining empty chairs. Portia, Dirk, Lauchmann the producer, Digg and a bald-headed dude who had to be Burt Mueller stood on the other side of the billiard table. Zach quietly took a deep breath. Damn, he was nervous. Of course having your job on the line and living in a perpetual state of lust and jealousy for the past few days would do that to a man.

Rourke walked in and sat next to Zach. Now that they were all here, Dirk moved to stand before the fire, striking a pose with one arm braced on the mantel.

"Congratulations, gentlemen, on making it through to the final round," Dirk said in his deep Southern accent.

Zach would've felt a helluva lot better if Rourke hadn't been one of the fab five left standing, as he'd been one of Andrea's kissing candidates.

Shit. He was a guy. He wasn't supposed to be plagued with all these post-sex insecurities. But then again, he'd never felt this way about a woman before. He was treading virgin territory emotionally.

"We have some important news to share with you," Dirk said. "First, however, let me remind you gentlemen of the agreement you signed before we began taping."

Dirk had definitely caught his interest. They'd signed a multipage document that essentially said if they did anything to screw up the taping and subsequent airing of the program, the studio would blackball them beyond redemption, which included suing the hell out of them for any current or future assets. Not a pretty thought. So what was such big news that Dirk had to bring up dire consequences before he could go there?

"Bearing that in mind, I'd like to turn things over to Mr. Mueller, the executive producer, who's flown in from L.A. to check in with us."

Zach barely refrained from rolling his eyes. People flew across country on a regular basis—it didn't exactly portend the second coming. He was testy and his nerves were definitely just a little jangled.

"As you boys know—" *Boys?* Take a hike, cue-ball head "—every show worth its salt has a twist. We've saved our twist for you final contestants."

"Is she an heiress or something?" Rourke asked. Trust an investment banker to come up with that.

"Not to our knowledge. Although we are compensating her handsomely for appearing on our show." He smiled and it wasn't a particularly nice smile. "It's better than that. Ms. Scarpini is unaware of just how thoroughly we know her…" Burt paused, looking like a big shark about to chomp down on an unsuspecting fish. Zach's gut clenched. This didn't sound good for Andrea at all. "…and just how thoroughly all of you and the viewing public are going to know her. Gentlemen, Andrea Scarpini is a virgin. The first among you to, shall we say, curry her favor—regardless of whether you're the one she chooses in the end—wins half a million dollars."

Andrea'd been a freaking virgin? A virgin? His body

tightened remembering the way she'd crawled up his body, her mouth turning him inside out. Sweet heaven, she hadn't made love like a virgin. Of course, technically, two out of the three times last night, she hadn't been.

Portia uttered a sharp sound of protest. Mueller cast her a censoring look. "Did you have a comment, Ms. Tomlinson?"

The blond woman stood a little straighter. "Sir, it doesn't seem quite ethical."

"That's life, Ms. Tomlinson. And this is reality TV, in case you forgot. This show will air, not as *The Single Girl,* but as *The Last Virgin.*"

She opened her mouth as if to register another protest, and then seemed to think better of it and clamped her lips together.

"No problems, Ms. Tomlinson?"

"No sir, no problems."

"So, let me get this straight, one of us bags her and you pay us to do that?" Tyler asked with a lecherous smirk.

Zach shoved his clenched fists into his pockets to keep from decking the guy.

Dirk looked down his pseudo-genteel nose, "May I remind you, this is a show location, not a locker room and we expect you to remember that. And, as we've mentioned before, we also expect you to remember that any physical contact must be completely consensual."

A number of thoughts rolled through Zach's head

in rapid succession. Andrea had deceived him. It was a deception of omission but a deception nonetheless. She could have mentioned it. Sleeping with a virgin was different from sleeping with regular women. Or it should be. He'd never made love to a virgin before. Well, now he had, but he hadn't known it at the time.

To his left, Rourke spoke up. "What if none of us sleeps with her? What if we're all men of ethics?"

Too late, bucko.

"It's a noble sentiment, Mr. O'Malley, but I assure you, half a million dollars buys a lot of things. And from what I've seen of the earlier tapings, you certainly stand a good chance of walking away with that money. But to address the unlikely outcome you propose, the winner will then be the man she selects and that man will be awarded ten thousand dollars."

Burt Mueller was a bastard. Andrea would be devastated and humiliated. Or was there a twist beyond this one? Was Andrea in on this and were they simply setting up the male contestants? His gut told him no. His gut also told him she deserved the truth. The easy thing to do would be to let her find out at the end of the show, the way the studio planned. The right thing to do was to come clean with her as to what the show was all about and why he was here. And he'd never been able to keep his mouth shut, even when it was in his own best interest. She wouldn't be thrilled about his role, but wouldn't giving her a heads-up exonerate him?

"Any more questions about the real side of reality TV, gentlemen?" Dirk asked.

Zach shook his head. Damn if he knew any more what was real and what wasn't. The only things he knew with any measure of certainty were that he now had the inside scoop on a story bigger than he'd ever hoped for, that the studio no longer had their virgin and that he'd netted half a million dollars.

He should be ecstatic, on top of the world that he'd come so far, so fast. But if he'd just been handed everything he wanted, why did he feel so low?

ANDREA PULLED ON a T-shirt. She'd change later. The guys had some big meeting this morning, so she was free to slob out in her own clothes, which was a nice change. She dreaded another five days of wining and dining when she'd rather spend that time making love with Zach.

No doubts. She'd made up her mind. Zach was her man. But an agreement with the studio was an agreement with the studio, and she was bound to honor it. She really couldn't complain because she'd found a great guy, The Guy, and they'd paid her to do it.

She ran a brush through her hair, grinning at herself in the mirror like a simpleton. Love was great. Love was grand. And the sex was fabulous. Life was good. She knew it was passé to fall in love with the first guy you slept with. It simply wasn't the way of a Manhattan, *Sex and the City* sophisticate. But she'd never exactly mastered that role anyway. At heart, she was just a girl from Brooklyn who'd found her guy.

The French door opened and she whirled around as Zach slipped inside. Speaking of her guy…

"Hi…" Her spontaneous joy at seeing him died once she caught a glimpse of his grim face. "What's the matter? Did anyone see you coming in here?"

"I could care less if anyone saw me coming in here," he said through clenched teeth, steadily advancing across the room.

"Zach?" What the heck was wrong with him?

"Were you a virgin last night?"

Stunned, prevarication never occurred to her and she answered truthfully. "Yes."

He shook his head and scrubbed his hand across his face. "It didn't occur to you to tell me?"

This wasn't the morning after she'd hoped for. "Actually it did. As you know, I decided not to."

"Because?"

His attitude was beginning to wear on her patience. Perhaps because she was feeling just a little guilty, which in turn left her just a little defensive. "Because it would've gone something like this. 'Well, you see, it's this way. I'm a virgin because I've just never found quite the right guy that I wanted to do it with. But, you really get my jets going, so how'd you like to help me out with this?' Oh, yeah. That'd be one way to find out just how fast you could run…in the other direction."

"You could've given me a little more credit—"

She threw up her hand, interrupting him before he could get on a roll because, by God, *she* was on a roll. "Right. Look at how you're acting now. Guys are weird. I've seen it too many times with my friends over the years. You men find out you're sleeping with a vir-

gin and you freak. You either act like we expect you
to marry us or you treat us with kid gloves. Either way
it's a bummer. And what are you complaining about?
What difference does it really make? It wasn't good
for you?" She knew that wasn't the case. Men couldn't
fake an orgasm the way women could. You pretty
much knew where you stood.

"You know damn well it was better than good. But
I feel used."

"Then I'm sorry. I never meant for you to feel used."
And now that they'd talked through her surprise and
his outrage, it occurred to her to wonder just how he
knew. "Zach, how did you find out?"

He shoved his hands in his pockets and looked
grimmer than ever. "You might want to sit down for
this."

Oh. That didn't sound good. "I'll take it standing.
Go ahead."

"That's the twist. They brought the five of us in and
announced you're a virgin. Whoever sleeps with you
first wins. The show will air as *The Last Virgin*."

All the blood seemed to drain from her body. "If
this is a joke…"

"It's no joke."

Sitting had been good advice. She plopped on the
bed. "And I assume there's more than my virginity as
a prize."

Zach nodded, his eyes sympathetic. "Half a million
dollars."

Great. Just what she wanted, to be an object of pity.

Not. She'd never felt more demoralized and dirty in her life. The pity factor had her kicking the only dog in the room. "Well, isn't it convenient you found out the morning after?"

Zach's eyes narrowed. "What are you implying?"

"I'd say it was pretty clear." She embraced her anger. It kept the tears at bay and she refused to further humiliate herself by crying.

"Andrea, I know you're angry, but you need to stop and think about this. You invited me to the stables that night. And I didn't have to come in here and tell you this."

"Why not tell me? Any way you look at it, you've won. Surely you know me well enough to know I wouldn't turn tail and run like a coward? Any other surprises up your sleeve?" Zach hesitated and her stomach dropped a little farther, which she hadn't thought possible. "What?"

"I'm not a salesman. I'm a journalist. The magazine I work for had a corporate buy-out. My job hinges on me getting an inside story on this show."

Andrea closed her eyes. Maybe she'd open her eyes and this would all be a bad dream. Nope. Her eyes were wide open and Zach was still standing there, hands in his pockets, remote.

This man was a stranger. And foolish her, the man she'd fallen in love with had been a fabrication. Could she have been that wrong, that delusional? She had to make one more effort to see if there was still a glimpse of that man. "I love you. And I thought you might feel the same way. What if you don't tell them? What if you don't write that story?"

His green eyes were unfathomable as he stood silent for a moment. Then he said, "To paraphrase you earlier, isn't it convenient that you decide you love me after we start talking money? Do you realize you're asking me to walk away from half a million dollars and saving my job?"

That pretty much told her everything she needed to know. "What if I deny that we slept together?"

"There aren't any cameras in the stables, but somewhere there's footage of us both going in and then us coming out together, hours later."

She clenched her hands into fists at her side and smiled bitterly. "I was closer with my gigolo comment than I knew. I suppose I should thank you. I didn't fully appreciate at the time just how thoroughly I was getting screwed."

"JUST A LITTLE MORE BLUSH," Tamsin, the makeup artist fussed about her, "and then we'll comb out your hair."

Andrea didn't even glance in the mirror. She didn't care. All that mattered was that this whole fiasco was about to end. It had been the longest, most miserable week of her existence fighting off the advances of three guys determined to get in her pants or die trying. She'd actually thought about killing one or two of them. As for the other two, Zach had the good sense not to go there again and Rourke was the consummate gentleman.

The night she'd had to sit through Zach wining and dining her, a smile on her face for the camera, had proven nearly unbearable. The worst of it was, she still felt so tuned into him it made her ache. Even knowing he was here to write an exposé, knowing he held the power to humiliate her before the world, she hated him, but wanted him with the same breath. Sick. Twisted. Miserable.

On a positive note, she and Rourke had spent lots of time together cementing a fast, firm friendship once they'd both acknowledged there was no spark of romance between them and it wasn't likely to develop. Rourke would make some really lucky gal a great husband. Too bad she'd wasted her heart on Zach, but she had and that was the reality of it.

"Okay, you're gorgeous," Tamsin proclaimed.

Portia walked over, her ever-present clipboard in hand. "I'll second that. Are you ready for the big moment?"

Portia had been another bitter pill to swallow. She'd liked this woman. It hurt to know she'd participated in the deception. "As ready as I'll ever be."

Tamsin rushed off to give Dirk a final pre-air check, leaving Portia and Andrea alone.

"Want to give me any hints as to who the winner is?" Portia asked.

"No."

"Oh, I think I've got a pretty good idea."

Andrea shrugged. "You'll know soon enough, won't you?"

Portia stilled her with a hand on her arm. She turned off the microphone wired along Andrea's neckline. "Andrea, I need for you to know that whatever happens… well, sometimes there are things about my job that are out of my control, that I don't particularly like, but I need this job. I'm a single mom supporting me and my son."

Andrea raised her head a notch and looked the other woman in the eye. It *almost* made it better. "I understand. Money drives most of the decisions in life, doesn't it?"

Portia appeared both stricken and almost relieved at the same time. "You know, don't you?"

Andrea offered a curt nod. "Yes."

"I'm sorry." Tears glistened in her eyes.

"I know." Andrea did know. If she was supporting herself and a kid, would she walk off of a job she found ethically offensive? Probably not. Ethics didn't put food on the table.

"For what it's worth, I didn't know, none of us knew, until Mr. Mueller flew in last Friday."

So, Zach hadn't been lying about that. "How did the studio find out?" She thought she knew. She'd had plenty of time to figure it out, but she wanted it confirmed because the only other option was that one of her friends had ratted her out and she refused to believe that.

"A scout overheard you and your girlfriends at lunch one day."

And there's something special about you. Exactly what she'd thought. "Yes. I remember that day."

"I'm so sorry," Portia said again, nearly sobbing.

Andrea found herself in the perverse situation of comforting the other woman. "It's fine. I'm fine. I'm healthy. It's been an experience. And they can only take away my dignity if I allow them to, and that's not going to happen. It'll be fine."

Portia hugged her and Andrea hugged back. "You're a heck of a woman."

"I know." She grinned in an effort to dry up Portia's impending tears. And actually she felt better than she had all week. "You know what they say, if it doesn't kill you, it makes you stronger…so, let's get this over with."

Portia signaled Jacey who came back at her with a high sign. Then she switched Andrea's audio feed back on.

"Okay. Let's go find out who the lucky guy is." Portia swept her along and into the formal living room. Andrea didn't look at the any of the five men sitting in a semicircle. She felt curiously calm and while Dirk went on, building up the suspense for the audience, she took a deep breath.

"So, Ms. Scarpini, we're all on pins and needles to know. Who is your man of choice?"

Another deep breath. "All the guys were great. At some point, I really had a special time with each of them. But I have to go with my heart on this one. Rourke O'Malley."

She *was* going with her heart. Zach had broken it. Now was his opportunity to take home his fortune. But it would be at the expense of his pride. Let him broadcast sleeping with her. She'd just picked another man in front of the whole world.

"Well, I know we all want to congratulate, Mr. O'Malley," Dirk said. "But first I need to ask if there's anything special about this week any of you gentlemen want to share with us?"

Andrea held her breath. Literally. Against her will, she looked at Zach. He sat there, silently, wearing a bland expression.

"Gentlemen?" Dirk prompted.

Zach sat forward, his green eyes boring into hers. "I have something I'd like to say."

Andrea's stomach bottomed out and she sat up a little straighter. Here it came. But she'd take it like a woman. She wouldn't show the whole world he'd taken her heart along with the virginity she'd willingly offered.

In the midst of the room thick with tension, a few pings sounded on the windowpane. Rain. It had started to rain. The sound grew as it picked up momentum, slanting against the glass.

Zach never looked away from her as he stood and crossed the room to where she sat. "It was an honor and a privilege to meet you, Andrea Scarpini. I wish you a lifetime of love and happiness." In a gesture reminiscent of the day he'd read his poem, he brought her hand to his lips and pressed a kiss to the back of her fingers. She was hot and cold and thoroughly confused. Zach turned and walked back across the room.

"That's very nice, but are you sure there's nothing else you'd like to tell us, Mr. Roberts?" Dirk asked.

"No. I've told all I have to tell."

Dirk looked very sly and the rest of the guys looked very confused. "We've been reviewing some video footage and it appears you and Ms. Scarpini spent quite a bit of time in the stables one evening. Anything you'd like to tell us about that?"

Zach shrugged. "We talked, it started to rain, and we were stuck there."

"Anything else you want to tell us about your time in the stables?"

"She's a great conversationalist."

Honest to God, maybe she was verging on hysteria, because she barely stifled a giggle at that. Just tell them, her mind screamed, and get it over with. Quit stringing me along, waiting for the axe to fall.

"Anything you want to tell us about that *conversation*?" Dirk Sherwood was practically begging to give Zach half a million dollars and he kept walking away from it. This wasn't making any sense.

"It was a *private* conversation. And no, I don't want to tell you or anyone else about it. It was between me and Andrea and it'll stay that way."

Comprehension flashed through her as the rain turned into a full deluge. It made perfect sense. What kind of man walked away from half a million dollars? There was only one possible answer. *Her* man. And what kind of woman would let him? Only a woman with no sense of adventure, unwilling to expand her boundaries. A woman afraid to live in the real world. And she no longer knew that woman.

Andrea stood, her legs shaking, her heart pounding. "I have something else to say."

WHAT THE HELL was she doing? She was home free. He'd walked away from the money. What could she possibly add to that?

Zach hadn't slept at all last night. Digg's words had kept playing through his head, *live in the moment...tomorrow's not even a promise...they never had a chance to say "I love you" again.* He'd realized he'd been so damn angry all week with himself, more so than the studio executives. Yeah, he'd landed a plum story and half a million dollars, but what had it cost him? His self-respect and a love that only came along once in a lifetime. Several times in the night he'd almost gone to her room to tell her how he felt. But he was pretty sure she'd think his declaration was a ruse for her to pick him today. Instead he'd spent the time re-writing his article with a slant he felt good about. Whether reality TV was real or not wasn't the issue. The issue was the reality each of them left the show with. The issue was the truth. He'd already lost her, and he hoped like hell he didn't wind up losing his job, but if he did, at least he had some measure of self-respect left.

Andrea cleared her throat. She looked beautiful

and brave and he had no idea where she was going with this.

"I agreed to come on this show for two reasons," she smiled, "and no, it wasn't for the fame and fortune. I came because it was an adventure. And it's definitely been that. I also came because I was searching for a special man. I have to confess, I wasn't really sure I'd find him. I almost didn't recognize him when I did." She looked straight across the room and into Zach's eyes. His pulse took off like a trip hammer but he didn't dare hope…. "But I finally did. I'm going to apologize to Rourke O'Malley who's a heck of a nice guy and a good friend, but not the love of my life. And now, I'm exercising my woman's prerogative and changing my mind." She held out her hand to Zach.

His heart damn near pounding out of his chest, he stood, but didn't move forward. "Are you sure about this?"

"Never surer of anything."

God, he loved this woman to distraction. Zach grinned. Wearing his heart on his sleeve for the whole world to see, he crossed the room and took her hand.

He turned to face her. He didn't care about the crew, the cast or the cameras. He had something to say to her. "I love you."

"I know." She smiled just for him. Then she turned to face the crowd. "And just for the record," she said, addressing Dirk, the smiling Portia, the rest of the crew, and the whole freaking world, "we had several long, deep, intimate *conversations* in that stable," she shot him a sly arch look, "and I no longer qualify as the oldest virgin in Brooklyn. So give my man his money, gentlemen."

EPILOGUE

"SHE PLAYED that absolutely brilliantly. It couldn't have gone better if I'd scripted the whole thing myself." Burt leaned back in the chair of the office he'd commandeered while visiting for the last few days of filming, feeling very pleased with the show's outcome and life in general. And, he realized with a start, for the first time in days, he wasn't desperate to suck on a cigarette.

Jacey nodded. "The show's gonna blow off the charts. It's going to be an uproar when Rourke the hottie gets picked and then dumped. But everyone will be okay with it cause who can resist the triumph of true love?"

Not that he was willing to admit it to anyone, but it had warmed the cockles of his atrophied heart to see that money hadn't bought Zach Roberts. And then it had warmed him even more to have the Last Virgin stand up and demand her man's money. Damn, that chick had balls. "And speaking of the triumph of true love—"

Jacey cut him off. "Can it, Daddy Matchmaker. Digg and I are okay." His smart-ass daughter grinned at him and he was amazed yet again that she was his. "We're better than good. We're great. My permanent address is changing to Digg's. He's going to try not to get killed in a fire or dump me, and I'm going to try not to kill his mother and get paranoid. I think we're in for a wonderful life. How's that for progress?"

"That's damn good news, Pumpkin. But that wasn't really where I was going…." Crissakes, he couldn't believe he was nervous about breaking this to Jacey. "I'm getting married." There he'd said it.

A grin lit her face and he let out a breath of relief. "Rachel?"

Burt smoothed his hand over his shaved head. "Of course. You don't mind?"

"Hell, no. I've known my old man needed a keeper from the moment I met you. She'll keep you in line."

"You're a chip off the old block. You could use a keeper yourself."

Jacey smirked. "Rachel's not my type. Do you have a date yet for the grand event?"

"Sometime in the next month. We're gonna take a trip to Vegas."

"Cool. I could show up and we could tape Burt Mueller's reality wedding."

Burt offered a mocking grin that echoed her own. "Or not. We want winners so I'll be able to leave plenty of dough to you when I kick off and go dirt napping."

Jacey rolled her eyes at that and Burt threw out the idea that had simmered in the back of his brain since the final taping of *The Last Virgin*. "You pointed out that Rourke O'Malley's a hottie and that women viewers are going to go ape-shit over him. Whatdaya say we ride his popularity and give him his own show: *The Single Guy*?"

"Brilliant. He'll have momentum and we'll have viewers before we even begin taping."

Burt plunked down and reached for a notepad, his brain already allocating personnel and a budget. "Then I'd say we've got our next blockbuster reality TV show, Pumpkin."

And he already had a helluva twist planned....

* * * * *

*Everything you love about romance...**and more!***
Please turn the page for
Signature Select™ Bonus Features.

Bonus Features:

Behind the Scenes 374
How *GETTING REAL* Got
Real

Character Profiles 378

Sneak Peek 383
REALLY HOT!
by Jennifer LaBrecque
Coming in February 2005

Behind the scenes with Leslie Kelly
How *GETTING REAL* Got Real

Have you ever wondered how a collection of stories gets put together, where the ideas come from, and how three authors work together? We asked Leslie Kelly some questions about GETTING REAL, as her book KILLING TIME (August 2004) was the inspiration behind the concept for this book.

Where did you come up with this idea?
I'd just finished writing *Killing Time*, my Harlequin Spotlight book for August 2004, which was about a reality TV show. Having enjoyed watching some of the reality TV greats, I created this entire world, complete with a camerawoman who was the illegitimate daughter of a big-time Hollywood producer, when writing *Killing Time*. It seemed a shame not to do more with that camerawoman (Jacey Turner) and her has-been superstar TV producer dad (Burt Mueller). So I figured, "what would a 1970's TV producer superstar do in the world of 2004 television, if he wanted to make his comeback?" The answer was sooooo easy: reality TV! Starting with Burt, it was easy to come up with an idea for a connected series of

stories about his attempts to make it big again in
the new millennium riding the reality TV wave.

**Once you came up with the idea, how did you decide
on who you would invite to join the collection
with you?**
I first approached Julie Elizabeth Leto. She and I are
great friends, and had collaborated on the Bad Girls
Club series within Temptation. The two of us
brainstormed and together realized that Vicki Lewis
Thompson would be an ideal addition. And adding
Jennifer LaBrecque was an easy decision, since we'd
so enjoyed her books within the line.

**Once they were on board, did you tell them what was
going to happen or was there a more collaborative
brainstorming session?**
I actually wrote a foundation "bible" about Burt
Mueller. Who he was, what he'd done, what his life
has been all about and what he wants now, most of
all. Then I added tidbits about his illegitimate
daughter, Jacey, who had her own secondary romance
in *Killing Time*. She and Digg (firefighter Diego) had
been such an important part of *Killing Time*, I felt they
deserved a little more attention. After finishing this
basic "bible," which ended with the fact that Mueller
really wants to make his TV comeback with a bunch of
reality show ideas, I threw it at the other authors. We
established an e-mail group and began tossing ideas
for reality shows around, until we each lit upon one we
really liked. One of the things that blew me away was
the fact that my idea for a modern-day Pygmalion type

show (in the lead-in Temptation *Make Me Over*) caught the eye of a real Hollywood production company. They contacted me and asked me to write a treatment for a real reality TV show, which I did, and which they then optioned! I'm currently waiting to see if one of the networks picks up my show, which is now tentatively titled *School for Seduction*. But, in any case, I like my funny little race-car-driver-turns-into-a-lady idea, which is the premise of *Make Me Over*.

Once the idea was fixed, was there a lot of back and forth among the four of you?
Once we had the basic background bible, we each took time out to write our own proposal for our own story. As long as the reality shows didn't overlap, we didn't worry too much about the individual stories. The shows lent themselves to very unique romances...as evidenced by the novels and novellas we produced! We each decided how we wanted the mystery involving Burt Mueller and the threatening "notes" to progress, as well as the romantic relationship between Jacey and Digg. Beyond that, each story belonged entirely to the author.

> *"We realized Vicki Lewis Thompson would be an ideal addition"*

At what point did the editor step in and how did an editor's voice change/alter/affect the proposal?
Our editor stepped in when we originally pitched this idea as a four-book miniseries within the Temptation

line. While she didn't feel the idea could sustain a four-month series of novels, she strongly believed it could work as a lead-in Temptation, then a collection of novellas, then a lead-out. So we tweaked the proposal. Even though I'd come up with the overview of the series, and created the characters of Burt and Jacey, I really felt my *Make Me Over* story lent itself better to a full-length novel than a novella, and our editor, Brenda, fully supported that. So I bowed out of the *Getting Real* anthology and offered to write a lead-in Temptation instead. It worked out beautifully.

One major point I'd like to make: It takes some serious cooperation to do an intertwining series. And egos need to be left at the door! When working with other authors on recurring characters/plotlines, it's simply imperative to play fair with your fellow authors. You can't stick the characters in a snowstorm in your story when they're supposed to be enjoying an unseasonably sunny day in someone else's! So it takes a great deal of coordination, and friendly cooperation, to pull all the stories together. Fortunately, it wasn't difficult to find authors who enjoyed collaborating and made every effort to accommodate each other.

For complete interviews with Vicki Lewis Thompson, Julie Elizabeth Leto and Jennifer LaBrecque visit eHarlequin.com 〆

Getting to know the
CHARACTERS

*Burt, Jacey and Digg are characters who appear in all
three of the GETTING REAL stories, and also appeared in
MAKE ME OVER by Leslie Kelly (Harlequin Temptation
2004). The romance that bloomed between Jacey and
Digg was first introduced in Leslie Kelly's KILLING TIME,
a story that was originally targeted to be in this anthology!
If you can't get enough of these dynamic characters,
read on!* ✑

BURT MUELLER:
Once upon a time, Burt Mueller had it all. A Hollywood
insider, he was the king of TV back in the early
seventies. The creative force behind a dozen of the
most popular shows ever, from campy musical variety,
like *Paw Come Git Your Dinner*, to game shows like
The $15,000.00 Power Tower, Burt had the magic touch.
He carved out a place for himself in boob tube history,
becoming the stuff Hollywood legends are made of.
He was the champion of camp, the ten-hit wonder. He
even crowned his achievements by earning himself a

place in the pop culture archives as a Trivial Pursuit question.

Burt became an American idol and landed in the fast lane by exploiting one very simple, easy truth about the television industry: Why create something original when you can steal and rework an idea somebody else already thought up? So he perfected the art of capitalizing on other networks' ideas. *The Gong Show* was a success? He answered with *Buzz That Bozo.* Everybody went nutty for *Petticoat Junction?* He hit them with three buxom hillbillies in *The Farmer's Daughters.* Yes, indeedy, Burt Mueller became a regular Joe Millionaire by taking other people's shows and turning them into faster, racier, trendier successes.

Then the rich bachelor went through a string of bad relationships. Bankruptcy. Failure. And though Burt had always been a real survivor, no matter how hard he tried, he'd never been able to recapture those glory days. Somehow, it just wasn't so easy anymore. In the eighties, he'd had no cheap answer for *Dynasty* or *Dallas*—not with those location shots, gowns with four-inch thick shoulder pads, and high-priced, spoiled starlets. And in the nineties, what could compete with fresh-faced youngsters like those little Olsen twins, who'd owned Thursday night? His amazing race to success crashed to a halt.

But things are changing. TV's gone around in a big wide circle, and it's finally returning to the world Burt recognizes. *His* TV-land. The territory of the con man, the shyster, the smooth-talker who can still manage some P.T. Barnum sleight of hand in front of the adoring public.

Welcome to the new millennium. The world of the reality TV show. Where the king has made his comeback.

JACEY TURNER:
Born to a single mom in L.A., Jacey grew up never knowing her real dad was Burt Mueller, the king of TV. The product of a brief relationship between Burt and a wannabe actress, Jacey wondered about her roots while growing up in South Central L.A. In the meantime, she fought to stay clear of the gangs and the drugs, and lost herself in her three favorite hobbies: skateboarding across the aqueducts, photography and dreaming of getting out.

At age seventeen, after cleaning the floor with a scumbag gangbanger who wouldn't take no for an answer, Jacey needed to get away and fast. Her mom, with no other choice, finally admitted the truth—that her dad was somebody famous. She'd kept Jacey a secret for fear of losing custody.

Inspired by the knowledge—not to mention the gangbanger out for revenge—Jacey took off and tracked down dear old Dad. Showing up on his doorstep with a ratty backpack and a bad attitude, she half expected to be kicked to the curb. But Mueller, to her surprise, had a heart of gold to go with his shiny bald head. She came to know, respect, and even care for the eccentric old guy. Best of all, he fully backed her up on her lifelong love of photography.

A high school dropout, Jacey had earned her degree

in life by the time she hit puberty, but she mastered her profession by working on the sets of several of her father's floundering TV projects. Gaining a reputation for excellence in the cinematography world, she began expanding her repertoire, working for other producers. Until finally, on the set of a smash hit murder-mystery reality TV show called *Killing Time In A Small Town*, she met her fate.

Not death. But Digg. Digg Martino. The man who made the street kid believe in true love.

DIGG MARTINO:

The youngest son of a big Hispanic family of New York City firefighters, Digg grew up knowing his place in the world. From the Catholic school up the block, to his grandparents, aunts, uncles and cousins littering the neighborhood, he was completely encapsulated in his own ethnic world. And he knew from a young age that he wanted to follow in the footsteps of his father, grandfather and uncles, and become a New York City firefighter.

Never had his decision made him feel more proud—yet more completely devastated—than on September 11, 2001. No, thankfully, he didn't lose any of his brothers, or family members, but he'd watched several friends go into that tower and never come out.

So when the chance came for him to participate in a murder-mystery reality TV show, he went for it. The show would be a welcome escape, a chance to get away from the expectations and the *sameness* of his New York City life, where his family watched his every move...and felt free to comment on it. But he also had the chance to earn a lot of money—money he could use to help the families of those killed, as well as his own family.

But Digg never expected when he landed on the set of *Killing Time In A Small Town* that he was going to completely lose his heart over a saucy, smart-mouthed little camera operator. Jacey Turner's black clothes and bad attitude screamed "stay away," but the warmth in her eyes and the sassiness of her wit appealed to him like no woman ever had.

Things seemed perfect. Until he and Jacey returned to the real world—*his* world—and his family got a load of the Hollywood wild child who'd tamed his calm, steady, hero's heart.

Here's a sneak peek...

REALLY HOT!
by
Jennifer LaBrecque

Enjoy this excerpt from Jennifer LaBrecque.

CHAPTER ONE

⑥

"ROURKE O'MALLEY is an orgasm waiting to happen," Portia Tomlinson read aloud. She rolled her eyes and scrolled down the screen, following the postings on the fan site that had sprung up for the latest reality show she'd worked on as associate producer, *The Last Virgin.* "Give me a break. Some women don't have good sense."

Rourke had been the favored contestant, but the show's bachelorette hadn't picked him. He had, however, captured the hearts of female viewers around the world and they were in a veritable lust frenzy. Amazing. She swung around in her office chair.

"You mean you don't think he's an orgasm waiting to happen?" Sadie Franken, an administrative assistant, asked.

More than once, Rourke O'Malley had intruded on her dreams. And she wasn't happy about it. Portia shrugged. "He's okay. Great face, great body, but that's nothing new in Hollywood. Of course, this," she gestured over her shoulder toward the computer screen, "should mean great ratings for our new show." This time around, they'd signed Rourke on as their star bachelor and lined up twelve wealthy single women for him to choose from. She'd read an article citing the latest trend among the twenty-something idle rich was to push their parents' buttons by putting themselves in a controversial spotlight. They had twelve young women who were living proof. Portia, however, was the lucky duck saddled with babysitting Rourke, the star, through production. She eyed the petite redhead. "Obviously you've joined the legion of women ready to drop at his feet."

Sadie raised her hand. "Guilty as charged. I've enjoyed several orgasms with him lately. I just crank my vibrator, close my eyes and Rourke O'Malley and I have a grand time."

Brash and uninhibited, Sadie usually left Portia laughing. "*That* was so much more information than I *ever* wanted to know. Please, feel free *not* to share in the future."

Sadie arched a brow. "Can you honestly tell me you've never fantasized about him after working with him and seeing him day after day?" Portia opened her mouth but Sadie cut her off before she could utter the denial. "You've never thought about kissing that fabulous mouth? Never imagined that hot bod naked and sweaty and getting down? Never imagined him touching you, you touching him?"

Enough. "No, no and no. I haven't." But now thanks to Sadie, she had. A warm flush spread inside her and she mercilessly exorcized the erotic imagery.

"Well, maybe you should—"

"Not." Portia cut her off and finished the sentence. "I should not."

"A little fantasy never hurt anyone."

"I don't have time for fantasy." And if she carved the time, reality lurked right around the corner. The stark contrast between the two proved too painful. Portia lived in the here and now.

She'd found out nine years ago where fantasy got you—single, pregnant and shattered. The ensuing reality had been waiting tables, changing diapers, several long years of night school and working her butt off to get ahead and make a better life for her and Danny.

Sadie shook her head. "A woman without time for fantasy. That's just not right."

Portia grinned. "Sorry, Toots."

"When's the last time you had a date?"

She shrugged and lied. "Not that long ago."

"Ha. Name the day, place and man."

Sadie was fun and they laughed together, but she'd just crossed into nunya territory, as in none of your business. Portia'd had one date in the past nine years. She had neither the time nor the inclination. Guys thought single moms were easy marks, desperate for sex. Thanks, but no thanks. The only thing she was desperate for was more hours in the day and a good pedicure.

Portia smiled to herself. Poor Sadie'd really be wrecked if she knew Portia hadn't had sex since the last time she'd slept with Mark, Danny's dad—wait, Mark hadn't been a dad at all, make that sperm donor—just before she found out she was pregnant. Sweet-talking, pretty-boy Mark, who'd promised to love her forever, had dumped her before the word pregnant was out of her mouth. And he'd turned out to be one rung lower than a deadbeat dad. The last she'd heard, he was a crack-head shacked up in East L.A.

"You're not going to answer me are you?" Sadie asked.

"Nope." Portia smiled to take the sting out of it.

"Well, okay. Don't date, don't fantasize. I'll handle all of that for both of us." Sadie nodded toward the computer screen crammed with fan postings. "Me and the other women without good sense."

"Good deal. You can drool enough for both of us."

"What a wasted opportunity. It's not fair you get to spend a couple of weeks shooting this new show with him. Fourteen days in a romantic setting with those blue eyes, that black hair, those chiseled features, that body…I've got chills just thinking about it."

388

"I know." Portia heaved a dramatic sigh, fluttered her lashes and cooed in a falsetto voice. "Just me, him, the moonlight, the hot tub…" Portia lost the simpering tone and added dryly, "…a dozen poor little rich girls and a production crew. Cozy, intimate."

"Go ahead, make fun. I'd be content to just breathe the same air he does."

"You need to breathe a little more air *now* instead of waiting on O'Malley. Obviously your brain isn't getting enough oxygen." Portia glanced out the window. "Are we on red alert today?"

Actually she thought the Santa Ana winds had blown through and temporarily cleared the combination of car exhaust and heat that smothered the city in smog so wretched they issued breathing codes.

"Very funny."

"I was just reminding you that even if I were remotely interested in Boy Toy O'Malley, and I think we've established that I'm not, he's there to pick from a bevy of wealthy beauties and I'm a drone, there to produce a show that'll pull in ratings."

"Drone? That has such an ugly sound to it."

"Ah, but apropos." And nothing was going to stop her. This was her proving ground. One last two-weeker away on location. If she did well, she'd been promised a studio position. No more long stretches of time away on location, where Danny had to stay with her parents and her sister. He loved them and they loved him, but the poor kid only had one parent as it was. He deserved to have her around a little more. Yeah, she'd still work brutal hours, but she *would* be home every night and he'd wake up to her there every morning. She had high stakes riding on this assignment.

"I WANT TO HAVE your baby!"

Rourke ducked into the elevator and watched in horror as the woman chasing him brandished a pair of purple thong panties and almost lost a few fingers in the closing door. "I love you," she yelled, dropping the panties and yanking her hand out at the last minute. "Call me."

He slumped against the wall, relieved the stranger, nutso or not, wasn't an amputee because of him. "The whole world's gone insane."

"Nah, man. Just the female portion. And, yeah, they're all crazy about you," his baby brother, Nick said.

"I'm pretty sure I'm crazy agreeing to do this show

and all of…this." He gestured at the undies on the floor. No way. A piece of paper with a phone number was pinned in the crotch. Totally looney.

"You're a good brother. You know I appreciate what you're doing for me." Despite his words, Rourke wasn't sure if Nick realized exactly how close he'd come to jail time. Embezzlement was a constant and serious temptation when you handled large quantities of money on a daily basis. A temptation his baby brother hadn't resisted. If Nick replaced the money, his employer had agreed not to press charges, preferring his money back to bad press. "Although women chasing you with their panties and choosing from twelve beautiful women with more money than God…I don't know how much of a hardship that'll be, Bro."

390   Nick really was clueless. "When people have that much money, they think they *are* God," Rourke said. He knew. He worked with them on a daily basis.

"Okay, sorry I sounded like an ingrate. Ya know, I can't thank you enough for helping me come up with the money." The elevator door opened. Rourke checked out the hallway for any other lingerie-wielding women. Coast was clear. He stopped over the purple thong. With a shrug, Nick scooped the panties up and shoved them in his pocket. "And it would've killed Mom and Dad."

Paul and Moira O'Malley had worked hard all their lives for a neat little house and yard in Quincey and an almost-comfortable retirement. They took pride in hard work, their home and their kids. If they knew how off-track Nicky had gotten…the shame of embezzlement and prison would damn near kill them. Not to mention they wouldn't hesitate to impoverish themselves trying to help him out of his jam. And Rourke wouldn't see that happen, or he'd die trying.

As an investment banker, he made decent money. Investment being the key word—most of his money was tied up. Ready cash simply wasn't that ready. Nick had pointed out that reality TV winners could bring in big bucks. It had seemed like a long shot, but more palatable than a loan shark.

It was too bad Nick couldn't have been the one on the show. Nick had good looks and the charm to go with it. All those women acting crazy about Rourke was just testimony to the power of suggestion and slick P.R. hype. In the past twelve years, his braces had come off, he'd filled in a hell of a lot and traded in Coke-bottle glasses for contact lenses, but Rourke knew he was still a geek beneath it all. And he still found mixing and mingling difficult. He could talk financial investments all day, but outside of that, he was pretty much at a loss. He'd heard himself referred to as the strong, silent type which made him feel even more like a fraud because he knew he was the quiet, I-don't-know-what-to-say geeky type. The truth of the matter was, women sort of scared the hell out of him.

But here he was, having blown the first opportunity to cash in on reality TV, moving on to round two, a sure thing to bring in the cash and keep Nick out of prison.

He unlocked his apartment door and Nick followed him in. He'd lived here two years and still loved the view from his place, the mix of modern skyscrapers, pre-Revolutionary redbrick buildings and Boston's legendary harbor.

"Thanks for looking after my place while I'm gone. Watson'll be much happier at home this time." Hearing his name, the miniature Schnauzer jumped down from the recliner he shared with Rourke and trotted over to him. Rourke bent down to scratch him behind the ears. "We'll go for a walk in a minute." He straightened and Watson walked over and sat patiently at the door. "You know Mom and Dad aren't really dog people."

Watson had stayed with his parents during the taping of *The Last Virgin*. Not only had poor Watson lost the comfort of his recliner, he'd been relegated to the yard. This time around, Nick was staying at Rourke's place and dog-sitting.

"It's cool. Wats and I are buds, but I hate scooping up the crap when he goes for a walk." Nick shuddered, wearing a look of disgust.

Rourke laughed with something close to incredulity. Nick could be so damned self-absorbed it amazed Rourke. "Probably not nearly as much as you'd hate being some tattooed felon's prison bitch. Keep that in mind while you're cleaning up after Watson. It'll put all the crap in your life in perspective."

Nick winced. "Where's a poop-scoop bag? Bring it on."

Rourke grabbed Watson's leash and passed the requested bag to Nick. Case in point, Rourke thought as he laughed with genuine amusement, it was impossible to stay angry with Nick.

"I'd love to trade places with you," he said as they headed back out the door, Watson leading the way. It hadn't been so bad on the last show, a bunch of guys and one woman. And he and Andrea, the bachelorette now known around the world as The Virgin, had actually become friends. But this time, it was only him and a legion of spoiled, high-maintenance women. And Portia Tomlinson.

He'd had mixed emotions when the studio listed her as associate producer. Portia fascinated him. Despite her friendly, easy demeanor, she had a way of looking at him with a trace of disdain, as if she'd judged him and found him lacking in some way. Perhaps if she got to know him better....

He'd thought about asking her out after the last show but they'd immediately offered him this upcoming show. And then there was the matter of him living in Boston and her living in L.A. And those were both nice excuses. The ugly truth was he'd figured she'd turn him down so fast it'd leave his head spinning. "Trust me, I'd rather clean up after Watson than be hounded by those pampered princesses."

They got on the elevator.

Nick, who ran through women like a slot addict in Vegas with a bag of coins, shook his head. "You are seriously warped, Rourke. Like maybe you need some therapy. I can't say I understand it, but I appreciate your sacrifice." Nick punched him on the shoulder. "Who knows? A dozen hot women, you might find your own true love."

Maybe he did need therapy. Twelve women and he was half smitten already with a woman who wasn't available. "Yeah."

"I don't want to step on your toes or anything, but I could give you some pointers. You know, I do okay with women," Nick said. *That* was an understatement.

Rourke wasn't exactly hitting any home runs on his own. Portia had treated him as if he were a piece of furniture, a prop, on the last show. And he didn't exactly want to humiliate himself by bombing with the twelve women. Best possible scenario would be to drag Nick along, a modern version of Cyranno de Bergerac, but that was impossible. He supposed the next best thing would be pointers. "I think I can use all the help I can get."

The door opened and Rourke was relieved to find the lobby empty. Nick shoved the poop bag into his pocket and grinned, "Welcome to Women 101."

394

...NOT THE END...

*Watch for REALLY HOT! from Harlequin Temptation®
in February 2005.*